The Woman Who Couldn't Scream

Center Point
Large Print

Also by Christina Dodd and available from
Center Point Large Print:

Obsession Falls
Because I'm Watching

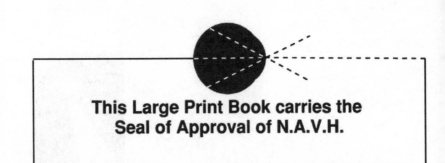

**This Large Print Book carries the
Seal of Approval of N.A.V.H.**

The Woman Who Couldn't Scream

Christina Dodd

CENTER POINT LARGE PRINT
THORNDIKE, MAINE

This Center Point Large Print edition
is published in the year 2017 by arrangement with
St. Martin's Press.

Copyright © 2017 by Christina Dodd.

This is a work of fiction.
All of the characters, organizations, and events
portrayed in this novel are either products
of the author's imagination or are used fictitiously.

The text of this Large Print edition is unabridged.
In other aspects, this book may vary
from the original edition.
Printed in the United States of America
on permanent paper.
Set in 16-point Times New Roman type.

ISBN: 978-1-68324-532-2

Library of Congress Cataloging-in-Publication Data

Names: Dodd, Christina, author.
Title: The woman who couldn't scream / Christina Dodd.
Description: Center Point Large Print edition. | Thorndike, Maine :
    Center Point Large Print, 2017.
Identifiers: LCCN 2017028408 | ISBN 9781683245322
    (hardcover : alk. paper)
Subjects: LCSH: Large type books. | GSAFD: Suspense fiction.
Classification: LCC PS3554.O3175 W66 2017b | DDC 813/.54—dc23
LC record available at https://lccn.loc.gov/2017028408

To Éowyn,
Brave, smart, and beautiful,
and the triumphant heroine of her own story.
I can't wait to see what deeds you'll accomplish
to make this a better world.

ACKNOWLEDGMENTS

A huge and amazing group hug with the people on my social media who, when I asked about American Sign Language and the Manual Alphabet (fingerspelling), were able to reassure me that many, many people learned to communicate in school, in Scouts, in college as a second language, and by studying on their own. Thank you for willingly offering your help whenever I need it.

Anne Marie Tallberg, Associate Publisher, and the marketing team of Jessica Preeg, Brant Janeway, Erica Martirano, DJ DeSmyter, thank you for your enthusiasm for *The Woman Who Couldn't Scream* and the whole Virtue Falls series.

The art department, led by Ervin Serrano, captured such a shocking, visceral image of the title.

To everybody on the Broadway and Fifth Avenue sales teams—thank you for placing *The Woman Who Couldn't Scream* in just the right places and at just the right times.

A huge thanks to managing editor Amelie Littell and Jessica Katz in production.

Thank you to Caitlin Dareff who keeps me up-to-date and on time.

Thank you to Sally Richardson, St. Martin's president and publisher.

Finally and most important, to Jennifer Enderlin, executive vice president and publisher at St. Martin's Press and my own editor; you provided the inspiration to build Virtue Falls and the guidance to make it the complex, marvelously interesting, and murderous small town that it is. No mere thank you could ever sufficiently express my gratitude.

CHAPTER ONE

Benedict Howard was used to having women *look* at him. He had money. He had power. He was ruthless. People saw that. In particular, women looked at him. As they always told him, they found him *interesting*.

Now, the most beautiful woman in the world looked through him. Not over him. Not around him. *Through* him.

The Eagle's Flight, the largest and newest sailing yacht in the high-end cruise line, cut through the waves with an authority that spoke well of the vessel's design as well as captain and crew. As the new owner of Birdwing Cruises, that gratified Benedict; his decision to buy the company had been sound.

But now at three days into the two-week transatlantic crossing, he stood by the port railing on the aft deck, and his whole attention was focused on the world's most beautiful woman.

Her skillfully tinted blond hair was styled in an upsweep with short tendrils that curled around her softly rounded face. Her nose was short and without freckles. Her neck was long and graceful. Her figure was without flaw, Barbie doll–like in its architectural magnificence, and unlike the other, determinedly casual passengers, she wore a designer dress with matching jacket and one-inch heels. Her wide blue eyes were set deep in an artfully tended peaches-and-cream complexion ... but they were blank, blind, indifferent. To him.

If she was trying to attract his attention by ignoring him, she had succeeded. But only for as long as it took him to recognize her machination. As he began to turn away, she looked toward a table set under the awning. She waved and she smiled.

Benedict was transfixed by her smile. He knew her. He was sure he knew her. From ... somewhere. Business? No. Pleasure? No. In passing? Absurd. Who was she? How could he forget the most beautiful woman in the world?

Stepping forward, he caught her elbow. "We've met."

She turned her head toward him, but as if his impertinence offended her, she took her time and moved stiffly. She shook her head.

"I'm sure we've met." He searched her face, searched his mind, seeking the time, the place. "You must remember. I'm Benedict Howard."

She wore a leather purse over one shoulder. With elaborate patience, she pulled it around, reached inside and pulled out a computer tablet. She brought up the keyboard and swiftly, so swiftly, she typed onto the screen. And showed it to him. It said, "How do you do, Mr. Howard. My name is Helen Brassard. I am mute, unable

10

to speak. DO NOT SHOUT. I am not deaf. I certainly recognize you. You're quite famous in the world of finance. But you don't know me."

"I don't believe you."

She gave him a look, the exasperated kind that without words called him an idiot.

He realized he had instinctively raised his voice.

She typed again and showed him the tablet. "I'm sure we'll run into each other again. It is a relatively small ship and an intimate passenger list. Now if you'll excuse me, I don't like to keep my husband waiting."

Benedict wanted to insist, but he glanced at the small dapper gentleman who glared at him with imperious fury, the gentleman who was old enough to be her grandfather. But wasn't her grandfather. Benedict recognized him; that was French billionaire Nauplius Brassard. That was the husband.

Trophy wife. Helen was a trophy wife: head-turningly beautiful, no doubt accomplished in bed . . . and mute. Perfect for the short, thin, elderly gentleman who had no doubt purchased her services for the long term.

Benedict let her go and turned away.

She was right. He didn't know her.

Helen Brassard seated herself next to her husband and used her hands to sign, "You look overheated

11

and ready for your afternoon cocktail. Shall I order you a sidecar?"

Nauplius flipped his bony fingers around, grasped her wrist and squeezed. "I saw him speak to you."

She groped for her purse and tablet.

"No! That's how you communicate with everyone else. Sign to me."

She shook her captured wrist, trying to free herself, to make it easier.

"Sign with one hand."

She did as he commanded. "Benedict did speak to me." She kept that gentle smile on her lips. Ignored the pain as the delicate bones ground together.

"He's lost his looks."

Signing: "He was never handsome." Although that was the truth; when she had known him before, Benedict's awkward arrangement of facial features had been offset by his youth and charisma. Now he looked . . . harsh, like a man who had tasted too much bitterness.

Nauplius adjusted his red bow tie. "What did he say?"

"He thought he knew me."

"Impossible."

Apparently not.

Nauplius was both jealous and selfish to the point of psychosis, but his skill at observing and interpreting others had brought him unimaginable wealth and a power he loved to abuse. Now he must have read her mind, for his grip tightened again. "You look . . . not at all like the woman you were when he knew you." Menacingly, "Do you?"

There was the paranoia she knew so well.

"I have not been in communication with him either on the ship or off. You know that."

He *did* know that. He knew what she said and to whom, what she did and when. He owned her, and she knew from experience he was infuriated by this unforeseen intrusion into the quality of his life. Especially *this* intrusion; during their nine-year marriage, they had lived in France and Italy, Greece and Spain and Morocco, anywhere she was isolated by language barriers, utterly dependent on him, and very, very unlikely to run into anyone she had known before.

Like the old man that he was, Brassard moved his jaw and chewed at nothing. "I didn't know Howard would be on this cruise. What is he doing here?"

Signing: "I don't know."

"He didn't tell you?"

She took a steadying breath before she signed, "All he said was that he knew me."

"What did you tell him?"

"That he didn't."

"I'll get us off this ship."

She glanced out at the turbulent blue Atlantic,

13

then up at the half-furled sails that caught the prevailing eastern winds. She signed, "How?"

"Helicopter. They can come out this far."

"As you wish." She bowed her head and waited.

His voice rasped with irritation. "But the helicopter—it's expensive and usually only used in case of emergency."

She signed, "That is my concern. A helicopter could cost possibly one hundred thousand dollars." Which Brassard could well afford. But wealthy as he was, he counted every cent and made sure she knew exactly how much she cost him.

He said, "I can call it in. I'm doing it for you."

She looked into his brown, deceptively soft eyes and signed, "You have no need. When I see Benedict, I feel nothing."

Brassard's grip tightened. "You never feel anything."

"Not true. Right now, you're hurting me."

In a swift, petty gesture, he tossed her wrist away from him.

As always, she was the perfect wife. In flowing, graceful movements, she asked, "Shall I order your cocktail?" and gestured to the hovering waiter.

For two days Benedict toured the working areas of the ship. He discussed meal preparation with the intimidated chef and the equally intimidated kitchen staff, inspected the lifeboats and their ongoing maintenance and gave orders to improve the air-conditioning in the stifling laundry area.

Then Benedict moved into the public areas, stalking the ship's photographer as she recorded the voyage as a video for purchase by the passengers. The invariably pleasant Abigail photographed passengers as they toured the bridge, arranged flowers, played bridge, ate and drank.

It was when he was with Abigail that he saw *her* again, the most beautiful woman in the world, in the midship lounge at the line-dancing class. Helen Brassard looked the same, tastefully dressed and in matching heels, and she frowned as she concentrated on the prescribed steps, placing each foot with a calm precision that created an anchor in the turbulently undisciplined line. She pulled the other dancers along, encouraging them with admiring gestures and warm touches to their shoulders. When the line completed the simplest dance step in unison, she smiled.

The most beautiful woman in the world had the most beautiful smile in the world, and Benedict was transfixed, enthralled, in need.

"That's Mrs. Brassard," Abigail said. "She's married to Mr. Brassard, who is possessive and quite . . . demanding." Her voice conveyed a distinct warning.

Benedict turned his cool gaze on her.

She respectfully lowered her eyes.

Abigail was afraid of him; all the staff were afraid of him. Yet she wanted him to know his interest would not be appreciated by a paying customer.

A good employee. A brave employee, one with guts and intelligence. He knew how rare those qualities were, and how valuable to the cruise line. He would see to it that she moved up in the ship's hierarchy and if she continued to do well, she would be sent to college and eventually move into his family's company. "Thank you for your insight." Which he wouldn't heed, but that was of no consequence to her. He indicated a burly black man with massive shoulders and a calm demeanor. "That's Carl Klineman, right? I always see him lurking near the Brassards. What is he to them?"

"He never speaks to them, and they never even glance at him," Abigail said. "For the most part, he keeps to himself."

"And yet?"

She spoke softly, "Speculation among the staff is that he's their bodyguard. Or an assassin. But no one really believes that Mr. Brassard would be oblivious to an assassin. He is a very astute man."

Benedict sensed she had more to say. "And . . . ?"

He had to lean close to hear her say, "Very

astute and very . . . dangerous. We, the staff, take care never to displease him."

A man could learn a lot from his employees, especially in these circumstances, and Abigail was genuinely frightened. "Then I will take care to tread carefully around Nauplius Brassard." He gave Abigail a moment to recover, then in a brisk tone asked, "What do you photograph next?"

"Musical bingo in the Bistro Bar starts in a half hour."

"Let's go."

Benedict despised trophy wives. He always had. And that name: *Helen.*

Helen of Troy.

The most beautiful woman in the ancient world, the woman whose face launched a thousand ships. He could hardly believe she had been born with that name. Probably she had chosen it when she created her persona to trap a wealthy man . . .

Benedict did his research and online he found out all about her.

Helen *was* the name she'd been given at birth. Her beginnings were humble; she had grown up in Nepal as the daughter of missionaries. When she was a teenager, her parents were killed in a rockfall and she was sent to the United States to live with her aunt and uncle in the south. She finished high school at sixteen and began college at Duke University, where her unusual beauty attracted Nauplius Brassard's attention. After a brief courtship, she graciously consented to be his wife and dedicated herself to him and his well-being. She did not work, did not express independent opinions, and during the days when he worked or during the evenings when he made public appearances, she never left his side.

Very neat. Very pat. But nowhere did any source explain why she could not speak. That single fact made Benedict doubt the whole story—although the numerous politically incorrect of the online community suggested that this disability made her the perfect wife for Nauplius Brassard.

The world abounded with snide jackasses.

And Benedict's curiosity was piqued.

Before the voyage had even begun, the crew had studied the ship's manifest and passenger list, memorizing every face and name. Now Benedict did the same. When he was satisfied with his ability to greet the guests, he joined the convivial table that nightly gathered after dinner at the aft main deck bar, a table that included five retired southern high school teachers making their annual pilgrimage to Europe, two university professors on sabbatical, a group of Spanish and Portuguese wine merchants, a skinny eighty-year-old corporate lawyer—and Nauplius Brassard and his wife, Helen.

Benedict turned a chair from another table and dragged it over. "May I join you?"

For a mere second, conversation faltered.

One of the middle-aged females scooted over. "We're all friends. Sit next to me." She placed her hand on her husband's arm. "We're Juan Carlos and Carmen Mendoza from Barcelona . . . and you are Benedict Howard."

Apparently he wasn't the only one who had studied the roster. "That's right, from Baltimore, Maryland, USA. I buy and sell things."

"On a grand scale," Juan Carlos said drily. "The Howard family is known for its business . . . acumen."

A nice way to say *ruthlessness*. "Yes." Benedict looked toward the opposite end of the long table. "But I interrupted the conversation. Please, continue while I sit and absorb the bonhomie." In fact, he had interrupted Helen Brassard, who had been animated and flushed as she recounted some story by signing while Nauplius Brassard translated in his faintly accented voice.

Cool and calm, she sipped her champagne and looked him in the eyes. She nodded. She put down her champagne, lifted her hands and signed, "Of course. I was telling this illustrious company about the surprise party my husband threw for me for my twenty-seventh birthday."

"Fascinating," he murmured.

With a turn of the head, she dismissed Benedict

and signed to the assemblage, "On the banks of the Loire in the month of June . . . he scheduled the Osiris String Quartet to play chamber music and had a catered picnic flown in from Vienna and laid on blankets on the grass. He hired a film crew to record each precious moment and he surprised me with a custom-made gift of polished amber stones set in a magnificent gold setting."

Benedict had trouble knowing who to look at—Helen, who was speaking, or Nauplius, who was interpreting. He glanced around and saw the others at the table seemed similarly stricken by uncertainty, and he wondered if they also found it odd to hear Nauplius Brassard praise himself so effusively . . . in her words. Certainly Brassard looked smug as he spoke.

Helen gazed at her husband as if she adored him, placed one palm flat on her chest, and with the other she spelled, "The memory is engraved on my heart."

The wide-bellied, rumpled academic nodded and in an accomplishment Benedict admired, at the same time sneered. Dawkins Cipre didn't want to offend Nauplius Brassard, a generous donor to European universities. Yet as a professor of literature he could hardly approve such a romantic gesture; it might reflect badly on his pretentiousness.

Elsa Cipre, the academic's thin, nervous, carefully unmade-up wife and a professor in her own right, said, "Nauplius has studied the inner workings of a woman's emotions."

One of the schoolteachers rolled her eyes. Another said, "Bless his heart." Apparently neither Nauplius nor the self-important academics had impressed anyone.

Unfazed, Elsa continued, "Dawkins is an expert on classic medieval French romance literature. Perhaps, Helen, for your twenty-eighth birthday he could consult with Nauplius and bring the full weight of French literature to bear."

Faintly Benedict heard Carmen Mendoza moan under her breath.

Dawkins took the opportunity to launch into a college-level literature lecture in which he cited his years at Oxford and the Sorbonne. His pontificating encouraged low buzzing conversations to start and swell, and Nauplius Brassard flushed with irritation—he did not enjoy losing his place in the spotlight or being told what to do—and tried to interrupt.

Oblivious, Dawkins rambled on.

Without asking, the bar staff delivered another round of stiff drinks.

The band came in; the musicians played guitar and keyboard; the singer was thin, young, attractive and handled the microphone with an expertise that spoke of long familiarity. They began the first set.

Dawkins held forth until his wife touched his

hand and they left to find the dessert buffet.

With a pretty smile, Helen pushed Brassard's drink toward him.

Brassard folded his arms over his chest, transferring his irritation to her.

She tried to sign to her husband, to cajole him into a better mood.

He turned his head away.

When she persisted, he whipped around to face her, caught her wrists and effectively rendered her mute.

At once she stopped her attempt, and when he released her, she contemplated the champagne in her flute and drank.

An interesting scene, Benedict thought. Helen was Brassard's whipping boy. What kind of background created a woman so greedy she would put up with that kind of abuse?

Of course, when Nauplius Brassard died, she would be wealthy beyond imagining. Legend had it that Nauplius had grown up on the streets of Marseilles, a scrawny vindictive thief; by the time he was twenty he had made his first million. Now he was still scrawny, still vindictive, but worth billions.

Carmen Mendoza began to hum and then to sing in a warm contralto, and within five minutes she had kicked off her shoes and stood before the band dancing. Before another minute had passed Juan Carlos had taken the female high school teachers onto the floor and the male high school teachers had joined them on the fringes, gyrating sheepishly.

Reginald Bardzecki, the eighty-year-old corporate lawyer, stood and offered his hand to Helen. She glanced at the still-fuming Brassard, smiled defiantly, removed her heels and joined Reginald. Unlike anyone else on the floor, they danced like experts. He led, she followed, the two of them staging a series of ballroom moves that only two people who reveled in the music could perform.

The musicians played. The staff and dancers stopped and watched.

Benedict leaned back in his chair and appreciated the sight. Then instinct led him to glance toward the other end of the table.

Nauplius Brassard sat glaring at the elderly man who spun his youthful smiling wife across the floor.

And Benedict remembered what Abigail had said about Nauplius Brassard: *He is dangerous. We take care never to displease him* . . . Benedict thought Helen would suffer for her insubordination.

The song ended. The dancers came back to the table, flushed and laughing. They ordered drinks and complimented Reginald and Helen on their skill.

Helen seated herself next to her husband,

keeping a few careful inches away from his simmering resentment.

The next song started. Carmen pulled Benedict to the dance floor and taught him flamenco. When he felt he'd made a fool of himself for long enough, Benedict started back toward the table.

The Brassards were gone.

The next morning, a helicopter arrived and lifted Nauplius Brassard and his wife off the ship.

Thirteen months later, Nauplius Brassard died of a brain aneurysm.

His children, all in their forties, moved swiftly to eject his young wife, Helen, from the Brassard Paris home.

They discovered her designer wardrobe, her jewels and all the furnishings intact.

The fortune Brassard had set aside in a bank account under her name had vanished—and so had she.

Less than forty-eight hours later, one of Nauplius Brassard's legal team was found murdered, slashed to death in her office.

The French police feared a copycat killer, one imitating the serial killer who two years before had died in a Canadian prison.

To their relief, no further murders followed.

CHAPTER TWO
Washington's Olympic Peninsula
In the mountains

Officer Rupert Moen steered the speeding patrol car around sharp corners, up steep rises and through washouts caused by spring rains. Sweat stained his shirt, ruddy blotches lit his cheeks and the middle of his forehead. He was young, with the sheriff's department for only a couple of years, shy and never the brightest bulb in the chandelier. But damn, put that kid behind the wheel and he could *drive*.

Sheriff Kateri Kwinault's only jobs were to lean into the curves and keep him calm. In the soothing voice she had perfected during her time as regional Coast Guard commander, she said, "Four wheels on the ground. Don't skid on the gravel. Your job is keep that car in sight. We've got a helicopter on its way and every law enforcement officer on the peninsula moving into position."

Like a Celtic warrior, Moen was all wild red hair and savage grins. "This road is a real bitch, isn't it?"

"It's . . . interesting." Kateri purposefully kept her gaze away from the almost vertical plunge on her side of the car, away from the equally vertical rise on the other side.

"Goddamn interesting." With flashing lights and a blast of the electronic air horn, Moen harried the black Dodge SRT Hellcat that raced ahead of them. "This time we'd better catch those bastards."

"Yes." The Terrances, father and son, were bastards and worse: drug dealers, meth cookers, jail escapees, drive-by shooters . . . and murderers.

Kateri corrected herself. *Attempted* murderers. No one was dead . . . yet.

She checked the dash cam; she wanted video of every last moment of this capture. "I hope the roadblocks stopped all unofficial vehicles. We don't want to meet someone in a head-on."

"Not much traffic up here this spring. Too much runoff. Good thing, considering."

Considering the steep and narrow gravel road, considering the speed, considering no civilian wanted to encounter John Senior and John Junior. Well, except for those few locals who monitored their police frequency radio scanners and were delighted when they could actively observe or participate in law enforcement activities— especially pursuits. So far, there hadn't been a problem; in this case, the public had been of assistance.

This was wild country. All the things that made the Olympic Peninsula a hiker's and boater's paradise—steep mountains, dense forests, wild beaches and hidden inlets—made it ideal for two fugitives intent on evading arrest. Except, oh gee, if the Terrances had been hidden in a cave or deep in the woods, they would have had no Wi-Fi, no radio reception, no way to contact the outside world.

The public and law enforcement had been put on alert and for three intensive days, the hunt had pulled in county, city and state police to patrol the roads as well as the Coast Guard to cruise the Pacific coast. The hunt had been publicized by local news media with the warning, "If seen do not attempt to apprehend; contact your local law enforcement agency." Finally alert citizen Pauline Nitz had spotted the black Dodge SRT Hellcat speeding along one of the isolated roads and the chase was on.

Now, spitting gravel and raising dust, Kateri and Moen led a line of Virtue Falls Police Department cars in hot pursuit.

Moen's white knuckles gripped the wheel. "Hold on." He steered them over a series of washboards that rattled everything in the car and made Kateri moan and press her hand to her side. He glanced at her. "Sorry, Sheriff."

"Not your fault," she said. Four days ago, while Kateri sat in the window of the Oceanview Café, celebrating her surprise election to the office of sheriff, the Terrances had sprayed bullets through the windows. One of their bullets had skipped off her ribs like a flat stone off the rippled surface of a river, leaving her broken and bloody and sore as hell, but not seriously wounded.

Instead, they'd put two bullets into Virtue Falls's beloved waitress, busybody, and local wise woman, Rainbow Breezewing. Now Rainbow rested in the hospital hooked up to ventilators and drips, unmoving, unconscious. The doctors told Kateri that Rainbow didn't have a chance. They said Rainbow's coma was a blessing, for she was dying. Dying . . .

"The Terrances are slowing down." Moen moved closer to the Hellcat's bumper.

"Maybe they're out of gas." That would be too wonderful—and too lucky since as far as Kateri could tell, the Terrances had stashed fuel and food all up and down the coast. "I don't believe it. Back off."

Moen sighed noisily, but did as he was told.

She leaned forward, trying to figure out what they were up to. "Be care—"

John Terrance, Junior or Senior, goosed the black Dodge SRT and threw it into a skid that sent the car sideways, passenger side toward the pursuers.

"Don't T-bone him!" Kateri shouted.

Moen downshifted, eased off the gas and in the excessively patient tone of the very young toward the very old (Kateri was thirty-four), he said, "I know what I'm doing, Sheriff."

The SRT's passenger door flew open. Some-thing tumbled out.

Someone tumbled out.

Moen screamed, "Shit son of a bitch!"

Kateri yelled, "Don't hit him. Don't run over him!"

Moen slammed on his brakes, locked up all four wheels, making the patrol car a high-speed toboggan propelled by inertia and momentum.

No way to avoid the collision.

The patrol car's left front tire caught the body. The car went airborne.

"The tree!" Moen shouted.

They rammed it, a giant Douglas fir, square on.

The airbags exploded.

Kateri was smashed against the back of her seat. She couldn't breathe. She couldn't see. *She was drowning.*

She fought the hot white plastic out of her face. The airbag was already deflating . . . she tore off her sunglasses. White dust covered them, covered the interior of the car. The siren blared. She needed to catch her breath—

Moen looked in the rearview mirror and yelled, "They can't stop. They're going to nail us!"

"Who?"

"Cops!"

Another explosion of sound and motion as they were rammed in the right rear fender. Metal scraped. Fir needles rained down. The impact spun the patrol car sideways, wrenched the stitches over Kateri's ribs. The wound opened, one torn stitch at a time. Icy-hot pain slithered up her nerves. Warm blood trickled down her side.

Moen opened his door.

Through the ringing in her ears, Kateri heard the roar of an engine. Was another vehicle going to hit them? Or worse—had John Senior escaped?

Moen unbuckled his seat belt. "You okay, Sheriff?"

"Yes." She pressed the pad of her bandage. "Go."

He leaped out and ran toward the unmoving body in the middle of the road.

Had they inadvertently killed a hostage?

Someone yanked open her door. "Sorry, Sheriff, when you fishtailed, we couldn't stop." A moment, then a face thrust into hers. "You okay, Sheriff?"

Kateri blinked at the star-pattern of pain before her eyes.

The face belonged to Deputy Sheriff Gunder Bergen. Good guy. Good law officer. Second in command. He knew stuff.

"Who did we hit?" she asked. "Did we kill him?"

"Moen's coming."

Moen stuck his head in the driver's door. He leaned a hand on the steering wheel and one on the seat and spoke to her. "The body was John Junior. He was already dead. Like . . . there was no rigor mortis so a few days ago, right?"

Bergen inched in farther, leaned a hand on the dashboard. "We're getting the coroner out here, but yeah. What killed him?"

Moen switched his attention to Bergen. "Gunshot wound."

"Close range? His father shot him?" Bergen asked.

The two men were talking over the top of her. Which was annoying as hell. "He shot his son so he could use the body as a diversion?" Kateri clicked her seat belt and let go.

The buckle smacked Bergen on the thigh.

He jumped back, bumped his head on the roof, looked surprised as the dog who ate the bumblebee.

"No. I mean, maybe, but the shot was long range, entered the right side at about the liver. He bled out." Moen looked hard at Kateri. "Sheriff, you don't look much better than the corpse."

Bergen nodded. "Ambulance just pulled up. We'll send her to the hospital."

Kateri said the obvious. "Don't be silly. I'm fine."

"You sound just like my wife right before she collapsed with a ruptured appendix," Bergen said.

"I'm fine," she repeated. The air coming in

the door was *hot*. Wasn't it? "Did we get John Senior?"

Moen clearly didn't want to give this report. "The diversion worked. He gunned it. Road was too narrow. No one could get past us. He's gone."

CHAPTER THREE

"Now I'm not fine." As her brief burst of hope faded, Kateri felt each torn stitch. "Hand me my walking stick."

Moen pulled it out of the backseat and passed it to Kateri.

Four years ago, an earthquake had hit the coast of Washington. Kateri Kwinault had been the regional Coast Guard commander. She had lost her Coast Guard cutter in the resulting tsunami, saved her crew, been sucked out to sea and drowned by the frog god . . .

She said, "Moen, move the cars and the body and get after John Terrance."

"If we do that, Sheriff, we'll compromise the evidence."

She looked at Moen. *Looked* at him.

"Right away, ma'am." He ducked out of the car.

She could hear him shouting instructions. "Good boy," she muttered.

Some people thought she was nuts thinking she had seen the frog god, that ancient god who lived in the depths of the ocean and whose leap caused the earth to move and the tsunamis to rise. Some people made snotty comments about her belief that she had died and been resurrected.

But after too much time in the hospital, too many operations, too many joint replacements and months of rehabilitation—after surviving when she should have died—she didn't care what anyone thought. She knew what she knew.

So she used a genuine *Lord of the Rings* Gandalf-tested polished walnut staff to help her get around . . . Maybe it wasn't truly Gandalf-tested. But it was genuine walnut.

To Bergen she said, "Terrance is up here for a reason. He's got a hideout and supplies. Find out where."

"Will do." Bergen stepped back. "As soon as I see you get yourself out of the car."

Cautiously she swung her legs around to the ground. Took a breath. Yeah, it was hot. Summer solstice, almost July, surprising for Washington State even-in-the-summer hot. Kateri put a hand on the door and one on the stick and tried to stand.

A few inches off the seat—and she dropped back.

Mistake. Such a mistake.

After The Earthquake, she had suffered so much pain, she should be inured to it.

Nope. Pain still hurt, and something about having stitches ripped out of already shredded skin nauseated her to the point of . . . She breathed deeply, staying conscious. "I'm not going in the damned ambulance," she muttered.

Bergen swore at her in some Scandinavian-sounding language.

"Mean. Considering." She crooked her finger to him, and when he leaned close she said, "Look. I'm not being stubborn or foolish. I was elected four days ago. By two votes. Had a drive-by shooting in the first few hours of my office. I was shot. Rainbow was critically wounded. Worse, the crime was committed by felons who escaped from custody. Tourists freaked out and left town. City council wants my head."

"Like they didn't already want it." But Bergen was beginning to comprehend.

"Business owners are screaming. July fourth is in two weeks. If I don't capture John Terrance, we're going to have a financial disaster. And we just lost him *again*." She stared Bergen in the eyes. "I'll go to the hospital, but not flat on my back in an ambulance. Get someone to drive me and I'll by God walk into the emergency room under my own power. You stay and handle this situation. We have to catch that guy and not just for the tourist trade or to keep Virtue Falls citizens secure. You know why? For Rainbow. She deserves to have justice."

Bergen stared right back at her. "You deserve justice, too, Kateri."

He didn't call her by her first name very often. Usually only when he and his wife, Sandra, had her over for dinner. Or in moments of great stress . . . Kateri supposed this boondoggle qualified as *great stress.* "We'll have justice. Bergen, make sure the memory on this dash cam is safe. Back it up as many times as you can. When we capture John Terrance and he tries to sue us for running over his beloved son, that's our insurance that we'll come out clean."

"Will do. I'll make sure we've saved the memory on any other camera that might have captured the action, too." He stood and glanced around, then leaned in briefly. "Someone's coming who can help you get down to the hospital on your terms."

"Thanks." She closed her eyes, listened to Bergen shout instructions to the assembled police, and hoped the someone who would drive her was not Moen. With her ribs, she didn't think she could survive a trip down the mountain at the same breakneck speed they'd come up.

A man's warm, reassuring voice spoke close beside her, "Don't worry. I'm here."

Familiar, but definitely not Moen.

Without hesitation, the guy slid an arm around her waist, down under her butt and *handled* her out of the patrol car.

She opened her eyes wide.

Oh. Now she knew who it was.

Stag Denali. Bouncer. Enforcer. A Native American with rumored connections to the Mob. A man who had served time for murder.

The guy who was bringing a casino to the local reservation. Rainbow had once expressed a wish to see him running through the forest naked. Kateri had . . . in a figurative sense.

She looked up into those dark, inscrutable eyes . . . eyes she had seen wild with lust and need and satisfaction. "What are you doing here?"

His smooth tones held an undercurrent of amusement. "I was out for a pleasure cruise through the scenic Olympic Mountains and came upon this scene, and like any good citizen I thought I should offer assistance."

"Bullshit."

"Okay, you got me. I was listening on the police scanner and decided I wanted in on the fun."

She judged that was bullshit, too. Stag Denali wasn't one of those guys who needed to join a police chase for his jollies. He'd already had plenty of excitement in his life. "Citizens who impede police action are a pain in the rear."

"I impeded nothing. Just tagged along and avoided the collision." He led her toward a gorgeous sedan. Really gorgeous. A Tesla . . . Expensive, too. He stopped beside the passenger door. "Here we are."

Stag's car, like the Terrances', was low-slung, fast and black, but where theirs had silver glitter in the paint, his was smooth with an undertone of dark, dark green that seemed to reflect the cool depths of the forest. "Nice," she mumbled. "New?"

"Yes."

"You shouldn't drive it on gravel roads."

"Today I got a chip in the windshield." He opened the passenger door and supported her as she lowered herself onto the seat. He lifted her feet inside, took her walking stick and shut the door. As he walked around the hood, she watched and thought it was one of God's little ironies to build a Native American into the living embodiment of John Wayne, all long legs, narrow hips, broad shoulders and calm confidence.

Stag opened the driver's door and suavely slid in.

Could the action of getting your butt into a car be described as suave?

Probably not. But Stag made it work for him. Maybe he was a mashup of John Wayne and James Bond . . .

She must be getting punchy from heat, pain and loss of blood. She pressed her hand hard against her ribs. Hot. Inflamed. That couldn't be good.

"Take this," he said.

She opened her eyes to see him holding a pill in the palm of one hand and a bottle of water in the other.

"What is it?"

"Percocet for the pain."

"Percocet is a prescription drug. How did you get it?"

"I strained a groin muscle lifting my girlfriend

up against the door so I could bang her brains out." He stared meaningfully at her. "She's a tall woman, I'd guess five-eleven."

She plucked the pill out of his palm. "Not since the hip replacements. Now I'm maybe five-nine." She swallowed the pill with a long drink of water. "The strained muscle? Was it worth it?"

"Yes." He lowered her seat all the way back. "If you weren't bleeding and looking like a ghost, I would lift you up on the hood and do it again, strained muscle or no."

The guy might be a crook. But damn, he was charming. If only she didn't have this ugly suspicion floating in the back of her mind . . .

Since the day Stag had strolled into Virtue Falls, he had been surrounded by a firestorm of gossip. Gossip about his past, about the casino, and inevitably, gossip about them.

They'd slept together. Which was nobody's business but their own—except at the time, she had been running for office and that made it everyone's business. In a small town where prejudice ran deep, electing a female sheriff had been a huge step. Electing a Native American female sheriff had been groundbreaking. Electing a woman who slept with the guy, also Native American, in charge of building a casino on the reservation . . . from here she could see beacon fires of indignation blazing all up and down the coast.

But none of that was why *she* felt conflicted about Stag Denali.

He pulled a blanket out of the duffel bag in the back and wrapped it around her. "Going to ask me why I carry a blanket?" He sounded testy.

"Emergency kit?"

He placed his index finger on her nose. "Right you are."

She should ask him what he'd been doing outside the window of the Oceanview Café at the time of the drive-by. Why, before the shooting started, he dove toward the ground. Why, although bullets riddled the pavement, the sidewalk, the trees in the park and the building, he hadn't been hit.

Virtue Falls was a small town. Gossip ran rife. Yet no one seemed to think anything suspicious about Stag Denali's miraculous escape. Except Kateri.

And she was the last person who should be having doubts.

CHAPTER FOUR

"What's wrong? You look funny. Are you going to vomit?" Stag looked around at his wonderfully glossy, polished wood interior. "Because this is a new car with all-leather seats and I can open the door in a hurry."

Clearly a man who kept his priorities straight. The breeze of the air conditioner grabbed her, and Kateri shivered. "I'm cold."

He touched her forehead. "You're clammy." He started the car and flipped on her seat heater. "You were in a wreck. You're in shock."

"None of the other officers are in shock." Testy. She was testy.

"No one else was shot four days ago."

She put her hand on her side. "It's nothing."

"I've been shot. It's never nothing." He put the car in reverse, made an efficient three-point turn and headed toward town. "It'll take us about an hour, hour and a half to get to the hospital, so close your eyes and try to get some sleep."

"I want to know what's happening." She sounded like a fretful child.

One hand on the wheel, he reached around and clicked a switch. The police scanner blared to life, then faded, then blared, then faded, but from the jumble of voices, the news didn't sound good. "In these mountains, it'll be in and out, mostly out." He reached back again and clicked it off.

"*Why* do you have a police scanner?"

"I like to keep track of my girlfriend."

Her mind clicked along to the next thought. "John Terrance has a police scanner, doesn't he?"

"Most likely."

"We could . . . do something with that information. Something . . . sneaky. Fill the scanner with misinformation."

"Isn't that as likely to confuse your men as John Terrance?"

"We have a secure channel . . . you didn't hear that." She took a couple of breaths and felt herself relax.

"John Terrance will likely figure out what you're doing."

"Yes, but maybe that'll help us catch him and even if it doesn't, won't he be frustrated?"

Stag laughed, warm and deep.

She had a plan. A stupidly obvious easy plan, and Stag had helped her figure it out. "Remind me later to tell my cops."

"I will. I'll even make up some fake stories for you."

"That would be lovely." She looked at his profile and appreciated how intently he concentrated. He drove well, not like Moen on the chase, but smoothly, competently, speeding around corners as fast as he could without tossing her from side to side.

The car's interior was nice. Really nice, with a computer console that looked vaguely like a *Star Trek Enterprise* control panel. From the latest movie. The new-car scent made her dizzy. Or maybe it was the bleeding. Or maybe it was Stag's scent. Whew. She closed her eyes. She thought she dozed.

John Terrance and his son . . . bullies, the kind who liked to harass women on the street, to fight when they were the only ones with firearms. Worse, they made meth, sold it all over Western Washington, were responsible for all the misery that addiction caused . . . and made a fortune. They owned the fast car, they owned the speedy boat, they escaped . . . but now John Jr. was dead. No one would mourn him except his father, and his father would mourn. His father would wage war on her and her men . . .

Kateri had a vision of John Terrance Sr., skinny, dirty, leering, eyes aflame, screaming he would come after her, rape her, hurt her, make her sorry. She heard his voice in her head . . . "I'll leave you more deformed than you already are!"

She came awake on the whiplash of *that* nightmare.

Stag must have been watching, because he asked, "How is Rainbow?"

Kateri breathed to calm her racing heart.

He repeated, "How's Rainbow?"

"Rainbow?" Kateri tensed, fought the drug, then inevitably relaxed again. "Dying. She's dying." Oh, God. Percocet helped the pain in her ribs. It did nothing for the pain in her heart.

He glanced at her. "The story I heard is that since meeting the frog god, you can bring people back from the brink."

Because Stag was Native American, she was comfortable talking with him about the gifts the frog god had forced upon her. "With her, I can't. There's no elegant way to do it. I have to *blast* life into a dying body. I've only done it a couple of times—once was my dog—and only when it was almost too late. If I blasted life into Rainbow, I'm afraid it'll be like blowing too hard on a dying flame. It will flicker out."

"You're afraid to try."

"Don't accuse me. Try to understand—I can't take the chance I'll kill her. She brought me into this world."

He'd been kind of guiding the conversation, giving her something to think about besides pain and worry. Now he was clearly riveted. *"What?"*

"Rainbow delivered me. She arrived in Virtue Falls, a kid with a backpack and a woven blanket and nothing else to her name, and of course my mother took her in. My mother was always taking in strays . . ."

"Including your father?" Stag slowed the car.

She felt the gentle bump as the wheels hit the pavement. "Yes. Perhaps. But that was like offering to carry the scorpion across the river. When she had helped him, loved him, adored him, given him everything of herself . . . When he had sucked all the life and youth out of her . . . he walked away. She never recovered." Her mind wandered to memories of her mother, of the smiles, the love, the time spent together . . . the well-hidden unhappiness, the slow disintegration into alcoholism, the broken body and soul.

In a gentle voice, Stag said, "You were telling me about your mother and how Rainbow delivered you."

Kateri focused. "Right. They went out to dig clams by the full moon. Mom was pretty pregnant—her due date had been the week before . . ."

"Good God. It was night? She was overdue? And they went out to the beach to dig clams?"

"Once I asked Rainbow what they were thinking and she said Mom was fat and uncomfortable and depressed about my father."

"How old was your mother?"

"Eighteen when she met him."

"And he was . . . ?"

"I don't know. In his thirties, I guess, visiting Virtue Falls for the game fishing. Of course she fell in love and gave up her V-card to him because she thought he was going to marry her. He romanced her for a couple of weeks, then when she asked about the wedding . . ." She looked up and out the window at the tops of the evergreens and the fringe of the sky. "He didn't stay."

"Jesus." Even Stag, who had probably seen plenty of brutality, sounded shocked.

"He wasn't about to sully his precious eastern white heritage with a short, black-haired, red-skinned Indian wife. What with being a blue blood and being married to a blue blood and having a pure blue blood kid." Why was Kateri confessing her darkest, most painful secrets to Stag Denali? She never told anyone about her screwed-up heritage . . . must be the Percocet. Or maybe the experience of lying back in a warm, soft leather seat knowing someone was in charge and she didn't have to tell him where to go or what to do or worry that Stag would blab her confessions to the world.

The side of his mouth was drawn up in a cynical crease. "What did this guy say when she told him she was pregnant?"

"She didn't tell him."

"Your father doesn't know you exist?" Stag was shocked again.

"Do you want me to finish this story or not?" Snarling was unpleasant, although sometimes necessary.

"Right. One thing at a time. So your mom was overdue and depressed . . ."

"And nineteen years old and Rainbow was seventeen, and everyone told them the first baby always took hours of labor . . . so they headed out in Mom's crummy old pickup down to Grenouille Beach—"

"Rough road." He clenched the steering wheel hard.

"Right. They hit enough washboard to knock the teeth out of a woodpecker."

"Woodpeckers don't have . . ." He caught himself. "Never mind. What happened?"

"Once they got there, they made a fire out of driftwood and started digging clams. They planned a picnic, a feast in the moonlight. Mom always said the best clamming was in that place where the waves and the currents intersect, so that's where she was digging. Rainbow was up the beach by the cliff and she said the waves were backing and forthing, as they do, and she was digging, and all of a sudden she realized it was quiet." Kateri had heard the story so many times she could see it in her mind. "Deadly quiet. She looked up and saw this giant wave rise up over the top of my mother." She lifted her hands and let them hover. "Rainbow screamed. Mom looked up in time to be slammed down to the sand. She disappeared. Just disappeared. The water rushed up the beach. Rainbow ran toward the spot where she had been. To hear Rainbow tell it, it was long

47

minutes before my mother washed up at the tip of the wave." Kateri allowed her hands to wilt down onto her chest. "When she crawled out, she was in labor."

"What did Rainbow do?"

"Delivered me. I came fast. They'd brought a knife and a blanket. For the picnic. They used the knife to cut the cord and the blanket to keep me warm by the fire."

Stag whistled softly. "I'll bet when the elders heard that story, they made some interesting predictions about you."

"As far back as I can remember, there was talk that I had been marked by the frog god. Like I wasn't already marked enough for being half-white on the reservation and half-Indian in the Virtue Falls schools."

Stag laughed, not like he thought it was funny, but like he understood all too well. "Get beat up a lot?"

"Conflict is a half-breed's lot in life." She managed the balance between pitiful and sarcastic very well. Years of practice had perfected the art.

Stag slowed, turned, hit a couple of speed bumps.

Lights flashed in her eyes; the car stopped and she could see the sign that proclaimed EMERGENCY ROOM in bright white and red.

He raised her seat back. "Ready to go in?" he asked.

"They're going to yell at me. Then they're going to hurt me."

"That's the price you pay for being a half-breed sheriff marked by the frog god." He managed the balance between pitiful and sarcastic pretty well himself. "I'll get the wheelchair." He got out and leaned back in to say, "I liked that story, but someday you'll tell me how you met your father."

"I didn't say I had met him."

"Sometimes, Kateri, what you don't say speaks as loudly as what you do."

CHAPTER FIVE

WELCOME TO VIRTUE FALLS
FOUNDED 1902

YOUR VACATION DESTINATION ON THE
WASHINGTON COAST

HOME OF THE WORLD FAMOUS
VIRTUE FALLS CANYON

POPULATION 2487

For a sweaty hour and a half, Merida Falcon had been sitting on the hood of her recently acquired Kia Soul, on a side road underneath the WELCOME TO VIRTUE FALLS sign, waiting for the roadblock to clear. She was first in a line of seven cars. She kept herself entertained by reading the latest Bill Bryson travel memoir on her iPad—on the cruise ship, the very superior Professor Dawkins Cipre and his equally condescending wife, Elsa, had characterized Bryson's books as puerile. Merida considered that a recommendation.

"There she goes," said the law enforcement officer in charge.

Merida looked up to see a black Tesla whip past. She raised her eyebrows at the officer.

"Not too much longer to wait." The name tag

50

above his badge read SEAN WESTON. He was tall, broad-shouldered, thirtyish with sandy brown hair, a nice tan, good teeth and a superior opinion of himself. He had been glancing at her with greater and greater frequency; now he made his move. "The police chase is headed in the opposite direction." He waved a hand toward the mountains. "That car was carrying our new sheriff."

Merida nodded.

He took that as encouragement. "Stag Denali's driving. He's her boyfriend. He's taking her to the hospital."

So far Merida had managed to get along with smiles and nods, but this required a greater response. Reaching into her canvas shoulder bag, she pulled out her computer tablet, switched it on, typed a few commands and passed it to him.

As he read, his lips moved. "My name is Merida Falcon. I am mute. I AM NOT DEAF. PLEASE DO NOT SHOUT!"

Of course he raised his voice. "Is that why you haven't said a word? I guess that makes you the perfect woman." He laughed.

She didn't. It wasn't funny the first time she'd heard it, and it wasn't funny now.

Removing her sunglasses, she turned her icy blue eyes on Officer Weston and smiled with her teeth clenched tight. Retrieving her tablet, she briskly typed, "Something about being without

51

the faculty of speech makes some people think I'm mentally impaired. This seems to free them from the most elementary of common courtesies. I certainly hope you, a public servant, are not one of those people?" She also typed in excess of one hundred words a minute, far faster than the average person could read, but she didn't feel the need to slap him upside the head with that information . . . yet. She passed the tablet.

He read what she wrote. "No! I didn't mean that you . . . Or that anyone . . ." He was smart enough to shut his mouth before he dug himself even deeper. "Um, sorry."

She retrieved the computer, inclined her head and typed, "Why is Mr. Denali taking Sheriff Kwinault to the hospital?" She turned the tablet for Officer Weston to read.

"She got all shook up in the high-speed car chase." He hooked his thumbs in his belt and hitched up his pants. "I worked for a female sheriff on my last position. She used to cry in her office. Women can't handle the stresses of the job."

Merida didn't look like the most beautiful woman in the world anymore. She'd made sure of that. She wore blue jean bib overalls, a white sleeveless T-shirt that showed off her new tattoo and ragged canvas sneakers. One side of her head was shaved, a long shank of hair grew on the other, and that hair was her natural brown with a bright streak of white—also natural—and an equally bright streak of blue—self-applied. She wore moisturizer with sunscreen, no makeup. There'd been no waxing, no Botox, no filler. She wore no rings, no earrings, no jewelry of any kind. In fact, she didn't own jewelry of any kind. She had left all decoration behind when she walked away from her last life . . . except for that tattoo, and it wasn't really a decoration. It was a declaration; a hunting falcon, talons outstretched, diving for some unidentified prey. Most men, if they were smart, would be afraid of her.

Yet somehow this officer was posturing in front of her, saying the dumb stuff that some men say when they equate beauty with a clinging need to be cared for. She typed, "Didn't I read that Sheriff Kwinault got shot a few days ago?" and passed it to him.

"She sure did. She was sitting in the Oceanview Café with Deputy Bergen, celebrating her victory with homemade donuts, and those wack jobs, the Terrances, drove by and shot her."

Merida typed, "So Sheriff Kwinault isn't feeble. She's injured." She turned the tablet and narrowed her eyes at him.

"Well, sure." He started to squirm. "But she said the injury wasn't bad."

Irritation heated Merida's cheeks and the tip of her nose. She typed, "What did you expect her to say? That she was so hurt she couldn't fulfill her duties?"

"No, Sheriff Kwinault would never say that. I mean, I don't think she would. I'm new in town. When they called for extra officers to deal with the crisis, I applied. She gave me a temp job. Three months. I appreciate that, but we're not old acquaintances. Or anything." He took off his cap and wiped his brow. He'd been standing in the sun, and suddenly seemed to feel its heat. "Do you know Sheriff Kwinault?"

"When we were children, we were friends."

"So you're from Virtue Falls?"

Now Merida was sorry she'd said more than she should. More slowly, she typed, "I knew her in Baltimore."

If he was faking confusion, he was doing a good job. "I thought Sheriff Kwinault grew up here."

"She lived with her father for a few years."

"*Really?* I knew she'd been in the Coast Guard and went around the country that way, but not—"

The radio hooked to his belt announced, *"The chase is done for the day. Let the roadblocks go."*

The guy in the car behind her must have heard, because he cheered and turned on his engine.

Merida put her tablet into her shoulder bag, slid off the car, dusted her rear and looked pointedly at Officer Weston, then at the barrier across the road.

He didn't move. "Are you staying in Virtue Falls or headed down the coast?"

Patiently she dug out her tablet again. "Staying."

"Vacation?"

"Rented an apartment in town."

"Really?" Now he was openly eager. "Since I'm new and you're new, what do you say we get together and explore the coast?"

She could have simply said no, but she didn't trust men, especially not men who worked at jobs that put them in charge. So she put on her grieved face and typed, "I'm recently widowed."

"Oh. Oh, I'm sorry."

She nodded and climbed in the car.

Sean Weston removed the barriers and waved her forward to the stop sign.

She figured that was that, but he put his hand on her door and leaned over. "I'll look you up."

She looked at him as if he were nuts and shook her head.

The guy behind her honked.

Officer Weston took his hand away.

She drove into Virtue Falls to create a new life . . . and at last, to get her revenge.

CHAPTER SIX

The old house was a monstrosity, a huge wooden gingerbread house, a parody of early twentieth century Gothic architecture set back on the lot on Lincoln Avenue. Dark Douglas fir trees overhung the dark stained wood, moss clumped on the cedar shingles, the windows were grimy, the yard was overgrown. This place was run-down, ill-kempt and eccentric, unlike anywhere Merida had lived before—and precisely what she wanted.

As she made her way up the front walk, she stumbled on the uneven concrete broken by huge tree roots. She clung to the railing as she climbed the porch stairs and watched her footing on the warped boards. A plaque beside the doorbell said:

GOOD KNIGHT MANOR BED AND BREAKFAST
IF NO ANSWER, WALK IN.

So she pushed the button and as she waited, she looked around. Next door, in gaps through the towering hedge, she saw a once-luxurious mansion that was now boarded up and dilapidated. On the other side, that home was smaller, newer, a tall and brightly painted Victorian house now undergoing renovation.

Interesting! This was a neighborhood in transition.

She pushed the doorbell again, then knocked loudly and tried the knob. The door opened with a creak.

To her delight, the interior matched the exterior in eccentricity. The dark wood-paneled walls and worn Oriental carpet made the giant entry feel like an expansive cave. Suits of armor stood on either side of the door, battle-axes clenched in their metal gloves. The candle-like bulbs in the brass chandelier barely emitted enough light to illuminate the dark corners, and if one were fanciful, a goblin might lurk at the top of the shadowy stairway.

Merida was not fanciful. She already knew that the real monsters lived in the material world: men with too much power, women without kindness or caring.

A ship's bell hung from a hook on the wall, a silver mallet hung beside it. A plaque announced, I'M PROBABLY IN THE KITCHEN PREPARING TOMORROW'S YUMMY BREAKFAST ROLLS. RING, PLEASE!

Merida tapped the mallet to the bell.

The sound echoed up toward the chandelier.

In less than a minute, a stylish, middle-aged woman bustled out from the back, wiping her flour-covered hands on her apron. "There you are! You must be Merida Falcon. I expected you sooner!"

Merida dug out her tablet and brought up her message about being mute, not deaf, please don't shout.

The woman did not stop talking long enough to look at the tablet, much less notice its message. "I'm Phoebe Glass, your new landlady. I'm delighted to meet you. Follow me and I'll show you your rooms. As requested, I gave you a *whole half of the house*." She beamed. "You're going to rattle around in all those big rooms, but since you took it for the year, I thought you might change bedrooms occasionally." She laughed merrily, stopped in front of a huge solid wood door, inserted a big old-fashioned key into the big old-fashioned lock, turned it and opened the door.

A dining table long enough to accommodate a dozen Queen Anne chairs—five on each side and one on either end—filled the long room. Four shiny suits of armor each holding a medieval weapon—long sword, mace, lance, spiked club—stood guard against the dark wood paneling.

Phoebe said, "You can see that this is the dining room and also see why I named my bed and break-fast Good Knight Manor. Eccentric, isn't it?"

Merida took to her tablet again.

Without heeding, Phoebe again swept on. "The home was originally built in 1900 during the first lumber boom by lumber baron Ernest Hagerjhelm—quite the name, isn't it? The manor is six thousand square feet on three levels, including a full attic where, of course, the servants resided. When Ernest died childless and unmarried in 1932, the house was sold and has been variously a private home, a boardinghouse, apartments and now my B and B. Every morning between eight and nine, I serve breakfast in the kitchen. If you're not able to attend, there'll be a pot to make coffee, a basket of fruit and breakfast bars on the buffet, and in the little refrigerator, cold drinks."

Merida slipped her tablet into her bag. Phoebe's dark snapping eyes, curly graying hair and rapid-fire delivery obviously did not require a response.

Phoebe moved into the room at the front of the house. "This is your small parlor. Most of the wood furniture is original, really grand antiques, but the chairs are new and comfortable. You have your own delightful little gas fireplace. It's on a timer. Those windows have a view of the street if you're a curtain-peeper—and aren't we all?"

Merida could truthfully say she didn't care who walked the sidewalks as long as they left her alone.

"Two months ago, I moved to Virtue Falls, bought the manor and ever since have been madly working to clean it up. You have no idea how difficult it has been to find help! Summer in

Virtue Falls is the high season and with the robust economy not even high school students need a job. I did manage to hire a local woman—poor thing, Susie Robinson has a worthless womanizing husband and four children to support. She'll be cleaning your rooms." Phoebe ducked into what looked like a dark cupboard. "Right through here, the stairs go up. They're narrow and steep, originally built for the maids and staff, but darned convenient for you! Follow me."

Merida followed and idly wondered if Phoebe had bought a bed-and-breakfast based solely on her need to talk incessantly.

Phoebe continued, "You have three inter-connected bedrooms on the second floor. There are five others on the other side of the corridor, but for your privacy I've blocked off all but one of your doors. Here we go, the sitting room for your master bedroom."

Merida stayed on the landing and when Phoebe turned, she gestured questioningly up the second flight of stairs.

"That leads up to the servants' attic. It's an apartment—I just rented to a gentleman and his wife." Phoebe must have correctly read Merida's expression for she said hastily, "I installed a deadbolt and sliding bolt for security on both sides. All of the outer doors to your rooms have a key-operated dead bolt, a chain and a sliding bolt for security."

Merida cautiously considered Phoebe. Before she rented, she had investigated Phoebe Glass. The woman had a few glitches in her background: two dead husbands, a son currently occupying a prison cell and a charge of embezzlement against her which she had soundly beaten. While Merida didn't entirely trust her—she didn't entirely trust anyone—still she suspected Phoebe was more sinned against than sinning. Merida had come into the situation knowing she was going to change the locks; she needed more than a mere old-fashioned key, chain and dead bolts to feel safe. Electronics would provide an extra layer of protection; she had brought everything she needed to install a thoroughly secure system and when she was done, she would have surveillance cameras inside her rooms and keyless electronic locks on every outer door.

Inside the master suite, the nine-foot ceilings, tall windows and creaking wooden floors provided ambiance with a vengeance. The velvet curtains, feather comforter and thick Oriental rugs exuded warmth and luxury. The old-fashioned touches were masterful: a ceramic chamber pot under the bed, a corded rotary phone from the twentieth century on the table, a black-mottled, wavy mirror over the antique dresser.

Merida could do her work very well here.

Phoebe asked if she had any questions.

Merida examined the thermostat.

"We don't have air-conditioning," Phoebe said. "The folks around here keep talking about this heat wave. I can't help but chuckle. I'm from the south"—a lie and Merida knew it, Phoebe was from the Midwest—"and I know what real heat is. But it's no problem. The trees around the house are shady, the windows are easy to open, and the ocean breeze so cool and constant, we don't really need air-conditioning. Isn't that right?" She beamed.

Merida could have disagreed. If she could speak.

But if Phoebe noticed Merida's silence, she didn't show it. Instead, she led the way out the one door into the upstairs corridor and down the stairs back to the entry, talking all the while, telling Merida to move her car around to the back by the old carriage house. "I turned that into a cottage for rent, too. On Tuesday, I have a gentleman moving in for the summer. When I bought Good Knight Manor Bed and Breakfast, my sister predicted disaster." Phoebe nodded, clearly pleased with herself, although Merida could not tell whether more for her own success or proving her sister wrong. "Leave your car unlocked. Susie can fetch your luggage when she arrives to clean."

Merida shook her head; she had no intention of allowing anyone to handle her bags.

"As you like. You have to haul the bags up the stairs, though. The dumbwaiter is broken and I've got to finish prepping tomorrow's breakfast rolls. We're having pecan sticky buns and a yogurt parfait with fresh strawberries." Phoebe headed toward the back of the house, then turned. "If this season is as prosperous as it's starting out to be, come this winter I'll install an elevator."

Merida smiled and gave her a thumbs-up.

Phoebe hurried back and enveloped her in a hug. "I knew as soon as we met you would be as positive a personality as I am!"

As Phoebe hustled toward the kitchen, Merida wondered if merely by being silent she had been elevated to a positive personality. And whether Phoebe would ever notice she didn't speak.

She parked as instructed, then in two trips she lugged her luggage in through the kitchen, past Phoebe, and into her new home.

Phoebe followed and ceremoniously turned over the keys. "I almost forgot! Merida, dear, every night at five I serve wine and port in the large downstairs living room, and the guests take that time to get to know each other. It's so lovely and convivial! On Tuesday night I fix an international buffet, and I promise I am an excellent cook. Make sure you plan to be there!" With a smile and a wave, she left Merida to unpack.

Merida shuddered inwardly. She didn't want

to—couldn't stand to—go into a room of strangers and be mute, have people avoid her gaze, or stare, or try to make awkward conversation with her. No, she would not attend Phoebe's convivial evening.

Shutting the dining room doors, she locked them, then stood and hugged herself.

For the first time in many years, she was alone; she didn't have to smile, to pretend interest in stories she had heard a hundred times, to wait on a cantankerous old man and make his needs and wants her primary responsibility. Her only responsibility was to herself. She headed for the stairway, laboriously carrying the bags into the master bedroom.

Following instructions, she attached the computer-sized safe to the wall beside the giant antique dresser and behind the large flowered easy chair—she would pay Phoebe for the damages when she left—and inside placed her two laptops and her extra iPad. She set the code, locked it and unlocked it, locked it again, and dusted her fingers in satisfaction. She lugged her suitcase into the dim, spacious closet. A bare bulb with a bead pull-chain switch hung from the ceiling. She reached up and gave it a tug—and touched the sticky thread of a spiderweb. Something landed on her head and scuttled across her ear. She jumped, screamed silently, bent down and thrashed at her hair. The spider—large, shiny, black, horrible—fell onto the faded carpet. She stomped at it in a panic.

The segmented body crunched.

She flinched. She shuddered. She stared at the smear of the corpse. Got a tissue and wiped it up. Let her breath out. No servants. No help. She had taken care of the matter herself.

This incident was not an omen.

CHAPTER SEVEN

Kateri opened the door to Rainbow's dim hospital room and peered inside.

Rainbow rested on the bed, immobile, blank-faced, not there. A tube ran down her throat. An IV dripped fluid into her arm. The side rails were raised; for what reason, Kateri did not know. It wasn't as if Rainbow would suddenly wake, move, try to leave the bed.

An elderly woman sat close, doing a crossword puzzle under a reading light. From the back, she looked vaguely familiar. But who . . . ?

Kateri slipped into the room.

The woman turned her gray head.

Crap. It was Mrs. Branyon, who said with her usual lack of charm, "Oh. It's you. I was due for a break anyway." Grasping the arms of the chair, she leveraged herself to her feet. Leaning over Rainbow's still form, she said loudly, "Honey, that Indian woman is here to see you, the one you took the bullet for. I know you like her, so I'll leave you two alone. I'm going to get some dinner—the food here is okay, better than at the nursing home, but nothing like the grub at the Oceanview Café. Since you got shot and gave up the job, even that food is not much good. Dax is too busy crying in his soup. I'll be back, don't you worry. You'll be okay for a few minutes." Without wasting a glance at Kateri, she creaked past to the door. She opened it and said, "Young lady, don't you open those blinds. She doesn't need the sun shining in her eyes. By the way, you look like hell yourself. You got the sheriff's job. Do us all a favor and try not to die before you take the oath of office." On that caring note, she left.

Kateri hurried to Rainbow's bedside. "Do you know who you had sitting with you? Mrs. Branyon! Holy cow, what did you do to deserve that? Something bad in a former life?" Kateri tucked in the blankets, and picking up Rainbow's hand, tsked. "Your fingers are frozen. Let me get you a warm blanket. And"—she lowered her voice—"I don't care what *she* says, I'm going to open the blinds. The sun is shining outside and I know how much you love the light." Kateri did as she said; let in the late-afternoon sun, got a blanket out of the warmer. She brought back the blanket, doubled it, placed it over Rainbow's body from her neck to her toes. "I remember how cold I was when I was in the coma. Seemed like I was in the opposite of hell, but it sure wasn't heaven."

Rainbow didn't indicate by a flicker of an eyelash that she knew Kateri was here.

"I thought I'd better bring you up to date. You know your parents are in Nepal doing social work and learning the local techniques and patterns of weaving. We've got people looking for them, but no one's found them yet. They sure know how to wander away, don't they?"

No response. Of course.

"I just got out of emergency myself. Your local law enforcement spent a useless day chasing after the Terrances. We did find out only one Terrance is left. John Senior dumped John Junior's body on the road as a distraction. It worked. Moen and I were in the lead, saw the body hit the ground, slammed headfirst into a tree trying to avoid it, got hit from behind, and I ended up getting hauled to the hospital by none other than Stag Denali." It seemed like Rainbow would say something now. Something raunchy, something funny, something earthy.

But no, she didn't move. Her heart monitor beeped quietly, slowly, steadily.

Kateri continued, "I know, I know. You approve. I approve, too, or rather my loins do. Unfortunately, my brain's kind of worried about the guy. If you'll recall, he was walking past the Oceanview Café when the shooting occurred. He dove for the ground a split second before we heard anything. And he came through it unscathed. We've been digging bullets and buckshot out of every tree and every building in the square, while he laid right on the sidewalk in full sight and didn't get a scratch. Which is lucky . . . unless he planned the shooting. I mean, he waltzes into town, romances me in a big way, announces he wants to build a casino on the rez that's going to cause no end of trouble for law enforcement, and when I say I oppose it and I unexpectedly win the election, I'm gunned down?" Kateri put her hand on her ribs. "As dear Mrs. Branyon pointed out, you're the one who actually got gunned down. In my place. Like I didn't already know that." Kateri found her throat was getting tight. She swallowed. Waited. Swallowed again. "But the point remains, did Stag help the Terrances plan that drive-by? Not that a drive-by is tough to work out, but for them to escape for four days . . ." Kateri realized she was staring at Rainbow, expecting an answer. Rainbow was so interested in people, she had such insight into people's minds and hearts, Kateri depended on her, listened to her . . .

She wanted to hear Rainbow again. Hear her voice.

"Right now they're doing an autopsy on John Junior. Apparently he was shot during the drive-by. We've lost John Senior in the mountains. But Bergen and the guys did find his campsite—or one of them—and his car. He escaped in an off-road vehicle, the bastard." Sliding her hand under the blanket, Kateri took Rainbow's cool, still fingers. She leaned close and whispered, "We will get him. I swear to you, we will get him." She leaned back quickly before her tears could fall on Rainbow's face.

Behind her, the door opened. She wiped at her face, then faced Mrs. Branyon.

But it wasn't Mrs. Branyon. It was Officer Moen. "Sheriff, you heard what happened with Terrance?"

She nodded.

"I'm sorry we screwed up." The pale, redheaded boy scraped his foot across the linoleum.

"We didn't screw up. We simply didn't realize the cold bastard would treat his son's body like garbage." Truer words she'd never spoken. "We know better now, and we won't underestimate him again."

"I can give you the details on the way to City Hall."

She cleared her throat. "Dr. Frownfelter told me to go home."

"Um, I don't think you should. Or . . . or can."

For the first time, she focused, really focused, on Moen. He had brown stains on his cuffs and a brown smear across his chest—bloodstains—and the kid looked tired. Grasping his arm, she turned him toward the door and pushed him into the corridor. "Moen, you have to be off duty. Why are you here?"

"Monique Ries came to the hospital in an ambulance. I came in with her."

Monique Ries was a local, probably in her

thirties although she looked older, overweight, overly affectionate when intoxicated—and she was always intoxicated. But for all that, no one disliked Monique enough to hurt her. "What happened to Monique?"

"We had a slashing incident behind the Gem Lounge."

"Slashing?" Man, this week just got better and better. "Who? How?"

"Unknown perp."

"Unknown perp . . ." Yep, better and better.

"Miss Ries was at the bar getting her morning refreshments . . ."

"Right."

"She met some guy lurking outside the ladies' room, he made an offer, she followed him into the alley and he tried to slash her throat with, like, a box knife. Something really sharp."

"Slash her throat?" Good God almighty. "He . . . missed?"

"She started shrieking and body-butted him." Moen looked at Kateri meaningfully. "She carries a lot of body."

Kateri waved at him to continue.

"She slammed him into the wall, shrieking all the time. Bertha Waldschmidt heard her and came out the back door with a knife." Moen was getting enthusiastic in his telling. "Bertha chased him to the end of the alley, then came back for Monique. She's okay, he missed her throat, cut her along the jawline, but man, you should have seen the blood!"

"Really. No. I don't need to see any more blood." She'd seen enough of her own. "Was she admitted?"

"I dunno. They're stitching her up right now. She's drunk, of course."

She and Moen were going to have to have another chat about being careful with his politically incorrect commentary. "Do we have a perp description?"

"Monique said he was tall, dark and handsome."

"*Not* helpful. What did Bertha say?"

"Bertha said she wants to talk to you."

"Then we'd better go to the police station." She held up one finger. "Let me say good-bye to Rainbow."

"She won't know—"

Kateri shot him a look that made him pale so much his freckles glowed like tiny beads of embarrassment.

"I'll wait out here," he said.

Kateri pushed the door open. She knew a moment of terror while she listened for the beeping of the heart monitor, but it sounded quiet, slow and steady. She walked to the bed. "I've got to go to the police station. You know Monique Ries . . . she got cut by an unknown perp. If you were here and talking, I'll bet you would have a suspect for me. Wouldn't you?"

No answer. Rainbow did not move. The flame of her life flickered so dimly, Kateri could scarcely see it.

Come on, Rainbow. Wake up! Lightly, Kateri put her hand on Rainbow's chest. "I'll be back soon. Stay alive. Please. Stay alive." Turning, she hurried toward the door.

She met Mrs. Branyon coming in.

Mrs. Branyon took one look at the brightly lit room and shrieked, "You wicked girl! Do you never follow instruction from your betters?"

Tired, impatient and grieved, Kateri snapped, "I do. But I so seldom hear from my betters." She stalked past Mrs. Branyon, down the corridor and out the exit into the sunshine Mrs. Branyon so despised.

Okay. *Now* she was ready to interview Bertha.

CHAPTER EIGHT

Moen babbled all the way into town. First he apologized for hitting the tree, asked how Kateri was feeling, then without waiting for a reply he told her that they'd lost John Terrance, he'd gotten away in an all-terrain vehicle, but they found his camp and confiscated his car. She didn't try to interrupt, to tell him she already had heard a briefing from Bergen, and sure enough she picked up a few more details she stored away in her mind. Like the fact that Moen's eyes were gleaming with excitement and the young man who usually only spoke to put his foot in his mouth spewed forth words as fast as he could. Virtue Falls didn't usually see such drama, and he relished every moment.

The Virtue Falls City Hall housed the Virtue Falls Police Department. City Hall was in the Historical Registry so when the building survived The Earthquake—everyone in town referred to that life-shattering event as The Earthquake—monies had been collected to fix it. They got more than they hoped and less than they needed, and the resulting fight about whether to restore the ornate façade or strengthen the structure had left them with a lot of seriously peeved citizens on both sides of the fence and a levee to raise enough money to pay the contractor when he overran his estimate.

Speaking as someone who worked in the big old stone building, Kateri thought all the money should have been spent on the seismic design upgrade. But nobody asked her or any of the other officers.

The walk through the police department to her office proved enlightening. She had left the chase in bad shape and returned in decent shape; she had expected to be inundated with mockery about her female frailty. Instead she heard mumbles of, "Sorry we lost him, Sheriff."

When she got to the door of her office, she faced them and said, "Guys, a dead body is a great diversion. Time and again, I've gone through it in my mind and I don't know what else we would have done. Do you?"

Heads shook.

"Let me talk to Mrs. Waldschmidt about this attack, then we'll figure out our next strategy for catching John Terrance."

Heads nodded.

Bergen asked, "You don't suppose Terrance slashed Monique Ries, do you?"

Kateri shook her head. "There's no way he could have gotten down here so fast." But of course he could, and a smart move that would be with every law enforcement officer in the state chasing around the mountains. "Let me see what Bertha has to say."

Bertha Waldschmidt was in her seventies, around five foot two and ninety-five pounds soaking wet. She wore black boots, black leggings, a slender coral sweater and a bulky black cardigan. Her inky-black hair was cut in the same pageboy style she'd worn for as long as Kateri remembered. The Gem Lounge had been in business for forty-five years and Bertha was the original owner. She was the toughest broad who had ever owned a bar in Virtue Falls.

Kateri adored her.

"Sweetheart!" Bertha sat in Kateri's office, drinking the vile police department coffee as if she liked it. "Congratulations on your election. Sorry about the shootings. John Terrance and his son are pigs. Sit down and I'll tell you what I know about Monique and her hookup."

Kateri wandered behind her desk, leaned her staff against the wall, placed her hands on the arms of her chair and lowered herself into the seat. "Good to see you, too, Bertha. Mind if we record this?"

"Go for it, honey." Bertha waited while Kateri pulled out her computer tablet, hit Record and placed it on the desk between them. Then, at Kateri's nod, she launched into her story. "The attacker was never in the bar. I figure he came in by the unlocked back door."

"Why was it unlocked?"

"Because I'm always going out into the alley

to smoke my cigarette. Damn stupid state laws, won't even let me smoke in my own establishment." Bertha took Kateri's agreement as natural. "The door's always unlocked, sometimes the street people come in for a snack, but what do I care? I give them some popcorn, a few sticks of pepperoni, a baggie of vegetables and they wander off again."

Beneath Bertha's gruff exterior beat a kind heart.

Kateri knew better than to point that out. Bertha was tough; she could also carve out your liver with a broken beer bottle. And she'd break the glass to do it.

"I went out to smoke, and as soon as I opened the door, there was Monique shrieking at the top of her lungs and beating on this guy. I wasn't going to interfere. When she's been drinking, Monique has her 'sexy moments.'" Bertha used air quotes. "But I took a second look and she was bleeding all down her neck and her shoulder. I yelled a word I don't use in polite company, grabbed a knife and the guy started running toward the street."

"No motivation that you know of?"

"None. Monique told me she had never seen him before, but she was swimming hard toward the drunk end of the pool."

Exactly what Moen had said. "Can you identify the slasher?"

Moen stepped into the doorway. "Sheriff, you want me to—"

Bertha cut him off. "I saw him from the back while he was getting the hell out of there. He's white. Or at least not African-American. Dark brown hair. I think he's tall, but I'm five one and seven-eighths and I'm no judge of men when they're vertical."

Horror painted Moen's freckled face, and he ducked away.

Bertha glanced toward the suddenly empty doorway. "Poor kid. I probably scarred him for life."

"He'll survive." Kateri wished Bergen hadn't raised the specter, but now she had to ask, "Was the attacker John Terrance?"

"I don't know. I wouldn't know John Terrance from a hole in the ground." Bertha's sharp blue eyes snapped with fury. " 'Bout thirty years ago, that smartass swaggering woman-hating hood came into the Gem Lounge selling his filthy drugs. When I told him to get the hell out, he said, 'What are you going to do about it, old lady?' "

Kateri leaned her head against the back of her chair. She was going to enjoy this.

Bertha continued, "I came around the bar. He stood up. I grabbed him by the nuts, lifted him up on his tiptoes and walked him backward out the door and onto the sidewalk. Told him to never return."

Torn between amusement, admiration and horror, Kateri asked, "*Did* he return?"

"Of course he did. That night with a pistol. I pulled my sawed-off shotgun out from underneath the bar, pointed it at him and asked who he thought he was going to harm with that little popgun. Haven't seen him since." Bertha examined her fingernails and smiled. "I did hear he had to fight a lot of men before they stopped laughing in his face." Her smile faded. "He ambushed them, usually. Nasty punk."

"He's gotten nastier."

"I know, dear. I am so sorry about Rainbow. I recall when she was young. I recall when she delivered you. I recall your mother."

Of course she did. Kateri remembered going into the Gem Lounge to fetch her mother after those long bouts of drinking that rendered Mary limp, jolly or sometimes . . . violent.

"Mary deserved better than your father, but damn, she raised you good. She would be proud."

Kateri blinked away tears. Yes. For all the problems she had experienced with her mother, she had never doubted Mary loved her. Kateri had never stopped working for her mother's approval. She had always believed that some-how, somewhere Mary knew what Kateri had accomplished . . . She really needed to get home before she dissolved into a puddle of damp emotion. "Thank you, Bertha. I'm glad you think that." She leaned forward, put her elbows on the desk and fixed her gaze on Bertha's face. "Listen—John Terrance is a lot more dangerous now than he was thirty years ago, or even last week. He's out to settle some scores and he's already proven he can get into town for a shooting. So why not come in and slash a woman's throat?"

"Why not try to shoot you again?"

"Why not make women afraid to come to your bar and destroy your business? And at the same time make me look incompetent as sheriff?"

Bertha nodded, but doubtfully. "He would have had to think awfully fast and be sort of subtle, and I never heard he was any too bright."

"He's not intelligent, but he's got an underhanded way of figuring things out."

"Like a weasel with rabies?"

"Yes. I don't know whether to hope it's John Terrance and when we've got him we've got the slasher, or to hope we've got two criminals and both are fools." Kateri rubbed her forehead.

"If Monique has never seen the slasher before, then he's not a local because she's known every man in town, most of them in the biblical sense. So maybe after screwing up his little crime, he'll move on."

"From your mouth to God's ears. But I'm afraid, after your story about getting a grip on John Terrance's testicles . . ."

"Not much there, and I grabbed 'em hard enough to know."

"One of the scores he wants to settle is yours. Men don't forget stuff like that. You'll be careful?"

"You bet. A few years ago, I installed a good security system at the Lounge. I live over the bar. So he's going to have to catch me out in the open to work me over." Bertha pulled back her bulky cardigan to reveal a holster and pistol. "I've got a concealed carry permit."

"Of course you do."

"If I see that worthless piece of shit, I'll shoot first and ask questions afterward."

Kateri should give her standard speech: *Call law enforcement and do not try to apprehend.* She decided against it. After all, Bertha wasn't going to try and apprehend him. She intended to kill him.

Bertha continued, "As for Monique's slasher, I'd recognize him from the back."

"For the love of God, don't shoot *him* until we prove—"

Bertha stood up. "I'm old and cranky, but I'm not stupid. Got any other questions about the slashing, Sheriff Kwinault?"

"That about does it. Thank you for coming in. If you remember any other details, please call and one of my officers will be by to take your statement."

Bertha pointed her finger at Kateri. "*You* come. Come by for a drink."

"I don't—"

"I know." Bertha waggled that finger. "You don't drink alcohol. Come by for a Coke and some corn nuts. When you were a kid, you always liked corn nuts. It would do my barflies good to know the sheriff was interested in their welfare."

When Bertha was right, she was right. Kateri painfully pushed herself to her feet. "I'll do that. Thank you."

Bertha winked and headed out the door.

Moen eased into Kateri's office. "Bergen sent me in to take you home."

"Great. I've got a pain pill calling my name." Kateri got her walking stick.

Moen looked distressed. "You don't suppose Mrs. Waldschmidt meant she likes men to be horizontal? As in . . ."

"As in sex?" Kateri grinned as she wound her way through the patrol room. "What do you think?"

"I don't want to think. She's got to be six hundred years old!"

Dumbass kid. "You know Bertha's been married five times? To a couple husbands I never met, to the same guy twice, to one guy who was half her age . . . I heard she wore the poor guy out."

Moen plugged his ears.

Kateri laughed uncontrollably. Maybe the pain shot Dr. Frownfelter had given her had taken effect at last. She laughed again when they stopped to pick up her dog, Lacey, from Mrs. Golobovitch the dog-sitter. Lacey danced with such joy her long, cocker spaniel ears flapped adorably and Kateri leaned down to pet her soft, blond head.

When Moen stopped at her apartment, Kateri opened the car door.

Lacey leaped out, put her nose to the ground and started sniffing.

Kateri followed much more slowly.

"Want some help, Sheriff?" Moen asked.

"I can make it." Because in Virtue Falls, you could always figure someone was peeking out the window and Kateri needed to give the impression of health. She climbed the stairs and got out her key.

Lacey raced after, placed herself between Kateri and the apartment. Bared her teeth, faced the door and growled low in her throat.

Taken aback, Kateri gazed at her usually charming dog, then took a long slow step backward. "Moen!" she called. The door stood ajar the smallest bit. With one finger, she pushed it open . . . and saw all the lights on, pillows tossed and the sparkle of broken glass.

Someone had trashed her apartment.

Turned out getting her dog was a smart move.

CHAPTER NINE

Kateri sat on a folding chair on her tiny porch as her officers went through her apartment, assessing the damage, dusting for fingerprints, holding hushed conversations with her neighbors.

There was no need for the hushed conversations; Kateri's pain meds had taken over. When she nodded off, as she occasionally did, Lacey would give her a nudge and Kateri would straighten up.

The sun had begun to set when at last Bergen came out, put his hand on Kateri's shoulder and said, "Come on. We're going to be a few more hours. I'll take you to my house so you can catch some shut-eye."

"I want to go to Rainbow's."

"Rainbow's . . . house?"

"I have her keys. She wouldn't mind."

Bergen got that stern, *I know better than you* face that he wore so well. "John Terrance is out there. He probably did this."

"That's true. He is out there and he did probably do this. So I'm not going to put your wife and children in jeopardy."

Bergen paused, and his *I know* face turned into his *Darn, I wish you hadn't thought of that* face.

"Hard to argue that, isn't it?" Kateri added, "After a day like today, I want to be alone."

"I'd rather you weren't."

"Send a patrol by every half hour."

"I'll put someone on guard at Rainbow's house."

"Make yourself happy." She allowed him to help her to her feet. "But Lacey is as good a guard as any you can set."

He leaned down to pet her dog. "She knows who did this."

"Yes. If only she could speak." Kateri thought a minute. "I suppose she will somehow tell us when she spots the perp."

"Another reason to keep her close." He put Kateri and Lacey in his patrol car and as they drove the three blocks to Rainbow's tiny corner house, he reported, "John Terrance—or whoever tossed the house—didn't do much damage. A broken vase. Furniture upended. The back door was open. We think you interrupted him—the perp—and he fled."

"Doesn't sound like Terrance to me. He's wily, but he wouldn't run from a girl. Except if that girl had a chance of hurting him. Spiteful bully."

"He had no idea how many officers you had called, so in his mind, he was running from overwhelming testosterone-driven odds."

She laughed and as they turned the corner, she almost toppled sideways onto the console.

"Whoa, girl." Bergen pushed on her shoulder.

She teetered back into a sitting position.

They pulled into Rainbow's driveway.

Another patrol car pulled in behind them.

Bergen came around to help her out. "Sean Weston volunteered for the first shift. I think he's bucking to get on full-time."

She glanced back at her newest temporary officer.

He smiled—he had one of those square smiles that showed all his teeth—and gave her a thumbs-up.

"I hate a brown nose," she muttered, then realized her mutter was a little too loud.

"You hired him." Bergen held her arm.

"Good credentials." They climbed the stairs to the front porch. "Glowing recommendation from the Carson City police chief."

"So the chief either wanted desperately to get rid of Weston . . ."

Kateri winced.

"Or he really is that good."

She handed Bergen Rainbow's keys. "What do you think?"

"I think we'll find out." He opened the front door and gave her a push inside.

Lacey followed, clearly delighted to once more visit Rainbow's home.

Bergen asked, "Can you get yourself to bed or should I call Sandra to help you?"

Kateri drew herself up. "I've been putting myself to bed for a lot of years." She considered him. "But I need my toothbrush and a change of clothes."

Bergen got that panicked look that men get when asked to dig around in a woman's panty drawer. "I'll call Sandra to come and pack you a bag."

"You do that. And thank you both. You are dear friends."

"Yeah, yeah." He waved that away and headed for his car.

Sean Weston parked himself at the curb.

Kateri walked inside, shut and locked the door behind her, slithered onto the couch on the way to the bedroom, dropped her walking stick on the floor beside her and slept the sleep of the dead.

Kateri woke up with her head kinked funny, one arm numb and a dog curled behind her bent knees. She half-opened her eyes and stared at the back of the couch.

God. What time was it?

Not that it mattered. She had to get up. Her ribs hurt. She was due to take an antibiotic. She had to pee. Plus she probably should brush her teeth and maybe try to climb into Rainbow's bed, which had to be more comfortable than this saggy old sofa.

With a groan, she rolled onto her back, dislodging Lacey, then over to the other side— and gave a half-scream.

Someone—a man—was sprawled in the armchair, watching her.

Lacey stood up and wagged her whole body.

"Stag." Kateri put a hand over her thumping heart and slowly worked herself into a sitting position. "You scared the hell out of me."

"*You* scared the hell out of *me*. Your place got broken into and you didn't even call?" He wasn't actually relaxed, she realized. Each muscle was tense.

Lacey stopped wagging.

"What were you going to do that the rest of the department couldn't?"

"Guard you."

"Oh. Yeah. I didn't think of that." Kateri dropped her eyes, because she hadn't thought of it, and if she had, that uneasy suspicion that he'd set up the drive-by lingered. Stupid, but one of the things that appealed to her on a visceral level—that was to say, made her horny—was how very dangerous he was, like a tiger in a sideshow that could at any moment turn feral. He'd been a bouncer. He'd served time for murder. Now he was involved with setting up a casino at the edge of her town, a casino that would ultimately make her life a hell with prostitution, drunkenness and gambling addicts.

She pushed her hair out of her eyes and looked up. A small wheeled bag sat on the dining room table. *Her* small wheeled bag. "Look.

88

Sandra must have sneaked in while I was asleep."

"Yeah . . . I could have packed your bag instead of her. I know my way around your bedroom." He still looked ready to spring, and his deep voice had a dark, edgy tone.

Lacey edged herself into Kateri's lap and fixed him with a stern eye.

Kateri petted her dog's head.

He said, "For God's sake, you stupid animal, I'm not going to hurt her."

The way he snapped at her dog, like Lacey had hurt his feelings, made Kateri relax and smile. She glanced toward the closed front door. "How did *you* get in?"

"I told the kid out front I intended to come in."

"The kid? The cop? He let you walk in?" Sean Weston was in big trouble.

"I may have frightened him. You might want to tell him you're still alive before all of Virtue Falls law enforcement arrives."

"Right." Gently she shoved Lacey out of her lap. Leaning down, she groped for her walking stick. She braced it on the floor, braced her other hand against the arm of the sofa and tried to rise.

She couldn't quite make it. Pain stabbed at her side, her wobbly knees gave out, and with a wince, she fell back—and that made her flinch, moan and hold her ribs.

Immediately Stag was on his feet and at her side. "For God's sake. Ask for help." He wrapped his arm around her butt and lifted her to her feet.

"Thank you." She hobbled toward the front door, Stag on one side, Lacey on the other.

"You don't know how to ask for help." He sounded surprised.

"It doesn't come easy."

He opened the door for her.

It was dark. Three cop cars had already arrived, lights flashing, sirens silenced. Neighbors were gathering on the sidewalks. Damn. She'd made a scene. She took a careful step out onto the porch and grasped the railing for support. "Sorry, guys. I'm fine. Really."

"How do we know he hasn't got a gun on you?" Sean sounded more than a little belligerent.

She shut the door in Stag's face, opened it to reveal him glaring balefully, shut it, opened it and said, "He's my boyfriend. He was overly concerned and I'm sure too pushy. I hope he didn't injure you?"

"Only his pride," Stag muttered.

"No, he . . . no." Sean shook his head.

Another cop car pulled up. Bergen got out of the driver's side, leaned an arm on the top of the car and called, "No prints, Kateri, and we've got a mess to clean up before you can go home."

"Okay. I'll stay here for the night. Stag and Lacey are here. I'll be safe. You all can go"—she waved a limp hand—"find John Terrance. And isn't it Saturday night?"

Bergen answered her unspoken question. "Yes, we've already got a few DUIs brought in."

She nodded. "Give me twelve good hours of sleep and I'll be riding with you again. Go on." She watched them reluctantly get in the cars to leave. Turning back to Stag, she said, "Please. I need some food, some meds and . . . can you help me take a shower?"

He got a crease in his cheek, the kind that meant he was holding back a smile. "See? Now that didn't hurt at all."

She pinched his butt. Hard. Which was no easy thing because his cheek was rock-hard firm muscle . . . really nice and tight . . . damn him.

He laughed, pulled her close, and together they headed into the bathroom.

Lacey stayed right on their heels. She sat looking into the bathtub while Stag gently soaped and rinsed Kateri. She watched him dry Kateri and put her into the nightgown Sandra had packed.

He kept his arm around Kateri as they made their way to the master bedroom. When he flipped on the light, he stopped, viewed the decadent queen-sized bed and asked, "Why are there scratch marks on the headboard posts?"

Kateri grinned. "Handcuffs?"

Her big, tough bouncer/lover turned her toward the guest room.

"I wish Rainbow was here, now, and well," she

said. "She'd make John Terrance sorry he was ever born."

"You'll have to do that for her." As he helped Kateri into the narrow double bed, Lacey leaped onto the middle of the mattress.

Stag eyed her.

She eyed him.

He went into the kitchen and came back with canned soup in a mug and a peanut butter and jelly sandwich. It was the *best* canned soup and the *best* PB & J Kateri had ever eaten. He gave Kateri her meds, took away the dishes, then came back and stripped down to his shorts—Kateri noted his chest was in the same condition as his butt—and climbed in on the other side of the bed.

Lacey stood up, leaped over, snuggled against his shoulder, then looked back at Kateri smugly as if to say, *Look who has him now.*

"You little traitor," Kateri told her.

Lacey playfully flipped her ears and put her head against his throat.

Stag chuckled deep in his chest. "She knows who the alpha male is and she knows his place at the top of the pack."

Kateri's eyes were already closing. "At the top of the pack . . . right under the alpha female."

"Exactly where I want to be."

She went to sleep smiling.

CHAPTER TEN

The next morning, Kateri woke to find herself alone except for one small blond cocker spaniel who now draped herself over Kateri's outflung arm. "Traitor," Kateri again told her sleepy-eyed girl dog, and scratched her between the ears. While Lacey lolled on the comforter, Kateri discovered her walking stick carefully propped up against the wall by the bed, and with that and the support of the end table, got to her feet.

She felt better. Still bruised, still achy, but with the sleep she needed she was ready to catch her some bad guys. In the kitchen she found coffee ready to brew, bread in the toaster, dog food and water in bowls on the floor and a note: *Bed is short. I am long (but you knew that). Went in early to work. Take it easy today, sweetheart, or suffer my wrath.*

"I am afraid," she said out loud.

While Lacey feasted, Kateri buttered her toast and considered how to tackle the day. Head on, as always.

She walked outside, over to the patrol car parked at the curb, leaned down and asked, "Anything happen I should know about?"

Officer Norm Knowles sighed deeply. "Tourists using a hibachi on a picnic table and setting it on fire. Fender bender on Main leading to a fistfight and a night in jail. Speeders. Public intoxication."

"So . . . the usual."

"Yep. No sign of John Terrance. That sick bastard." Norm had one adult son, the apple of his eye, and the idea of using his body as a defense made Norm's lip curl.

"Thanks. I'm going to drop Lacey off at Mrs. Golobovitch's, then head downtown for breakfast. Why don't you go home and put your feet up?"

"I'll do that." He tilted his hat back. "You look better, Sheriff. Keep it that way."

She slapped the top of the car. "I will." She walked the two blocks to the Oceanview Café, braced herself, pushed open the door and walked into an atmosphere smelling of bacon, coffee and avid speculation.

Conversation stopped. In unison, all eyes turned to her.

She waited for the accusations of incompetence in the matter of the capture of John Terrance.

From the corner geezer table, Mr. Caldwell asked, "How you doing, Sheriff?"

Which on the surface sounded like a perfectly friendly inquiry. Except that Mr. Caldwell was an old sonofabitch who hated uppity women in principle and her in particular.

Kateri replied cautiously, "Pretty good."

"You look like shit."

There was the Mr. Caldwell she knew and despised.

He continued, "This your first time in here since the shooting?"

Her throat unexpectedly closed. She nodded.

"We're all missing Rainbow," Mr. Harcourt said.

The new waitress, a thin buzz saw of a woman with frizzy blond hair fixed in a long tight braid, turned away from the counter and held the coffeepot in a manner that could only be described as threatening.

Mr. Harcourt added hastily, "Not that Linda isn't doing a great job taking care of the customers. But Rainbow is in our prayers."

"Amen," Mr. Caldwell said loudly and glared at Linda.

Linda snorted, slammed down the coffeepot and delivered a plate of pancakes with such vigor that syrup leaped into the air like Old Faithful.

In unison, the customers leaned away.

Kateri raised her eyebrows at Mr. Caldwell.

He mouthed, "Meanest woman in the world."

Coming from him, that said a lot.

"You ought to sit down before you fall down." Mr. Setzer was a real charmer, too, and Mr. Caldwell's best buddy.

"Thanks. I will."

Mr. Edkvist was the fourth at the geezer table, an Oceanview Café institution that consisted of four slightly deaf old guys loudly predicting the end of America while disparaging today's politics, today's shiftless youth and today's lousy manners. Their own discourtesy, of course, was never a topic of discussion, at least among them.

Kateri started toward the long counter and an empty stool, then caught sight of a beautiful woman sitting alone at a four-person table.

The woman smiled at her and using American Sign Language, spelled, "Hi, Kateri."

Kateri blinked. She looked closer at the woman. She didn't recognize her.

The woman spelled, "Do you remember how to do this?"

Kateri spelled, but much more awkwardly, "I learned long ago. Do I know you?"

The woman offered her iPad and gestured to the chair next to her.

Kateri seated herself so she could observe the café and read the message on the iPad. "My name is Merida Falcon. I am mute. I AM NOT DEAF. PLEASE DO NOT SHOUT!" Again she looked up at the woman. There was something about her . . . but she would *swear* she didn't recognize that face.

The woman turned so her back was to the customers and with her hands low and swift, she spelled, "It's been many years since we met, but I've never forgotten you."

Kateri looked from those hands, at those long,

nimble fingers, to the unknown face, then back at the fingers. Memory carried her to a day long ago when two giggling little girls sat in a Baltimore attic learning the manual alphabet for the deaf. They thought it would be cool if they could silently speak to each other in a secret language. The two children, one a foster child, the other an alien in her father's home, said it would be great if no one else—parents, teachers, siblings—could understand them. Looking back, it had been silly and the phase hadn't lasted long; they quickly discovered the manual alphabet took practice to do and to read. Still, Kateri remembered . . .

Reaching out, Kateri snagged Merida's wrist and turned her left hand over. The tip of her thumb had a notch-shaped scar where she'd used the screwdriver to pry the panel off the door to the attic . . . She whispered, "Merry. Merry Byrd."

The woman smiled, nodded. She touched her chest. "Merida now. Merida Falcon."

Kateri moved her chair closer to the table. Instinctively she lowered her voice. "You're now a person who is mute? What happened to your voice? And what happened to your face? You were always pretty, but now you're . . . gorgeous."

Merida pulled the iPad close, typed, pushed the iPad across the table. "There was an explosion."

"What kind of explosion?"

Merida made a flying motion.

"Airplane?"

Merida nodded.

"You always wanted to fly. You dreamed of flying." When Merry had talked about her future, it always included somehow becoming a pilot and flying high above the clouds. "And your airplane exploded? On the ground? It had to be on the ground."

Merida spelled, "Of course."

"Right. So you had to have plastic surgery?"

"A lot." Merida gestured up and down at her figure, then spelled, "Too much. Too much pain. Too much anger, too much resentment. Merry is dead. I am sorry."

"Yes. I see." The woman beside Kateri bore no resemblance to the bright, outgoing girl she had been so many years ago.

Linda stomped up with glasses of ice water. "You want anything, Sheriff? Ask your friend if she wants anything, would you?"

"I'd take coffee, black, and a Denver omelet. And you can ask my friend—she can hear, she's merely mute."

Linda leaned close to Merida and asked loudly, "You want anything?" She gestured like someone drinking coffee from a mug.

Merida laughed silently, then typed and passed the iPad.

Linda read it. "Bacon, crisp. Eggs over easy.

98

Wheat toast. Hash browns. Orange juice and hot coffee?"

Merida slapped her hands together, pointed at Linda and nodded.

"You *can* hear, can't you? There's something to remember." Linda walked away muttering, "Every time I turn around, we've got more weirdoes in this town."

Kateri blushed for Linda. "I'm sorry. Honestly, we're not all so rude here."

Merida typed, "Better that then the over-solicitous kindness when they think because I can't speak, I'm mentally challenged. Or unbalanced. I love that one, too."

Kateri glanced around the café.

Everyone was watching them, openly or surreptitiously or avidly.

"You must get tired of the curiosity."

"I'm used to it." Merida put down the iPad and with her hands spelled, "You've changed, too."

"Yes." Remembering Merida's casual explanation of her transformation, Kateri said, "There was a tsunami."

"I've followed your career. I know about your . . . mishap. I never doubted you would triumph."

Kateri's eyes filled with tears again. Her campaign manager would tell her sheriffs didn't cry. And usually, she didn't; no woman survived what she'd survived without being tough as nails. But seeing her friend Rainbow shot and in a coma, then losing John Terrance while in hot pursuit, had created a relentless guilt and pressure. Now to have her best friend from so long ago appear and express such confidence in her—turned out Kateri was sentimental after all.

Linda whipped past and tossed silverware and paper napkins on the table, followed by cups of coffee. "You girls want cream or sugar?"

"Actually, I'd like sweetener," Kateri said. "Do you want anything, Merida?"

Merida spelled, "Cream."

"She'd like cream," Kateri told Linda.

"I know!" Linda left and returned with cream and a small container full of pink, green and yellow envelopes. "You know, Sheriff, this stuff will give you bladder cancer. Food'll be up in a minute." And she was gone once more, headed away to torment the customers at the other tables.

"Why are you here? In Virtue Falls?" Kateri put one of the yellow cancer-causing packets into her coffee, stirred and took a sip. "The last time I heard from you, you were in Baltimore going to college."

Merida considered her and chose her words carefully, utilizing sign language rather than the easier-to-use iPad. "My life changed."

Kateri wasn't really guessing when she said, "Not for the better."

Merida shook her head.

"Why can't you . . . ?"

100

"Why can't I speak?" Now Merida changed from sign language to the iPad. "My face—much of the damage was to my jaw, teeth and lips." She kept her head down, typed rapidly without looking Kateri in the eyes. "The pain was terrific and I screamed so much . . . Well. You know what agony is."

"I do."

"By the time the pain was gone, the surgeries were over, the rehab . . . it was almost two years later. I just . . . couldn't." Merida picked up her coffee cup, but her fingers trembled and she put it back on the saucer.

Kateri thought about what Merida had said and what she wasn't saying. "Technically you should be able to speak?"

She typed, "The doctors tell me there's nothing wrong now."

"Oh, my friend."

Merida looked up, her eyes anguished, pleading. With her fingers, she spelled, "But you understand?"

In an odd way, Kateri did understand. She had suffered a catastrophe that changed everything: her livelihood, her affections, her pride, her appearance, her ambitions, her future. She had come away broken in so many ways; she had had to learn to deal with pain, to walk again, to live with limitations. Merida had a different limitation, one that was at the same time both emotional and real. "I do understand. But I am so sorry."

"Don't be. I'm free now. I'm content. Or I will be soon." Merida smiled, a curve of the lips that reminded Kateri of Cruella contemplating a new coat.

The expression did not fit well on that flawless face, and Kateri remembered it had been twenty years since she'd last seen Merry Byrd and thirteen years since Merry had cut communication completely. Everything about Merry had changed: her appearance, her method of speaking, even her name. Kateri didn't know this woman, this Merida Falcon, and that meant she should proceed with caution.

Linda arrived at the table, hands full of breakfast plates and eyes full of irritation. She slapped the plates down. "Eat 'em while they're hot," she ordered, and headed off.

Merida looked out the window, then typed, "Your officer is coming this way and he looks very serious."

Kateri looked, too.

Rupert Moen was jogging across the street toward the Oceanview Café, his copper hair standing on end and blotchy red in his cheeks.

Kateri checked her phone. No missed messages. If John Terrance had resurfaced, all the officers would be running for their cars, sirens would be wailing and someone would have called her.

She started working her way through the omelet as quickly as she could.

Moen charged through the door and toward Kateri.

The whole diner went on alert.

When he got close, she chewed, swallowed and asked, "Emergency?"

"No. Gosh, no! Well, maybe. There's this woman . . ." He caught sight of Merida. He stopped in his tracks. "Wow." He mouthed the word.

Poor kid. He wasn't equipped to handle movie star glamour in their little town.

"Ironic that he was struck dumb at the sight of you," Kateri said out of the corner of her mouth.

Merida laughed silently.

Aloud, Kateri said, "Officer Moen, this is my friend Merida Falcon. Merida, this is Officer Moen, a very valuable member of the sheriff's team."

Merida smiled and nodded.

Moen tore the hat off his head and nodded back. And stared. And stared.

Kateri took the moment to eat a bite of toast. One thing she knew about being in law enforcement—you ate when you could because you never knew when the next opportunity might be. "Moen, what's the problem?"

He yanked his attention back to Kateri. "You have a visitor."

Kateri's fork hovered in the air over the plate. "At the police station?"

"Yeah . . . A lady."

"*What* lady?" Why did he look like a meteor had landed in City Hall?

He looked around at the avidly listening customers. He leaned down and said softly, "A *bitchy* lady."

Kateri drank more coffee, ate another bite of eggs. "What's this bitchy lady's name?"

"She refused to tell us. Said you'd know her."

"Description?"

"Caucasian. Blond. Expensive. Thinks she's important." Now the true extent of Moen's foot-in-mouth syndrome burst forth. "So mean I thought she must have PMS but Bergen said no, she was just scary. For sure. She scared the hell out of me. She's waiting in your office."

Kateri wondered how it was possible for Moen to drive a narrow mountain road and grin with excitement, but when he faced a malicious woman he displayed the hollow-eyed terror of a two-year-old on Santa's lap. "Is there no one else in the station who can handle this woman?"

"No."

That was blunt. "All right. I'll come." She handed Moen her toast, handed her card to Merida and said, "Text me. Let me know where you're staying."

Merida nodded, her eyes wide, as if seeing Kateri in action startled her.

Walking stick in hand, Kateri headed across the street and around the square to City Hall, Moen pacing beside her. She asked, "So do you figure this is an uppity tourist? Or a reporter who thought she could bully her way into a story?"

"I don't think so." Moen's tone was ominous, but he chewed through the toast with relish.

As she entered the police department, she called, "Hi, guys, thanks for last night!"

No laughter. No teasing. Just a lot of quiet, tense officers avoiding her eyes, and mostly filling out their reports without being nagged.

Something had spooked them. Or *someone* had . . .

Kateri's curiosity hitched up a notch. She stepped into her office, looked at the woman sitting before her desk, at the back of that blond, perfectly coiffed head—and almost backpedaled all the way to the Oceanview Café.

It was Lilith Palmer. Her very own wicked stepsister.

CHAPTER ELEVEN

Merida watched Kateri and Moen leave. It had been good to see Kateri again, to reestablish the bond between them. It had been sad to see Kateri's sudden wariness, too, but she supposed not surprising. She wasn't the optimistic, hopeful Merry Byrd that Kateri had once known. Too many years of rigid self-discipline and meticulous plotting had changed her, made her cold, made her hard, made her a woman fired by fury and driven by vengeance.

Bending her head to her tablet, she brought up her spreadsheet and checked her figures. Last night, caught up in the excitement of putting her plan in motion, she had worked later than she meant to. Financial revenge would be satisfying, but if she handled this correctly, one man would be very sorry that he had ever crossed her path.

The door opened. A breeze swept through the diner.

Linda yelled, "Hey! You born in a barn? Shut the door!"

Merida glanced up.

There, holding the door open and viewing the diner and its customers as if they were a bucket of worms, stood Professor Dawkins Cipre. He looked the same as he had on the cruise: tall, white-haired, round-bellied, wearing a rumpled tan suit and a blue oxford button-up shirt with the top button open to accommodate his sagging, jowled neck.

Merida ducked her head. All too well she remembered those horrific days aboard the yacht: meeting Benedict, listening to Dawkins's lectures until she wanted to fall into a coma, and dealing with Nauplius's increasingly outrageous jealousy and aging temper.

"In or out!" Linda yelled.

Merida raised her iPad and peeked over the top.

Dawkins looked astonished to be addressed in such a manner, but he stepped in and let the door swing shut behind him. Again he looked around the café and before Merida could avert her eyes, he saw her.

She froze.

He looked her over.

Her iPad drooped.

His lip curled. Deliberately he turned his shoulder and headed to a far table. With his back still turned, he sat down and started texting.

He had snubbed her.

Or . . . or perhaps he hadn't recognized her.

She put her hand to the buzzed side of her head. She brought the long strand in front of her eyes. She looked down at her outfit: a bright orange sleeveless T-shirt that showed off the colorful falcon tattoo on her left bicep, ragged jeans and her worn college-era Birkenstocks.

He really hadn't recognized her. That shallow snob, that pompous academic, had looked at her, seen a badly dressed woman with hair dyed the colors of the United States flag and immediately decided she was not the kind of person with whom he wanted to associate.

She wilted with relief. Her disguise, such as it was, had passed the test.

But she couldn't stay here and take the chance he would remember her. Standing, she gathered her tablet and purse, put a twenty on the table and hurried toward the door. She extended her hand to push it open—

And met Elsa Cipre coming in.

Merida tried to turn her head away, but of *course,* Elsa recognized her immediately. She never seemed as self-absorbed as her husband. She caught Merida's outstretched wrist. "Helen!"

Merida shook her head.

"How good to see you. I never expected to find you in this little corner of the world. How did you get here?" She looked around the café, spotted her husband and said, "Dawkins is right over there. Come and sit with us."

Merida shook her head more emphatically.

"Dawkins will be so pleased to see you again."

Merida set her heels.

Without any seeming effort, Elsa dragged her toward Dawkins.

For a skinny, nervous academic, the woman had impressive upper body strength. "Dawkins, look who I found in this godforsaken town."

Dawkins gave Merida his patented superior sneer, then visibly started. "Helen Brassard! I didn't realize . . ." He rose to his feet. "Helen, my dear, we had no idea we would find you here."

If I had known I would find you, I wouldn't be here. But Merida couldn't say it, didn't sign it, smiled tightly. Pulling out her iPad, she typed, "Not Helen. I'm Merida now. I don't tell anyone about my husband."

"Why not?" Dawkins boomed.

Elsa lowered her voice. "Because of the money. Of course. We understand."

Merida nodded.

"Do you still have your bodyguard? What was his name? Carl Klinger?" Dawkins didn't know how to lower his voice.

"Carl Klineman, dear," Elsa said.

Merida shook her head, put her finger to her lips.

Dawkins leaned forward and in a piercing whisper said, "You should get him back so you could use your real name. It's not safe for you to be alone."

Merida typed, "Most of the money went to Nauplius Brassard's children. I don't need a bodyguard for my small savings. What brings you to Virtue Falls?"

"I'm on sabbatical from Oxford and Washington State University begged me to come and lecture on French medieval poetry and its influence on the customs of romance and chivalry."

Merida could see a free lecture coming at an unstoppable speed, and she clutched her backpack closer in preparation for a panicked escape.

Elsa didn't wait for him to get rolling. Instead she stroked his ego. "They are so lucky to have you."

"They know it." Dawkins folded his hands over his belly. "The semester starts in August and until then, I gave in to Elsa's desires and we're touring the Washington coast. It's very . . . picturesque."

The way he said *picturesque* reduced the Pacific Ocean to the level of a lap dance.

"What are *you* doing here, Hele . . . Merida?" Elsa asked.

Merida typed, "I'm touring, also."

"We should tour together!" Elsa exclaimed.

"That would be lovely, but I've taken rooms at the Good Knight Manor Bed and Breakfast for the next year and they're nonrefundable." Merida congratulated herself on a nice save.

"That's where we're staying!"

Fatal mistake.

"Dear Dawkins, couldn't we extend our stay longer to visit with our Merida?"

Dawkins's cheeks turned a slight purple that made him look like he was strangling. "Virtual

Falls is ridiculously busy this time of year. And expensive. We barely got a reservation as it was!"

Gently, Elsa corrected him, "It's *Virtue* Falls, dear."

"I know that!"

Elsa smiled at Merida companionably, as if she expected her to understand Dawkins's peevishness. Of course she would think that; she had seen Merida catering to her husband the same way Elsa catered to hers. What Elsa didn't realize was that Merida had hated every minute of her servitude, and before she was done, someone would pay.

What was more, she couldn't stand to sit by and watch this kind of abuse. It made her want to slap Dawkins—and Elsa.

Merida stood, gathered her tablet, touched her brow in a farewell salutation.

"Wait, dear! We should exchange phone numbers!" Elsa called.

Not while I have breath in my body. Merida again started toward the door.

Behind her, she heard Elsa say, "The poor dear was obviously overcome by our repartee. She must be missing Nauplius."

Merida fled. She drove her car out to the beach, parked and walked along the sand, letting the wind, the salt air and the joy of being alone and at no one's beck and call drive the distasteful memory of the Cipres out of her brain.

CHAPTER TWELVE

On occasions like these, Kateri wondered what kind of crapshoot was going on in the wonderful world of genetics.

Lilith had naturally blond hair that she styled in an upsweep with enough texturizing spray to make a Texas debutante coo with joy. Her fair, carefully tended skin glowed like an English maiden's, and her makeup had been so carefully selected and applied one could not tell where the cosmetics left off and nature began. Her figure had been given the advantage of a lifetime of dance and a daily fitness regimen with a physical trainer. The only sign of Lilith's age—she was thirty-nine—was mild wrinkling at the corners of her eyes and age spots on the backs of her hands, and she was so short—five-two—and thin that Kateri should be able to snap her like a toothpick.

Kateri knew better. Lilith was one frightening woman and Kateri would never, repeat never, run afoul of her. Making Lilith angry was akin to poking a stick in the tiger's cage in the belief that your reach was longer. Being wrong could leave you bleeding and possibly eviscerated.

The fact Kateri had to take a fortifying breath to walk into her own office irritated her. So she fixed an artificial smile on her lips, took that fortifying breath and walked in. "Lilith, how good to see you after so many years."

Lilith didn't get to her feet. She smiled with the same artifice Kateri had utilized—Kateri realized Lilith's mother had taught them both that smile—and she looked her over from top to toe. "Darling Katherine, you really were battered by that big wave, weren't you?" Which was Lilith's less than subtle way of saying Kateri looked like hell.

With her words, Kateri immediately felt every ache and pain. "The bullet four days ago didn't help, either." She headed around her desk for her chair and hoped she didn't pitch forward in a faint. It wouldn't do to show this woman any sign of weakness.

"I heard the men out there saying that you'd hit a tree, too."

Another less than subtle suggestion that Kateri was a lousy driver. "Officer Moen hit a tree. I was the passenger."

"Ah." Like the manipulative bitch she was, Lilith held out her arms. "Katherine, an embrace of sibling affection."

Kateri paused, halfway into a seated position. Damn. Really?

Of course, really. Lilith had to establish her authority swiftly, and if she did not she would stretch out this whole wretched ordeal until she was satisfied she was dominant. With Lilith, it was simply easier to let her have her way.

Kateri leaned on her stick and her desk to straighten herself, walked around the desk and met Lilith as she half-rose.

Lilith offered her cheek.

Kateri kissed it.

There. Dominance established.

Lilith's nose wrinkled. "This place smells like dirty socks. You should command your staff to get in here and do some serious cleaning. Then get an interior decorator in to improve the décor."

Oh boy. People unclear on the concept. "The sheriff's department gets its funding from the county council and the county council and the city council work in absolute opposition to each other until it comes to funding. At that point they agree that luxuries like excess janitorial staff and raises for public servants are unnecessary."

"What does that mean?"

"It means I can't afford an interior decorator." Kateri retreated to her desk. "What can I do for you, Lilith?" For there was never a doubt she would be doing the favor.

"Katherine, I bring bad tidings." Lilith donned her sad face. "Our father, Neill Palmer . . . is dead."

"I *know* what his name is." Kateri only wished she did not. "On the other hand, my name is Kateri. Not Katherine."

"Isn't Kateri the Native American version of Katherine?"

"Yes. They are as similar as Sean and John. One is not an acceptable substitute for the other."

Kateri might as well be finger-spelling for all the notice Lilith displayed. Lilith said, "Yes. About our father . . ."

Kateri sighed. "Our father." The man had twice ruined her mother's life, once when he got her pregnant and abandoned her, and again when he had snatched his bastard daughter Kateri from the wilderness of Western Washington, took her to Baltimore and placed her in his bleak and glorious marble mansion. He cared nothing about Mary's grief at losing her daughter. He had cared nothing about his wife and daughter's horror at being saddled with a Native American savage. Most especially he had cared nothing for Kateri's homesickness and unhappiness.

Now he was dead.

Kateri wished she could say she didn't care. But every time she thought of her mother's broken life, she burned with loathing. And to say she burned was not a metaphor; her hatred made her blood hot, her face flush, her stomach . . . burn.

Rainbow had lectured her about carrying that kind of destructive baggage, and in theory, Kateri agreed. But although she had meditated, prayed and lectured herself, still the mention of her father's name made her remember . . . and burn.

Lilith said, "He departed this life as he had lived, a good man who fought a good fight—"

Kateri gave herself extra points for not snorting.

"—But in the end he could only succumb to the cancer that broke his body . . ." Lilith was watching Kateri all too closely. "You don't seem surprised."

"I suspected."

"Why did you suspect, sister?"

"He sent me a package. Since I hadn't heard from him since I begged him to get me into the Coast Guard Academy, I figured something was up. Imminent death. Sudden insanity." Perhaps that was a little cold.

Lilith seemed not to notice. "What did the package contain?"

"The raven."

"Edgar Allan Poe's raven."

"That's right."

"What else?"

What else? A photo album filled with pictures of her father and her mother taken during that summer when he romanced the Indian maiden named Mary and Mary fell in love with a man who didn't exist. "Nothing."

Lilith's eyes narrowed. "Do you still have the raven and the box it came in?"

Did Lilith not know about the album? "No."

Lilith leaned forward. "What do you mean, no?"

"I mean I wanted to toss the whole thing into the ocean—"

Lilith gasped in outrage. "That raven is of historical importance!"

"—but my friend took it so I could not." Probably Lilith didn't know about the album. Even if she did, why would she care about photos of her father and one of his affairs? The answer was clear; she wouldn't.

"Your friend . . . your friend took it? The raven?" Lilith clutched the arms of the chair so tightly her stacked Tiffany rings lifted off her skinny fingers. "You allowed that?"

For the first time, Kateri began to enjoy herself. "One does not *allow* Rainbow to do anything. She is a force of nature."

In that East Coast patrician accent that was for Kateri like nails on a chalkboard, Lilith said, "That raven is a precious artifact that belongs to the family as part of our noble inheritance. I would emphatically request of your friend that she give it back to you and you give it to the estate."

Yes. This was definitely enjoyable. "That's not possible."

"Why not?"

"Rainbow took the box and didn't tell me where she put it. I don't know where it is."

Enunciating clearly, Lilith said, "Go ask your friend where she put it."

"She's in a coma."

"You're joking."

Kateri's wisp of enjoyment evaporated. "Would that I were. Rainbow was shot in the same incident that put a bullet through me. She's in a coma. She's not expected to live."

"Let's search her house!"

There was the sister Kateri knew and despised. No compassion, no interest in another's welfare, no kindness, only a determination to get her way at any cost. "Rainbow is still alive and searching her house would constitute breaking and entering."

"Surely she has designated a guardian in case . . ."

"In case she got shot? Unlikely." Kateri was Rainbow's emergency contact, but she felt no need to tell a sister who would view that as an open invitation. "Her parents are currently in Nepal. We're unable to reach them." That, at least, was the truth.

"Unfortunate." Lilith tapped her well-manicured nails on the arm of her chair. "Yet I don't see what harm would come of searching her closets . . ."

"The main harm would be that I'd have to arrest my own sister. I am the sheriff, you know." It was amazing how the thought of putting handcuffs on Lilith revived Kateri.

"Yes. I'm aware. Naturally, *I* wouldn't do it."

Foolish Kateri, thinking Lilith would do physical labor. "Nor would I."

"I suppose not. You do have a staff."

"A staff." Kateri glanced at the stick near at hand, then with a start comprehended Lilith's meaning. "Ah. The Virtue Falls law enforcement team. They're also opposed to breaking and entering. On principle."

"I suppose it's required. They seemed unaware that you have a sister and a family in Baltimore."

"My sister always seemed surprised that she had a sister. And no, I don't brag about my time in Baltimore with your family."

"Your family, too. I would have thought it would lend you credibility to have our family in your background."

Kateri's hackles went up. "My family is here. On the reservation. In town. Up and down the coast. My family looks like me, not you."

"I don't understand your attitude. You achieved your success in the Coast Guard due to our father's influence."

Kateri's hackles got hedgehog high. "I got into the Coast Guard Academy due to your . . . our . . . father's influence. I succeeded because of my own efforts."

Lilith smiled that tight-ass smile that caused wrinkles in her upper lip. "Father liked you, you know."

Kateri blinked. Of all the things she expected

to hear today, that was at the bottom of the list. "I can't imagine that's true. Especially after the tsunami when I was court-martialed and discharged from the Coast Guard. Being the town librarian seems nothing that would excite his admiration."

"At that point, he did stop unfavorably comparing me to you. That was a relief. I was tired of that." Lilith stood. "Where is your home? The trip was exhausting and I need to rest."

Kateri's jaw dropped. She knew it was unattractive and gave too much away. But . . . "You can't stay with me. I've got a one-bedroom apartment. With a single bed." No. She was not contaminating her house with this woman's presence.

"I had assumed you—"

"No! Not unless you want to sleep on the couch."

"You could—"

"I'm wounded." Inspiration struck. "Also, yesterday there was a break-in."

"A break-in? Why? Surely you have nothing anyone would want."

True. Kateri had nothing anyone would want. "Maybe the raven?"

"Yes. You do have that. Somewhere."

"We believe it's the criminal who is currently at large and causing havoc in the county. You simply cannot stay at my house. It isn't safe."

"Where should I go?"

Kateri noted that it never occurred to Lilith to wonder if Kateri's home was safe for Kateri. But not to cavil; at least she had easily abandoned her intention to freeload off Kateri. "It's summer. This is a tourist town." She experienced a flutter of panic. "You mean you showed up here without making reservations?"

"I had hoped to finish our business and leave within the hour."

Of course you did. Kateri used a tissue to blot her suddenly hot forehead. "No reservations . . ."

"Perhaps one of your friends . . ."

My poor, unsuspecting friends. No. "A new bed-and-breakfast opened in town. Good Knight Manor Bed and Breakfast. Nice old mansion. I've heard their meals are superior. Maybe you can get a room there."

"A bed-and-breakfast?" Lilith made it sound like a brothel. "Is there no other hotel? A Four Seasons or a Hyatt?"

"In Seattle." *Go!*

Lilith opened her Ferragamo purse, fished out a small leather notebook embossed with her initials, removed the affixed Tiffany's pen and clicked it officiously. "What's the name of the bed-and-breakfast again?"

"The Good Knight Manor Bed and Breakfast."

Lilith pulled out the smallest cell phone on the market, found the number, called the proprietor, asked for a room and said that she needed it tonight, asked for a room and said that she needed it tonight, asked for a room and said that she needed it tonight . . . and somehow, through the process of sheer nagging, she got her way.

Kateri reflected that she should feel guilty for siccing Lilith on the inexperienced and unsuspecting proprietress, and maybe she did. But not enough to share her apartment.

Lilith held up her hand. "Don't get up on my account. I can find my way out and around your little town."

"You do that. I need to do some paperwork." Actually Kateri needed to think. She watched her sister leave, then leaned back in her chair and tapped her pencil on the desk. And waited.

As expected, Bergen showed up. "Who was that?"

"My sister."

In tones of doubt, Bergen admitted, "That's what she said."

"Then it's unanimous."

"I didn't know that you . . . I thought you were . . . What does she . . . ?" Kateri watched him struggle to think of an appropriate tactful response. He must have decided discretion was the better part of valor, for he sank down in the chair Lilith had just vacated. "No fingerprints for your apartment. Nothing unexpected. You. Rainbow. Stag. Someone came in and searched the place. Someone who was smart enough to wear gloves."

"John Terrance is smart enough."

"But why would he care? Seems as if he'd want us to know he'd been there."

She and Bergen had arrived at similar conclusions. Which meant there was a pretty good chance it was a solid conclusion. "I'll tell you what. Today we'll get someone in there to clean up my place and I'll move back in."

"Not a good idea."

"I think it might be."

"Who do you think . . . ?" He glanced out the door. "Your *sister?*"

"It's just a suspicion."

"Why?"

Kateri tapped the pencil again. "Family heirloom."

"You've got a family heirloom? How did you get it?"

"Our father sent it to me."

"Ooh. You share a father. Makes sense." Bergen stared into Kateri's face, trying to see a hint of Anglo-Saxon.

"I'm tall," she said. "I've got long arms. That's what I got from him. My father. Neill Palmer. Hopefully that's all I got from him."

"And the family heirloom," Bergen said helpfully. "Miss Palmer doesn't seem the type to go in for breaking and entering."

"She's the type to believe she can get away with anything. And she's usually right. I'll go clean my stuff out of Rainbow's house"—*and look through the closets myself*—"then let's all keep an unofficial eye on Rainbow's house and see if anything happens there in the way of unauthorized entry."

Bergen contemplated Kateri. "I have a sister with a sense of entitlement . . . she's a pain in the keister. But my grandma always said to remember this one piece of wisdom—there are no functional families."

Kateri liked that. "Your grandmother sounds pretty smart."

"Scary smart. That's why my grandfather killed her."

CHAPTER THIRTEEN

Since that moment when Merida woke in the hospital to discover she no longer had a nose and all the bones in her face were broken . . . she had not slept well. She used to lay in the bed next to Nauplius and listen to him snuffle and snore, get up to pee and grumble about his prostate, watch the dawn arrive and wish that she were dead. Or he were.

He had finally obliged, toppling without warning into hell, and she was free, and although she was trying to regain the habit of slumber, she only achieved sleep in short bursts. In her periods of wakefulness the psychological cancers of the past gnawed at her, and so she had developed the habit of rising with the sun and going out for a run.

After Merida's arrival in Washington, she had discovered that in June, the sun rose very early, and by Tuesday, she had settled into a routine. As the sun began to lighten the sky, she slipped out of bed, dressed in yoga pants and a ragged T-shirt and quietly (very quietly) made her way out of the Good Knight Manor Bed and Breakfast. She ran along the sidewalk broken by tree roots, past tall hedges and along the shadowy street.

The years of living with Nauplius had changed her, kept her at all times on the lookout for treachery. Every day she varied her route . . . and yet somehow, she always found herself racing along toward the sea, where glorious eternity greeted her. With each step she felt as if she could fly into the wind. There on the shore, her restless fears blew away.

Today she returned to the B and B—she had so far managed to avoiding meeting anyone other than Phoebe—and went to work. In the afternoon, she explored Virtue Falls and its small cache of restaurants and take-outs. She kept herself fed, she advanced her revenge and she avoided the difficulties of socializing with Phoebe's other guests.

Or, God forbid, the Cipres. She'd seen no sign of them, but then, she'd been careful not to. Still, her isolation gave her hope . . .

Today she determined she would try a different adventure, and a trip to the grocery store with her new insulated grocery bag netted her a frozen dinner. Surely frozen dinners had improved since her college years . . .

Merida parked in her spot beside the Good Knight Manor Bed and Breakfast carriage house; through the windows, she caught a glimpse of someone moving around inside.

Phoebe's newest guest must have arrived.

Grocery bag in hand, Merida hurried past. When she opened the side door, a blast of rich, vibrant, appetizing scents rushed out.

That's right. It was Tuesday evening, that time when Phoebe served an international dinner with the intention of herding her guests toward conviviality.

Not just no. Hell no.

Intent on reaching her rooms unnoticed, Merida sneaked up the stairway to the second floor into the dim, empty corridor. She unlocked her bedroom door with both Phoebe's old-fashioned key and her own electronic security code, then jumped when beside her, a timid voice said, "Miss Falcon?"

Alarmed, Merida turned to face a tall, skinny, slump-shouldered woman with a bruise on one cheek and her left wrist in a brace. How had she crept up on Merida so quickly and quietly?

Still in that small, timid voice, so out of place in a woman of her age and height, she said, "I'm Susie Robinson. I'm supposed to clean your room. I couldn't get in."

Merida gestured to the locks.

"I can clean it now while you're at dinner."

Merida reached into her bag and pulled out her tablet. She showed Susie the usual message, then typed, "I have to work."

"I'm quick and quiet." Susie wrung her bony, work-worn hands. "Please, Miss Falcon, Phoebe takes pride in caring for her guests and if I don't . . ."

Merida remembered what Phoebe had said

about Susie's home situation, realized that she was inadvertently making the woman's life harder, and held up one finger.

At once, Susie stopped talking.

Merida went inside, locked the door behind her, collected her computer from the wall safe, opened her door and gestured Susie in.

"Thank you, Miss Falcon, I promise I won't disturb you." She looked anxious again. "I have to fetch my cleaning supplies."

Merida nodded and waited until Susie had lugged in her vacuum cleaner and cleaning bin, and shut the door behind her.

Susie's worn face brightened. "Aren't you going to Phoebe's dinner, Miss Falcon? She's a real good cook."

Merida's stomach growled; she hadn't eaten since her breakfast at the Oceanview Café. Even up here, the scents of bacon, caramelized onions and freshly baked bread permeated the air. But Merida smiled and patted her computer.

"I know. Phoebe says you're a real quiet guest and are here to work. Don't worry, she'll save you some leftovers. That's what she does for me. I take 'em home, feed 'em to my kids. My husband, he don't like that fancy stuff."

Merida took a slow step backward. *Please, no confidences. I don't want to hear how your husband beats you. I don't want to feel empathy.*

"Sorry, miss. I'd love to chat, but you're the

last room and I have to get home soon as I can."
Susie headed into the bathroom.

Merida hurried down the maid's back stairs to the dining room with its long table, its rows of knights standing guard—and the microwave.

She charred the frozen dinner. Apparently before you cooked it, you were supposed to read the directions. She tried to eat it and realized even if she hadn't burned it, it would have tasted like cardboard and ketchup.

So frozen dinners *hadn't* improved since she was in college.

No matter. When she had lived with Nauplius, she had learned to do without meals as necessary. When he tied her hands so she couldn't speak . . . and when she wished to aggravate him by refusing the food he bought her. She hadn't been able to do much to defy him. Just a few things.

Overhead, the vacuum cleaner started up.

Merida looked toward the door that led to the entry and from there to the large living room where every evening, Phoebe served appetizers and wines and ports in sparkling jeweled glasses. She was pretty sure the Cipres were gone from Virtue Falls. But she did really need to work. The program she had developed required daily tending, a sense of when to gamble, when to escalate the pressure and at the same time not call attention to her underlying purpose . . .

She bent to her computer screen and immersed herself in the labor . . . for fifteen minutes. Until her stomach growled so loudly she wanted to tell it to hush up—or feed it. Without the incentive of annoying Nauplius, self-denial wasn't nearly as much fun.

Another fifteen minutes, and she began to realize socializing might not be all bad. She didn't like it, but she knew how. Phoebe truly was a fabulous cook; the breakfasts Merida had grabbed in passing proved that. Maybe just this once . . .

She shut her laptop. What to do with it? She didn't want to take it upstairs and put it into the safe. Not with Susie watching. Opening the mirrored doors on the old-fashioned cupboard, she slid it into the bottom drawer underneath a stack of ironed tablecloths. She shut the drawer, shut the cupboard and looked around to make sure she was unobserved. She opened the door into the entry, heard the clatter of silverware, shut the door. No use locking it. Not with Susie inside. She had to assume no one was going to bother with a stack of tablecloths.

She tiptoed toward the open door of the parlor, toward the murmur of voices and the clatter of silverware. She peeked around the corner . . .

The sideboard sported a fabulous buffet. An arrangement of charcuterie, cheeses and breads was laid out on an olive wood platter. Candles flickered beneath a chafing dish. Champagne rested on ice in silver buckets. The smells tantalized and enticed.

A quick sweep of the guests relieved her mind. She saw a young couple, possibly honeymooners, snuggling on the old-fashioned love seat. Four men in various degrees of casual touristy garb stood around the mantel, eating off crystal plates and watching a soccer game on someone's computer tablet.

She saw no sign of the rotund Dawkins Cipre and his skinny scholar of a wife.

Still, so many people . . . so many explanations about her own inability to speak. So many difficult social niceties . . .

The thing that overcame Merida's last scrap of reluctance was Phoebe, sitting forlorn in the corner by the sideboard. The vibrant woman had prepared this lovely repast, yet she had been unable to coerce her guests into *visiting*.

Very well. Merida would *visit*.

Stepping in, she walked over to Phoebe and touched her hand, and when Phoebe looked up, she smiled and gestured at the buffet.

At once Phoebe came to her feet. "Merida, I'm so glad you joined us. We are having such a convivial time! This week the country I'm honoring is France. Everything is prepared with butter and cheese. I hope you're not worried about your cholesterol!" She laughed merrily.

131

Merida smiled and patted her fingers to her lips like someone using a napkin.

"Of course not. You're young and thin. You can eat anything." Phoebe led her to the buffet. "Let me take you on a tour. We have *salade niçoise*—the tuna is fresh off the boat! I prepared a simple quiche—eggs and chèvre in a pastry shell with bacon and spinach. I have a bowl of sour cream as a side. It's not traditional, but I think that tang improves the dish, *n'est-ce pas?*"

Merida nodded, but noted in a panic that at the mantel, male heads swiveled. She looked away.

"Make sure you try some of my *cassoulet au canard*. When I was in college in France, I learned from the best." Phoebe didn't seem to trust that Merida would properly serve herself, for she took a plate and dished up generous portions. "Here I have *pommes frites*. French fries, of course, but does it get any better than deep-fried potatoes?"

Merida glanced back at the men. Damn! One of them was Officer Sean Weston, the patrolman at the roadblock who had so clumsily made a pass at her. No, no, no. She did not want to do this.

She started to back away.

Phoebe handed her the plate and silverware wrapped in a linen napkin, tore off a crusty chunk of baguette. "Look at the desserts I've prepared. Napoleons, cream puffs, éclairs with homemade custard and, the pièce de résistance—crème brûlée." She clicked her miniature blowtorch. "I'm ready to caramelize the sugar whenever you're ready. I won't judge if you eat dessert first. Think of all the women on the *Titanic* who worried about their waistlines!"

Phoebe made a powerful argument for self-indulgence.

And Merida had lingered too long.

Officer Sean Weston stood beside her. "I was hoping to see you here tonight. How are you?"

Merida ate a bite of the glorious, garlicky cassoulet and realized this was worth whatever price she had to pay. She nodded at Sean, seated herself in a hard-cushioned antique chair, and went to work on the quiche. And the sour cream. As she ate, she liked Phoebe more and more.

Sean dragged up a chair and sat, elbows on his knees, leaning close. "I'm afraid I made you mad yesterday. Listen, I adore the sheriff. She's smart and she's tough. She let me guard her last night, so you know she trusts me."

Phoebe said, "Officer Weston, Merida needs a glass of champagne!"

He looked startled, leaped to his feet and said, "Yes, ma'am!" and dove for the crystal flutes.

In a distressed voice, Phoebe murmured, "He wanted to come to dinner, I was afraid no one would be here to enjoy all this food, I said yes, I didn't discover until afterward he was interested in pursuing you. I'm sorry, Miss Falcon."

Merida patted her hand.

"Thank you, Merida. You are such a wonderful woman. I knew it! A kindred spirit."

Then Phoebe, the traitor, faded away, leaving Sean hovering with a glass of champagne.

Merida took it with a nod of thanks.

Sean seated himself again. "Merida, do you know why I guarded the sheriff last night?"

Why no. She didn't.

"Yesterday someone broke into her apartment. She moved to her friend's house—Rainbow, who was shot when Sheriff Kwinault was shot—and the sheriff slept there. I protected her."

Merida moved to sign language, trusting that she would be comprehended. "Who broke into her apartment?"

Sean got it. "We don't know. We think it's John Terrance, the drug dealer we're pursuing. But . . . no fingerprints."

Merida had spent the last year looking over her shoulder, fearing to see the paparazzi on her trail, or Nauplius Brassard's children or some specter of her past . . . it had never occurred to her someone else could be in danger. That her friend Kateri Kwinault could also be looking over *her* shoulder. Maybe Dawkins and Elsa Cipre were not as bad as she feared. Maybe she needed to think about someone else for a change.

She glanced toward the other men by the mantel. One stood intently watching her and Sean. Intently, coolly, menacingly.

No. *No.* This wasn't possible.

Benedict Howard. In the flesh.

CHAPTER FOURTEEN

The meeting with Kateri had gone so well.

The meeting with the Cipres had been so unfortunate.

This meeting with Benedict was so disastrous.

Maybe that was why Merida lost her temper. Lost her temper in a way she hadn't since college.

She flew at Benedict. Standing toe to toe, with emphatic gestures she signed, "What are you doing here? Why are you here?"

He took a step away as if she intimidated him and observed her intently. A pause, then he said, "You know why I'm here."

"Sex? Intercourse?" Her signing was rapid, vulgar and explicit, and drew gasps from the onlookers—and everyone was looking. "Bullshit. Bullshit! No way. All you want is the one beautiful woman you couldn't have."

He spoke the words clearly and calmly. "Now I call bullshit. I haven't seen you in years. You've changed. Aged. I could have found a more beautiful and also less resistant woman than you."

That knocked Merida back on her heels, made her think, made her silently laugh. Her temper marginally cooled. "How did you find me?"

Again a pause that involved his close scrutiny.

"Pure luck. I had an investigative firm looking for you. Then my assistant saw you in the airport. She wasn't sure. She took your picture."

Merida had a flashback of rushing to catch a plane—she tried never to be early, to be caught standing around—and noticing a young, tall, smartly suited female fumbling with her phone.

Luck. Rotten luck. Damned fate.

And damn him. Benedict Howard. Always him.

Another man who wanted to make a deal. Another man who would use any leverage, no matter how abhorrent, to force her to sign a contract that would give him possession over her: her face, her body, her presence at his side until such time as he no longer wanted her—or, like Nauplius, he dropped dead.

"Go away," she signed, gesturing wildly.

He caught her wrists.

She didn't pause. She didn't think. She head-butted him in the chest. He stumbled backward, yet held on. She stumbled forward. He hit the fireplace utensils. The clang and rattle as they fell over seemed to awaken him and abruptly, he let her go. Seeking balance, one of his hands swept out. He knocked over the tray of delicate crystal goblets.

Purple port splashed. Glass shattered.

Phoebe cried out in distress.

All at once, Merida realized every eye in the room was fixed on her. She was doing the thing she most needed to avoid: she was causing a scene, calling attention to herself.

Turning on her heel, she stalked toward the entry.

Sean caught her arm and swung her around. "Do you want to file a complaint against him?"

In a fury, she glared.

He let her go.

Clothed in dignity and exuding offense, she left the room. Behind her, she heard the murmur of voices, the general rise of surprised, shocked and scintillated conversation, then Phoebe saying, "Can't she speak? She didn't tell me she couldn't speak. Why didn't she tell me?"

Merida hoped to escape into her room before Benedict caught up with her. She inserted her key into the lock and turned it. No problem. She tried to input her code into the keypad. She got it wrong. She tried again.

Benedict tapped her shoulder.

She thumped her head on the door, then faced him.

He held up his hands, palms out. "I'm sorry I held you. I've been practicing sign language, reading it and speaking it, but I'm slow and I couldn't keep up and you were . . . I'm not used to anyone swearing at me."

She thought about it, then nodded a grudging acceptance. Again she signed, "Why are you here?"

"Is sheer lust not a good enough reason?"

"For years?" Every gesture was emphatic. "With this woman who is so much older than your usual paramours?"

He sighed as if he didn't quite know what to say. "The thing is—I feel like I've known you forever."

No. "No! You don't know me. Go away and leave me alone."

"I can't. I tried to forget you, but there's something between us."

Yes. There was so much between them. Love. Lust. Joy. Betrayal. *Betrayal on a cosmic level.*

She wanted to grab him, shake him, demand he explain himself . . . pick up a knife and stick it in his chest, hurt him as he had hurt her.

"What?" he asked. "Tell me what it is."

God. She would so love to tell him what it was. She would love to hear him deny, grovel, be shocked and appalled.

He would be lying, but she would love it anyway.

Nine years of servitude, and they were all Benedict's fault. The explosion, the horror of waking and discovering she was broken in face and body . . . and discovering, also, she could be repaired . . . for a price, and that price was her freedom. Nine years spent knowing she *had* signed Nauplius Brassard's draconian contract, that it *was* her name on the dotted line, and learning all too painfully that Nauplius had no pity, no compassion, and escape, physically or mentally, was impossible.

The front door slammed open.

Merida's and Benedict's heads swiveled to look.

Dawkins and Elsa Cipre stood in the entry.

Dear God, they were still at the B and B. Was Merida cursed?

Dawkins looked indignant. Elsa looked disheveled, or maybe it was simply another one of her odd outfits.

Dawkins proclaimed, "That wave came right at me. Right at me, Elsa!"

Elsa brushed at his jacket. "Dear, surely you can't believe the ocean conspired to rob you of your dignity. That simply doesn't make sense."

"Are you saying I'm not sensible?"

Elsa struggled for words, then caught sight of Benedict and Merida frozen and staring. She seized on them like the diversion they were. "Darling, look! It's Merida and . . . and the young man from the ship!"

Dawkins turned to his wife and in an accusing voice said, "So much for your theory that Merida is pining for Nauplius. They must have made an assignation."

Merida shook her head and spelled, *No. No. No.*

No to the assignation. No to the Cipres residing here. No to the whole scene.

From the kitchen, another voice spoke, a feminine, high-class Baltimore, superior/nasty voice. With an indignation to match Cipre's, the woman said, "My God, what kind of disgusting spectacle have I walked into?"

Merida's and Benedict's heads swiveled in that direction.

The woman continued to complain. "I should never have made a reservation in a bed-and-breakfast. So . . . common."

Merida couldn't believe her bad luck. Lilith Palmer. *Lilith Palmer.* Kateri's sister, the one who had locked them in the basement. Merida and Kateri believed she had hoped to kill them.

She had met Lilith again, too, at some boring charity function she had attended as Nauplius Brassard's wife.

But . . . but Merida looked very different now. Different from her teen years. Different from those years of suited and high-heeled bondage.

Yet Lilith's Botoxed forehead almost wrinkled. "Do I know you?" She sounded scornful, but puzzled, too.

Merida shook her head. *No. You don't know me.*

Sean Weston stepped into the doorway. "Merida, do you need assistance?"

No. None of you know me.

Dawkins Cipre. Elsa Cipre. Officer Sean Weston. Lilith Palmer. And most horribly, Benedict Howard. Why were they here? Now?

In Merida's refuge? To her, it seemed as if predator birds circled overhead, waiting for the moment of weakness when they would swoop down and tear her to pieces. She rubbed her forehead with her fingertips.

Benedict touched her arm. "Merida?"

She flung him away. Her hands moved violently and her lips moved, too. "Leave me alone!" She turned to the door of her rooms, fumbled with the key. Her hands shook.

Everyone was looking at her. She could *feel* them looking at her. She tried the key again. That lock was open. She touched the right sequence of numbers on the keypad.

She was in! She stepped over the threshold, slammed the door behind her—and saw Susie, looking horrified and guilty, the open laptop on the table before her . . . the laptop Merida had so carefully hidden an hour before.

CHAPTER FIFTEEN

Susie's fingers were on the keyboard.

Merida grew cold with fear. She signed, "What are you doing?"

"Nothing, miss!" Susie answered as if she could read sign language. "That is . . . I thought you'd be longer. At dinner." She saw Merida looking at her hands and slammed the laptop shut.

"Where did you get that?"

Again Susie answered as if she could read Merida's hands. "I . . . I . . . I . . . found it when I went to get a new tablecloth for your parlor." She picked up the computer and offered it.

Merida advanced on her, took it, backed away.

"I didn't mean nothing by it, miss! My boys need a new computer for school. I don't know nothin' about them and I was just wonderin' whether this kind would do."

Merida stared at the woman with new eyes. Susie still looked thin, she still looked careworn, but her eyes held intelligence and cunning. And lies?

"Please don't tell Miss Phoebe, ma'am, she'll fire me for sure and I need this job. My husband will beat me if I don't bring home the money! He drinks, you know, and when he does that, he beats the kids. I put myself between 'em until he tires out. Please don't tell her!"

Merida nodded. Susie's story was all possible. Even probable. But Susie's use of a country accent had intensified. Maybe from nerves. Maybe to disarm her. As Merida observed her with more care, she saw a box knife connected to Susie's belt and a kitchen knife and a screwdriver in her carry caddy. Those weren't standard supplies for a cleaning woman, at least not one she had ever met.

"I'm almost done, miss. All I have to do is change that tablecloth"—she put her hand on the folded linen on the table beside her—"and dust in here. Then I have to go upstairs to the attic, up to clean for them Cipres."

Merida pointed up at the ceiling. *They were above her?*

"Yes, and that woman—she is the very devil for being fussy." For one moment, Susie looked dangerously peeved. "Can I finish with you now?"

Merida nodded again.

Susie shook out the tablecloth and brushed past Merida on her way to the parlor.

Merida stood where she was, the computer pressed to her chest, feeling suspicion crawl up her spine. For the first time since Nauplius had died, she felt . . . watched, as if someone knew more than she did and was spying on her.

The Cipres. Sean Weston. Susie. Everyone seemed corrupt. Even Phoebe's exuberance rang false.

And Benedict. Most of all, Benedict . . . was he here because she had somehow betrayed herself? Had he tracked her not to use her for sex, as he had suggested, but to at last wipe her from the face of the earth? Because he knew . . . who she was. Because he remembered . . . what he had done. Because he was afraid of her . . . as he should be.

She glanced at the video camera she had set up, the one that looked like an antique mirror. She had placed something similar in every room she occupied. She would review the videos and see exactly what Susie had been doing, and if she was telling the truth.

Susie hustled back into the dining room. "There you go, miss. The parlor's ready if you want to sit in there and wait for me to finish. I won't be ten more minutes!"

Merida went into the parlor and sat. She opened her laptop and surveyed the screen. As it should be, it was blank, with no way in without a password.

She looked at the key click history.

Susie had been typing nonsense words. Code? Merida saw no pattern, but she knew the basics and no more, and computer science progressed at the speed of light. If Susie was secretly a hacker . . .

But what should Merida be looking for? Who would Susie be working for? Benedict? His aunt and uncle? Or for herself because she knew anyone who had the cash to take half this house for a year must be rich?

Merida had made a mistake. She knew that now. She'd lived with so much money for so long, she had thought only of privacy, not that she had placed herself as a target to be hit up for money.

She used her handprint to get into the password screen, then used her password to advance to the security viewer.

She had always wanted to fly. With a name like Merry Byrd, that had seemed a natural. She didn't remember the mother who had given her the name and there was no father listed on her birth records, yet she confidently told the other children at the orphanage that Amelia Earhart was her aunt and on the day of her birth Aunt Amelia had taken her on a flight into the clouds. Merry told them she was fated to be a famous pilot.

That worked until one of the older kids scornfully informed her, and everyone else, that Amelia Earhart had been dead for about a hundred years and anyway she flew off course, crashed somewhere, disappeared forever and was a major loser.

To Merry Byrd, that made Aunt Amelia even more brave and romantic, and at night she made up stories about Amelia and how she had never meant to fly around the world at all. Instead she had deliberately landed on a remote tropical island and lived there forever with her foreign lover, and took him flying whenever he wanted.

Merry made the mistake of telling one of the other kids about that, too, and for that she was teased mercilessly. Then she stopped telling everyone about her destiny and began to quietly plan how to get what she wanted—to fly as far away from this place as possible and disappear forever.

Be careful what you wish for, Merry Byrd.

By the time she was eleven, she'd been working in the nursery as long as she could remember. Babies loved her because she sang them nonsense songs. Little kids loved her because she told them stories that took them far away to a mythical place where their parents lived. And she loved the little ones because they didn't mock her dreams. Merry didn't realize anyone had noticed, but when one of the men on the orphanage board heard that one of his rich friends was looking for someone to help his wife with his newborn triplets, he recommended Merry.

That was when her life really began.

Mr. and Mrs. Cole took her in as a foster child and treated her better than she could have ever imagined. She had a beautiful bedroom and a maid to pick up after her, and all she had to do was go to school—a private school!—and help with the babies. The babies grew into toddlers who adored her, and Mrs. Cole adored her, too. She gave her an allowance, more money than Merry had ever imagined, and told her friends about Merry and let Merry go babysit her friends' children. Merry had a savings account. Mrs. Cole listened to Merry's dreams and hopes, and promised Merry she would fund college and when Merry was old enough, she would pay for flying lessons.

Compared to the orphanage, it was heaven. Merry had a future.

At eleven, she was ugly, awkward and gangly, her ears and hands and feet too big for her too-skinny, too-tall, totally unformed body. Sometime in the next two years, she changed. She was too busy to notice—she'd been ugly, awkward and gangly her whole life, she never expected anything different—but boys started watching her in a different way.

She laughed and dismissed them.

Mr. Cole wasn't so easy to dismiss. He was a banker. He was important. At first he hadn't paid attention to her. She was hungry for a father's love, so she liked it when he teased her, hugged her. Then she got uncomfortable and avoided him, hiding in the nursery with the little ones, or at her friend Kateri Kwinault's house.

She knew about men like him. In the foster care system, they were legion.

Mr. and Mrs. Cole started fighting.

Kateri ran away to her home in Washington State and didn't come back.

Mrs. Cole cried when she told Merry she had to return to the orphanage, but she gave her her savings account and a bonus and a letter of recommendation. Merry immediately secured another foster home with one of Mrs. Cole's divorced friends who had two kids, and this time she negotiated a budget that paid for her school and a salary. She no longer called it an allowance.

By the time she graduated from high school, she had earned a scholarship to Johns Hopkins, the governor's award for the development and funding for a twenty-four-hour charity day care, and she believed she could change the world.

University was everything she'd dreamed of. She studied languages, pre-med, psychology. She dabbled in the humanities. She led the debate team and for fun she played broomball on a hockey rink with tennis shoes, a ball and brooms.

She met Benedict Howard.

He attended a charity event and stood around with a bourbon on the rocks, looking ruthless and cynical.

She'd heard of the Howards. The ruthless family owned a ruthless corporation with a reputation for ruthless takeovers. A good reason to hit him up for a donation for her charity day care.

He ruthlessly turned her down.

She told him about the difference her facility had made for poor single mothers and their children.

He told her poor people shouldn't reproduce if they couldn't support their children.

She got into his face and told him rich, ruthless scum shouldn't reproduce, either, but obviously his parents had.

In years to come, whenever she recalled his expression, she always smiled.

She then told him that before he

mouthed off about things he didn't know or understand, he should work at the day care center.

He said he would . . . when she did.

She told him she worked the 3 A.M. to 8 A.M. shift and she would see him there. She flounced off to importune a wealthy elderly gentleman who had watched the scene with chortling amusement and gave her ten thousand dollars for the day care, and promised another ten thousand if she could pry a single dollar out of young Benedict Howard.

She kissed him on the cheek and thanked him for the ten thousand, and told him she deserved the second ten thousand for not telling his wife about him sneaking cigars at the club.

She got the other ten thousand.

She didn't expect to ever see Benedict at the day care, much less the next morning still in his tuxedo with his jacket off, his bow tie dangling and his cuffs rolled up. He looked like a disreputable James Bond. Which wasn't a bad look when combined with a warmed bottle of formula in one hand and a teething toddler hanging on the opposite leg howling for its momma.

"Why do people need twenty-four-hour child care?" he asked with grinding impatience.

"Mothers who have no help sometimes have to work two jobs, one in the day and one at night."

"Strippers?"

He was a judgmental asshole. No biggie. The world was full of judgmental assholes. But this guy was young, in his early twenties, and privileged, and seemed to have not a scrap of compassion or empathy for the less fortunate. "Yes, strippers. If they're lucky enough and agile enough to perform the job. Stripping pays well. Waitressing at an all-night diner is more common, or working as a hospice nursing assistant. Also a lot of our mothers are going to school in the day while their kids are in school and working at night while their kids are asleep."

"Supposedly asleep." Leaning down, he scooped up the child and offered the bottle.

The child reached for it.

"Not until you smile first," he told her.

Her lower lip stuck out. Her eyes refilled with tears.

"One smile," he said, and he smiled at her.

The child, who had been crying intermittently for five nights straight, smiled back at him.

Merry exchanged an exasperated look with the director, Ms. Sandvig. Of course that baby would respond to him. When Merry saw him smile, she wanted to respond to him. She wanted to lavish him with smiles. She wanted to . . . well, hell. He was wealthy, privileged and a judgmental asshole. She shouldn't *really* want anything with him.

But she couldn't resist.

Merry believed in gun control.

Benedict believed in the Second Amendment.

She believed in liberty and justice for all.

He believed the world belonged to those who worked to win it.

She believed in education for every child regardless of race, color or gender.

He believed in educating the privileged.

She pointed out that she was less privileged than him. And smarter.

He argued for those who had earned their living or protected their inheritance or both.

She lost that argument because he was burping a newborn and seeing him wipe a big ol' puddle of formula off his suit made her grow soft with sentiment and estrogen.

They dated. They broke up. They dated. They had the best sex in the history of the world.

He was in Johns Hopkins Carey Business School and headed for the top job at his family's business.

She was an undergrad with nobody, not one person who cared about her.

He cared about her. Somehow, he cared.

Or so she thought.

He took her to meet his aunt and uncle, Rose and Albert Howard. On the death of his parents in a yachting accident, they had raised Benedict. The old couple was charming. So charming. Rather ditzy. Yet sharp-eyed and maybe faking it.

At the time, Merry believed in the good of all mankind. Well, not really. She wasn't stupid. She remembered Mr. Cole. At the same time, she believed everyone should have the chance to improve themselves, to be better, to be kind, to love as much as they could.

She simply didn't realize that some people . . . never love.

Benedict worked with her every morning at the day care center from 3 A.M. to 8 A.M. The children adored him. Ms. Sandvig adored him.

Merry loved him. She loved him so much. She thought she was making a difference in his life. She imagined because of her he saw the world with new eyes.

Then he did change her life . . . when he tried to kill her.

CHAPTER SIXTEEN

The corded phone rang beside Merida's bed, waking her out of a nightmare-haunted sleep. For a moment, she stared around the room, lost in the past. The lights were on, she still wore her clothes. What . . . ? Where was she?

Disoriented, she snatched up the receiver.

She said, "Hello." No sound came out of her mouth, but for the first time in years, she had tried to speak.

Unbalanced? Yes, and her bewilderment grew worse when a man's hoarse voice whispered, "Be careful. They're hunting you . . ."

She wanted to demand an explanation, to ask who was after her.

But that voice said, "Remember, Helen. You cannot scream." He hung up, leaving her clutching the receiver so hard her knuckles were white.

She didn't glance at the clock, didn't give a thought to the time. She grabbed her iPad in her shaking fingers, dropped it, picked it up again. Called Kateri's number and activated the video.

Kateri answered immediately. She was braiding her dark hair. Behind her Merida could see a shadowy living room and a brightly lit kitchen.

"What is it, Merida?" Her voice was clipped, anxious.

Merida tried typing, but her hands were shaking too hard. She propped up the tablet and spelled, "A man. A man! Called me here. He said . . . he said . . ."

At once, Kateri leaned close to the camera. "Are you in any immediate danger?"

Merida looked around. She was alone. The doors were locked. No one was watching her. Were they? The windows were dark. But she was on the second floor. All that was out there were those giant trees that overhung the mansion . . . no one would climb a tree to watch her.

No one.

Would they?

She signed, "He said, 'Remember. You cannot scream.' " She didn't tell the whole truth. She didn't say that he'd called her *Helen*. The name, for her, was a shameful brand that burned and burned and never stopped.

Kateri sucked in her breath. "Damn. Not surprised you were scared. I'll send a patrolman."

Merida pointed. "You?"

"I'm sorry, Merida, but I can't come myself. Right now, we've got a situation."

Merida glanced at the clock. Three A.M.

Kateri was awake, alert, dressed in her sheriff's uniform. She tied off her braid and flipped it back over her shoulder.

A man, a tall man, Native American and bare to the waist, stepped into range of the camera, kissed her on the cheek and murmured, "Take care."

"I always do," Kateri said to him. She leaned down and petted her dog and with tablet still in hand, she picked up her walking stick and walked out of her apartment and into the night.

Behind her, a young, red-haired patrolman followed, speaking into the radio clipped onto the shoulder of his uniform.

"A crime?" Merida asked.

"A murder."

That word, *murder,* jolted Merida into thinking logically and without that knee-jerk fear. "Don't send anyone here." Because she didn't want to make a scene at the B and B. She didn't want Sean Weston to be the patrolman who came to check on her. Most of all, she didn't want Benedict to know his scare tactics were working. Because it had to be him, didn't it? He had arrived in town and within hours a strange man called and "warned" her of oncoming trouble. "I'm fine. I'm safe. Take care."

Kateri understood. "I always do," she said again.

Merida cut the connection. She held the tablet and thought, then with every evidence of casualness, she turned off the lights—and dropped to the floor. She crawled to the window and looked out into the yard. She scanned the trees first—the moon was close to full and no clouds covered its face, and in the light she saw no suspicious shapes, no lurkers in the branches.

But when she peeked out into the shadowy yard, she saw furtive movement. A flash of eyes? A scuttle against the ground? Maybe a raccoon? Or a wolf? Or a . . . not a wolf. Not . . . it was human. Someone was watching.

She closed her eyes and leaned her head against the wall.

Who was watching? Paparazzi? Benedict? Someone who was after her?

Who?

And why?

CHAPTER SEVENTEEN

Officer Rupert Moen had parked the patrol car at the curb by Kateri's door. He opened the passenger side door.

Kateri slid in, placed her walking stick in the back and watched the young officer as he crossed in front of the headlights. His mouth was pinched as if he wanted to vomit, and he walked like a man suffering from a massive hangover. But he'd been fine yesterday . . . and he'd been on duty all night. The boy was not hungover. He was sick in his heart and soul. He started the car and headed out of town and down the dark and winding coast highway toward the crime scene.

"You were the first responder?" she guessed.

"Yes." In the dash lights, he looked scared . . . no, not scared. Haunted.

"You want to fill me in?"

"No." That was all. No description, no details, no excitement. The young officer was uncharacteristically silent.

So it was bad. Very bad.

She patted his hand on the steering wheel.

He jumped as if someone had sneaked up on him, as if what he'd seen made his skin hurt.

"Sorry." She removed her hand. "Sorry. As soon as you drop me off, you should go home.

See your folks. Talk to your father." Who was a former cop, disabled while in the line, but proud of his son and more capable of helping him than anyone she knew.

"I can drive you back."

"I know you can. But your shift is over and I think there will be plenty of police presence, don't you?" He did not need to view the scene again.

Moen nodded jerkily. "Okay. I'll drop you off and head back. I have to file the report, anyway."

She wanted to tell him to forget it until later that day. But if he wasn't going to talk, she needed that report. "Right. If you would." She pulled out her phone, dialed. "Let me video chat with Bergen. Get an update." Her phone connected to the car, rang half a ring.

Bergen's face lit the small screen in the middle of the dash. "Sheriff. Another slashing. No one local, not a big woman, not this time. A petite tourist, single, forty-five, taking the long way around to visit her kids in Portland. Stopped in Virtue Falls to pick up dinner, drove down the highway to Lupine Point. Got out to picnic. Cheese and crackers and baby carrots were scattered toward the front of the car. I'd say she pulled into the pocket park, found an isolated overlook, sat on the hood to eat her lunch and enjoy the sunset. He snuck up on her . . ."

Behind him, she saw floodlights, men moving

161

from one place to another, serious expressions and the occasional angry glance.

Bergen continued, "He used a scalpel? A razor blade? Something sharp. Mike doesn't know what. Not yet. Cut along her jawline, traced the line around one ear. I've never seen anything like it. She bled . . ." Bergen gestured randomly.

"Who is she?" Kateri asked.

"According to her driver's license, she's Carolyn Abner of Springfield, Missouri."

"Her driver's license was on her?" *Not good.*

"It was in her purse. Which was in her car. Keys in the ignition. Robbery was not the motive."

Which left little motive except . . . murder for the joy of it.

"Coroner is here," Bergen said. "Preliminary—Mike says she's been dead at least eight hours. At one point her killer crushed her windpipe. But cause of death was bleeding, not suffocation. She fought. She's got bruising and scrapes on her knuckles and two torn fingernails."

"Let me see."

"You aren't going to like it."

"Do *you* like it?"

He turned his camera and pointed it at the scene.

First Kateri saw the congregation of lights against the ground. Then she saw their coroner, Mike Sun. He moved back on Bergen's command. Bergen zoomed in and Kateri saw the body.

Carolyn Abner rested on her back, her eyes open, staring toward the sky. Blood had poured from the incisions along her jawbone and up past her ear and cheek. Blood had filled her blondish hair and turned the strands into a gruesome, clotted black. Her face was eerily clean, as if the killer had wiped any trace of blood away from her pale skin.

Kateri fought the same sickness that afflicted Moen and Bergen. "Mike, anything you want to tell me?"

"Look at this." Mike gestured Bergen closer. "I just found this. Right here, right at the point at her temple where he stopped cutting, there's a tear in the skin. I couldn't figure out why there wasn't some symmetry here."

"Right. Symmetry." Mike was five-foot-five, half-Chinese and half-Aleut, raised in Virtue Falls and had been with the city most of his career. He was a good guy, a good coroner, and Kateri trusted his findings—and his intuitions—implicitly. If he said there should be symmetry, then he was right.

"If he's going to cut half her face, why not the other half? But it looks like he screwed up, tugged at the delicate skin here and it tore." In a characteristic gesture, Mike swiped his shoulder-length straight black hair off his forehead. "That's why he stopped. I think otherwise he would have kept right on cutting."

Moen rolled down the window, slowed the car.

She glanced at him.

Maybe it was the dash lights, but he looked green.

He came to a stop on the shoulder of the dark, isolated highway, opened the door, unclicked his seat belt and vomited on the pavement.

She reached back into the first-aid kit, got a cold pack, broke it to release the chemicals and placed it on the back of his neck.

"Kid sick?" Mike asked.

"Aren't we all?" Kateri countered.

Around the lighted circle, heads nodded.

"We're almost there," Kateri said to the men on the scene. To Moen, she said, "Can you drive?"

He pulled himself back into the car and put the car in gear.

She wanted to tell him to put on his seat belt, but she knew he was afraid he was going to be sick again.

He slowed at the sign for Lupine Point, turned onto the narrow, winding road and pulled into the usually quiet parking lot packed with bright lights and grim-faced police.

"You going to be okay to get home?" Kateri asked Moen.

"Sure, Sheriff. I'm fine."

Stick in hand, she got out and watched him drive away. Moen had dreamed of illustrating graphic novels. Maybe this would give him the push he needed to follow his dream. Or maybe, like a hot flame, it would harden him into steel.

She limped over to the body and the men surrounding it.

Her officers had fanned out in the parking lot, the grass and up the dune toward the beach. Most of them were in uniform; all of them carried flashlights and occasionally one would call Officer Bill Chippen over to take a photo. These guys knew the procedure all too well.

She glanced at Carolyn Abner, but didn't quite look at her straight on. There was no need, and she had to be steady and on her feet for the next God knew how many hours. She asked the first, most important question. "Bergen, do you think John is doing this?"

"I sure as hell hope so," Bergen said.

He was so prompt and emphatic, she almost laughed. Except that the truth was so awful.

He continued, "Because if it's not John Terrance, we've got not just one sick bastard on our hands, but two."

"Don't sugarcoat it. Give it to me straight." But he only said what they all were thinking. "How did this guy arrive at the scene?"

"Don't know. Too much evidence, we're working to narrow it down. Car probably. All kinds of tracks. It's the high season for bikes, and those tracks are here, too." Bergen pointed toward the beach. "And he could have parked down at the dunes and walked up the trail or along the beach. It's only a couple of miles."

"Mike, any of his DNA?" she asked.

"She should have flesh and blood under her fingernails." Mike lifted one of her hands. "He cleaned them out. I'll have to get her back to the morgue to see if he dropped a hair or missed a molecule of skin."

Kateri stared at Carolyn Abner's circled, rigid fingers, at the wide silver ring, the torn nails and the broken skin over the knuckles. Then she had to look at her, all of her, and acknowledge the woman beneath the tragedy.

Carolyn Abner was dressed like a typical summertime tourist, in loose white capris and a pink sweatshirt jacket. Her hair was styled in a bob. She'd lost a sandal. Kateri thought of all the other tourists, some already spooked by the specter of John Terrance, some completely unaware, some determinedly going on with their vacations. She thought of Terrance, belligerent, skinny, scrawny, so mean he starved his own dog to ensure the beast was vicious. She was going to have to do something, and fast. "It's our second slashing, and fatal. When I get back to City Hall and pull the preliminary reports together, I'll call Garik Jacobsen at the FBI and see what he knows."

Mike Sun reached up and punched Bergen on the thigh. "I told you she'd think of it herself."

Bergen smiled with genuine relief. "Yeah, baby. That is best news I've heard this week."

So. They'd been talking about her, speculating what her next course of action *should* be. Kateri wanted to punch them both on the thighs. She contained the urge and in an excessively pleasant voice said, "It's the logical course of action. No one understands the situation in Virtue Falls better than Garik, who grew up here, whose wife was almost killed by the last serial killer in town. Garik, who was the former sheriff."

Mike and Bergen exchanged glances.

They were both married. Maybe they'd recognized something about her tone.

Because Bergen said, "He's in the position to know all about serial killers. That's why we need him. Not because we think that you . . ." He trailed off.

Mike picked it up. "Really, it's not that you aren't doing a great job in this case. It's not your fault Terrance threw his son's body out and disrupted the chase. Everybody knows that. And this slashing thing is just bad—"

Bergen surreptitiously kicked him.

They were so stupid. She said, "You guys never know when to shut up, do you?"

"No, ma'am," Mike said.

"That's what my wife tells me," Bergen said.

She pointed at them both. "I need reports and photos as soon as I can get them. Bergen, I'll take your car. You catch a ride with Mike. In the hearse."

Bergen groaned, then intercepted a withering glance from her. "Absolutely. You take my car. I'll ride in the hearse. And actually . . . someone should accompany the body to the morgue and talk to the family when they arrive."

That lessened Kateri's ire. "You're right, my friend, and thank you for thinking of that."

CHAPTER EIGHTEEN

Kateri sat at her desk in her office, pulled in the evidence from her guys, compiled the reports and the photos, and by nine A.M. she was calling Garik's private line. A female answered, her tone businesslike, proving not even his cell phone was his own during FBI business hours. Kateri said, "Garik Jacobsen, please. This is Sheriff Kateri Kwinault from Virtue Falls. I'd like to speak to him about a situation we have here."

"Let me see if he's in." Which translated meant, *Let me see if he wants to speak with you.*

He came on the line right away and for some reason, his voice sounded amused. "So . . . what's this I hear about the Virtue Falls sheriff shacking up with a bouncer?"

Kateri had been concentrating on the gruesome photos of the murder. Caught off guard, she stammered, "A . . . a bouncer? You mean Stag? He's more than a . . ." She realized Garik was pulling her chain, and said, "How did you hear about it?"

"When half the law enforcement in Western Washington is deployed to Virtue Falls to catch John Terrance and their chase comes to such a walloping finish, you know what they do afterward."

"They gossip. I know. But really? Why would they care who I'm sleeping with?"

"You're a female sheriff—that's still pretty rare in the business—you're famous and you're hot."

She looked down at her scarred hands, at the walking stick leaning against the wall. "Hot, huh?"

"Every day."

Yep. She liked Garik. He was smart, sharp, with a lot of law enforcement experience. When he recommended her for the interim position of sheriff, the city council had gone along. She'd had to win the election on her own, but he'd given her the push she needed. Maybe more important, he was dedicated to his mother, his wife and his daughter. Good guy.

He was still laughing at her. "Plus the cops all know I'm from Virtue Falls, so I got a call right away. Plus . . ." He let that dangle.

"Your foster mother told you."

"Margaret Smith knows all."

"She's almost one hundred years old. How does she hear this stuff?"

"She's charming, she has connections and she runs the Virtue Falls Resort. Everyone tells her everything."

Yep. Kateri liked Margaret Smith, too.

He continued, "Stag Denali, huh? I remember him. Good catch. He's quite the arm candy."

"I don't know that that's what he signed on for."

"He's a tough guy. He'll bear up under the strain."

They laughed, then Kateri got down to business. "We had a second slashing in Virtue Falls. This one ended in a death."

"Slashing? John Terrance?"

"We'd like to think so."

"But you don't."

"There is reasonable doubt." She filled him in, sent the files on the first slashing and the preliminaries on the second, and promised the autopsy when Mike Sun had finished.

"Looking at the pictures now . . ." She could hear him clicking through the photos.

"See anything familiar? Does the FBI have reports of similar attacks anywhere close? Or far? Past or present? Have you heard anything?"

"No clusters of slashing attacks that I'm aware of. The only things the victims had in common was that they're white and female?"

"And that the slashing was to their faces. That coincidence seems unlikely."

"Agreed. Let me look around at FBI reports, talk to some people, get back to you. In the meantime, you eliminate or confirm Terrance as a suspect."

"You mean, catch him?"

"You've only got a little time before Virtue Falls goes from quiet hysteria to a riot."

"I am aware. But he's gone to ground."

A short, portly man stepped into the doorway and rapped briskly on the sill.

This could not be good. "Garik, I have to go. City Councilman Venegra has arrived for a visit."

"Viagra Venegra? Isn't that the guy you arrested last week?"

"Yes, it is."

"Along with most of the city council and the school board?"

"Yes, I did."

"For getting involved in a fight between two members of the school board in front of the courthouse that became a riot involving every politician in town?"

Shut up, Garik. "That is correct."

"Think he might hold a grudge against you?"

She checked out Venegra's scowl. "Absolutely! I'll keep you posted as events unfold. Call me as soon as you've got something." She hung up on him and gestured to a seat. "Come in, Councilman. What's on your mind?"

He gripped the arms of the chair as he lowered himself down and he winced as he settled on the cushion.

On that fateful day last week in front of the courthouse, Venegra's wife had discovered he was having an affair with Mona Coleman and she had bunched up her fist and landed a good solid hit. That was part of what precipitated the riot . . .

Kateri refrained from asking how his nads were feeling.

"Who were you talking to, Sheriff?" Venegra asked.

As if he had the right to know. As if she reported to him. Which she did not. But she knew damned good and well he'd heard at least some of her part of the conversation and so she told him, "Garik Jacobsen at the FBI. In case you haven't heard, we have a situation here in the county."

"I'm glad to hear you admit that. For as little as you've done to apprehend John Terrance, I thought you were unaware of the danger lurking on every corner. When *are* you going to catch John Terrance? The citizens of Virtue Falls didn't vote you in and expect you to prove your incompetence in the first week."

He was a nasty little sexist creep. Kateri wondered what Mona saw in him—and Kateri didn't think much good of Mona.

"What do you have to say for yourself?" he demanded.

"Is this official business, Councilman? Because I've got citizens to interview, calls to make and—"

"This is *official business*. The Virtue Falls City Council is in charge of the finances of this city and this adverse publicity that you have garnered by letting John Terrance run around the county unchecked when the Fourth of July, the date of our country's independence and the largest moneymaking week for Virtue Falls businesses . . . this is ruinous!"

She was staring, she realized, with her mouth cocked sideways. "You're not complaining because the citizens of Virtue Falls are in danger, but because the city treasury is in peril?"

"When the town's profits are disrupted, do you imagine the citizens will be happy?"

She had been up for hours. She'd viewed the scene of a gruesome murder, grieved for a woman she had never met, worried that others would suffer the same fate, dealt with paperwork, listened to police reports, dealt with more paperwork, organized photos, called the victim's family, comforted Carolyn Abner's children, persuaded them to authorize the autopsy . . . and now Kateri faced an indignant, moneygrubbing politician who looked like a bug-eyed snake who had swallowed an egg.

But she had to be fair . . . "You have heard a woman was discovered early this morning at Lupine Point, murdered by a slasher?"

"What? What? Murder?" Venegra put his hand over his heart as if to still the palpitations.

Kateri thought he'd be better off putting his hands on his aching testicles.

In a booming voice, he asked, "Did you catch the killer?"

"We have no suspects."

"Is the victim someone local?"

"A tourist." Kateri's sarcasm got the better of her. "Is that better for business or worse?"

She was making fun of him, and Venegra was smart enough—barely—to know it. "At least you've done one thing right—you had the good sense to bring Garik Jacobsen into the case. Maybe our former sheriff will come back and catch the murderer before he kills again!"

In a voice that would have frozen a normal man, she said, "Garik would not so overstep his authority."

"Well, maybe we'll just vote him in after the citizens of our fair city impeach you!"

That's it. I am done with you. Kateri stood up and offered her hand. "Let's shake on that."

Venegra grabbed her fingers and squeezed. Hard.

Kateri dragged seething fire, molten rock, ocean-cold, angry-red power up from the earth and let it flow through her and into him.

First Venegra started trembling.

The earth jolted hard and fast, a brief movement the seismologists would categorize as an aftershock to the big one that had reshaped Virtue Falls.

Venegra's eyes grew wide.

Kateri pulled her hand away before she wholly gave in to her temper—and brought the walls down.

He flopped backward into the chair, his gaze fixed on her in horror.

With a fixed smile, she reminded him, "I did say, 'Let's shake.'"

CHAPTER NINETEEN

Kateri texted Merida. *Okay?*

Merida texted back, *No worries. I'm fine.*
Have errands. Will be there as soon as I can.
Headed out for a run. See you soon.

Merida left the B and B and ran a mile through Virtue Falls, then took the cutoff that descended toward the beach and there along the fringes of the sand, she hopped along the rocks and the old dock pilings. She did her yoga, made like a tree, stood on one leg, then the other. In a silly departure from discipline, she became a pelican and waved her arms. It was perhaps childhood reborn, but in those moments she gained balance and dexterity—and she tasted freedom. Freedom from memory. Freedom from worry. Freedom from anger and vengeance. Just . . . freedom.

Slowly she stilled. Exuberance changed to introspection.

She'd been here for less than a week, yet last night she had encountered too many people who knew her as Helen. Then early this morning someone had called her, warned her that "they" were hunting her, and today worry replaced joy and mindlessness. As she stood there, facing the ocean, she found herself listening, not to the waves ceaselessly rolling, but for the sound of footsteps behind her. Serenity had never seemed so far away, so at last she turned back, running hard up the path, testing her limits for speed and endurance. She turned onto the street where the B and B stood, saw a man jogging toward her, shirtless, in shorts, shirtless, beautifully sculpted, shirtless . . . *Lifts weights, shorts are too long, almost to his knees, such a shame, those thigh muscles must be awesome . . .*

Benedict, of course.

He lifted one hand in recognition and ran past her at a pace that made her feel like a sweaty underachiever.

She turned and ran backward—it was good exercise—and watched him.

"Wow." For a ruthless, conniving asshole of an autocrat, he looked good, probably because he had time left over from impaling his competitors to exercise.

He rounded the corner and headed for town, and he didn't turn to glance back.

"Damn it." She slowed to a walk. She was looking at him, and he didn't care to look at her. She turned to face forward, glimpsed movement out of the corners of her eyes.

A man hid in the hedges.

She leaped sideways, but too late.

He yanked her into the shadowy yard through a narrow gap in the towering boxwood.

She fought. Branches scraped her skin.

But he was powerful and skilled. He rendered her helpless, pulled her close and in a deep, familiar voice said, "Helen, I did warn that you couldn't scream."

CHAPTER TWENTY

The Gem Lounge hadn't changed a bit. It looked—and smelled—exactly as it had when, as a child, Kateri had crept in nightly to bring her mother home. Years of spilled beer, squeezed limes, tomato juice and Tabasco, cracked vinyl, the dishwasher's steam . . . and a whiff of tobacco.

Maybe Bertha wasn't paying that much attention to the smoking ban.

The afternoon crowd was quiet, fishermen mostly, early risers, intent on playing cards, cracking peanuts, having a beer before going home to bed.

Kateri lifted a hand to the guys, went to the bar and pulled up a stool. Today Bertha wore black boots, black leggings, a black cardigan and a purple collared shirt. Kateri envied the woman her style.

"Hey, darlin', good to see you here." Bertha got out a mug, poured it full of almond milk and slid it into the microwave. "Did you decide I was right and this was a good place for that sheriff to visit?"

Kateri watched her, knowing what Bertha was doing, appreciating the tradition and right now, needing the comfort. "You're always right, Bertha. Everybody knows that."

Bertha smirked. "That's true, and it's amazing that people don't always do what I tell them to do."

"The world would be a better place."

"Now take off your hat inside."

Kateri complied, setting down her sheriff's wide-brimmed hat on the bar.

"Hey, Sheriff." Berk Moore slid into the seat beside her. "How's Rainbow?"

"I haven't been in to visit her yet today. Things got hectic." An understatement. "But last night she was 'bout the same."

"Sorry. Really. That sucks. Geeze. I can't imagine . . ." *the Oceanview Café without her.* He didn't say it, but the words hung in the air.

Bertha whisked chocolate into the milk, topped it with marshmallow cream and slid it across the bar to Kateri. "How's you?"

Kateri pressed her hand to her ribs. " 'Bout the same. Sleeping in my own house, though. That makes me happy." She pulled the hot chocolate close, sipped and sighed with pleasure. "So does this."

"I know, darlin'." Bertha was watching Kateri a little too closely.

"There's nothing like your own bed," Berk agreed.

Kateri licked the marshmallow cream off her upper lip. "Berk, how's business?"

"Not much new construction. You know it's

about impossible to get permitted. But plenty of remodeling." Berk owned a construction company in town. "With the dry summer weather, we're hustling."

"So why are you in here?" Kateri didn't expect to like the answer.

Berk pulled off his baseball hat and ran his hand over his bald head. "I heard a rumor and when I saw the sheriff come in here, I thought I'd follow along and ask if it was true."

Kateri sighed. Small towns. Everybody knew everything about five seconds after it happened. "It's true. We lost a tourist last night."

Bertha put her hand on her skinny hip. "Something tells me it wasn't another dumb-ass who walked off the cliffs while he was texting."

"No, although we did have one come into the police station yesterday to demand we retrieve her phone from the ocean."

Berk and Bertha cackled.

Then Bertha sobered. "The way you're acting, I'm going to guess it's another slashing."

"Yes." Kateri pushed the half-finished chocolate away. "He, um, finished what he started with Monique."

"Slashed her neck?" Bertha guessed.

"Slashed around her face." Kateri gestured in a circle around her own face.

"What?" Bertha got loud.

Heads turned.

Bertha leaned across the bar. "What?" she whispered.

"Exactly what I said. Head wounds bleed, you know? I don't ever want to see that again." Kateri reached across and took Bertha's hand. "Listen, if this is John Terrance, and even if it's not, you're the sole witness to Monique's attack and I'm worried about you."

"I know, honey. But I'm not leaving town, and I'm not leaving my bar." Bertha was implacable. "No little prick with a box cutter is going to chase me away from my home."

"I figured you were going to say that . . . Got any objections to the occasional police presence?"

"Not at all. I'll give 'em peanuts, jerky, hot chocolate and maybe even iced tea." Bertha crossed her fingers and her heart. "No liquor for the boys in blue."

Kateri slid off the bar stool. "You take care of yourself, Bertha." She turned to Berk. "You, too. John Terrance worked for you once upon a time, and you fired him."

Berk turned a lovely shade of green.

Kateri said, "All of us, no matter who we are, need to be careful."

Kateri thought he'd turned green because he was considering how John Terrance might get his revenge. But the way Berk stared at the door made her look, and she recognized the form silhouetted against the light.

Luis Sanchez, the current Coast Guard commander. He had served under her when she held the post. He had been a steadfast friend through the horror of her drowning and the constant, dreadful effort of recovery. He had been her most constant friend . . . and then, almost lover.

That was when things got awkward.

Luis headed for Kateri. He was Hispanic, tanned, not too tall, toned, moved like a dancer and a dark curl of hair caressed his forehead. It was a miracle any woman ever resisted him.

Kateri had been so, so lucky.

Berk, the lousy coward, said, "Gotta go to work. Talk to you later, Sheriff!"

Bertha, the other lousy coward, moved to the far end of the bar and started assiduously polishing the glasses.

Even the fishermen leaned back in their chairs as if they viewed a possible blast zone.

Luis pulled up the stool Berk had so recently vacated. He leaned close and quietly said, "I've got news about John Terrance. Maybe."

Kateri sat back down. This was the best news she'd had in two days and it was delivered by a man who was all business. "Tell me," she said.

"Last night, a bunch of idiots, group of about twenty, were partying down on the beach. They had their zoom-zoom fast boat tied up against the rocks. They had a fire, they were smoking weed, drinking I don't know what. A lot."

Bertha called, "Commander, you want something?"

"The usual." Luis kept talking, his dark eyes fixed on Kateri with all the fiery excitement he had once displayed in his courting. "If I've got this right, this guy stopped in for a drink before he made his move. Then he went over and untied the boat."

"It was John Terrance?"

"Description matches. The group was laughing at him, teasing that he didn't know how to drive that thing."

Bertha placed a cold beer with a tequila chaser at his elbow. "I'll bet that pissed him off."

He took a long swallow of the beer. "They're damned lucky that vicious sonofabitch didn't kill a few before he drove away."

Bertha retreated, but not far.

Incredulous, Kateri asked, "They watched him drive their boat out into the Pacific Ocean? What time?"

"You know drunks aren't good with time."

Kateri most certainly did.

He continued, "They reported it to the Coast Guard this morning when it was finally clear the boat was not coming back either with the guy or on its own."

"Did he hot-wire it?"

"Of course not. They left the key in the ignition."

Kateri found herself shaking her head back and forth, back and forth like a bobblehead doll. "No sign of him or the boat?"

"I've got a cutter out looking, but the man has been manufacturing meth for years. He knows this coast as well as we do. He could be anywhere."

Kateri thought of the dead girl. "He could be back on land. If we had any idea of the correct time, we could figure if he's a suspect in the murder."

Luis knew about the murder; all of law enforcement in this part of the state knew about the murder. It made everyone itchy, and they were starting to squabble, to place blame.

Kateri was first in line for blame. "I've done so much wrong with this case and yet—I don't know what I'd do differently. Except keep an eye on the Terrances while we were arresting the school board and the city council."

"Sometimes there's no right. You know that. You're doing what you can. We're all doing what we can. It's just not enough." Luis finished off the beer, picked up the shot.

Kateri couldn't stand it. Couldn't stand to see her friend so frustrated he was drinking in the middle of the afternoon and while on duty. She put her hand over his.

He froze in place, staring down at her fingers.

"Luis, for so long, you've been one of my best friends. After all we've been through, can't we salvage a remnant of that affection?"

He traced one of the myriad of scars that crossed her hand, reminders of the tsunami, and the frog god, and broken bones and pain and recovery that would never end. "I don't see how that's possible. You know what I wanted from you."

He was pouting. A very handsome pout, but a pout nevertheless. "And you would have won me, if not—"

He pulled his hand away. "Are you going to nag me about that forever?"

Kateri's grasp on her temper was usually good, but he was being a pig. "You were dating me and you slept with Sienna."

"Only once!"

Bertha edged closer. Sienna had come to Virtue Falls as an ambitious young graduate. She had quickly opened a sandwich shop, then a pizza shop, and now it seemed she owned all of Virtue Falls. That was, of course, totally untrue. But she did own Luis, in ways Kateri did not choose to imagine.

Kateri said, "It's not a matter of degrees, Luis. Once is unforgiveable."

"Sienna and I have a casual relationship."

"That's great, as long as it's okay for the two of you." Kateri thought Sienna would be surprised to hear her relationship with Luis was casual; that young woman was beautiful, spoiled and determined to have him. "As long as I'm not involved."

Luis must have decided he was losing this argument, because he went on the attack. "After putting me off for weeks, you slept with another man. As soon as you got the chance!"

You started it! Kateri bit her tongue. Pretty soon they were going to be slapping at each other like two squabbling toddlers. "Sienna thought she was pregnant. You thought you were the father. I considered that infidelity. You got engaged. I was therefore free to do what I wished."

Bertha had her back to them, her elbow on the bar, but by the way her head was cocked, Kateri knew she was listening with all her might.

"You wanted to do . . . him? You slept with him after one night! Stag Denali. For fuck's sake. A gambler. Is *he* a casual relationship?" Heedless of Kateri's rising temper, Luis charged on in a voice that carried across the bar. "Because if you're into casual relationships, count me in!"

She didn't hesitate, she most definitely didn't think and she answered just as loudly. "I don't *do* casual relationships."

Bertha gasped.

Luis looked as if he'd been slapped.

Kateri couldn't look either of them in the eyes, so she glanced around the bar.

The customers sat, mouths agape.

She whispered, "Most definitely not with, um, two men."

Oh, shit. What had she said? What had she admitted?

Kateri picked up her hat, eased off the bar stool. "If you'll excuse me, I, um, have to go check on my friend at the Good Knight Manor Bed and Breakfast. Early this morning she, um, got a threatening call and I put her off because . . . you know. The murder."

Everyone was staring. Everyone was whispering.

"Luis—I wish you the best of luck in your next significant relationship, whoever it is with."

CHAPTER TWENTY-ONE

Kateri stood on the street corner outside the Gem Lounge.

Rainbow lay in a hospital room dying.

The criminal John Terrance was still free.

A female tourist had been gruesomely murdered by persons unknown.

Her best friend of years past had been threatened by persons unknown.

Kateri's ribs burned like sonsabitches. And within the hour, half the town would hear that Sheriff Kwinault had declared she didn't do casual relationships—and would be told, in case they had forgotten, that she was in a relationship with Stag Denali. Might as well brazen it out and hope to hell Stag wasn't among the half of the town who heard the story.

Yep. Being sheriff was as much fun as she had imagined.

Better get moving before the bar patrons got done texting their friends and they descended on the Gem Lounge to catch sight of crazy-in-love Kateri Kwinault.

She winced at the thought, got in the patrol car and headed toward Mrs. Golobovitch's apartment. While she drove, she called Bergen, who said everything was quiet. Then in an ominous tone, he added, "Too quiet."

He was quoting the oft-used movie line, and she said, "Very funny."

"I'm serious. Where is that goddamned sonofabitch John Terrance?"

She hung up carefully . . . because Bergen never swore.

She checked in with Mike Sun, who told her in a tone of intense annoyance he would call when he knew something about Carolyn Abner's murder.

Finally she checked in with Moen's father, Ron. Moen hadn't been at work and she was worried about the boy. She asked, "How is he doing today?"

"Thanks for calling about him. Thanks for sending him home and thanks for giving him a little time off. Rupert's sleeping." Ron's voice got rough. "He, uh, he was pretty broken up."

Which was code for: *He's been crying.*

Kateri felt so inadequate. She knew how proud Ron was of his son and his career in law enforcement. She also knew about Rupert's aspirations as an artist. So what was she supposed to say? Platitudes, she supposed. "He's a good kid. He's a good cop."

"He is. I'm just not sure if he . . . Well!" Ron drew a breath. "He'll toughen up."

Now Kateri did know what to say. "I hope not. I like him like he is."

"I'll tell him you called." Which was code for: *Butt out*.

"Thanks, Mr. Moen. Please do." She hung up.

This had been a long day and it was just past noon. She had hours of work and heartbreak to go. She needed her dog. She parked at the curb, rapped on Mrs. Golobovitch's door and when Mrs. Golobovitch opened, Kateri asked jokingly, "Can Lacey come out and play?"

"Dear, I don't have her."

"What?"

"When you didn't bring her to me, I was a bit surprised, but I called Stag and he told me Lacey seemed anxious and assured me he would keep her today." Mrs. Golobovitch patted Kateri's hand and beamed. "He's such a nice man. I'm so glad you have someone to take care of you."

"Um, he doesn't . . . that is, I don't need someone to care for me. I can take care of myself."

"Of course you can. But isn't it lovely that he's there to protect and cherish you anyway?"

Kateri shut up. Mrs. Golobovitch held Old World views of men and women and love and marriage and, well, hell, she was right. It was lovely that Stag Denali had her back.

Mrs. Golobovitch added helpfully, "I believe they're at the construction site on the reservation."

The casino construction site. "They've already started building?"

"Site preparation. Soil testing, then scrape it down a few feet and get ready for the foundation pour."

Kateri cocked her head. "Mrs. Golobovitch, how do you know all that?"

"Dear, I haven't always been an old lady. When I came from Yugoslavia, I was a structural engineer. Here they wouldn't honor my degree and give me reciprocity"—Mrs. Golobovitch waggled her finger at Kateri—"but I haven't forgotten everything I knew!"

"Of course not. Forgive me. I should have realized." Sometimes, Kateri felt as if she didn't really know anybody. Like Stag, who saw that her dog was anxious and took Lacey to work with him. "I guess I'll head over to the rez." Which was a tough show for her. She was related to half the tribe. Half were proud of their first Native American sheriff. Half thought she had betrayed them by succeeding in a mainstream world. There was a lot of overlap in those groups, but one thing was for sure: most despised law enforcement. Then there was the "chosen by the frog god" thing. To say feelings toward Kateri were mixed was putting it diplomatically.

Of course, Stag was building a casino, which would bring prosperity to Virtue Falls and the rez . . . also gambling addiction, alcoholism, prostitution and suicide . . . so Kateri's feelings were equally mixed. Toward her tribe, toward Stag, toward being involved with him . . .

Mrs. Golobovitch patted Kateri's shoulder. "Don't worry, dear. It will all turn out for the best. It always does."

Except for Carolyn Abner of Springfield, Missouri, who died last night. "Thank you. I'm sure you're right. Now I have to go get my dog."

CHAPTER TWENTY-TWO

Kateri didn't need the sign telling her she'd crossed onto the reservation. Here the air grew misty, shades of gray and gold tinted the sky, the tears of fifteen generations soaked the ground, the odors of evergreen, ocean and marsh combined to smell like home. And yet . . .

And yet.

Ten-year-old Kateri left the house where her mother was sleeping it off and went looking for Uncle Bluster, real name Willis Warner. She found him in the usual place, sitting cross-legged under the twisted cypress overlooking the ocean. He wore an orange game cap on his head, dirty jeans and a starched shirt with no buttons. He rested his elbow on the battered blue-and-white cooler beside him and stared at his bare toes. She could see his lips move; he was talking to himself.

She stood at a distance and eyed the frosty one-liter bottle of vodka in his hand. Conversation best occurred when the level of the clear liquid was between one-quarter and three-quarters full. Too early and Uncle Bluster was sharp, angry and sarcastic. Too late and he became a pitiful, tearful former mercenary plagued by the ghosts of the people he had killed.

Two more swallows and he would be in the golden zone.

He lifted his gaze, saw her, took the two swallows and gestured her closer. "What do you wish to ask?"

Kateri scooted close, sat down with her knees almost touching his and pretended to think. Actually, she *was* thinking; thinking she couldn't ask what she wanted to ask, which was, "Why doesn't my mama love me?" Instead she said, "Tell me the legend of the frog god."

Uncle Bluster narrowed his rheumy brown eyes. "I've already told you. So many times."

"Again. Please. I love it when you tell me."

"I wish all the kids listened like you. Showed some respect for the traditions. Learned about their collective pasts. Modern kids. No respect. They don't respect me." His voice rose. "Do you know I could kill you with one hand?"

"I know. You're tough and you're dangerous." She touched the bottom of the bottle, urging it toward his mouth. She watched him swallow, wipe his mouth,

196

and she asked, "When was the frog god born?"

Uncle Bluster belched; some of the belligerence eased out of him and he settled into the role of honored storyteller. In a sonorous voice, he began, "When the world was born, a giant monster grew in the depths of the ocean. He was the frog god, fearsome, dark and green, living in a universe lit only by fluorescent fishes that darted out of his reach, then died when he sucked them into his gullet. Yet the frog god hungered, for light, for heat . . . for love. He sought a mate. She spurned him, ran from him."

"She became one with the sun, right, Uncle Bluster?"

He broke off and in an irritated voice, he asked, "Who's telling this story? You? Or me?"

"You are. You are!"

"All right." He settled to the task again. "She became one with the sun. For centuries he brooded, growing more and more wrathful about the deprivation he suffered. Finally he pushed his great legs against the ocean floor and leaped toward the surface, seeking light and heat! Seeking her and the sun! When he did, the earth shuddered, the ocean rose.

Trees fell, waves pounded the shore."

Kateri caught her breath, imagining the cataclysm of earthquake and tsunami.

"In our lands, the harbor filled. Boats were swept away. Men, women, children disappeared, never to be seen again, swallowed by the angry blue boil of the sea. They were a sacrifice to the frog god's hunger. Yet"—Uncle Bluster paused, his arms lifted, his eyes on the horizon—"he failed. His mate escaped him. He sank once more into the depths. The sun continued its trek across the sky. Today and every day, he hungers. Soon the frog god will jump again."

"What about me?" Kateri shifted. Leaves and needles crackled beneath her bottom. "Tell me about me!"

"The frog god is a great god, yet he can live only at the bottom of the ocean. He is imprisoned by his monstrous size, his inhumanity . . . by a god loftier than himself. Far and faint, beyond the drumbeat of his heart, he can hear a woman's cry of defiance, of survival. She goes to the shore. She bathes her feet. She is not his love, yet he takes her, swallows her, kills her, disgorges her, making her a god of prescience and strength, an emissary on land of his greatness . . ."

"Is that me?"

"To every generation, a goddess is born whom the frog god loves . . . and destroys. Once upon a time, I foretold that your mother was that goddess. But she gave herself in love to a mortal man, she drowned herself in liquor and desperation." His voice dropped to a mere whisper. "Be careful, Kateri Kwinault. Don't go to the shore. Don't swim in the ocean."

"I have before and I've never seen the frog god."

"You will."

Kateri leaned forward eagerly. "Because I'm special, Uncle Bluster?"

He took a long pull of vodka, taking the level dangerously close to the three-quarter mark. "Don't ask me. I'm only a drunk old mercenary sitting under a tree waiting for the day when the ocean rises and sweeps me away."

With absolute certainty, Kateri said, "Uncle Bluster, the frog god will never take you. You keep his legend alive."

Uncle Bluster's gaze examined Kateri, and he saw too much. "Why are you really here? What is your real question?"

She shifted again, uncomfortable, hot, embarrassed. "I already asked—"

"You are special. But not so special I can't tell when you lie."

Kateri's hands slid down over her belly. She had the cramps. She was bleeding. This was gross, uncontrollable—and the first time. She wanted her mother to be with her. But her mother was sleeping it off. Kateri burst out, "I want my mother! I needed her last night and she . . . she was in the bar, she was drunk, she was with a man, she was laughing. She doesn't care about me!"

"Why did you want her, child?"

Kateri crossed her arms over her budding breasts. "I'm not a child anymore."

"Oh." He nodded. He understood. "No. You're not." Lifting his bottle, he took a long pull. "I remember the day you were born. I held your tiny body in my hands and saw you had the frog god's eyes. Now you have stepped across the line and become a woman. Here." He offered the bottle. "I guess you're old enough now."

Horror. Fury. Indignation. "No!"

"It'll make you feel better."

"Like *you* feel better? Like *my mother* feels better? Throwing up and drooling on yourself and complaining about your headache like it's a disease you can't

help? No! I will never drink that shit."
Kateri wasn't supposed to use words like
shit, but she used it like adults used it, for
emphasis and with contempt.

Still Uncle Bluster held the bottle out.
"I said that, too, when I was your age."

"Never!" she yelled, and stood up.
"No!" She ran down to the beach, away
from the sight of Uncle Bluster listing
sideways from the slight weight of the
outstretched bottle. She let the waves
wash over her feet, listened to the inhale
and exhale of the ocean as it advanced
and retreated . . . approached and tugged
at her.

She would *never* be like him. Like her
mother. She wouldn't. *No.*

Uncle Bluster always warned her never
to go swimming in the Pacific. But Kateri
couldn't stay away. The ocean rhythms
drove the beat of her heart and in her mind
she sensed the currents, the underwater
sway of the seaweed forests, the glorious
depths and unimaginable secrets. In those
places, she wouldn't be in pain. She
wouldn't be unhappy.

She would be loved.

A long wave rolled toward her, covered
her feet, rose to her knees, her thighs
. . . it was coming up, coming fast. She

started backing up. Backing up. Running backward. The water tugged at her, pulling the sand from beneath her feet, trying to make her fall, to submerge her in salt and wrap her in seaweed. Sure, she had imagined she could walk to the bottom of the ocean and still live and breathe. And sometimes—today—she wanted to sink into the depths and become one with the sea foam like the Little Mermaid. Not the Little Mermaid in the Disney movie, but the real Little Mermaid in Hans Christian Andersen's dark fairy tale.

But she didn't mean it. She didn't want her vee-jay-jay to get wet. Her pad . . . she wore a pad . . . it was gross. Everything was gross. She was disgusting. She started sobbing, crying like she hadn't ever allowed herself to do, her tears dripping into the ocean . . .

The wave retreated.

She wanted to turn and run, but she knew better now. She backed away, crying, bawling, broken apart by loneliness and anguish.

Hormones. Her teacher explained it was hormones. Yet Kateri's emotions were real. Maybe the hormones brought them close to the surface, but she recognized her own desolation. And her right to that desolation.

She trudged home, and when she got there, she discovered her mother throwing up in the toilet.

She didn't care. It was only later, when her father appeared, that she found out her mother wasn't merely hungover.

She was sick. She had cancer.

CHAPTER TWENTY-THREE

Kateri followed the plywood, orange spray-painted CONSTRUSHION! sign—someone could not spell—turned left onto a new, narrow dirt road cut through the forest and followed the increasing roar of heavy machinery. She parked at the end of the line of dusty, battered pickups, got out and walked over to the chain link that surrounded the job site perimeter. She arrived in time to see Stag gesturing wildly while he shouted directions at one of the excavator operators scraping the site.

Stag Denali. Square chin, cheekbones, dark intent eyes, dark hair. Denim shirt, washed and worn to a faded blue, hugging his shoulders. That perfect butt in the blue jeans . . . the old leather belt, the work boots, yellow hard hat and ear protection.

He looked like one of the Village People, only straight. He looked like the guy in the paper towel commercials, only not a cartoon. Plus, he was dirty.

Kateri wanted to *lick* the dirt off.

No. *Focus.* She had come for Lacey . . . who was nowhere in sight. There was only this gray shaggy mongrel who bounded toward her, ears flapping. "My God." Kateri slid to her knees to embrace her filthy dog. "What have you been doing?"

Lacey looked up and *smiled;* even her teeth were dirty.

"Oh, honey." Kateri petted her gingerly. "You look—"

"She's been helping prepare the site."

Kateri looked up into Stag's amused face. "By digging?"

He pulled off his hard hat and ear protection and hung them on a hook on the fence. "And rolling. I've never seen a dog have so much fun." Getting down on his knees beside Kateri, he licked his thumb and wiped her chin. "She got dirt on you." He was still smiling, right at her, into her eyes.

Her heart sank. He'd heard what she'd said at the Gem Lounge. She broke a sweat. Hot summer. Streak of heat. Long sunny days. She was warm. Too warm. Really warm. Embarrassed. Blushing.

The heavy equipment behind them slowed and idled. Someone whistled suggestively.

Stag whipped his head around and stared, eyes narrowed. Just stared.

There were no more whistles. The engines began to roar again; things got very busy on the site.

Stag stood and helped her to her feet. "Come on. We'll take Lacey to the stream and toss her in."

She dusted her knees. "You're going to toss my dog into a creek?"

"Naw, she'll jump in by herself. She's been in at least eight times today. In between rolling in the slash pile and bumming lunch off the guys. Come on, sweetie." The *sweetie* was directed at Lacey, not Kateri.

Lacey flung herself into Stag's arms and looked smugly at Kateri.

Stag headed into the woods. "All the guys adore her. Nifty threatened to steal her, but I told him she was your dog and he shivered and backed away. You inspire fear and awe, Kateri Kwinault."

"From you?"

"You bet. I was afraid you were only using me for my body."

He sounded so casual, so amused, and he looked so . . . so strong and manly.

Ugh. *Manly*. Who even thought stuff like that anymore? "I'm also using you for your dog-sitting abilities." *High five, Kateri! That was a smooth, noncommittal reply.*

"You can use me however you want—as long as it's forever."

She stopped cold.

He kept walking, strolling along the shady forest path toward the sound of burbling water. And the way he walked . . . swaggering like a conceited ass, like he knew she was watching. At the same time, he held her dog against his chest in the most heart-melting . . .

No. No melting hearts. Kateri needed to remember who he was and that she didn't entirely trust him. She hurried, and caught them as they reached the swirling pool under a rushing waterfall.

"There you go, sweetheart." He put Lacey down. "Hop in."

He only had to tell the little dog once. She clambered onto a fallen log that overhung the pool and leaped, landed with a splash, went under, came up and started swimming upstream, fighting the currents and joyously barking.

"I never knew she liked to swim," Kateri said.

"Sure." Stag sat on the log and unlaced his boots. "I figure in high school she was not only the prom queen, she was also the swimming champ and the girl voted most likely to succeed."

Kateri laughed, because he was so spot-on about Lacey's doggy personality. And she stared, because after he removed his boots and socks, he stood up and stretched, his long arms extending way up. "What are you doing?"

"It doesn't get hot here often, but when it does, it's a steamer. I'm going to cool off." He waded into the stream and offered his hand. "Want to come in?"

She almost put her hand in his, then common sense caught up with her. "No. No, I, um, I'm on duty and the shit has officially hit the fan."

"I heard about the tourist. I'm sorry. You deserve a break." That hand remained steadily outstretched.

She noted that he had a scar across his palm, a deep red mark, and his little finger curled almost into his palm. Seemed like the kind of thing she should have noticed before, but she'd always been involved with his other body parts. Right now, she stared fixedly at that hand. "I wish I could. I can't. Don't tempt me."

The hand clenched, disappeared out of her line of vision. "Wouldn't dream of it."

Out of the corners of her eyes, she caught a glimpse of him falling backward—and the cold splash drenched her, head to toe. "Damn you!" She laughed, and wiped at the water on her uniform. "You are the most—"

"Charming man you've ever met?"

"That, too." She watched him float seemingly without effort and oh, God, it did look refreshing. In more ways than one.

"Lacey's looking a little more herself." Stag gestured toward a branch. "Her towel's hanging over there."

Kateri took one look. "That's Lacey's towel?"

"She was in my car on the new leather seat. She does have dog claws, you know!"

"So you bought her a Barbie beach towel?" She knelt and called her dog.

Lacey paddled toward her.

"It was on sale!" He sounded defensive. As he should.

Kateri started to laugh.

Then he stood.

She froze.

Water ran off his hair and face in rivulets that slid under his collar and down his chest. She knew because his blue denim shirt was plastered to his chest and . . . muscles. In detail. His jeans sagged low on his hips. Really low. The kind of low that if she gave them a tug, she would see London and France, and probably all of the Iberian Peninsula.

This could not be good for her heart.

Too late she realized he was headed right for her. "No. Don't! You're—"

Gently he wrapped her in his arms, pulled her close and up onto her toes, and kissed her.

The cold water soaked through her uniform, opening the way to the blistering heat of his body. His mouth was wet and warm and absolutely intent . . . on her. He absorbed her. He consumed her. He . . . wanted her. Heat and cold. Forest and stream. The great, dark depths of the ocean rising up to envelop—

Lacey barked. Furiously. Imperiously.

Stag pulled away, looked down at the little dog at their feet and laughed. Taking the Barbie towel out of Kateri's hands, he leaned down and dried Lacey from head to toe, picked her up and cradled her. And slid his arm around Kateri's waist.

Stretching and reaching, Lacey licked at their chins.

Between Stag and Kateri, passion simmered beneath the surface.

At the same time, they shared an affection for the dog who adored them so.

For Kateri, this felt like family, close and tight. Support . . . for one moment, she allowed her head to rest on Stag's shoulder.

His big hand came up and pressed her into him.

They both straightened.

"Come on. I'll walk you to your car." Still holding the dog, Stag steered Kateri with his hand on her back. "When do you go see the doctor again?"

The switch of conversation startled Kateri out of her pleasant reverie. "What? The doctor?"

"About your ribs."

"Oh." She had winced when he embraced her; she had hoped he didn't notice. "I'm supposed to stop in when I visit Rainbow."

He stopped by her car, put Lacey into the passenger seat and strapped her into her doggie seat belt. "So tonight?"

"Yes."

"I'll go with you."

It was on the tip of Kateri's tongue to tell him

not to bother. But . . . no way around it, it was going to be a long day. She was tired and sore and grief-stricken about Rainbow. So she said, "Thank you."

Taking her face between his hands, he pressed a kiss on her forehead. "Good girl!"

Kateri muttered, "Woof."

He gave Lacey one last pet and strode away. Strode. Not walked. Not sauntered. Strode. Like Clint Eastwood on steroids.

"Whew." Climbing in the car, Kateri said to Lacey, "So he heard what I said at the Gem Lounge and he didn't get pissy or run away. Point for him."

Lacey gave her her best *I'm a starving doggie* look.

Kateri riffled around in the car door side pocket, brought out the plastic bag of dog treats and handed her a green one. "Coming out of that stream, all wet . . . he Mr. Darcy'd me." She looked down at her damp uniform. "And unless I miss my guess, when he kissed me, he was marking me."

The green treats were Lacey's least favorite, but she munched down with great enthusiasm, spraying crumbs on the seat and then daintily retrieving them one at a time.

"All that playing in the dirt will give a dog an appetite, hmm?"

Lacey put her head on Kateri's thigh.

"Yeah, yeah." Kateri dug out a brown treat and handed it over. "On the other hand, let us remember who he is and what he's done in his life. As law-abiding citizens go, he's on the shady side. Maybe he just has good reflexes, but during that drive-by, he hit the ground a little too promptly."

Lacey made a *humph!* sound, flopped onto the seat and closed her eyes.

"That's not the attitude to take. I'm trying not to be stupid. Or stupider. What kind of sheriff sleeps with Stag Denali, enforcer and convicted murderer, after one casual meeting? It's career suicide. Plus, to trust a guy with his reputation simply because he seems solid as a rock and is good in bed. Really good in bed." Kateri looked over at Lacey.

Lacey was curled up and asleep.

Kateri started the car. "I know. If we don't catch John Terrance and the slasher, I won't have to worry about being the sheriff much longer." The trouble was, when dealing with Councilman Venegra's threat of impeachment, the unexpectedly vicious streak of crimes and Rainbow's slow, long slide into death, it seemed as if Stag Denali's arms were the one place she could safely sleep.

CHAPTER TWENTY-FOUR

While Lacey snored in a manner totally unlike any prom queen, Kateri drove to the Good Knight Manor Bed and Breakfast.

Kateri needed to take a moment to see her best friend; this morning Merida had been scared to death, and a law enforcement presence might help frighten off the mouth breathers and knuckle draggers—although possibly not the murderers and rapists. Still, hope springs eternal.

Of course, while she was at the bed-and-breakfast, she'd get to see her sister, too.

God help her.

When she parked at the curb, Lacey was on her feet, wagging her tail and ready to go. The clear message was that thirty minutes of sleep could be refreshing.

Kateri could only imagine.

Together they walked the shadowy path, up the rickety stairs and over to the grand front door. Kateri read the plaque:

GOOD KNIGHT MANOR BED AND BREAKFAST
IF NO ANSWER, WALK IN.

She knocked. No one opened the door, so she did as the sign instructed and walked in.

Lacey trotted in on her heels.

The entry looked like an *Addams Family* nightmare. To the left all the doors were shut. To the right a parlor had been attractively arranged, set up for an evening of wine and appetizers. On the wall, Kateri saw a cutesy sign inviting her to use the ship's bell and small mallet, but from the back in the depths of the mansion, she heard raised voices.

She moved slowly toward those voices, reluctant to get involved in a domestic dispute—they were always messy and seldom rewarding—yet one voice was male and abusive, one softly female and pleading.

Trouble. Kateri had walked into trouble.

What else was new?

With a whispered word and a soft gesture, she instructed Lacey to wait in the entry. She eased toward the back of the house, through the empty kitchen, then stood to one side of the large, walk-in pantry. She couldn't see the occupants, but she could hear them.

"You owe me!" the male voice said.

"If you would simply work for me . . ."

"Work! Why would I work? For you? After everything you did to me?"

"I didn't do anything to you!"

"You let me go to prison!"

"You were robbing convenience stores!"

"You wouldn't give me any of the money."

"I told you. They caught me. I had to save myself. You could have run—"

"And never come back to plague you again. Yeah, thanks."

Kateri heard a clatter, a crash, a woman's cry, and rushed to stand in the doorway.

A tall young man, red-faced and furious, swept cans, boxes and bottles off the shelves. Flour flew. Glass crashed. Fruit and pickle juice sprayed.

The older woman grabbed at his arm and hollered, "No. Stop! Or I will—"

"Excuse me," Kateri said firmly and loudly. "Is there a problem?"

The two froze.

The man glimpsed her uniform, dropped his arm, turned his head away. He spoke in a quiet, orderly voice, like a second grader caught feeding the dog his homework. "I was, um, going out to work on the garage. 'Scuse me." He brushed past Kateri and out the kitchen door.

Kateri watched—and wondered. In the short time she'd been listening, she'd heard the guy go from threatening to violent to impressively orderly. Was this the man who'd terrorized Merida? "Are you okay?" Kateri asked the older woman.

"Fine. I just . . ." She looked around. "What a mess!"

"Do you want to press charges?"

"Against . . . him? No. No, not at all. He's
. . . new here. My new handyman. Evan. Evan
doesn't want me to criticize his efforts, but he'll
be . . . he'll work out. I am not someone who is
easily intimidated." The woman edged her way
out of the pantry. "Oh, dear. Susie will not be
happy."

"Susie?"

"My cleaning lady, Susie Robinson. You . . .
you're the sheriff."

"Yes, I'm Kateri Kwinault."

"Then you probably know her all too well. The
poor dear has four children and a husband who
beats her. I imagine occasionally you get called
to her house?"

"No, I don't recall any Susie Robinson."

Phoebe said bracingly, "Don't feel bad. You're
new at the job. I'm sure soon you'll remember
the names of your regulars."

"Actually I was the interim sheriff and—"

The lady interrupted. "I'm Phoebe Glass, the
proprietress of the Good Knight Manor Bed and
Breakfast. What can I do for you?"

Kateri shook hands, noting Phoebe's fingers
were trembling and her gaze slid away to the
side.

Her body language said she knew Kateri could
and probably had heard the altercation and was
drawing unfortunate conclusions. And in fact,
Kateri would do a little poking around in Phoebe

Glass's background. "I came to see Merida. She lives here?"

"Yes. Lovely girl. She went for a run. I'm sure she'll be back soon." Phoebe frowned. "Did you know she can't speak?"

"I am aware."

"You can wait in the parlor. This way." Phoebe led the way out of the kitchen and toward the entry. "I wish she had told me. She must be self-conscious about her handicap, but I am the last person to judge someone for being unable to properly communicate." Phoebe seemed to realize her faux pas, and rattled on. "Not that she can't properly communicate, of course, in her way. Isn't the computer tablet a grand invention when it comes to helping all of us, especially her, get by? Here's the parlor." Phoebe's tone cooled perceptibly. "Oh! Miss Palmer, I see you found our parlor more acceptable this morning than you did last night."

Lilith sat in a high-backed, cushioned chair turned sideways to the door. Lifting her head from her book, she icily stared at Phoebe Glass. "I could hardly expect to spend all my time in that tiny bedroom you assigned me."

"I had to bump another guest to fit you in!"

"Yes." Lilith transferred her attention to Kateri. "Katherine, do you never groom before you go out in public?"

Kateri thought about the 2:30 A.M. call, the

bloody crime scene, the subdued officers, the coroner pointing out the tear in Carolyn Abner's skin where the killer had abandoned his work, the reports, the paperwork, the visit to the Gem Lounge . . . "This is as groomed as I get."

"I heard there was a murder this morning?" Phoebe asked. "I didn't expect that kind of crime when I moved to Virtue Falls."

"You weren't paying attention, then," Lilith said. "A few years ago they had quite the string of ghastly murders. It was in all the news."

"The visitors' bureau certainly never mentioned any killers!" Phoebe huffed.

"No. They wouldn't, would they?" Lilith lifted the hardcover in her lap. "Yet here on your shelves is a fictionalized accounting of the murders. Perhaps you should peruse it."

"A lodger must have left it here," Phoebe said. "I'll read it when you're done."

To Kateri's astonishment, Lacey popped her head up over the arm of Lilith's chair.

But Kateri's astonishment was nothing compared to Phoebe's. "Miss Palmer, I had no idea you brought a dog into the bed-and-breakfast. I'm afraid that's not permissible."

"Lacey is my dog." Kateri moved toward the chair. "I'll remove her at once."

"Nonsense!" Lilith shut her book. "Mrs. Glass likes dogs. Don't you, Mrs. Glass?"

Phoebe smiled. She wasn't happy, but she

smiled because liking dogs was required, and not liking the sheriff's dog might lead to trouble. For some reason, Mrs. Glass was anxious to avoid trouble. "Of course Lacey is welcome as long as she's visiting and not staying. Since you ladies wish to visit, I'll be going to the kitchen to clean up and start tomorrow's breakfast."

"Next time you indulge in an argument, do try not to shout." Lilith watched Phoebe for her reaction. "Sound echoes so through these old houses, don't you know?"

Phoebe smiled again. Still. With clenched teeth. "Sound is deceptive in these old houses. Really . . . deceptive."

Lilith scratched Lacey's head. "Katherine, this is a beautiful cocker spaniel. Who's the breeder?"

"I don't know that there was a breeder. I don't know that Lacey is a purebred. Someone dumped her in a ditch half-starved and I found her."

"Oh, no! Who would abandon such a beautiful girl?"

Lacey leaned her head against Lilith.

Kateri had forgotten. Whatever awful accusations could be made about Lilith, she had a way with animals, all animals. Usually Kateri trusted Lacey's judgment. Now she wished that wasn't the case.

"I assure you, regardless of the circumstances in which you found her, this is a purebred dog." Because Lilith was never wrong.

"It doesn't matter to me. I love her anyway."

"Of course you do." In that abrupt fashion of hers, Lilith said, "Katherine, you have blood on your cuffs."

Kateri looked down, saw the brown stains, remembered too many deadly details and leaned a little harder on her staff.

Lilith said, "Mrs. Glass, would you bring the sheriff some ice water?"

Phoebe zeroed in on Kateri's face. "Of course!" She headed for the kitchen.

"Sit down before you fall down." Lilith pointed to the chair opposite her. "One doesn't suppose being sick at the sight of blood is much of an endorsement of your law enforcement skills."

"That question never came up in the campaign." Kateri sat down. "I didn't vomit, unlike two of my men."

Lilith waved the men's queasiness away.

Tail wagging, Lacey stood up on Lilith's chair and eyed Kateri.

Kateri broke into a smile. "Come on, sweetheart." She patted her lap.

Lacey leaped and slammed into Kateri's ribs.

Kateri winced, but considered it a fair price to pay to hold a wiggling blond cocker spaniel with warm brown eyes and luxuriously long ears. As she rubbed that soft head, she could feel her blood pressure go down and her annoyance fade. Not that Lilith wouldn't get both roiling again.

Lilith learned forward and in a quiet voice confided, "I met a young woman who is staying here."

Oh, no. "Merida?"

"You know her?"

"I met her the other day at the Oceanview Café." That was the truth. Not the whole truth, but Kateri needed to tread carefully. Lilith was far too sharp for comfort. And nosy. So nosy.

"Merida wasn't her name when I met her. I was in India at a fund-raiser for the preservation of ancient monuments in Pakistan. Her husband was Nauplius Brassard."

That rocked Kateri back on her heels. "You're sure?"

"Of course I'm sure." Lilith's fist clenched. "Dreadful man. Nauplius Brassard told me about his admiration of the Indian tradition of suttee, where a wife sacrificed herself on her husband's funeral pyre. As if any woman would sacrifice herself for *him*."

"Huh." Kateri hadn't had time to speculate on what had happened during the years Merry had disappeared from her life. "Did Merida love him?"

"She stood by him, indulged him, did everything in her power to anticipate his every whim. She was a doormat."

"Merida?"

"Her name at the time was Helen. Helen

Brassard." Kateri must have looked disbelieving, for Lilith said, "Look her up. I did. There are photos online. She is changed, but it is definitely her."

"Changed how?"

"She was . . . classic. Now she has no style whatsoever."

"Hmm." Merida hid so many secrets . . .

Lilith stared at Kateri. "You know her."

Damn Lilith! No one was more selfish—or, if it profited her, more likely to be perceptive to the point of discomfort. Kateri bent her head to look at Lacey, and to hide her face. "I didn't say I knew her."

"I think you do." Lilith sat back in her chair and tapped her finger to her forehead. "*Why* wouldn't you want to admit it? The only sensible answer is—because I know her, too. From Baltimore, I suppose. That's the only place our acquaintances intersected. I never forget a face . . . but faces can be changed, and she does remind me of someone else." Again Lilith leaned forward and bent the force of her formidable will on Kateri. "Where did you say you knew her?"

CHAPTER TWENTY-FIVE

The front door quietly opened, quietly shut, and careful footsteps made their way across the entry.

From the direction of the kitchen, Phoebe Glass called heartily, "Miss Falcon, you have arrived exactly on time. Sheriff Kwinault and Miss Palmer are in the parlor waiting for you. We're about to have refreshments. Won't you join us?"

The footsteps paused, then continued.

"Do come. We're so convivial!"

Merida followed Phoebe into the parlor. She wore purple cotton yoga pants, a man's wide-armed T-shirt, a pair of white leather running shoes and carried a small one-shoulder leather backpack. She had a bloody scratch across her cheek, and sweat rimmed her hairline. She wiped her face with the hem of her shirt, leaving a damp stain, and she was silently panting.

She looked glorious.

She smiled widely at Kateri. Nodded politely to Lilith. Spelled, "A good day for a run. I've got to grab a shower," and looked meaningfully at Kateri.

Kateri patted Lacey and when Lacey jumped down, Kateri came to her feet. "Now that I know you're settled here, Lilith, I'll go on my way."

Lilith's narrow face grew chill with scorn.

"Wait. You haven't yet given me your report."

As if Kateri owed her a report. About *anything*. "About?"

"Any word about the box our father sent you?"

"Rainbow is not . . . not out of her coma yet. No one expects that she will live through this."

"So you're going to give up on the possessions our father sent you?"

Sudden irritation scratched at Kateri, like sea salt on an open wound. "Are they important?"

Her snappishness gave Lilith the chance to be calm, logical and patronizing. "The raven is of historical importance. You know that, Katherine."

"That raven is almost alive. If he wishes to return to me, he will." Kateri pivoted on her heel and, using her stick, stalked out of the room, past Phoebe with her tray of ice water.

Phoebe must have enjoyed the little scene, for she smiled smugly.

Merida hurried ahead toward the door on the left. She used a key in the lock, tapped in a code on the keypad and used her thumbprint to get inside. She held the door for Kateri and Lacey, then shut the door behind them and locked them in.

Kateri felt she locked Lilith out. "That woman. Lilith. My sister." She could hardly speak for annoyance. "I've set a watch on Rainbow's house because I believe she is going to try and search it. What does that say about me?"

Merida took the small backpack off her

shoulder, put it on the table and pulled out her tablet. She typed, "What does it say about *her?*"

"That she's desperate. And I'm suspicious. Has there ever been anything Lilith wanted she didn't get?"

"Actually, I think many things. When I look at her, I see a woman eaten up with envy. Of you."

Kateri laughed a litle. "No. She couldn't be so patronizing and still envy me."

Merida sank into one of the dining chairs, and leaned down to offer her hand to Lacey.

Lacey seemed cautious with Merida, sniffing her fingers, allowing her to pet her, but not snuggling as she had with Lilith.

Merida gave Kateri such a look of wisdom, Kateri laughed again.

"I shouldn't let her irritate me so."

Merida nodded.

Her calm combination of signing and text soothed Kateri's ire, made her feel a little less exasperated and more rational, and helped her focus on her errand here. "Let's talk about this morning. Someone called you and threatened you."

"Yes," Merida signed.

"A man?"

Merida nodded again.

"Tell me exactly what he said."

Merida straightened up, started to pick up her tablet.

Kateri stopped her. "No. Use your hands. Tell me what he said." She wanted to see the look on Merida's face, interpret her expressions, her gestures. More and more, she didn't trust Merida.

Merida signed, "He said, 'Be careful. They're hunting you. Remember, you cannot scream.' "

"Did you recognize his voice?"

Merida shook her head, but her eyes held that faraway expression as if she was looking at a time past.

"What happened to your face?" Kateri pulled a line on her own cheek where the bloody scratch marred Merida's skin.

Merida lifted her fingers to the mark, then signed, "I was running. I fell into the hedge next door."

She was lying. Kateri was sure of it. "Merida, don't discount this as a prank. Threats like that are serious."

"It wasn't really a threat, was it? More of a warning."

"Who would warn you? Who are *they*?"

Again Merida shook her head, but she spelled, "I thought I had left everyone behind. But your sister is here."

"She recognized you from India. She said . . . you were married then, and your name was Helen."

"Yes. Nauplius created me out of the ashes. He remade me. He named me. I was his . . .

invention." Merida looked at her hands as if she could not believe the things she had said. "He's dead. Someone else must be here." Merida leaned her palms against the table, pressing hard as if she could shove her troubles away. "None of them have any reason to waste their time chasing after me. I'm not news. Nauplius's children are vindictive and foolish, but I walked away with comparably little money and I'm not worth tracking."

"It's not always money."

"No one knows that better than me."

Kateri watched Lacey wander toward the door and lean against it as if the emotions in this room urged her out. "Do you know anyone in Virtue Falls you trust?"

Merida looked at Kateri.

"Besides me. I'm the sheriff and I'm dealing with big problems. Last night we had a woman slashed to death. Every female in this town is in danger."

Merida nodded acknowledgment. She signed, "I do have someone I can trust. For the moment, at least. Please, concentrate and find the murderer. That is the best thing you can do now."

CHAPTER TWENTY-SIX

Merida locked the door after Kateri and leaned her head against the wood. She could not believe this. It was impossible, and yet it was happening.

Damn Nauplius Brassard. Damn his soul to hell.

Going upstairs, she retrieved her laptop. She got to her browser and made a dinner reservation, then entered her code and got into her charts, her spreadsheet, her projections. She surveyed the current updates. Every indicator pointed to a rousing success, provided she took it slow and easy. But not much longer . . .

She pushed a few more triggers and left the program to update while she showered. She dressed in a red sleeveless shift that showed off her bird of prey tattoo to perfection. She applied makeup, maximizing her smoky blue eyes and minimizing the scratch on her cheek. Again she checked the laptop. At five, she backed up her drive, locked up the computer and put the backup in her silver Miu Miu handbag. She dug in her closet and found her red patent Fendi fuck-me heels, the heels she had promised herself she would only ever wear again in an emergency.

This qualified as an emergency.

She slid her feet into the heels, stood and

silently sighed at the discomfort. She made her way downstairs to the dining room, where rows of knights held their weapons erect in, she was sure, appreciation. Without her previous hesitation, she left the safety of her rooms, locking the door behind her, and ventured out, seeking a champion. She walked to the parlor, where the guests were already gathering for their wine and appetizers, and posed in the doorway.

Conversation died.

Sean Weston loudly whispered, "Wow."

Dawkins Cipre said, "That's more like it!"

For a moment, Elsa's eyes flashed with envy—the same envy Merida saw in Phoebe's eyes, and Lilith's.

Benedict Howard said nothing, but he watched her over the rim of his glass like a cat watches a mouse hole.

She understood each reaction. The foundation, the highlighter, the eye shadow, the mascara, the clothes, the shoes—she had once more created the fantasy, becoming Helen, the face that launched a thousand ships.

But she was only interested in one ship. She walked to Benedict and put her hand on his arm. She showed him her tablet and waited while he read, "I've made reservations at the Virtue Falls Resort for this evening at seven, if you'd like to go."

He looked at her hand, looked at her face, put

his drink down. "Thank you. Let me go put on a tie."

She took her hand away. "I'll meet you at my car." She watched him leave.

Ironic to think that the man who now she trusted was the man who had once tried to kill her. One thing she'd learned from that experience: Benedict Howard didn't murder until he got what he wanted.

And he hadn't yet gotten what he wanted from her. Not this time.

She was safe with him.

CHAPTER TWENTY-SEVEN

Bergen slapped the flat of his hand on Kateri's office door. "When are you going home?"

Lacey lifted her head from the chair where she snoozed.

Both dog and sheriff glared at him blearily. Kateri said, "When the paperwork's done."

He snorted. "Then you're never going home."

"I know." She tucked strands of hair back into her braid. "I've got to hire a replacement for Mona."

"Mona's unemployed. You could always hire her again."

"Are you *nuts?*"

He laughed. "Yeah . . . the only thing she ever did well was mess around with Councilman Venegra. Because, you know, sequined knee pads." Bergen came around the desk, handed her her walking stick and lifted her to her feet. "You've been working for sixteen hours straight. You're in pain. You're irritable. We're in crisis mode. We need our sheriff to be alert."

She hated that he was right.

She hated that Lacey leaped down and frisked around.

Kateri needed about ten hours of sleep before she could frisk. Yanking her arm free, she leaned heavily on her stick and marched into the patrol room. "What about you? You've been on duty longer than I have."

"I did a face-plant in the break room for three hours this afternoon."

She started to laugh. "You fit on that puny love seat?"

"I didn't say I fit on it. I said I slept on it." He pushed her toward the outside door. "Go get some food and some sleep. For Lacey's sake."

All the irritation oozed out of her. "Yes. I think I'd better." With Lacey at her heels, she headed for the door and met Moen walking in.

He looked better, less haunted, recovered as only a young man with a clean conscience could be. He asked, "Need a ride, Sheriff?"

"No, thanks, Moen. I think we'll walk home, work out the kinks."

"Okay. G'night, Sheriff." He headed inside.

She opened the door. She stepped outside.

From somewhere, she heard a deep, muffled boom!

Lacey barked once, sharply.

On the northern outskirts of town, a dark plume of smoke rose.

She stepped back inside. "Moen," she called. "Now I need a ride."

The scene was carnage; one small house exploded, houses on either side burning, three fire engines parked at the curb while their men battled the flames, and two of Virtue Falls's policemen stood over the prostrate form of a tall, skinny, sobbing man.

She recognized him. Kevin Wilson, official loser.

"Moen, you come with me. Lacey, you stay here." When Lacey whined pitifully, Kateri said, "We don't want the firefighters running over you and we definitely don't want you on the ground if there is, God forbid, another explosion."

As always, Lacey seemed to understand. She stayed in the car, paws perched at the edge of the rolled-down window, watching eagerly.

Police officer and friend Ed Legbrandt gestured to Kateri. "You'll want to hear this, Kateri . . . um, Sheriff."

She limped over, Moen at her side. She knelt beside Kevin, grabbed his greasy hair and lifted his head. In a deliberately charming tone, she asked, "Little man, what's the matter?"

He had a bruise across his chin, a busted lip and big wet tears. "I rented that place. Paid good cash for it. And he blew it up."

Suspicion made her voice deepen. "He?"

Kevin sniffled. "John Terrance."

She looked up at Legbrandt.

He nodded and mouthed: *Told you so.*

She did not smash Kevin's face into the

sidewalk. She thought she should get points for that. "John Terrance blew up your rented house. Why?"

"I figured . . . figured . . . figured if he wasn't making meth anymore, someone could cash in big time. Why not me?"

"Why not indeed?"

"So I rented this place, was cooking the stuff, sold my first on the street yesterday and today I'm in the kitchen and I smell something funny. Not what I'm cooking, you know? So I turn around and there's John, looking pissed as a yellow stream. He's holding a can of gas, pouring it in a circle around me, and he says, 'Better get out while you can, you miserable little . . .' I didn't hang around to hear what he called me. He was smoking a cigarette and I thought . . . damn it!" Kevin twisted his head so hard Kateri lost her grip on his greasy hair. He looked at the blackened explosion site. "Yesterday I bought the first ripe organic tomatoes from Joe's Garden and he blew them up!"

Moen perked up. "Joe's Garden has a new crop of tomatoes? They're the best!"

"I know. Right?" Kevin said.

Kateri wiped her hand on her pants, got laboriously to her feet and grabbed Moen by the lapels. "Never mind the tomatoes. John Terrance is in town. Somewhere. Make the call, make sure every officer is looking for him. I'll take the patrol car. And Lacey. You stick here, coordinate with Legbrandt, supervise the cleanup."

"Where are you going?"

"To the Gem Lounge." Her phone rang. Her pager vibrated. She answered and looked at her message "Yep. The Gem Lounge. That bastard is looking for revenge. Against everyone."

CHAPTER TWENTY-EIGHT

Kateri flipped on her lights and her siren and drove hell-for-leather toward downtown.

Officer Weston reported shots fired at the Gem Lounge.

Bergen reported John Terrance was headed for the harbor; Bergen had alerted the Coast Guard, and he and Officer Chippen were in hot pursuit.

"You've got that covered?" she asked. "Because I'm backup at the Gem Lounge."

"Go for it," he said.

Three minutes later she parked along the curb where two of her cops were trying to interview the thirty excited citizens who milled around gesturing, talking and slapping each other on the back.

She took a long breath. Back-slapping constituted a situation well in hand.

She keyed into Bergen and heard him shouting, "We've got him cornered. He's cornered!"

"Good man." This would all be over soon. For now, she needed to know that Bertha was alive. With Lacey at her heels, she hurried toward the saloon. People turned to her, shouting various versions of, "He was here! John Terrance was here! And Bertha—"

"Is okay or you all wouldn't be smiling so broadly." She hurried through the door.

Broken bottles and glasses littered the floor, and the odor of beer, whisky and gin almost drove her backward over the threshold.

The place was empty except for Sean Weston, who stood at the bar holding a sawed-off shotgun and murmuring soothingly up at the red-faced and obviously livid Bertha . . . who stood on the bar kicking at the shattered liquor bottles and cursing John Terrance's name in English, Norwegian and a few languages Kateri didn't recognize.

Calm descended on Kateri.

The bad-tempered woman was apparently unhurt.

Kateri scooped up Lacey to protect her paws from the broken glass, strolled over to a bar stool, used a napkin to dry it and seated herself, Lacey in her lap. She waved Sean Weston away and waited until Bertha wound down. "So, Bertha, how's it going?" she asked.

That started Bertha off again. "I just had Tom in here to build me a new bar, solid walnut, and that limp prick John Terrance slashed the wood and ruined the finish. Ruined it!"

"I can see that." Big cuts in the bar. Deep. "What'd he use?"

"A machete."

"And . . . ?"

"I pulled my sawed-off shotgun out from under the bar and aimed it at him. Told him he was an idiot to bring a knife to a gunfight. I thought he was going to take another swing at me—"

"Wait. Back up." Kateri shed a little of her professional calm. "When did he swing at *you* with the machete?"

"He came in through the back. Sneaked up behind me, the snot-nosed little coward, and he would have got me, too, but Berk Moore shrieked like a trussed-up opera singer. I dove for the floor. That's when Terrance took the first chunk out of the bar. There." Bertha pointed. "He buried the blade deep enough he had trouble prying it loose, and that gave me the time to grab the shotgun. By now the crowd was screaming and running outside, which was a goddamn good thing since Terrance started backing toward the back door. I yelled at everybody to hit the deck and when John Terrance turned to run I peppered his behind with buckshot. I was hoping to kill him but the last I saw he was still moving. You got him in custody?"

Kateri checked. "Not yet." She cradled Lacey in one arm and offered her hand. "You look silly up there. Let me help you down."

"I'm going to need more than your help." Bertha looked sheepish. "When I jumped up here, I think I broke something."

"Like a bone?" Kateri asked. "You jumped?"

"I was just so goddamn mad."

Kateri called, "Sean, you need to call the EMTs."

Sean reappeared at her side. "I already did. She was listing a little to one side, so . . ." He climbed onto a bar stool, wrapped his arms around Bertha's waist and asked, "That okay?"

"Okay? It's great." Bertha grinned at him. "I don't often get a young, handsome, buff guy hugging me."

He smiled back. "I can hardly believe that."

"Shitkicker." She braced herself while he lifted her. He did not place her on the stool.

Kateri reached up and helped steady her.

Bertha looked down. "Honey, in your shape, what are you going to do if I topple over?"

"Break your fall?"

"That's fine, but I don't want to land on the dog."

Kateri chuckled and stepped away.

Sean Weston climbed down, took Bertha by the waist and lifted her to the floor. "Mrs. Waldschmidt, with all due respect, next time when you get mad, would you stay on the ground?"

Damn. Kateri was starting to like Weston. To counter that, she asked, "Give me a report on the surveillance at Rainbow's house."

He sighed. "It's okay. I haven't seen anything."

Kateri put her hands on her hips.

Weston looked sulky. "I need to go back and

check. After I'm done here, I will. I promise . . . it's just so boring."

So much for liking Weston.

The two-way on Kateri's shoulder vibrated, and she clicked it on to hear Bergen's toneless voice report, "We lost him."

Bertha slapped the bar. "Sonofabitch!"

Bergen continued, "On the dock. We had a civilian who decided to capture the criminal for the incompetent cops. That is, by the way, what he shouted as he jumped out of his yacht. 'Incompetent cops.' "

"Yacht?"

"A Marquis Sport Bridge."

"Big boat."

"Right. Our hero tripped, made a face-plant onto the dock at John Terrance's feet and when he lifted his head, Terrance had a pistol pointed right at his bloody nose. We ceased pursuit."

Weston and Bertha were leaning toward the tiny speaker.

"Go on," Kateri pressed.

"Terrance forced the civilian—tourist by the name of Henry H. Henning—back into the yacht, made him start it. The guy's wife came up from the galley and screamed bloody murder. Terrance grabbed her, put the pistol to her head. Henry H. drove them out of the harbor. If I'd had a sniper rifle . . . but I didn't." Bergen had put in a stint with the Vegas police department.

He didn't talk about what he did, but Kateri knew he'd been on a sniper team—and returned to Virtue Falls hardened and weary. "The Coast Guard waited an appropriate amount of time, then gave pursuit. They found the Hennings floating without power close to the shore. Terrance had disabled the motor, took a scuba tank and mask, shot Henry H. in the hip and jumped into the water."

Kateri filled in, "The Coast Guard stopped to render aid to the Hennings and secure the boat. No sign of Terrance in the water."

"Are you giving this report or am I?" Bergen sounded humorous; he knew all too well her expertise acquired from years in the Coast Guard.

"Terrance doesn't have a dive suit, right? That would have taken too much time and effort to put on. Right now, water temperature's running about fifty-three degrees. Hypothermia in ten minutes plus. Rough currents out there." Kateri thought about the area outside the harbor, the tides, the terrain. "He'll probably make it to shore, but it'll be rough on him."

"Send armed deputies?"

"Yes. Flood the area. Extreme caution, blah, blah. I'll get there as soon as I can." Turning to Sean Weston and Bertha, she said, "You can take care of this?"

"Go. Get. Him." Bertha had an ugly twist to her face. "And for me—make him suffer."

Kateri owed Bertha the truth. "He's going to get away again. Too much terrain, too rugged, too much cover, he knows every inch of it, and night is falling fast."

"Maybe not. I did shoot him in the ass."

"Oh, yeah." Kateri smiled.

Bertha put her hand on Lacey's head. "Leave her here with me. And try your damnedest to get John Terrance."

CHAPTER TWENTY-NINE

The dining room at the Virtue Falls Resort matched the luxury of any world-class restaurant, but the table was not at all up to Benedict's standards. It was small, set against the wall and close to the kitchen. He had to crane his neck to see the lavish view across the Pacific toward the setting sun. Even the maître d' had apologized for their placement, but as he said, it was the tourist season and their late reservation had provided them with the last table in the house.

Benedict had come within inches of making it clear he would take the table against the windows, a table set up and waiting for another couple. He had power and he knew how to get what he wanted.

Yet Merida inclined her head with a smile. She chose the chair that put her back to the room, allowed the maître d' to seat her, and signed, "Harold, this is perfect."

Harold was apparently the maître d's name; of course Merida had somehow figured it out and remembered. Harold's smile blossomed and he awkwardly signed back, "Very good, madam." An apt skill for a man who worked with the public, and one he had cultivated as part of his job as maître d'.

Merida's smile stayed in place during cocktails and appetizers. As she signed, her every motion was graceful, and she showed no impatience when Benedict's command of the language failed and she had to resort to her tablet. She was his hostess and clearly she had set out to make herself agreeable and put him at ease—which put his teeth on edge a bit, because it reminded him of her manner with Nauplius Brassard, and he did not like the association.

After they ordered their salads and entrees, she signed, "The table is perhaps not what I would have chosen, but the service, the presentation and the food are exemplary."

"The wine list, also," Benedict said. "If you will allow me to choose, this Sangiovese from Bella Terra is excellent and would go well with your salmon."

She nodded and touched her chest over her heart.

"Excellent choice, sir," the sommelier said warmly.

He might be speaking of the wine, but he was looking at Merida.

"We'll have that." Benedict handed the steward the list and waved him away. Putting his elbows on the table, he studied Merida. "You're lying."

She lifted her eyebrows. "About what?"

"You prefer this table."

In the smooth, smiling lines of her face, he

observed a shift. He had called her a liar; she had tensed. He had told her why he thought she was a liar; she had relaxed. Relaxed because a disagreement about the table was relatively minor.

Very good. He had learned two things: Merida was a very good actress, and if he wanted to delve into the mystery of her past and personality, he would have to watch carefully. Her outburst the night before had been atypical; she scrupulously guarded her emotions. He said, "You like this table because it's private, your back is to the room and no one can easily stare while you sign."

His insight surprised her, and that reaction she did not bother to hide. "Acute," she spelled.

"Now that we're here, I prefer this table, also."

She gestured in question.

"You're so beautiful. The sommelier and the maître d' are enthralled." In fact, so was Benedict. Enthralled . . . and wary. "Having everyone stare at you would make you self-conscious, and I prefer you to be comfortable."

"And concentrate on you?"

Now he nodded.

Her smile became less gracious, more real. "I'm glad to do that." She glanced around and moved her shoulders uncomfortably. "I don't like being the center of attention."

"That's why you changed your looks."

"Partly. But also to feel as if my youth had

not totally passed me by." Abruptly, she put her hands in her lap, as if she'd said too much.

She'd been married to a rich man who showed her off like a trophy and demanded she maintain the beauty standards of his long-departed youth. Now she was free and she reveled in that freedom to dress, groom and behave as she wished.

"I wonder why you married Nauplius Brassard."

Her smile disappeared. Her eyes narrowed on him. "My boyfriend forced me."

He never foresaw that answer, or the hostility with which she signed. "Forced you . . . how?"

"He made it impossible for me to do anything but marry Nauplius. It was a matter of life or death. I chose life. I made an agreement, and I kept it."

Their waiter and Harold approached with the salads, and in unison they placed them on the table.

She thanked them with the flat of her hand to her mouth, and they departed looking dazed.

Benedict picked up his fork. "You're a wealthy woman. Have you revenged yourself on this boyfriend?"

Her smile was back, that gracious, blank, indecipherable smile. "I am in the process."

"I suppose I should feel sorry for the bastard. But he deserves it."

"Yes." She ate a bite of her salad, put down her fork, pulled out her tablet and typed, then handed it to him. "This is excellent. The Stilton is perfect with these greens and the citrus dressing provides a lovely backdrop for the flavors."

"Yeah, mine's good, too." She had stepped away from the intimacy of sign language and returned to the mechanical form of communication. Subtly, she was placing him into a category with everyone else.

He couldn't figure her out. Why she had suddenly approached him when before she had so clearly resisted? Maybe she was on the hunt for another wealthy husband and she was playing him? Or maybe everything about her reeked of deception. Maybe . . . oh, the possibilities were endless.

The closer he got to her, the more determined he was to comprehend her. It almost seemed knowing her was more important than having sex with her. If he'd had a lick of sense, that realization would alarm him.

Yes, like every other man in Virtue Falls, he was enthralled.

CHAPTER THIRTY

Kateri stumbled going into Rainbow's dim hospital room. She caught herself before she fell, but the stitches and sore muscles protested, and she gasped at the pain.

Dr. Frownfelter turned away from the bed. He was rumpled, overweight, with bags under his eyes and he wore a white coat that needed to be ironed and white running shoes that needed to be cleaned. He was officially retired, and officially on duty whenever he was needed. "About time you got here. Let me look at those ribs."

Kateri didn't move. "Rainbow?"

"She's still with us. Sit down. You look like hell."

Kateri took her time getting to the chair and sinking onto the seat. "Long day."

"So I heard. Unbutton that shirt." Dr. Frownfelter pressed the nurse's call button. "Peggy's on duty. You two can catch up."

After the tsunami, Kateri had spent so much time in the hospital she knew all the nurses from here to Seattle.

Peggy came through the door, and Dr. Frownfelter told her, "We need to examine Kateri's injuries. I'm thinking pain relief, some disinfectant, a good-sized brick to knock some sense into her."

Kateri tried to laugh and winced.

Peggy was sixty, tall, solid, practical and she didn't crack a smile. "Of course, Doctor. Do you want the brick sterilized?"

"Dirty as hell should do it."

Peggy headed out the door and Dr. Frownfelter sat down in front of Kateri. He watched her try to get out of the shirt.

Her fingers were shaking too much to deal with the buttons.

With a sound of disgust, he brushed her hands aside and finished the task. "Did you get him? I suppose not, or you would be less despairing."

"We didn't get him. John Terrance has been sneaking around the countryside delivering his drugs. He knows what he's doing, and he's smart."

"Like a fox."

"That's a slur on all foxes. But yes. Sly and well prepared."

Peggy returned with a tray covered with a white cloth, placed it on the small table and rolled it close to Dr. Frownfelter's elbow. She knelt beside Kateri, carefully removed the adhesive, peeled the bandages back and muttered darkly.

Kateri didn't ask what she had said. She was merely glad to get the adhesive off.

Dr. Frownfelter delved into his coat pocket

and retrieved a bottle of Tums and a battered flashlight. He offered Kateri the bottle. "Want a Tums? Even if you haven't got indigestion, they're good for your calcium."

Kateri took one, popped it in her mouth and shuddered. "That's awful."

"Probably a fruit flavor." Dr. Frownfelter pointed his flashlight at Kateri's ribs. "This looks better than I would have expected, considering. The stitches are holding this time. Whatever else you can say about the frog god, he gave you remarkable recuperative powers." The doctor might not be Native American, but he knew the local legends.

Kateri craned her neck to see the red, jagged wound over her ribs. "If only that included pain relief."

Dr. Frownfelter pulled on his gloves, lifted a syringe and prepared to inject it close to the stitches. "If the frog god had provided that, you'd simply do more stupid things to injure yourself."

"I didn't injure myself," she snapped. "I was shot."

"Most patients would lie down and recover. It *is* considered the wise move to make. Let's use some pain relief and clean this up." He couldn't resist adding, "Again."

Peggy lifted the cloth off the tray and revealed an impressive array of instruments.

Dr. Frownfelter placed the syringe in the

disposal container. "Mike Sun called me about the autopsy he's doing. Asked me about Monique Ries, where exactly the slashing was relative to her face and neck, wanted to know what I thought had been used to cause the injury."

"What did you tell him?"

"She was slashed along the jawline, right at the bone, with something incredibly sharp because she didn't realize at first that she was being cut. That accounted for the clean line along the first two inches. After that, not even booze could dull the pain. Monique went berserk and the cut got ugly." He went to work cleaning up Kateri's ribs. "I thought the assailant had aimed for her throat and missed, but Mike said the slashing on the deceased was exactly in the same location—and then some."

"All around the jaw, up . . ." Kateri realized she'd better not visualize that again, not while Dr. Frownfelter was working on her ribs. "It was such a precise cut. About two hours ago, Mike sent me the report. I forwarded it to Garik Jacobsen, but I haven't had time to read it. Did Mike tell you what was used to make the incision?"

"He didn't know. I suggested a scalpel, but he said no. Not a razor blade, not an X-Acto knife . . . How long's it been since you've eaten?"

Kateri couldn't remember. "Why?"

"Because your stomach's growling so loud we can hear it," Peggy said.

"Can you round her something up?" Dr. Frownfelter worked on the injury, dabbing and pressing. "She'll need something in her gullet before she takes any medication."

"Gullet? Is that official medical talk?" Kateri asked.

"Soup. Jell-O. Pudding. Rice. The usual for this time of night. Then I'll call down to the cafeteria and have them bring up a meal." Peggy whipped out the door.

"Saw my old friend Bertha Waldschmidt and ordered her an X-ray," Dr. Frownfelter chuckled and shook his head at the same time. "What a woman. Holds off a maniac with a machete, chases him out of her bar, shoots him in the butt, then fractures her hip jumping up on the bar in a rage."

"Is she going to have to have surgery?"

"Hairline fracture. She saw the orthopedist. If she uses crutches, keeps the weight off of it, uses heat and cold and the X-rays show normal healing—no. But she's older, so I give a fifty/fifty chance of it healing on its own. If it doesn't, *I* don't want to be the one who tells her she has to head to Seattle for a hip replacement." He opened a wide package and pulled out a sterile dressing.

"No." Over Dr. Frownfelter's shoulder, Kateri observed Rainbow's still figure, her waxy complexion, the shallow rise of her chest. "Is she worse? I can't tell."

"Still hovering on the brink. Every day someone from town comes in and sits with her, talks to her. That anchors her, I believe. Most nights she's alone and she slips a little farther along the path." He taped the dressing in place.

Kateri wanted to go home, to sleep in her own bed with Stag and Lacey, but she said, "I can stay tonight."

To her surprise, Dr. Frownfelter didn't argue. "We'll bring a cot in."

Peggy came back with chocolate pudding and a cup of beef bouillon.

Kateri drank the bouillon and burned her mouth. She used the pudding to soothe her tongue.

Dr. Frownfelter stripped off his gloves and tossed them. "You got any other injuries that require attention? How's the hip, the knee, the . . . how're all the artificial joints?"

"I'm stiff. But this food was *amazing*."

Dr. Frownfelter laughed creakily. "We don't hear that every day."

"I've got a tray on the way," Peggy said. "And a cot. Is there anybody you want us to call?"

"Stag Denali. I can do it. He's probably going to yell, and it might as well be at me." Kateri started to stand.

Dr. Frownfelter and Peggy each grabbed an arm and helped her up.

"Thank you." Kateri limped over to the bed, leaned over Rainbow's face, smoothed the hair away from her forehead. "Rainbow," she called softly. "I'm here. I'm staying with you tonight."

Dr. Frownfelter shoved a chair under her knees. "Sit down before you fall down, at least until the cot gets here."

Kateri sat and held Rainbow's cool hand between both of hers. "So much is happening, Rainbow. Did you hear any of what I was telling the doctor? It's very exciting. My life is full of adventure. And you wouldn't believe the stupid thing I said today about me and casual relationships. Or maybe you would." She half expected to hear Rainbow laughing at her, booming out wisdom, talking so fast the words tumbled over themselves.

Yet except for the whoosh of the door as Dr. Frownfelter left the room and Peggy's careful cleanup of the tray, the room was silent.

When Dr. Frownfelter returned, a mug in each hand, Peggy indicated Kateri, head resting on the mattress, sound asleep. "Still holding Rainbow's hand."

"This is going to be a tough one for her."

Peggy took a blanket from the warmer and tucked it around Kateri. "Do you want me to call Stag Denali?"

"I already did it. He's a big guy. Young. When

he gets here, he can move her to the cot." Dr. Frownfelter handed Peggy one of the mugs. "Come on, old girl, let's do our final rounds and when the next crew comes in, we'll head for home."

CHAPTER THIRTY-ONE

Benedict stared out the windshield at the dark, windy coastal road lit only by the sweep of the headlights. "I don't think I've ever had a woman buy dinner for me before."

Merida was driving; she had limited herself to one glass of that very fine wine, so she couldn't blame the alcohol. But without thinking, she lifted one hand from the wheel and signed, "Yes, you have. Remember—" Horrified, she caught herself.

"Remember what?" His head turned toward her and he stared.

Remember when I dragged you to the Hickory Barn for barbecue and I paid? "Nothing. I was thinking of . . . nothing." She put her hand back on the wheel before she blurted out another word.

The trouble with using Benedict as protection was that, other than the fact he had tried to kill her, she liked him. Tonight, as before, they talked, they argued, they laughed. Her hands hurt from signing so much.

He looked back at the road. "I still believe we've met. But how could I have forgotten you?"

They were coming into town, thank God. She could drop him off at his coach house, park the car and get herself inside where she was safe.

Safe from the killer. Safe from him. Not safe from herself, though. She'd just proved that.

"Maybe when I was young, before my parents died? We traveled all over the world. That way you wouldn't remember, because I was eight when they were killed and you're younger than me."

She shook her head.

"According to your online bio, you grew up in Nepal. I don't remember Nepal, but I do remember India."

She shrugged.

He pressed her. "Your parents were missionaries?"

As she turned into the driveway, she gestured noncommittally. Damn it. He knew the story Nauplius had concocted to give her a personal history. Should she admit it was all a fabrication? No, if she did that, he'd want to know her real background. If she didn't answer, he would research her, or think more deeply about where they could have met . . . He was suspicious already, of course. He was too intelligent not to be.

In a reflective voice, he said, "We have a lot in common."

She wanted to snort. They had nothing in common. They never had.

He continued, "Our parents were killed and our young lives both altered beyond all recognition.

Do you want to come into my cottage for a drink and more conversation?"

She shook her head. Most definitely not. Not if she wanted to keep her cover story. Not if she wanted to stay out of his bed—and stay alive.

"I'm not a rapist," he said.

She shook her head again, quickly, in surprise.

"I thought that a woman who can't scream for help might worry about that."

He was the second man in twenty-four hours to worry that she couldn't scream. Which wasn't something she had worried about . . . before.

She pulled up beside the B and B carriage house.

He gestured toward her designated parking space. "If you won't come in, fine, but I'm still going to walk you to your door."

She glanced around at the Christmas lights Phoebe had strung in the trees, at the shadows lurking at the property's borders. Right. Good plan. She drove forward and parked. She started to open her door.

Gently he caught her arm and when she faced him, he released her. "My poor male ego has been flattened enough by you driving and buying dinner. Don't you think you should kiss it and make it better?"

He made her want to laugh out loud. She signed, "Your male ego? Is that what we're calling it now? It's deflated? Am I supposed to believe that?"

"At least take advantage of me for one kiss, on the lips if you must."

She examined him in the dim light. He was not handsome, not with those mismatched features and those ears, but that crooked smile and those warm eyes made her want to kiss him. Worse than that, to trust him.

Silently she sighed. She was a fool, the worst kind of fool. She wouldn't trust him. But it had been a very, very long time since she had kissed a man in passion—in fact, since the last time she'd kissed Benedict himself. A kiss filled the space where words could not explain or express. One kiss . . . Leaning across the console, she put her hands on his shoulders and pulled him toward her. She tilted her head and put her mouth to his. She closed her eyes and tried to remember how to do this right . . . Lips, brushing softly. A careful opening, breathing together, a tentative exploration, then the reward for patience, a taste of red wine and Benedict. A little more pressure, his intrusion, then hers, then his . . . Both of them breathing faster. Her heart hammering. Her fingers tangled in his soft hair . . . her arms around his shoulders, her breasts pressed to his chest. She strained toward . . .

She opened her eyes. She caught her breath. She pushed away, banged her elbow on the steering wheel, hit the horn for one sharp beep.

Scream? She didn't need to scream.

She needed to *swear*.

He'd always been a good kisser, slow, tender, touching, breathing, loving every moment. He'd only improved with time, and what was worse—in this short span of time he had brought her almost to ecstasy. She looked for his hands. They were clasping the car seat.

She had been ready to fling herself across the console onto the tiny seat and ravage him—and he hadn't touched her.

He was a *show-off*.

She had been trying to remember how to kiss and got caught up in the warmth, the softness . . . the long, slow slide into wetness and anticipation . . . the intimation of further pleasure . . . Her mistake.

Now she needed to remember that this man had tried to kill her. This man had been the cause of nine years of unhappiness and abuse.

Worse, he was a show-off. *Show-off, show-off, show-off!*

As she watched, he opened his eyes. He looked almost sleepy. Deceptively sleepy. She knew what that meant: he was ready.

The car was hot and steamy and this time, no matter what he said or did, she was *leaving*. She slammed out of the car and headed for the house, half expecting his hand to catch her arm.

She readied her best self-defense move, one that would knock him into the dirt.

He caught up. Didn't touch her. Walked beside her, opened the back door, followed her as she stalked through the kitchen and escorted her to the door that led into the dining room and her suite.

She could hear conversation and the clinking of glasses in the sitting room. She didn't want to talk to anyone right now. See anyone right now. Not when she was flushed with arousal. Not when Benedict waited while she worked her way through the locks to get her door open. Too many conclusions—accurate conclusions—would be drawn.

Then he grasped her hand and lifted it to his lips. "Thank you for a lovely evening. Perhaps we can meet tomorrow?"

Which reminded her—he might aggravate her, but she was supposed to be using him for safety. She signed, "Want to go for a run in the morning?"

Maybe her suggestion surprised him. Maybe her obvious irritation intrigued him. Something made his eyes narrow in suspicion. Still, he agreed right away. "Sure. Nine?"

"Seven." *Want to argue about that?*

"See you then." Hands in his pockets, he strolled away.

She shut the door behind her, set all the locks,

checked the progress of her program and gave it a nudge—a little more aggressively than usual, but she was frustrated with the stately pace of her revenge. Nothing more.

Looking at her purse, she hesitated. She didn't want to talk, but if she didn't call, she wouldn't sleep knowing he would call her . . . and be angry. Maybe if she texted . . . No. He'd never let her get away with that. Pulling out her tablet, she made the connection.

He answered immediately. "What do you think you're doing, going out with Benedict Howard?"

He'd been watching her. Somehow, watching her, tracking her. Rage hit her like a freight train, the old rage, dark with dreams of vengeance and long years of bondage. She propped up the tablet, signed, "It is none of your business what I do, who I date."

"It's my business if I—"

"No. No!" She gestured emphatically. "I will not exist under surveillance ever again. If I die, I die. But I will *live* for the brief moments that are allowed me."

"So you're sleeping with him."

Very softly, she hit the disconnect button.

For one long moment, she stood straight, shoulders back, chin up, fists clenched, hating them all. Then, leaning over her computer, she gave the program another nudge, tiny and subtle, but a nudge.

The phone rang again.

She answered and he said, "Come over."

She stared at him.

"I'm sorry. I won't say anything else. But come over. You need to practice."

She nodded and hung up. She changed into dark clothes, pulled on a black hoodie and slid out into the entry. She debated; the front door would take her past the sitting room, where guests still sipped wine and chatted. The back door would take her past Benedict's cottage.

She took a chance with the front door. She pulled her hood up over her head, slipped past and hoped no one saw her, or at least no one identified her. The door was a challenge. It creaked. But she got onto the porch without being hailed and after that, it was easy to slip through the hedge and into the yard next door.

If the bed-and-breakfast looked as if the Addams family inhabited it, this place looked like Hill House: haunted, abandoned, ill-treated.

But she came here anyway.

Because he'd told her to. And about this, at least, he was right.

CHAPTER THIRTY-TWO

The coach house at the Good Knight Manor Bed and Breakfast suffocated Benedict with its bric-a-brac and ruffles, china cups and flowered wallpaper. Yet tonight, Benedict felt at home. The evening had gone well. Very well. Better than he could have imagined. Sure, he knew that Merida was up to something, using him for some reason. Yet the wine had been excellent, the conversation scintillating.

He removed his jacket, his tie, his shoes.

And if that kiss was anything to go by, he'd be glad to let Merida use him any way she wanted, all night long.

His phone rang. For one brief, forgetful moment, he thought it was Merida. Then he checked the number.

His aunt. Last he'd heard, Rose and Albert were on a leisurely cruise across the North Atlantic to view the glaciers and fjords. Even if they were in a port, it was very late there and unless there was an emergency, those two believed in early to bed. He picked up. "Rose, what's wrong?"

His aunt's voice held that slight old age tremor she had developed. "Dear boy, it's good to hear your voice after so long!"

264

Right away, his suspicions were aroused. "It's only been a week since we spoke."

"I know, but I recall the days when you lived with us and I saw you every day. I do miss that!"

"Hmm." When his parents were killed, Rose and Albert took him in without a single sign of distress and raised him as their own, but Aunt Rose was not one to show affection. "Is Albert okay?"

"We're both fine. We're at sea steaming our way toward the Isle of Man. We may be in our seventies and leaving the corporations to you, but we like to keep our fingers on the pulse!"

Of course. The business. "What's wrong with the corporations?"

"Where are you, dear?"

"In Virtue Falls, Washington."

"What's there?"

"Vacation."

"I suppose if we are enjoying ourselves more than we should, you can, too." The old age tremor grew more pronounced.

Sometimes it was hard for Benedict to believe that he was related to these people, that Benedict's father, Troy, and Albert had been brothers, and that Rose and his mother, Carla, had been sisters-in-law. Troy had been the younger son, irresponsible, traveling the world, making friends everywhere, handing out the family fortune to anyone who told him a sob story. His mother had been the practical one, insisting they live where Benedict could attend school, making sure they had shelter over their heads and regular meals. Yet Carla had adored Troy and whenever she woke Benedict in the early morning hours and handed him his backpack, he knew he was in for some form of delightful madness. Good times. Even today he missed his parents, the love, the laughter, the spontaneous travels.

With Albert and Rose, it was all money, greed, profit and an almost psychotic disregard for the world, its people and its future. "What's wrong with the corporations?"

"Dear, I was checking the records for the next board meeting . . ."

What her on-board Wi-Fi charges must be!

"—and something caught my eye. Just the tiniest niggle."

"What kind of niggle?"

"The stockholders' information and the actual records don't match." When it profited her, Rose pretended to be a feeble old lady, but she knew her numbers. "Dear boy, you ought to check it out."

"All right. Send me the information. I imagine someone keyed something incorrectly."

The voice tremor disappeared, and Rose sounded more like the woman who, with her husband, had transformed the family business into a multibillion-dollar corporation. "Heads will roll."

"Of course." She had drilled into him a simple truth: little discrepancies were sometimes harbingers of big trouble. "I'll look it over."

"Tonight?"

"In the morning. Give Albert my greetings, and enjoy your voyage." He hung up, more annoyed than he should be, and flung one shoe across the bedroom. With a satisfying punch, it hit the wall inside the closet. When Benedict talked to Rose, she always made him feel as if he was a slacker, a disappointment, a failure. As Albert had once said in his hearing, his father's son.

His parents' deaths had changed Benedict. The joy was gone from the world, and by the time he had struggled up from the depths of his grief, he was living a scheduled life of education and work experiences. That was what Uncle Albert called having Benedict spend his summers in the company mail room: "work experiences." Albert and Rose taught Benedict their values: earn a profit at all costs, make more tomorrow than today and be damned to joy, to leisure, to love. He had grown up responsible, the valedictorian, a man of measured tastes and careful passions.

Never again had Benedict experienced anything like his parents' brand of delightful madness—until Merry.

Merry was dead, too. Yet lately, she had been on his mind, a sweet, sad ghost. He had never had the chance to say good-bye . . .

He wasn't going to sleep now, so he might as well look over those reports.

Rose returned to their stateroom, where Albert sat at the desk, computer open, scrolling through the reports and making notations. "He's found her," she said.

Albert turned away from the screen. "Who? Benedict? Found who?"

God, Albert could be annoying. "Who do we not want him to find?"

"Merry Byrd? Impossible! Why would he even want to find her?" Albert asked the obvious question. "Where's the profit in that?"

"Remember when he first met Merry? The way he acted?" Rose looked down at her hands. The skin was spotted, thin, wrinkled. Every bone, sinew and vein showed. "Business took second place to her and her do-gooding."

"He's had other women, more practical women. He needs to marry. He needs to have a son to pass the business on to. Why not one of the women who live for the business?"

"He said he loved Merry Byrd."

"Stupid name!"

"Yes." She was too old to deal with this nonsense: from Albert, and from Benedict.

"All cats are gray in the dark," Albert said.

She eyed him: tall, bony, bad eyes and wispy hair. "So they are." Knowing Albert, he didn't even start to comprehend the irony of her answer.

"Why do you say he found her?"

"He's on vacation in Virtue Falls, Washington."

Albert squinted at her, his reading glasses making his blue eyes wide and round. "Where's that?"

"I don't know, dear. In Washington, I suppose. But Benedict sounded happy, and he refused to immediately look over the reports."

"You told him there was something wrong."

"Yes."

Albert leaned back in his chair and stroked his forehead. "Could be a different woman."

"Could be. But *she* disappeared."

"Merry did?"

"Yes, dear." She hated when Albert played stupid. "When Nauplius Brassard died, his wife, Helen, disappeared. We know who that really was."

"Merry Byrd."

"The question is—does Benedict realize that Helen and Merry are one and the same?"

"If he's found her, it's only a matter of time." Albert pointed at Rose. "Better take care of that." Turning away, he returned to his work, muttering darkly as he traced down the discrepancies Rose had found.

CHAPTER THIRTY-THREE

Benedict and Merida started out slowly, warming up, their feet pounding the sidewalk, dodging overgrown branches and a bicycle left lying on the sidewalk, avoiding barking dogs. He let her set the route. They ran a mile through Virtue Falls, then turned onto the well-worn path along the cliffs above the Pacific. There he began to stretch his legs, taking longer strides, pushing her harder than her usual pace. For her, it at once became a contest, one she couldn't stand to lose.

When she began to pant, he slowed. "I forget. You're short."

She held out her hands, using them like a selfie stick, so he could see her talk. "I'm petite."

"Right. Petite."

She pointed down the steep path to the beach.

He said, "Sure. Good idea," and gestured for her to lead the way.

She loved this part of the run, leaping down the slippery trail like a mountain goat. She loved more that she left him behind.

At the bottom, she stopped, placed her hands on her knees and got her breath. When he came up behind her, she straightened and hopped along the rocks toward the pilings of the old dock.

Behind her, he called, "Great food last night."

She nodded.

"Good kiss."

She stopped, turned, signed, "Not a great kiss?"

"You need practice."

She shot him the universal gesture of fuckoffery.

He laughed. He looked tired, as if he'd been up all night, but he sounded happy.

She returned to her rock-hopping. She was happy, too. The day had dawned with a rare blue sky, the air was cool, the ocean rolled and sparkled, she was with Benedict and her revenge was coming to fruition. Right now, the fact that she was revenging herself on *him* seemed irrelevant.

She jumped down onto the damp sand, then climbed onto the pilings and did her karate-movie poses, balancing on one leg and then the other. He watched for a few moments, then jumped onto a piling, wavered and fell off into the sand.

Clutching her side, silently laughing, she fell off, too.

"Really? Laugh at me?" He crawled toward her. He was on the prowl.

She crawled away. It was stupid, playful—she could have stood up and run. Instead she got sand in her shoes, scoured the skin off her knees, and when he caught her hips, found herself toppled onto her back, looking up at him silhouetted against the sky.

She thought he would be laughing. He wasn't. He *looked* at her, searching her face, trying to peer beneath the features, seeking the truth.

He'd know the truth soon enough.

But not now. She wanted to live. A distraction. She needed a distraction.

Reaching up, she twisted her hands in his sweaty T-shirt, pulled him down on her—and practiced her kissing.

Stupid distraction.

By the time she was done, he had touched her. By the time she pushed him off, he was hard and hot and she knew she had made him suffer.

If only she didn't still feel the pressure of his hands cupping her breasts, the thrust of his hips against hers. If only she wasn't suffering, too.

She stood and set off across the sand, running fast, desperate to get away until her flush had faded and her pulse roared aerobically rather than lustily.

The sand ruined that plan. She had to stop, sit, shake out her shoes and empty her socks.

By the time she was done, he was standing, waiting. He set the pace up the steep path onto the cliff and he didn't slack off to accommodate her. Or maybe he did, which made her gasping at the top even more humiliating. She wanted to take a break; she couldn't because he kept running. Once again it had become a contest, and she wasn't going to catch him without a strategy.

She'd traveled this path before; he probably hadn't. She tracked him until he followed the trail as it cut inland, through a stand of cypress trees, and disappeared from sight. Then she took the shortcut, thrashing through the underbrush to cut him off.

She barely made it, leaping out in front of him where the path cut sharply back toward the sea. His competitive smile changed to surprise and he skidded to a stop. "How did you do that?"

"I cheated," she signed, and grinned and plucked cypress bark from her hair.

"Wish I'd thought of that." He looked beyond her. "Hello."

She swung around.

The maid from the Good Knight Manor Bed and Breakfast stood there in her drab garb, holding her bag of cleaning supplies. Susie looked more surprised than Benedict or Merida, then annoyed, then embarrassed. "Sorry. Sorry! I'm in your way. Seems like I'm always in the way." She shuffled off the trail and back into the trees. "Go on. Finish your run. I'll stand here and wait."

Merida gestured in question.

"What? Oh. What am I doin'?" Susie shifted her bag from hand to hand as if it weighed her down. "If I've got time before I go to work, I like to come look at the view. Refreshin', it is, like a really good bathroom cleaner."

"Oh." Merida mouthed the word, began to sign, then stopped in frustration.

"Go ahead," Benedict said. "I'll tell her what you're saying."

To Susie, Merida signed, "I thought you didn't start work at the B and B until later. Around eleven." As she spoke, Benedict translated the sign language into spoken English.

Interesting. When Nauplius translated for Merida, he used her gestures, her expressions, to bring attention to *himself*. With Benedict, she felt as if he was simply making her life easier.

"I've got another job today, cleanin' a house down here by the ocean. Please don't tell Mrs. Glass. She's real funny about me workin' for someone other than her."

Merida pantomimed zipping her lip, then signed, "Enjoy your quiet before your busy day."

"Right. I'll see ya at the B and B. You going to let me in to clean your room today?" Susie looked so worn down by life, so eager to please. "I promise not to touch any of your stuff, not ever again."

Merida nodded. Reluctantly, but she nodded.

"Miss, what time you want me in there?" Susie asked.

"I'll go out for lunch about one. You can do it then." Merida would make sure she locked her computer in the safe.

"Okay." Susie looked at Benedict. "You going out with her? To lunch?"

Benedict raised his eyebrows to Merida.

She nodded.

Susie said, "I'll prep your room, too. There'll be clean sheets." Susie looked horrified. "Which . . . I mean . . . when you get back, everything else will be clean, too, not just the sheets."

Merida was already flushed from the run. Thank God, for Susie made such a big deal covering her blooper that Merida blushed.

Benedict, naturally, seemed unaffected. "Sounds good, Susie. We'll leave you to your view." He gestured to Merida to go ahead, and when they were out of earshot, he said, *"Bathroom cleaner?"*

Merida turned around, ran backward and spelled, "She's . . . odd."

He slowed to a walk to watch her. *"Clean sheets?"* He obviously thought it was funny.

Merida did not want to go there. She spelled, "Probably some new wrapped slivers of soap, too." She faced forward and took the right into Virtue Falls. They walked through little pocket neighborhoods, past tiny shotgun houses built in the thirties that were now worn from constant exposure to the winds off the ocean and the salt in the air.

"Soap would be good. Yesterday she forgot to leave towels. I had to call before I showered." Exasperated, he asked, "What kind of maid forgets to leave towels?"

"As I said, odd. And not too bright. Don't leave out any belongings you don't want her to investigate."

"Right. Thanks for the warning."

As they got closer to the Good Knight Manor Bed and Breakfast, the houses got bigger and usually better kept. Although not always—there was that mansion behind the hedge next to the B and B . . .

She gave the place a wide berth, stepping into the street and tugging at his arm to steer him around.

"Is it haunted?" he asked. "That house? Is it supposed to be haunted?"

She looked skeptical.

"I wondered. At night, I've seen lights over there. Vagrants probably, rather than spooks."

Sure. Vagrants. Good cover story.

"You going to partake of Phoebe's excellent breakfast?"

Merida rolled her shoulders uncomfortably.

"Come on. I'm starving and if I go in by myself, Phoebe sits on one side and talks to me and that Palmer woman sits on the other side and talks to me. Phoebe chirps about everything being delightful and Lilith bitches about everything in Virtue Falls including the unceasing sound of the ocean. She seems to think it should be on a sound machine with an off switch." He perfectly captured the two women's personalities.

Merida signed, "Wow, you know how to sweet-talk a girl into getting your way."

He waited.

"All right, I'll come to breakfast."

"And lunch."

"And lunch. But in between, I have to work."

His voice went from amused to grim. "So do I."

She glanced at him.

He *looked* grim. Good. Maybe he sensed the shift in the ground beneath his feet, the violence of the oncoming earthquake, his inevitable destruction.

She hoped so. She hoped he had started to worry.

CHAPTER THIRTY-FOUR

Kateri woke. She lay on her side. Her arm was asleep, dangling off the cot. Her mouth was dry and tasted like cotton.

All in all, she felt better.

She opened her eyes. She didn't remember falling asleep, didn't remember anything after promising Rainbow she would stay, but now she rested on a cot in Rainbow's hospital room, a weight on her waist held her down, and if she was supposed to be keeping Rainbow company through the night, she had been a miserable failure.

"You awake?" Stag's deep voice spoke in her ear; he was spooning her on the narrow cot. Nice. Comforting. Poor guy must be cramped as all hell. The weight at her waist—his arm— disappeared.

"Yes. Better." She lifted herself onto her elbow and looked across at Rainbow—who was still unmoving, unconscious, barely breathing.

Stag's thoughts ran parallel to Kateri's. "She's alive. That's something."

Lacey popped her head up; she rested on the hospital bed against Rainbow's side, and she stared at Kateri, her big brown eyes sad and pleading.

"Ohh." Kateri sighed softly. "You brought the dog." The dog who believed Kateri could fix anything. The dog whom Kateri had rescued from certain death.

"Lacey loves Rainbow and I thought she might . . . help Rainbow, or at least wish to say good-bye."

Kateri wished she had been so thoughtful. But she'd been too busy chasing John Terrance and examining dead bodies to think of the connection between Rainbow and Lacey. "The hospital let her in?"

"It was late, and Dr. Frownfelter put her on the bed himself . . . Did you know you drool and snore at the same time?"

Kateri used a well-aimed elbow to shove him off the cot and onto the floor.

He landed with a thump, chuckling low in his chest. "I'll walk Lacey." Going to the bed, he lifted the dog off, taking care not to joggle the mattress. "I brought you clean clothes. Go shower."

"Right." Kateri glanced at the clock. Six A.M. She checked her cell. No messages. No crises, no murders. So far, so good. She gathered the bag Stag had shoved into the corner. Going to the bed, she lightly touched Rainbow's head, her chest, her hand.

No change. Barely a flicker of life. "Dear friend . . ." she said, and remembered

Lacey's sorrowful eyes. Guilt. So much guilt.

She hurried into the bathroom. Her ironed uniform was wrinkled; Stag wasn't the best at packing. But he'd thought about how she would want clean clothes and that gave him all the points. After a day filled with blood and sweat, bullets and worry, and a night of black exhaustion, nothing was as glorious as a shower and clean clothes. She came out to a room empty except for her friend Rainbow, whose soul awaited transport across the cold depths and into that last, glorious warmth of light.

Perhaps letting her go was the kindest thing. Perhaps that was Rainbow's destiny. If Rainbow survived, she faced a road ahead of pain, challenge and change.

But what was a world without Rainbow? She was the heart of Virtue Falls, the woman who knew everyone, the waitress who listened to dreams, hopes and troubles, the counselor who gave advice, both wanted and unwanted.

The memory of Lacey's pleading eyes made Kateri decide she had to try. Yes, Rainbow's life was barely a flicker, but if death was inevitable . . . Going to Rainbow's side, Kateri took Rainbow's hand. "It's me. It's Kateri. You know what I can do . . . sometimes. Save someone's life . . . sometimes. If the conditions are right. I want to try. With you. Is that okay?"

The hospital had removed Rainbow from all

the machines except the monitor that tracked her heartbeat, and that had been silenced. The room was quiet, the hush almost holy, and although Kateri listened, she felt no stirring in Rainbow's mind, no response to her question. Going to the window, she opened the curtains and let the dawn into the room. Returning to the bed, Kateri could smell death in the scent of Rainbow's exhalation. But there was also life, wanting to take control. Kateri breathed Rainbow's breath into her lungs, let them mix, exhaled close, hoping her essence would mix with Rainbow's and together they would feed life's fire. "My gift comes from the frog god," she whispered to Rainbow. "Sip it. Taste it. Inhale and let it warm your blood and bring you strength."

Rainbow's chest rose and fell, rose and fell.

She was breathing more deeply, absorbing Kateri's essence.

"That's it, Rainbow. That's it!" Kateri had been a fool to worry; she could do this! She could save Rainbow!

Then . . . Rainbow's chest collapsed. The heart monitor went flat.

"No. No, Rainbow!" Kateri blew air at Rainbow. "Listen to me. You have to live!"

A nurse rushed in. Another nurse. They pushed Kateri out of the way, took Rainbow's pulse, lifted her lids. Significantly, they didn't speak.

Kateri had done it, all right. She'd killed Rainbow.

Dr. Frownfelter came in, white coat flapping. He caught Kateri's arm. "Don't," he said. "We knew this was coming. There was nothing you could do." Letting her go, he hurried to the bed.

She blundered out into the corridor, into Stag's solid form.

He took one look at her face, picked up Lacey and put her into her arms, and disappeared into the room.

Kateri hugged her dog, rocked her while Lacey licked her face in distress.

Stag stepped out of Rainbow's room. "She's going now. Do you want to go in and be with her?"

"I'm afraid to go near her."

"What happened?"

"I had to try."

"To save her?"

"I thought I would be okay with whatever happened. I'm not. I was afraid I would blow out the flame of Rainbow's life. I did."

"Oh, honey." Stag put his arm around her, enveloping Kateri and Lacey.

Kateri stood straight and stiff.

"Hey. Stop blaming yourself."

"I don't blame myself. *I* didn't shoot her." She pushed away.

Again Stag tried to hug her. "The Terrances shot her."

"It was such good timing, with me and Bergen in the Oceanview Café."

Now Stag stiffened. He stepped away. "What are you trying to say?"

She looked up at him.

His eyes were blank, black, closed off. Like a storm, he was gathering fury.

She wet her lips.

He took another step away. "You might as well say it, Kateri Kwinault."

Now that she'd started this, she was afraid. Afraid she'd made a mistake. "I just wondered if you . . ."

"No. If I had arranged it, you would be dead." His tone was flat, implacable.

Giving voice to her suspicions was the worst mistake of her life.

He continued, "It's one thing not to trust me to bring home almond milk. It's another thing not to trust me to run a law-abiding construction site. And it's another to believe I orchestrated the shooting at the Oceanview Café."

One look at his flinty eyes and she discarded any flippant suggestion that she trusted him with the milk.

Lacey whimpered.

Kateri petted her and tried to explain, to backtrack. "You were walking down the street. Your reflexes were so fast. You hit the ground before anyone else heard the Terrances' car or noticed anything . . . I'm sorry, but I couldn't help but think how much easier it would be for your casino if the sheriff and the deputy sheriff were replaced by people more . . . amenable to . . ." Her voice petered out.

Stag stood in that cool hospital corridor, hands loose, staring at her. He didn't look defensive, or indignant, and as she watched, his fury dissipated, leaving only grief.

That frightened her.

Taking her face in his hands, he leaned forward and kissed her forehead. "Good-bye, my beautiful Kateri." Turning, he walked away.

There was a finality about that kiss that at last drove home what she had done. She had killed Rainbow and now, she had killed something beautiful, something she would never find again.

Worse, if his expression was anything to go by, she had hurt Stag Denali as he had never been hurt before. "Oh, Lacey," she said. "What have I done?"

Lacey struggled in her arms.

Kateri placed her on the floor.

Lacey trotted after Stag, then looked back at Kateri, then trotted a few more steps, then looked back at Kateri. Kateri understood her clearly: *What's wrong with you? Let's go. We belong with Stag.*

Kateri's tears welled in her eyes. She hurt. She hurt all over. For Rainbow. For Lacey. For herself. And for Stag. But she didn't sob out loud; that wouldn't be fair to Lacey.

The little prom queen of a dog got all the way to the door before she turned around and trotted back to Kateri.

Overcome with regret, with anguish, with old fears that drove her to foolishness, Kateri dropped to her knees and hugged her.

Then the radio on her shoulder crackled to life.

CHAPTER THIRTY-FIVE

In all her life, Kateri had never been so glad to be interrupted.

"Weston here." The cocky, overconfident law enforcement officer sounded as if he were a kid talking to the principal. *"Sheriff . . ."*

In the background she heard Bergen say, *"You have to tell her. I'm not gonna."*

Weston's voice quavered. *"Sheriff, Rainbow's house was broken into and, um, searched."*

Kateri wanted to shout, to rage about his incompetence and his inability to follow orders.

But all he'd done was fail to protect Rainbow's property.

Kateri had killed her.

So in a reasonable tone of voice, she asked, "Is it trashed?"

"Nothing's hurt, but it's not neat anymore. Like . . . like your place when someone searched. Everything shoved around, but nothing's broken, nothing's missing that I can see."

Kateri rubbed her forehead. "You don't know who did this?"

"No."

"Or when?"

"Sometime in the last twenty-four hours?"

"You don't sound sure."

286

"Maybe thirty hours."

"Weston."

"Yes, ma'am?"

"When you decided to not follow my orders to protect Rainbow's property, did it not occur to you to install some kind of security in her home?"

"No, ma'am. I thought that . . ."

"I was overreacting?" God save her from superior young men. "Rather than be fired for this blatant incompetence, I suggest that you spend your off-duty hours cleaning up the mess in Rainbow's house."

"Even in her bedroom?"

Kateri could hear him squirming. "Even in her bedroom."

"She's got . . . in there, she's got . . . it's red satin and there are these . . . toys . . ."

"I don't expect you to enjoy it. I expect you to do it."

"Yes, ma'am." For once, Sean Weston sounded subdued.

She cut the connection and softly, with Lacey on her heels, made her way into Rainbow's room.

Dr. Frownfelter and the nurses were turning away from the bed.

Kateri could hardly speak for grief and remorse. "Is she gone?"

"The crisis is over. She's stabilized once more." Dr. Frownfelter patted Kateri's shoulder. "She wants this life. I wish I could help her."

One by one, the nurses left the room, and each of them patted her, too.

Alone with Rainbow, Kateri went to the bed once more. And cried.

Kateri drove with Lacey to City Hall, turned off the car, stared at the entrance, then started the car again and drove to the harbor, to the Coast Guard office. She parked and with Lacey on her heels, went in, and just . . . stood there.

The tsunami had swept away the old Coast Guard headquarters. She had never worked in this building. But in a glass case on one wall, a series of miniatures told the history of the Coast Guard in Virtue Falls. Kateri wandered over and saw the representation of the tsunami, recognized a tiny Kateri doll and saw, beneath the giant waves, two glassy green eyes peering up. Somebody had respected the Native American legend enough to represent the frog god in the story. Which was nice, but those eyes were real enough to make Kateri remember why she no longer went too close to the ocean. To see that cold, enormous face once more would freeze her soul with fear. Even now, years later, the memory sent a shiver down her spine.

Petty Officer Tyler Kovavitc came out of his office and welcomed Kateri with a grin. "Good to see you again, Sheriff Kwinault! I imagine you've come to talk to Commander Luis about yesterday's incident on the docks."

"Sure. Of course. That makes sense. That's why I'm here."

If a dog could snort, Lacey did it.

Kovavitc took Kateri and Lacey to an open door and ushered them into Luis's office. "Sheriff Kateri Kwinault to see you, sir."

Lacey realized who sat at the chair behind the desk, gave a yip and raced around to greet Luis.

Kovavitc added, "And her dog."

Luis looked up from his paperwork. "Baby, it's so wonderful to see you!" He dropped to his knees and came up holding Lacey. To Kateri, he said, "You, too, Kateri. Come in! You must have read my mind. I was just finishing up this report."

Kateri sat down in the chair in front of the desk and started to lie. "Yes, I came to hear the . . ." But she couldn't finish. "I wanted to be somewhere I felt at home."

Luis smiled and he honest-to-God looked pleased. "You feel at home here?"

"I do. My twenties were spent trying to be the best Coastie I could be. I'm not that person anymore, but I remember how much I loved the job and the camaraderie. If the tsunami hadn't changed our world, I would still be here, and gladly."

"I'd be glad if you were still in this chair." He rubbed Lacey's head, then placed her on the floor. "I'm proud to be the commander, but . . ."

"I know," Kateri said. "I am so tired of being . . ."

He finished her sentence. "In charge."

Kateri remembered now why they had been friends. They completed each other's thoughts.

Lacey trotted over and sat on Kateri's feet.

Luis said, "We had some overnight developments. We got a distress call from Bardsey Island."

"Ruth Blethyn's place?" In Kateri's opinion, nothing was more unlikely. Kateri remembered Mrs. Blethyn as English, stout, organized, dignified and wealthy.

"Right. Turns out Mrs. Blethyn has a secret life. She's a 'friend' of John Terrance's." Luis used air quotes.

"You are kidding." Only too well, Kateri remembered John Terrance's appearance. Scrawny, smelly, with greasy hair, dirty fingernails and that nasty leer that showed off teeth that had seldom seen a toothbrush.

"He appeals to her 'wild streak.' " More air quotes.

"Like . . . you mean . . . she . . . they . . ." Kateri wanted to plug her ears. "I don't want to think about that."

"She believes that deep down inside he's 'a good man worth saving.' " Yet more air quotes.

"She's an educated woman. It's not like his appearance is the worst part of him, although it's . . . ew. Ruth Blethyn and John Terrance. He hates women! Not just me, all women!"

Luis suspended his air-quoting fingers in midair. "I'm not arguing."

Kateri continued as if he were. "She has a PhD in psychology. Does she know what this says about her?"

"He just 'needs the right woman.' " Eye roll and air quotes. "He showed up at her house with buckshot in his ass. She removed it for him. He was worried someone—land-based law enforcement, the Coast Guard—was going to track him. So she carried him away to her private island to canoodle."

"Canoodle?" Kateri laughed. "Her words?"

Luis looked surprised at himself. "Actually, my grandmother's. But that was the meaning. Mrs. Blethyn was vague on the details, but I do believe there was some canoodling, also some food and drink and fresh clothing. Then he stole her boat and left her stranded on the island."

Sarcasm spilled from Kateri. "I'm stunned that he would betray his lover in such a manner. You'd think she could recognize his character. Or lack of it." Then she realized—who was she to mock? She had talked with Stag, slept with Stag, allowed him to scold and care for her. And she still hadn't known him. Pain twisted her heart.

She must have gotten an expression on her face, because Luis asked, "Ribs hurt?"

To her horror, she burst into tears.

Luis leaped to his feet and shut the door, came back and dug around in his desk drawer and produced a box of tissues. He offered them to her. "What's wrong? Did Stag get mad because you announced you two were in a relationship?"

She shook her head.

"This is about Stag, isn't it?"

She nodded.

Luis knelt before her. "What did that bastard do?"

"He was nice about the relationship. And I . . ." She cried harder.

He put Lacey into her lap. "What did *you* do?"

"Asked . . . accused . . ."

"Accused him of what?"

"The *shooting*."

"What shooting?" Luis's voice dropped to a hush. "At the Oceanview Café?"

Kateri nodded.

Lacey sighed.

Luis's voice got loud. "What in the hell were you *thinking?*"

"That . . . he . . ."

Luis didn't wait for her to stammer through her words. "He wouldn't work with an amateur like John Terrance."

"If he . . . shot law enforcement . . . his life would be"—Kateri took a long breath and wailed—"easier."

Luis was unrelenting. "Are you kidding? If Stag Denali wanted you dead, you'd be dead."

She nodded. Apparently everyone knew that. Except her.

"As it is, he wants you alive so he can bang your brains out. All the time."

And she was here to testify that he was good at it. "How do you know . . . anything?"

"It's logical. You got a guy who's been in prison for murder. I'd guess a rough early life, learned a lot of skills necessary to survive. He could get a job anywhere doing enforcement, legal or otherwise, or obtain a 'position' as a stud for Ruth Blethyn"—more air quotes—"or work at any number of lucrative jobs. He showed up in Virtue Falls, the piddly-poop outback of nowhere, and he's working as financial wizard on the rez in Virtue Falls for their new casino. I figured he'd move on as soon as he got the funding set up. Makes sense, right? Then he comes after you. Specifically after you. He sleeps with you and all of a sudden, he's construction superintendent on the site, working all hours, living in an apartment over the flower shop that's so small he bumps his head on the hood when he uses the stovetop. And you don't know if he loves you?"

"*Loves* me?"

Luis handed her another wad of tissue. "I used to think you were smart. Then you turned me away and that was the first nail in that coffin."

She laughed explosively. And cried some more. "Last week I had won a brutal election for sheriff and I was on top of the world. Now I'm wounded, women are being slashed, I can't catch the fugitive who shot up the Oceanview Café, I tried to kill Rainbow—"

"You . . . what?"

"Tried to help her. I did it wrong. Then I screwed up with the one man who . . ." She couldn't continue. She didn't have the breath. Leaning forward, she wept into Lacey's fur.

Luis waited until her crying had calmed a little, then handed her a bottle of water. "What are you going to do about getting him back?"

She remembered Stag's expression when he kissed her on the forehead. That was *farewell*. "He doesn't want me back."

Luis snorted. "Yes, he does. You might have to crawl . . . But you can fix it."

Easy for him to say, and considering his track record . . . She wiped her eyes and her nose. She took a sip of the water. "Speaking of a screwed-up situation, how's Sienna?" His girlfriend, the woman who had gone out of her way to show Kateri that Luis was hers, even going so far as to fake a pregnancy.

Luis stood up and sat on his desk. "I really did break up with her. I'm a Coastie through and through. Sooner or later I'll get transferred. Sienna put down roots here and now she'll never leave. You be careful, Kateri. She's a smart girl, and ruthless. Before she's done, she'll own Virtue Falls and be mayor, and she's got it in for you."

"Goodie. Another challenge." Kateri leaned back in the chair and pressed her hand over her swollen eyes. "Let me try to sort this all out. John Terrance managed to find someone to remove the shot from his butt, stole a boat—another one—and landed somewhere along the coast?"

"When we were transporting Mrs. Blethyn back to her home on the mainland, we found the boat adrift. No John Terrance."

"Right. So we can assume he's still alive and holed up somewhere waiting for his next chance to get his revenge on Virtue Falls for a thousand real and imagined slights. Plus—you have once more become Virtue Falls's most eligible bachelor. Plus—I'm an idiot."

"Nice summation. That covers it."

She put Lacey on the floor, hauled herself to her feet and tossed the wad of tissue into his trash. "Thanks for the news, the talking-to and the bottle of water. Now I have to go speak sternly to my sister about breaking and entering."

That made Luis stand up straight. "I didn't even know you had a sister, much less a larcenous sister."

"Not larcenous in the usual sense. But determined to get what she wants." Kateri's voice wavered. "Luis, I've missed having you as a friend."

"I've missed you, too."

Spontaneously, they hugged.

Unexpectedly, Kovavitc opened the door. He stared, coughed and said, "I thought you two were broken up!"

"We are." Kateri stepped out of Luis's arms. "He was telling me I'm an idiot. In a loving way. Like a brother."

"Geeze, Sheriff Kwinault, why don't you just cut off his balls?" Kovavitc had a way with words.

Kateri saw Luis's pained expression and backpedaled. "What I meant to say was I could no longer refrain from flinging myself into Commander Sanchez's arms, but he nobly fought me off and gently told me we could never be one."

"Yeah . . . that didn't help. He's still a nutless wonder." Kovavitc turned to Luis. "Commander, Mrs. Blethyn called to report her car as stolen."

The radio on Kateri's sleeve vibrated.

Bergen said, *"Sheriff, we've got a call from Garik Jacobsen at the FBI. He has the report you've been waiting for."*

Luis and Kateri faced off with each other, then each gave a nod and she walked toward the exit, Lacey on her heels.

When she was out the door, Luis turned to

Kovavitc. "I deserve a fucking medal for what I just did. I convinced her that she needed to convince Stag Denali they were the ideal couple."

"You still want to bang her?"

"Yeah."

Kovavitc punched him on the shoulder good and hard. "Wow, man. You *are* a nutless wonder."

CHAPTER THIRTY-SIX

The trouble with police work was that it was so damned unreliable. One week it was all slashings and car chases and break-ins and confrontations and murders. The next week, you were handing out speeding tickets and earnestly explaining the danger of crossing the street against the light.

That sucked, especially when Kateri had a moping dog, a sister who refused to admit to breaking and entering and yet always managed to find Kateri no matter where she hid, a worrisome FBI report, no lover in sight and *way* too much time on her hands.

Thank God it was Thursday evening. She asked Moen if he wanted to go with her to the quilting group, grinned at his horror, and waved a cheerful farewell to the thoroughly bored and testosterone-soaked police station.

The Scrap Happy Stitchers, a group of ten to twelve regulars, usually women, met in the library, an old hardware store that had survived the earthquake and now housed books, children, maps, crafts, computers, toys, women, men, teenagers . . . After the tsunami, Kateri had been physically unable to continue in the Coast Guard. Coast Guard policy had put her through a court-martial for the loss of her vessel, and when she was cleared she was medically retired with pay and benefits. So . . . she became the town librarian. Because no one else wanted the job. Because the pay was crappy. Because she was handicapped and in pain, and the job didn't require too many hours.

She had learned who lived in this small town, what they thought, who they loved, what they hoped and dreamed and did. Her command at the Virtue Falls Coast Guard had prepared her to lead, but her time at the library had given her insight into the people.

Now in its third year and under Mrs. Golobovitch's direction, the Scrap Happy Stitchers patched together quilts for church sales, charity functions and to show at the county fair. They also talked, listened, gossiped, advised, suggested and fought. And ate. They ate whatever anyone else made or bought and loved it, because they didn't have to prepare it themselves.

Tonight was Kateri's night to bring snacks, so she headed to the Oceanview Café to pick up the sandwich plate she'd ordered. She walked in; the place was packed. Locals, tourists . . . everybody but their local dysfunctional genius, Cornelia Markum. Kateri walked up to the counter where Mr. Caldwell, the meanest old man in the world, sat hunched over a cup of coffee. "Hi, Mr. Caldwell, where's Cornelia?"

Mr. Caldwell lifted his morose gaze from

the counter. "That bitch of a new waitress told her she wasn't going to fix her weird pie every day and she was sucking up all the Wi-Fi, and Cornelia left."

"Linda? Said that to Cornelia?"

Mr. Caldwell slid an evil glance toward the thin, blond waitress as she whipped around the restaurant with a coffeepot. "Why don't you ask me what she said to ol' Setzer?"

Kateri looked around. His three friends from the old geezer table were nowhere in sight. She leaned her elbows on the counter and quietly asked, "*What* did she say to Mr. Setzer?"

"She used that 'nails on a chalkboard' voice of hers and told him she was tired of having his baggy old ass taking up a chair a paying customer would use, and from now on he could get his coffee elsewhere."

Kateri straightened up. "Dax owns the place. Can't he do something?"

"Are you kidding? Dax is a pushover all the time, and right now, he's a blubbering mess because he's in love with Rainbow. Not that I know why, Rainbow never gives it to him."

"Unrequited love," Kateri suggested.

"Right. Like a teenager. So between Dax crying in the soup and the tourists taking every seat, Linda's got this place held in her iron fist."

"What about you?"

"I actually am mean enough to take up a bar

stool for an endless cup of coffee. Not that I can get coffee. She won't serve me anymore."

"Not a problem, Mr. Caldwell. I'll serve you." Taking his cup, Kateri whipped behind the counter. She dumped out the old, cold coffee, rinsed the cup, poured it full of the fresh brew and put it on the saucer in front of him.

"Thank you," he said. "Here she comes."

Linda arrived, her blue eyes snapping. "Sheriff Kwinault, you are not allowed behind the counter."

Kateri batted her brown eyes at Linda. "Poor Mr. Caldwell's coffee was cold, and there are so many people in here, I knew you needed the help."

Out of the corner of his mouth, Mr. Caldwell said, "Well done. She's speechless."

But not for long. Linda's voice went up an octave. "It's illegal for non-kitchen staff to go behind the counter!"

"I won't arrest myself. But since I have your attention, Mr. Caldwell needs a slice of pie. With ice cream. Right, Mr. Caldwell?"

Mr. Caldwell was no longer hunched over his coffee. He was gloating over it. "That would be wonderful, Sheriff Kwinault."

"I am not serving that old stool-sitter," Linda snapped.

"Are you refusing service to a man because of his *age?*" Kateri contrived to look shocked. "I'm afraid that is a much more serious crime than me illegally serving coffee."

"I'm not refusing to serve him because of his age. He hangs around all the time, his bony old hands clutching that one cup—"

"Mr. Caldwell, are you not paying?" Kateri asked in her most scolding tone.

Mr. Caldwell put his hand on his chest. "Every day."

"One cup," Linda said. "He pays for one cup. And he wants endless refills!"

"Which is what the menu offers. As a customer, elderly or not, he has that right. Now, he's asking for pie and ice cream. Is that a problem?" Kateri saw the moment when it clicked with Linda that she was overmatched.

The thin, snippy, perpetually irritated waitress marched to the pie case, pulled out the mixed berry pie, slid her spatula under the smallest slice, placed one tiny scoop of ice cream on the top and slammed it down in front of Mr. Caldwell.

Who said, "Thank you," picked up his fork and burrowed right in.

Linda sneered and stormed away.

Mr. Caldwell told Kateri, "I'm digging black-berry seeds out from my dentures all night. But that was worth it. Thank you, Sheriff Kwinault."

He was really piling on the respect for her title.

She liked that.

Her phone vibrated in her pocket. Pulling it out, she looked and moaned.

"What is it?" Mr. Caldwell asked.

"The Good Knight Manor Bed and Breakfast. Where my sister is staying. This cannot be good." She picked up.

Phoebe shrieked in her ear, "Would you come immediately and arrest your sister for refusing to leave the great room so I can set up for the evening's social hour?"

"I . . . don't think that's illegal." Kateri made her eyes wide and appealing, and stared at Mr. Caldwell.

He chortled and kept eating.

Phoebe shouted, "She's disrupting the schedule!"

Kateri took a breath to explain why the sheriff couldn't answer a call like this—and collapsed in defeat. "I'll come over and see what I can do. Yes. Right away." She hung up, and asked Mr. Caldwell, "Anything else?"

"I'm going to give you some advice, young lady."

"I'm listening."

"Kipling said, 'The female of the species is more deadly than the male.' " He nodded toward Linda. "If I were you, I wouldn't turn my back on that woman. Or accept food from her. Or coffee. Or cross the street in front of her."

"Thank you, I'll keep that in mind." Stepping behind the counter, she picked up the tray of sandwiches. "However—I'm female, too."

"So you are, my dear." Mr. Caldwell was still grinning. "So you are."

CHAPTER THIRTY-SEVEN

Merida had spent almost ten years in an environment controlled by a despotic man who demanded the kind of peace and quiet one might experience in a sepulchre. To stand in the entry of the Good Knight Manor Bed and Breakfast and listen to Phoebe shout, "No, that is not your private sitting room, Miss Palmer, and you may not forbid our entry so you can enjoy your privacy!" made Merida hug herself with glee.

To hear Lilith reply, "My room has not yet been cleaned and the evening is approaching, so where else would I enjoy my privacy?" brought a silent chuckle.

Phoebe took a shuddering breath. "I told you. Susie didn't show up for work today. I'm working as quickly as I can, but I work from the most expensive room down and your room is at the bottom of the list."

"Whose fault is that? I required the most expensive room when I registered." As Lilith spoke, her voice got more and more superior and contrasted strongly with Phoebe's high-pitched indignation.

"You should have called sooner. Months sooner! It's the tourist season!" Phoebe waved her fists. "As it is, you've overstayed and I've completely angered two different sets of guests who believed they had rooms reserved in the Good Knight Manor Bed and Breakfast!"

Lilith sniffed with such disdain Merida thought Phoebe was going to fling herself into battle armed with a serving fork.

Someone edged into the room from the direction of the kitchen.

A young man; Merida had seen him loitering on the premises, living in the supply shack at the far back, occasionally dashing toward the house and coming away with food and drink. She recognized him from her research: Phoebe's son, Evan Glass, recently released from prison. Now he watched his mother, listened to the battle, smiled and swung his arms like a fighter against an imaginary opponent.

As much as Merida hated to miss the rest of the fight, if he was going to get involved, she would consider a retreat to her rooms.

A knock sounded on the front door. It opened.

More combatants?

Kateri walked in holding a plastic catering tray in one arm, her walking stick in her hand.

Phoebe's son speedily backed out of the room.

Yes, he definitely had something to hide.

Merida signed, "Hello!"

Phoebe shrieked, "Sheriff Kwinault, thank God you got here." She pointed. "Arrest that woman!"

Kateri said, "Hello, Merida, good to see you. How's the entertainment?"

Merida gave her a thumbs-up.

From her chair, Lilith called, "Katherine, is that you?"

Kateri walked to the arched doorway. "Yes, Lilith. Please, per your innkeeper's request, would you vacate the parlor?"

"Not until my bedroom is cleaned."

Phoebe started shouting again. "My maid didn't show up for work. I can't hire someone else because everyone in this town is already employed. I can't get it all done by myself. *Make her move!*" She seemed to expect Kateri to draw her pistol.

Instead Kateri said, "Lilith, tonight I go to my quilting club. Would you care to go with me?"

Lilith's struggle between staying to annoy Phoebe and going out with her sister was almost audible.

Kateri slid Merida a sideways, conspiring glance. "Come on, Lilith." She headed into the parlor. "I know how important your support of early American crafts is to you. Here's a chance to see a contemporary quilting group in session. It is, I believe, exactly like the historical gatherings and a fascinating glimpse of culture in the western states." She came out, arm in arm with her sister.

They were a contrast: Lilith with her blond hair,

perfectly made-up face, casual vacation dress and superior irritation and Kateri, so very Native American with long dark hair pinned under a sheriff's brimmed hat and amused brown eyes.

Kateri smiled brightly at Phoebe. "We're going out." To Merida, she said, "Want to come?"

Merida did want to come. Not because her sewing skills were any better than Kateri's, but because she had spent much of the last twenty-four hours with Benedict and things were getting . . . worrisome. As if she should have taken her chances with the slasher. Not that Benedict was pushy. Not in the slightest. In fact, there hadn't been even a suggestion of another kiss. Worse, when he thought she wasn't looking, he watched her as if he suspected . . . something. When she thought of the somethings he might suspect—her long-ago identity or her plan for vengeance or both—she wanted to get as far away from him as possible. He had tried to kill her once before. He was not the kind of man who would fail a second time.

In answer to Kateri, she held up one finger, hurried into her room, grabbed her purse and a sweater—evenings so close to the ocean often became chilly—came out and activated the locks on her door. She turned to find Phoebe and Lilith locked in a glaring contest. She wanted to tell Phoebe she didn't stand a chance; instead she took Lilith's other arm and started toward the porch.

Her gesture broke up the impasse and earned her a look of gratitude from Kateri.

As they stepped outside into the early evening, Lilith asked, "We're *walking?*"

"Yes," Kateri said. "My only vehicle is a patrol car. I left it in its parking spot at City Hall in case someone needs it. Anyway, if I'd brought it, you'd have to sit in the back." In the back with the cage between the front seat and the doors with no handles.

"*I* have a car," Lilith said. "I rented it in Seattle and I've hardly driven it."

"The library is only a few blocks. Almost everything in Virtue Falls is only a few blocks." Kateri gestured north. In a solicitous tone, she added, "Unless you have difficulty walking?"

"Of course not! Every day I walk vigorously for exercise!" Lilith started swiftly in the direction Kateri had indicated. "Although I do prefer the gym. There's quite a sufficient gym here, but it's very busy. After my first time there, they have not had room for me to work out."

"I'll bet," Kateri muttered.

Merida shook her finger at the sheriff.

"My concern was for you," Lilith said to Kateri. "With your disabilities, will you be able to go so far?"

Lilith's solicitude made Kateri aim the tray of sandwiches at Lilith's head.

Merida removed them from her grasp.

Kateri thumped her walking stick on the sidewalk. "I'm fine, thank you, sister."

"Good." Lilith forged on, forcing Kateri and Merida to hurry and catch up. "Katherine, where is your charming doggie?"

"While I work, Mrs. Golobovitch babysits Lacey. They adore each other." Kateri walked on one side of Lilith. "Mrs. Golobovitch also leads the Scrap Happy Stitchers."

"The Scrap Happy Stitchers." Lilith struggled between mockery and her excessive good breeding. She managed, "How quaint."

"Mrs. Golobovitch has won so many blue ribbons at so many Washington county fairs she's a legend in the Pacific Northwest quilting world."

"I believe I've heard of her." Because Lilith would never admit ignorance about any matter.

"Of course you have." Kateri sounded the tiniest bit sarcastic. "Mrs. Golobovitch leads us as we talk and sew. Usually Bette Abrahamson, Gladys McKissick and Rosa Sage come together and sit together. They're friends from high school. Emma Royalty is an electrician from Berk Moore's construction crew. The electrical work she does has taught her such dexterity, she can do rocking stitches like nobody's business. Lillie and Tora Keidel are sisters who are friends." She sounded as if sisters/friends were an unusual occurrence, and hastily added, "Frances Salak is always there. Her mother, a cranky old woman if there ever was one, lives with her and Frances will do anything to get out of the house."

"That's too bad. I always got along with our mother very well. People said we were very much alike." Lilith looked smug and somehow managed to convey pity for anyone who experienced a parental problem.

Merida admired that Kateri managed to say as much with her silence and her tight smile as most people did with their words. "At the SHS, we're all friends, sometimes confidantes."

Merida walked on the other side of Lilith and signed, "Will we be intruding?"

"Of course not!" Lilith replied. "Katherine wouldn't have invited us if that was the case."

Both Merida and Kateri stopped in the street and stared at Lilith.

"How did you know what she said?" Kateri asked.

"Oh. That." Lilith smirked. "I've been studying signing so I can understand what Merida says when she speaks."

Merida blinked in astonishment. Nauplius had learned sign language . . . after two years, when he finally had to admit his ideal woman, his Helen, would never speak again. He had come to like the fact she was mute; it kept her isolated.

Benedict Howard had learned sign language, but he had a motive—he wanted in her pants.

What was in it for Lilith?

Lilith didn't wait for her to ask. "I like to know things. I find ignorance a disgrace to the human condition, and this time in Virtue Falls has reminded me of Kateri and her childhood friend who used to sign to shut me out of their silly conversations." Lilith did a double take and stared at Merida, then at Kateri.

Kateri walked on.

Merida widened her eyes and stared back.

Lilith shook her head slightly. "Not that I cared, but while I'm still woefully slow at understanding, I will do my best to keep up."

Merida nodded and touched her mouth in thanks.

Lilith signed, "You're welcome," then, obviously pleased with herself, she turned on Kateri. "Katherine, why are *you* going to a quilting club? Mother despaired of teaching you to sew on a button. She always said you were spectacularly unprepared to take care of yourself."

Merida remembered that. Kateri's stepmother had made it quite clear Kateri was not a daughter of the house and would someday have to fend for herself.

"Yet non-seamstress that I am, I facilitated the very first Thursday night quilting group." Kateri sounded determinedly matter-of-fact.

"After you were court-martialed, left the Coast Guard and were forced to become the town librarian." As Lilith remembered Kateri's fall from grace, her stride lengthened as if satisfaction fed her energy.

Merida envied Kateri's serenity whether it was real or feigned . . . Lilith was so annoying that with very little provocation, *Merida* could have shouted at Lilith.

They reached downtown and the concrete building with a sign beside the door proclaiming, VIRTUE FALLS LIBRARY.

Kateri ushered them in.

Lacey raced toward Kateri, barking in ecstasy, and danced around her, front paws in the air.

Kateri murmured endearments.

A dozen strange women sat around the quilting frame, a dozen strangers' faces turned in their direction.

Merida shrank back.

One woman stood at a library table wearing an eccentric all-black outfit with half capes over the long black sleeves, a half skirt over capri leggings and black woven flats with a sparkle of silver. She was thin, elegant and European, and she rolled a rotary blade along a broad wooden straight edge, cutting perfectly straight strips of red cloth that she lifted from the table and set aside. She glanced over her shoulder. Her cool gaze met Merida's.

Elsa Cipre.

Animosity swept Merida. Fear, too. *How were*

these people everywhere she went? She backed out the door and retreated to the sidewalk out of sight of the open door and the quilters.

Why had she come tonight? What had she been thinking? She didn't like strangers. She had been lured by the pleasure of a few moments spent with Kateri, and by the knowledge that Kateri needed her to help handle Lilith.

Friendship and compassion, both guaranteed to destroy her. Would she never learn?

CHAPTER THIRTY-EIGHT

Lilith and Kateri joined Merida on the sidewalk.

Lacey came out of the library and stood on the top step of the porch, head cocked.

"What's wrong?" Kateri asked.

Merida shook her head and pointed inside, then shook her head again.

Lilith answered for her. "It's Elsa Cipre. She and her husband are staying at the B and B with us. He's a visiting professor at Washington State University. Wherever that is."

"In Pullman, across the state," Kateri said.

"I stand shoulder to shoulder with our friend Merida when I say—the woman is truly obnoxious." Coming from Lilith, that comment was either funny or a damaging indictment.

"The Cipres are very superior people," Merida signed, and if signing could be sarcastic, this was.

"Except when it comes to fashion?" Kateri muttered.

Merida gave a twisted smile. "She takes a special interest in me."

"I've seen evidence of that interest. Elsa Cipre seems almost motherly toward you." Lilith frowned, her brow knit in confusion. "Why would any woman feel motherly toward another woman? You're obviously capable of taking care of yourself."

Merida and Kateri again exchanged sideways glances. Lilith was so completely unself-aware in her judgments and of her own personality, they didn't know whether to laugh or sigh.

"She is"—Merida seemed to search for the word—"tiring."

"We don't have to stay," Kateri said.

Lacey gave a bark, ran down the stairs, did her dance around Kateri, around Lilith, around Merida, then put her paws on Merida's leg and looked up enticingly.

Merida stroked her soft head and felt the return of her courage. She signed, "I can shake it off. Let's go in."

At their return, a spatter of applause came from the regulars.

Kateri loved these people. They were her friends, the backbone of her life in Virtue Falls, always there, always dependable, showing their support in discreet and loving ways.

As always, Mrs. Golobovitch sat at the head of the quilt directing operations. "Hello, Kateri, I'm glad you decided to join us. Would you introduce us to your friends?"

"My sister, Lilith Palmer, from Baltimore." No one audibly gasped, but a few opened their eyes wide, as if they didn't dare blink at the news Kateri had a sister. "My friend, Merida Falcon, currently living in Virtue Falls." Merida commanded her own kind of reaction: she wore lavender coveralls, a purple sleeveless T-shirt and had recently shaved the hair over her left ear. Which put her in the mainstream of Virtue Falls fashion. But she was so beautiful, the women looked and looked away, as if she was difficult to view.

Kateri introduced the women around the table, and when she introduced Lillie and Tora Keidel, Lilith said, "Oh. The sisters who are *friends*."

Damn. Lilith had noticed Kateri's slip.

Kateri showed Merida where to place the sandwiches—on a table as far away from the quilt as possible—then they went to sit among the group, and everyone shuffled their seats to make room.

Kateri pointed Merida to a chair between Emma Royalty and Rosa Sage, then seated herself across the table with Lilith beside her. To the table in general, she explained, "My friend Merida can hear, so don't shout! But she can't speak. Lilith and I will translate as needed."

An awkward silence. A little chitchat asking how Merida and Lilith liked Virtue Falls. Mrs. Golobovitch gave them quilting needles and showed them the basics of putting the patches together. Then Gladys McKissick asked, "How are your ribs, Kateri?"

Kateri touched her side. "Better, thank you. Since we lost John Terrance and we're dealing with a period of relative calm—except for some of the less sensible tourists—"

Knowing laughter.

"—I've had time to heal."

"And Rainbow? No change?" Tora Keidel's voice trembled.

The room grew very quiet; the only sound was the zip of the rotary cutter in Elsa's hand. Rainbow was a regular at the quilting group; she was sorely missed and they all waited on the sad news with tears and prayers.

Kateri cleared her throat. "No change."

Lilith looked around in surprise; apparently it hadn't occurred to her that people other than Kateri might harbor a love for Rainbow.

Frances Salak said, "Kateri, can you tell us what Garik said about these . . . these slashings around town?"

Everyone here knew Garik, most had known him all their lives, and Kateri had tried to make sure gossips knew she'd consulted him and his FBI database. She told them, "In the last twelve months, slashings in the U.S. are up, but only slightly. Most of the perpetrators are accounted for—drug cases or spousal abuse. The three fatalities that are still without a suspect are in different parts of the country and the methods and weapons are not similar."

"Where were they?" Frances asked. "What were the weapons?"

Kateri counted down on her fingers. "New York, Chicago and Birmingham, Alabama. A paring knife, an X-Acto knife and a butcher knife. Weapons everyone has access to."

Without looking up, Elsa Cipre corrected Kateri. "*To whom* everyone has access."

Kateri wanted to smack her.

Merida put her fingers to her forehead and massaged.

Lilith moaned softly.

And dear, sweet Mrs. Golobovitch stood up and stalked over to Elsa Cipre. "Please stop cutting that material. We don't need so many strips for this quilt!"

Elsa Cipre didn't even look up. "Yes, you do."

Mrs. Golobovitch's Eastern European accent got heavier. "I have been quilting for sixty years. Do you dare tell me I'm wrong?"

"You *are* wrong. Do you have a degree in Home Sciences?" Elsa answered. "No, you do not. I have designed this quilt in my mind and with the additional three inches it needs at the top and the bottom—"

"It doesn't need anything at the top or the bottom!" Outrage brought Mrs. Golobovitch to attention.

"Of course not." The rotary cutter slid past the tips of Elsa's fingers. "If you want the proportions to be incorrect."

At the quilting table, all needles froze in midair.

Every eye was fixed on the scene between Elsa Cipre and Mrs. Golobovitch, and no one knew what to say, what to do, how to alleviate the tension.

Mrs. Golobovitch said, "Mrs. Cipre, I have led this group to four blue ribbons at the county fair—"

"I guided young women's lives for *years*. Do you hear me? Years! Do you know who I am?"

"No." Mrs. Golobovitch leaned her hands on the table and tried to catch Elsa's eyes. "Nor do I want—"

The rotary cutter swerved within millimeters of Mrs. Golobovitch's fingertips.

Kateri half-rose, expecting to have to render aid.

Mrs. Golobovitch leaped back, saving herself, and her outrage changed to wariness, caution, suspicion.

Elsa Cipre never noticed. Or if she did, she didn't deign to show it. "*I* taught Home Sciences at Northeastern Christian University, and within ten years I had vanquished all other contenders and I was the head of the program. I taught those young women more than sewing and cooking. I taught them how to make a house a home. I taught flower arrangement, interior decorating, gardening. *Quilting*. I taught them creativity."

"You were like Martha Stewart," Emma Royalty said.

Elsa whipped around and faced the quilting table, still clutching that rotary cutter. "That *faker*. If I had accepted a television show, my Home Sciences program would still be in place. I would still be guiding young ladies to seek the pinnacle of their womanhood. Yet I would not lower myself to anything so vulgar."

"I *like* Martha Stewart," Emma said, but she muttered under her breath as if Elsa Cipre intimidated her.

Bette Abrahamson, who had her own background of academic honors, asked, "Mrs. Cipre, were there no young men in your classes?"

"None seriously. Not at first. Some, of course, thought to get an easy A by attending my basic baking classes." Elsa stacked the strips she had cut, turned them 45 degrees and began to make small triangles for some design she had created in her mind. "But they found out soon enough they were expected to knead dough into a loaf of white bread with a good crumb. They were expected to produce a pie crust so crisp it crumbled in a stiff breeze. Their angel food cakes had better be light and heavenly. Some of them thought to cheat, to get their girlfriends to do the work for them, but I watched closely and they performed those tasks or their easy A dropped to a big fat F. I would not sacrifice the integrity of my courses, not even for those young men who thought themselves privileged sports stars.

As the seventies progressed, some brave young men came to realize the value of my instruction and enrolled for their own sakes. I updated the program, adding knowledge about car mechanics, horticulture, technology. I kept up to date!"

Merida signed, Lilith translated. "What happened to your classes?"

"I should have had tenure. It was time for me to have tenure. And the college . . ." Elsa stopped, head down, and breathed heavily. "The college canceled the whole program. They said Home Sciences was a dated concept, that young women—young people—didn't need to learn good housewifery, that getting a job was more important than making a home." She threw out her hand in a grand, dramatic gesture. "In this day and age when so many people work so hard to succeed in a daytime job, and in the evening provide succor for their families, it's obvious that—"

The library door slammed back.

Everyone turned, gasped.

A man's hulking silhouette loomed against the light.

Dawkins Cipre stepped inside.

Everything about Elsa's demeanor changed; she went from wildly indignant instructor to cowed female. "Dawkins! Dear! I didn't know you were . . . close. To here."

"You disappeared, Elsa, darling. I didn't know

where you were or what you were doing. You know I need to keep track of you." He sounded so genial . . . and he looked so threatening.

Kateri slid her hand off the quilt and loosened the snap over her 9mm semiautomatic.

Like a bug caught in amber, Elsa struggled to get free. "I wasn't trying to escape . . . you. I simply . . . I saw the flyer for the quilting group. You know how I love to quilt."

"At all times, I need to know where you are." He was a big man, and as he advanced into the room, fists clenched, every woman there shrank back.

Especially Elsa.

His whole attention was fixed . . . on Elsa.

She scrambled to put the table between him and her.

He caught her arm and dragged her.

Her hip smashed into the corner of the table.

He brought her close. His fingers squeezed her flesh.

Kateri said, "Mrs. Cipre, I'm the Virtue Falls sheriff. If I can render aid . . ."

"No. No, of course not. There's nothing wrong, Sheriff." Elsa never took her frightened gaze from her husband's face. "Dawkins and I are simply . . . very close."

"Say good-bye to your new friends, my dear." His light brown eyes glowed a sickly amber.

"Good-bye. I . . . I enjoyed myself," Elsa said.

He acknowledged the group by not even a glance. All his attention was for his wife. "Sorry, ladies, I don't like losing control of her." He dragged at Elsa, making her move too quickly.

She stumbled.

The door slammed behind them.

Silence reigned for a long moment.

Mrs. Golobovitch looked at her fingers, then looked at the door. "That poor woman."

Merida began to tremble. "That's why she wears those clothes," she signed. "To cover the bruises."

Lilith gave voice to her words.

Emma turned to Kateri. "Can't you do something?"

"Abused women sometimes are afraid of their abusers and refuse to report them, but more often, they're in love and won't leave and won't file a report." Kateri snapped the cover over her 9mm semiautomatic once more. "I'm sorry. We see this more often than you know."

In a low, shamed voice, Tora said, "I was abused. I didn't leave him until . . . he almost killed me. If it wasn't for Lillie . . ." She hugged her sister.

A murmur of sympathy swept the room.

The radio at Kateri's shoulder vibrated. She stood and walked away from the group, listened to Bergen's low-voiced report and said, "Oh, my God. Her whole face?"

"It's . . . so much worse than last time," he told her. *"You can't imagine."*

"I'm trying not to."

"I've got Moen on his way to pick you up."

"See you soon." Kateri hung up and returned to stand over the quilting frame. "Ladies, we have a situation. I don't want to cause panic, but I would ask that none of you walk alone tonight."

"Another slashing?" Emma Royalty asked.

Kateri nodded.

"Killed?" Mrs. Golobovitch asked.

"Yes."

"Who?"

"We haven't been able to identify the body."

Nine women dove for their cell phones to call the people important to them. A babble broke out. There were exclamations of relief and warnings.

Meanwhile, Mrs. Golobovitch clasped her hands at her ample bosom. "The Cipre man was out there alone, without his wife. She is so afraid of him. Do you think that he . . . ?"

"Right now, we don't have a suspect, not on our radar and not in custody. But yes, until Dawkins Cipre provides an alibi, he's a suspect." The room fell silent as everyone listened to Kateri. "So are a lot of men. And women. Please don't make accusations. I can tell you that the sheriff's department's official statement will be that we are investigating and hope to have a suspect in custody soon."

The women returned to their phone calls. Word would spread fast.

Kateri switched her attention to Lilith and Merida. "You'll walk back together."

"I'll call a cab. We'll share." Lilith got out her phone and proceeded to do exactly that.

Rosa Sage got out her car keys. "We'll stay with Mrs. Golobovitch and help her clean up, then we'll take her home."

Bette Abrahamson and Gladys McKissick nodded agreement.

"For the moment, I will keep the darling Lacey and she will protect me." Mrs. Golobovitch rubbed Lacey's adoring face. "Won't you?"

"So Lacey is an alpha bitch?" Lilith asked.

Takes one to know one. "She is," Kateri said.

Lilith gave her approval. "She will be your best protection, Mrs. Golobovitch."

"What about you, dear Kateri?" Mrs. Golobovitch asked. "I worry about your safety. Will Stag Denali be with you tonight?"

"Who's Stag Denali?" Lilith asked.

"Her boyfriend," Mrs. Golobovitch told her.

"Really." Lilith's eyes narrowed. "Is he Indian?"

"Native American," Kateri snapped. "Yes, he's one of the People. But he's not my boyfriend. We're not committed."

Everyone stared at Kateri, then looked at each other.

Mrs. Golobovitch began, "Dear Kateri, Stag is—"

Kateri spoke over her. "Moen's coming for me to take me to the murder scene. I'll be safe since I imagine I'll spend most of the night at the police department. Someone needs to take the sandwiches to the women's shelter." She picked up the rotary cutter. "Mrs. Golobovitch, can I take this with me?"

Mrs. Golobovitch nodded. "Of course, dear. Just be careful. That is new, and very sharp."

Kateri tested it on her fingertip and gasped when she drew blood. "Yes . . . isn't *that* interesting."

CHAPTER THIRTY-NINE

Mike Sun had thoughtfully placed the body in a bag and zipped it up—which is why Kateri was able to stand beside it without vomiting. "Do we have an ID yet?"

Looking pale and sweaty, Bergen, Norm Knowles and Bill Chippen stood huddled together over the body.

Bergen said, "Nothing positive. Phoebe Glass at the Good Knight Manor Bed and Breakfast reported her maid as missing. She told us the woman, Susie, lived away from town with her philandering husband and four children. Mrs. Glass was worried not only for the maid, but for the children. She was so insistent . . . and we didn't have anything to do except ticket jaywalkers . . . and Weston said why not come out looking?"

Kateri glanced over; Sean Weston sat on a fallen log, hands in his pockets, watching the scene.

Bergen wiped at his brow with his sleeve. "She wasn't at the address Mrs. Glass gave us. The lady who lived there denied knowing this Susie. But the buzzards were circling on the hill, so we hiked up here. And found her in the trees."

"Why don't we have an ID?" Kateri asked.

Mike Sun sat on the ground filling out a form on a clipboard. "She has a bullet hole in her forehead, no face and her fingertips were removed."

Moen paced back and forth on the path they'd taken. Kateri thought he couldn't hear what was going on, but he paused and looked their way in horror.

Kid had good ears.

"Mrs. Glass believed this Susie was originally from Virtue Falls," Bergen said.

"But Mrs. Glass isn't local so how would she know?" Officer Chippen asked.

"Why did she think Susie was local?" Kateri asked.

"Susie told her so. All the information we've got here—her address, the philandering husband and the four children—comes from Susie herself via Mrs. Glass. Mrs. Glass was really concerned."

"Also she can't find someone else to clean." Kateri waved that away. "Sorry, not the point."

"The body is dressed like a cleaning woman," Officer Knowles said.

"She didn't have the hands for it," Mike Sun said.

"How do you know? She didn't have finger-tips!" Knowles said.

Mike Sun didn't like Knowles lipping off to him, so he unzipped the bag from the bottom and brought out one of the mutilated hands.

Norm Knowles turned his back.

Mike said, "I recognize these calluses. These weren't caused by cleaning. She's practiced self-defense for a long time. Karate at the least."

"That's interesting." Kateri contemplated the news. "So we have a corpse with no ID and no fingerprints who has apparently been lying to her employer about just about everything. She ran into our slasher. He shot her and used her to experiment on, and if his goal was to remove his victims' faces intact, he apparently managed it this time."

Mike Sun said, "You've got one thing backward. He took her face first. Then he shot her."

That did it for Bill Chippen. He headed for the bushes and they heard him throwing up.

Kateri rubbed the side of her head. "This is one sick bastard."

"We can officially label this 'escalating violence,'" Bergen said. "Although it almost seems as if he shot her to put her out of her misery."

"Suspects?" Kateri had one, but she wanted to hear everyone else's thoughts.

"John Terrance," Knowles said instantly.

"Maybe." Kateri believed it less and less. "But according to Bertha, she filled him full of buckshot, and according to Mrs. Blethyn, he was hurting pretty badly when she removed it.

She was worried about him, thought he needed antibiotics and he wouldn't be able to get them."

"Poor guy!" Knowles said sarcastically.

No use popping back at him. Knowles was a good officer and right now she needed every one she had. "I'm saying if this woman knew karate and was capable of defending herself, John Terrance might not be able to handle it."

Chippen came back out of the bushes, his complexion tinged with green. "Maybe Terrance has picked up a partner."

"I think whoever is doing this has got to be an out-of-towner," Knowles said. "It doesn't seem as if someone local could have hidden this perversion for long."

"It's summer, and as Councilman Venegra has kindly pointed out, we're coming into our busiest tourist time of the year." Kateri sighed. "So that doesn't eliminate very many people."

"If it's a tourist, it has to be someone who summers over." Mike consulted his files. "The first slashing was a week ago."

"The first slashing that we *know of*," Bergen said. "If Mrs. Glass hadn't called this in and Weston hadn't wanted to come out and if we hadn't seen the buzzards . . ."

"Right." Kateri didn't even want to consider that. "Listen to this. Which probably means nothing. But tonight at quilting, I was watching this woman—tourist, older, Elsa Cipre—use a rotary cutter. She was whipping that thing along a straight edge, cutting material. I was looking at her in a new way. Then her husband showed up. He grabbed her and dragged her out of there. She was afraid of him, and I was thinking—"

"A rotary cutter?" Mike Sun made a note, then looked delighted when Kateri pulled it out of her pocket and handed it to him.

"Be careful." She showed him her bandaged finger. "It really is sharp."

He twirled it. "Promising . . ."

"Know anything about this Cipre guy?" Bergen asked.

"He's a college professor," Kateri said. "So's she, or was. She doesn't teach anymore."

"I know, I know, all abusive husbands are scum, blah, blah," Chippen said, "but that doesn't mean Cipre is the killer. Not any more than the next guy."

Kateri viewed Chippen in a new light. "No. But he's a big guy, strong if the way he hauled her out is any indication, and his wife could have taught him everything she knows about . . . cutters."

The guys were unconvinced.

Officer Ed Legbrandt came puffing up the hill, followed by Ernie Fitzwater.

"At least let's keep an eye on the Good Knight Manor Bed and Breakfast," Kateri said.

"What are you thinking?" Bergen asked.

"I'm thinking my friend Merida Falcon is

staying there and got a threatening phone call. Susie worked there and she's dead. Phoebe Glass, the proprietress, is new to Virtue Falls. Dawkins Cipre and his wife are staying there." It sounded worse when Kateri said it out loud.

Sean Weston stood up. "It is sort of the center of the vortex."

"Don't forget your sister's there," Moen said.

Kateri sighed. "I only wish I could."

General, subdued laughter across the site.

Moen bent down and picked something up and examined it.

Kateri prepared to make the hike down the hill. "Pardon me, gentlemen, I'm going to call Garik and fill him in on this one, then we're going to hold a press conference if anybody would like to stand behind me for support."

General head shaking.

"Bergen, you stand behind me on the right. Moen, you stand behind me on the left."

"No, Sheriff Kwinault."

Kateri turned to Moen. "What?"

Moen advanced toward Mike Sun and offered him something from the palm of his hand.

Sun let out a huff of air, dug in his bag, pulled out a pair of tweezers and lifted the little black piece of—"It's a piece of skin. It's a fingertip. I think we can pull a print off this. Sonofabitch, Moen, you just saved the case!"

"Good for me." Moen wiped his hand on his

trousers. "I'm done with law enforcement. I thought I could do it. And I can. I can drive and fill out reports and arrest citizens for drunk driving. I can handle accidental shootings and bar fights and traffic deaths. But I can't do"—he gestured at the body bag—"this."

The officers got quiet. They understood the difference, nobody better.

Kateri asked, "What are you going to do, Moen?"

"I'm going to school, get better at graphics, get some kind of job in the field. Maybe go to Japan. I've been studying the language. I want to get my graphic novels published." Moen looked at his palm and wiped his hand again. "No matter what, I'm done with police work."

Bergen handed him a wet-wipe pack. "What about your father?"

"He'll have to be disappointed in me." Moen cleaned his hand, and cleaned, and cleaned. "I'm done. Sheriff, can I leave or do you want me to work my two weeks' notice?"

Kateri almost gave him a pass and said he could go. Then she remembered—slashings, John Terrance, the Fourth of July . . . "Moen. If you would stay for the two weeks. We'll make sure you stick with traffic violations and intoxication and littering. I'll get someone else to stand behind me at the press conference."

"Thank you, Sheriff." Moen took off his hat and

held it, and looked at Kateri. "It's been a privilege to work with you, ma'am, and I was wrong when I said you were too old to be interested in sex." He put on his hat and started down the hill.

The officers who were left fought back grins.

Kateri sighed. "He was doing so well. Then he had to add that last bit."

Bergen sobered. "I hate to see him go. But we always knew he didn't have the stomach for it."

"Smart kid," Chippen said. "He's getting out while he can."

That was the trouble with crimes like these—they took the heart out of the whole department. Kateri asked, "Knowles, about the press conference, would you stand behind me on the left side?"

"Sure, Sheriff." Knowles touched his hat brim. "When the citizens start lobbing the tomatoes, I'll even throw them back."

CHAPTER FORTY

"Sheriff. Kateri!"

Kateri lifted her head off her desk and blinked at Bergen.

He pointed at the blinking light on her phone. "Call for you from Garik Jacobsen."

"Right." She looked at the time. Just after midnight. She cleared her throat, picked up the phone and said, "Tell me again we don't have an unusual spike of slashings in the U.S."

Garik's voice sounded grim. "Virtue Falls has always been an overachiever. The photos you sent . . ."

"I know." She had tried not to look at the pictures of the faceless corpse, but a few glimpses would suffice to give her nightmares forever . . . and strengthened her determination to catch this sadistic bastard.

"The FBI will send someone to coordinate with your law enforcement."

"You?"

"I've requested to be sent."

"How soon?"

"Tomorrow." He must have checked the time. "Today."

"Are Elizabeth and the baby coming down?"

"Tomorrow Elizabeth has to give a seminar on

tsunamis. Because, you know, she took the Virtue Falls tsunami video right after the earthquake and since then, she is *the* geological expert for the area." He exhaled as if he had explained this far too many times. "Kateri, the *baby* is five—"

"Good Lord." Kateri couldn't believe it. "Since when?"

"We took Bella to the flight museum *one time* and now she loves airplanes. That *baby* can tell me what kind of plane is overhead, and if I watch a war movie she calls out the name, the class, the . . . whatever. Bella will be a pilot."

Kateri remembered how much Merry Byrd had wanted to fly, the way her face used to shine when she talked about soaring toward the heavens, and she imagined little Bella wearing that expression, too. "Smart kid. You must be proud."

"I am. I didn't think I'd be her dumb ol' dad until she was a teenager, but it appears I was wrong."

Kateri laughed, then sobered. "You didn't want her to be an expert in serial killers, did you?"

"No. God. No. I'm putting my bag in the car right now."

"We'll be here."

"You sound like you need some sleep."

"I think I just got some."

"Get more. See you later." He hung up.

Bergen lingered by the door. She filled him in. "I'm glad he's coming. He's probably the one person who can reassure the citizens and get Venegra off my back."

The press conference had not gone well. Neither had her meeting with the city council.

Bergen said, "You really ought to go home."

She *looked* at him.

"I know. Paperwork. I'm going to go sleep on the love seat in the break room. It's uncomfortable enough that I can't sleep long."

"I'll wake you if we need you."

"I know you will." He staggered a little as he left.

She had been asleep long enough for her screen saver to be activated, but not long enough for everything to automatically shut down. She watched the series of cute baby animals roll across the screen—after today, she *needed* to see cute baby animals—and contemplated the interview she had done for the *Virtue Falls Herald*. It probably needed a final read before she pressed Send. She probably needed to add some warm fuzzy assurances to the frightened public. She would have already done it, but right now, she didn't have any warm fuzzy assurances in her arsenal. She was as frightened as anybody; Virtue Falls had a monster in their midst and if—when—he killed again, it would be her fault. She was in charge. The buck stopped only one place. Here.

She located the cursor and typed a few words,

deleted, typed, deleted. She needed to figure this out . . .

She wasn't surprised when she dreamed. After today, she expected one nightmare after another. Not to find herself in Rainbow's hospital room.

Dr. Watchman was a friend, a veterinarian, a Native American, a wise woman. She stood beside the bed, eyes closed, breathing deeply, holding Rainbow's hand. In a faraway voice, she said, "Her soul is wandering in a far, cold place, and the further she goes, the harder it is for her to find her way back."

Kateri moved to the side of the bed. "Maybe she doesn't want to come back."

Dr. Watchman's eyes snapped open. "If she didn't want to come back, Kateri Kwinault, she would already be gone from the home that has nurtured her."

Kateri picked up Rainbow's other hand and cradled it in both of hers. "She's gone so far I can't see her."

"I can."

"I don't know what to do, how to bring her back."

"Yes, you do. You're afraid."

Now Kateri closed her eyes.

"What do you want to live with your whole life, Kateri Kwinault? Your failure to rescue your friend or your cowardice and failure to try?"

Kateri gave a dry, hard sob.

"Make up your mind. And take action now. Time is running out."

Kateri's eyes snapped open. She lifted her head from her desk. She stood and walked into the break room.

Bergen woke with that wide-eyed, *I'm alert!* expression. "What's happening?"

"Nothing."

"Damn it."

"That being the case, do you think law enforcement can do without me tonight?"

It took a moment for him to assimilate her question, work himself into an upright position and examine her as if she'd lost her mind. "Sleep deprivation getting to you?"

"Even worse. I'm going to talk to the frog god."

A startled moment of silence, then Bergen laughed aloud. "I wish you wouldn't joke about that. It scares the hell out of us Scandinavian boys."

If you only knew . . . "You scare easy. So you'll cover for me?"

Bergen's voice sobered. "The only thing that we'll call you for is if we spot John Terrance or . . . or whoever is killing the women."

"I'm headed to Grenouille Beach." The beach where she had been born. "I'm going to dump my phone for the night. If you want me, send someone. Otherwise . . . talk to you in the morning." As she turned away, she muttered, "If I'm alive, still have a mind and am in one piece . . ." She turned back. "Oh! Can I borrow your car?"

For this ceremony, Kateri thought she should be wearing the garments of an Indian warrior maiden, fringed buckskin and beading. But she didn't own the outfit—among her coastal tribe, it had never existed—so she dressed in the outfit she felt most at home in: jeans, T-shirt and flip-flops. She needed a gift, an offering . . . she headed to the Gem Lounge. It was, predictably, crowded, and as she wended her way through the small tables she was glad she'd come in. Press conferences were official; this was her moment to speak to locals and tourists, one-on-one, reinforce her request that no one walk home alone, reassure them that law enforcement was out there and get a little reassurance herself. They looked to her for protection, and they hadn't given up on her yet. By the time she got to the bar, that terrible feeling of failure had faded, leaving her with merely the abject fear of what she was doing next.

Bertha sat on a stool against the back wall, holding her sawed-off shotgun and telling handsome young Jeffrey Jerome Porter how to mix drinks.

Kateri quelled the urge to ask JJ for his ID. He didn't look old enough to be in a bar, much less to be learning the trade. But Kateri had noticed that for every day she got older, twenty-one-year-olds looked more youthful.

"Honey! Sheriff. Good to see you here." Bertha grinned at her. "The usual?"

"I don't think so. If I drink a hot chocolate, I'll throw up." Kateri leaned across the bar and said quietly, "I'm going to see the frog god."

Bertha nodded. " 'Bout time."

"Can I get your best bottle of ruby port? For no reason I know, I think the frog god would like port."

"You bet. JJ, reach up there on the top shelf and get me the Bella Terra Nonna Ruby Port."

While he climbed up on the ladder, all the women in the bar turned for the view.

Bertha said to Kateri, "That's why I hired him. So I could watch him climb that ladder. Makes me wish I kept more stuff up top." She tapped her hip. "See how good I am about staying off my feet?"

"I'm impressed." Kateri was; as busy as Bertha liked to be, she imagined sitting and watching must be killing her. "What does the doctor say about that hip?"

"It's healing good. With any luck, I'll avoid surgery. Any word of John Terrance?"

"Not a peep."

Bertha rubbed the barrel of her sawed-off shotgun. "When I fill a man's ass with buckshot, it stays filled." She looked at the deep gash on her bar top where Terrance's machete had landed. "I hope he dies a miserable, festering death in the wild."

"It would be impolitic for me to agree," Kateri said.

"But you do. Thank you, JJ." Bertha used her sleeve to dust the bottle. "I've been saving this for a special occasion. I guess we just found that occasion."

"How much do I owe you?" Kateri asked.

"If I can help with Rainbow's recovery, that's the payment I'm looking for. Hell, if I thought it would do any good, I'd get up on the bar and do a frog god dance for her." Bertha threw Kateri a kiss. "You take care."

"I will." Which was absolutely not true. No sensible person would do what she was doing. But sometimes sensible took a backseat to love and gratitude.

As she drove the winding highway, the stars twinkled, indifferent, cold and white in the black night sky. As she got close to Grenouille Beach, she slowed way down and still almost missed it. She made a late turn, drove down the narrow paved road, parked in the deserted lot and took a fortifying breath. Stashed her pistol, her radio and her cell phone under the seat. She got out and took another deep breath: the air filled her lungs with salt and the memory of cutting through the storm with a Coast Guard vessel beneath her.

How she had loved that sensation of freedom from earthly concerns, of flying without wings! The blessed freedom was what drew her to the ocean, to a career in the Coast Guard. She knew there was danger in the violence of the waves. Of course. She had thought of drowning. It was, after all, the single most common fate of unlucky sailors everywhere. But she'd had no fear. She had considered how she would swim to shore or to another vessel, if that was possible, and if not, she would breathe in the salt water and make a swift, brave end of it.

How could she ever have imagined the earth-quake, the tsunami, the duty that drove her and the horror that broke her?

Kateri Kwinault, the child who used to play in the waves, run on the sand, sing mocking songs to the legendary gods . . . now trembled with fear.

CHAPTER FORTY-ONE

Bottle in her fist, Kateri took the path to the beach. A kind of weird twilight lit her way on a twisting, turning path over the dunes to the frigid ocean. The wind blew off the Pacific, rearranging the dunes like a fussy housekeeper. The long beach was eerily empty. She hustled to get settled before dawn arrived and work consumed her once more. At that line where the land turned to sand, she removed her flip-flops and walked barefoot. There, where at high tide the waves met the shore, she seated herself, crossed her legs, made her hands loose, closed her eyes and tried to find her way into the frog god's presence.

At the sound of the first wave crashing and rolling, her fear roiled within her, her eyes sprang open and she couldn't *not* look.

When she remembered how much she used to love this place, knowing that here Rainbow and her mother had labored to bring her into the world, knowing that she had drawn her first breath here, she wanted to weep.

For so long, she had avoided contact with this beach—any beach—sand, waves, ocean. Frankly, a dense fog gave her the creeps. If she had wanted to speak to the frog god, to demand answers, she did so from the highest cliff away from any immediate danger . . . but always she had known if the frog god wanted her, he could crack the earth open and take her.

He had taken her once before; he tore her from the wheelhouse of her cutter, broke her every bone and joint and sucked her into the deep. There she came face-to-face with a legend of power and terror . . . the frog god. Mottled, slimy, slick skin; a pleased green smile; fronds of seaweed for his cushion; large, black, glassy eyes and long green fingers that plucked her up, examined her, thrust her into his mouth and swallowed her.

After that, there was only terror and pain, struggling and being unwillingly bound to a will and a strength that were not her own. Then rebirth into a new Kateri. She had been broken and rebuilt by pain, struggle and anguish. Now she shared his powers.

She could make the earth shake.

She could make the waters rise.

She didn't want those powers; when she used them, she became less human, and each time she didn't know if she could find her way back to humanity. But knowing she could change the course of events, right wrongs, serve justice— that was a constant temptation, and she knew her resistance displeased the frog god.

Now she went to him in abject supplication to wholeheartedly offer herself.

As she gazed across the midnight sea, the full

moon rose in all its splendor and laid a white path across the roiled waters leading her to eternity.

It was a sight she'd never seen before . . . because she faced west across the Pacific, and the moon did not rise in the west. "Oh." She was on a metaphysical beach. Or maybe metaphorical. Whatever it was, the frog god had brought her here so they could speak. She lifted the bottle. She spoke. "I have a gift for you. I think you'll like it."

The wave rolled to her knees and retreated, rolled to her knees, paused and retreated. She placed the bottle in the sand. The wave rolled to her knees, captured the bottle and sucked it into the depths.

He was listening. Foolish of her to doubt it.

"I come in supplication. I wish to bring life to my friend Rainbow. You remember her. She delivered me. She has stood by me steadfastly through many trials. She always loved nature, loved the sea, and she believed me when I said you had taken me. She believed me. That counts for something, doesn't it? She was hurt because of me, and she deserves life. I would give my own life for hers." Kateri stretched out her arms to the ocean and waited.

The waves kept rolling, in and out, ceaseless and uncaring.

"Rainbow is dying. There have been times in the past when you let me bring someone back from the brink. Lacey. You let me save Lacey. I thank you for that gift. She is dear and wonderful. This time, with Rainbow, the situation is more delicate and I need—"

A wave rose high, crashed hard, rolled up the beach to touch her toes. And retreated.

"Okay. You know why I need help. I know for this large favor, I owe a sacrifice beyond even a bottle of port. Really good port. Expensive port. Bertha said so and you know Bertha knows her liquors."

The ocean sloshed and somehow managed to look bored.

Hastily Kateri added, "I've wondered what might please you. Do you want me to serve you and you alone? I can quit the job of sheriff and become a hermit and be your devoted servant, trying always to do as you wish."

A wave crashed again, rolled toward her . . .

Before it could touch her, she said, "But I would like to say I believe that would be a mistake. I'm a damned good sheriff and as a representative of the Native Americans, I impress the citizens, no matter how reluctant they are, and the media."

The wave retreated.

Telling the frog god *that* was probably a mistake.

"I can sacrifice other things of importance to me. What would you wish? I can give you chastity, should you demand it. If you wish me to be a chaste vessel dedicated only to you, I will do so. Stag isn't speaking to me anyway. I don't believe you give a damn about my body or you would have kept it in the first place. But I have to offer it. It's traditional."

Bored ocean. Again.

She said, "I can sacrifice my ambitions. Perhaps my emotions. My loves, my hates."

More waves, sloshing back and forth, back and forth.

"You can't have my dog," she said definitively.

More waves. More sloshing.

"I can sacrifice my . . . I don't know. My grudges?"

Far out at the edge of the inlet, a wave rose, silent, menacing, glistening with moonlight.

"My grudges? My grudge against . . . my baggage? My . . ." Oh, God. Here on the edge of the continent where she'd been born to a woman broken from her lover's betrayal, Kateri had to forgive the man who had taken her mother's heart and ripped it like tissue. "You want me to forgive my father." The wave climbed higher. She stood up. She shouted, "What difference does it make? He's dead. Even if he wasn't, my judgment meant nothing to him. No one meant anything to him. All he cared about was duty, success, being untouched by scandal. Why would you even care whether I forgive him?"

The frog god didn't answer. Except that wave crashed and retreated.

But she heard the sound of Rainbow's voice in her head saying what she had said so many times before: *Your baggage is weighing you down. Forgive him. Forgive your whole family. You think they care what you feel? You're carrying around a grudge all the time and they're out dancing at a party. Let it go.*

The grudge against her father had been a part of Kateri for so long. Like a bad habit, she was used to it. It was ingrained in her, with tentacles in every dark crevasse of her soul, and to dig it out would take concentration and effort.

She sighed. She sat down and shut her eyes.

Why not? If she was on a beach created of rubble from the frog god's imagination, watching for him would do her no good. Probably never had.

She tried to find her hatred to rip it out. She couldn't quite grasp it. Something about it was slippery, slimy, like a well-told lie. In her mind, she caught a glimpse of the frog god, implacable, impatient, disdainful. "Look," she said, "I'm doing the best I can, and if this isn't what you wanted, I don't know what it is."

The disdain flared brighter.

She opened her eyes.

A wall of water reared itself off the sand in front of her and, before she could move, slammed down on her.

CHAPTER FORTY-TWO

Kateri rolled, over and over, clawing at the sand, unable to tell up from down, salt in her mouth, water in her throat. She choked, cried. The water grew frothy; she reached up a hand into the air— and irrevocably, the wave sucked her toward the ocean, tumbling her like a rock that needed polishing. She fought, maddened with fear, afraid to go to the depths again, to see the frog god gloating over her return.

She had to get out. She had to go up. She needed to breathe, to be human, to be alive and part of the earth. Yet the current pulled her along the pale moonlit path and she kept sinking, sinking, into waters black and thick as memory.

Fourteen-year-old Kateri walked down the narrow wooded dirt lane. She had hitchhiked and hopped trains and walked and worked and rode buses from Baltimore to Virtue Falls. Now . . . she was almost home. Home. To her mother. Home. Where someone loved her. Home . . . In the twilight, she spotted the trailer house, the white metal siding dented by hail, the sloped roof covered in moss. She broke into a run, leaped up the listing porch steps. She grabbed the loose doorknob, jiggled it frantically until the metal door opened, raced into the living room and dropped her backpack. "Mama, I'm home!"

Faded flowered sheets covered the windows, letting in only the feeblest of light. Yet Kateri could find her way in the dark. This was the place where she belonged. Nothing had changed. Nothing . . . the stench hit her first. She remembered the smells. Mildew. Sweat. Spilled beer. Vomit. Rancid bacon. "Mama?"

A faint moan came from the couch.

Kateri turned, hurried toward the sound, knelt beside the short, skinny, half-clothed body resting on the sagging cushions. Kateri ran her hand over Mary's feverish forehead, felt the skeletal shape of her shoulders.

The worst of the smells emanated from Mary.

But her mother was still alive. Mary's cancer had brought Kateri's father and delivered Kateri into hell, yet it had not killed Mary. That knowledge had been what kept Kateri moving across country, facing hardship, attempted rape, hungry days and cold nights. Cancer had not killed Mary, and Kateri could be with her again. Leaning close, Kateri hugged the limp body. "Mama, I'm home."

Mary struggled a little, moaning slightly; Kateri felt as if she hugged a skeleton held together by thin, fragile, old skin.

Mary was only thirty-two.

"Mama?"

Rainbow's quiet voice spoke from the sagging easy chair against the opposite wall. "Her remission is over. She's dying."

Kateri turned to face the shadowy form. "She's . . . drunk."

"Yes. She said she didn't have enough money for food and drink, and she'd rather drink."

"You let her?"

Rainbow chuckled, a dry, pained sound. "Let her? Kateri Kwinault, you have been gone five years. Do you remember your mother? Did anyone ever change her mind about anything? We warned her about your father, but she would have him, and he broke her heart. We told her to take you away, to take the money the government offered and get an education and make a life for herself and you. She would not leave Virtue Falls. She set her mind to this death; she will die from cancer and starvation, and she will die drunk. Hopefully the liquor will at least dull the pain."

Wet seeped into the knees of Kateri's jeans; she didn't want to know what it was. "But I'm home."

"I know, dear." Rainbow's voice was gentle. "She's not dead yet. She'll wake in the morning, and she'll be happy to see you." She sighed and stood, hauling her big-boned form out of the broken easy chair. "Since you're here, I'll take the night off and sleep. I'm tired, Kateri. Tired of watching and weeping alone."

"Did she get my letters?"

"She did. She loves those letters. She reads and rereads them. She quotes them. She says you're funny. She says you're smart. She knows that you love her, and she talks about how she loves you."

Hostility rose in Kateri, unwelcome and unconfessed. "If she loves me so much, why didn't she ever write me back?"

Rainbow walked over to Kateri, cupped her cheeks in her hands and kissed her forehead. "She loves you. She cries for you every day. In the difficult times ahead, never doubt that."

Now Kateri was dying, again, in the depths while a pair of large, black, glassy eyes watched her . . .

She had to get rid of this weight. She had to . . . in an instant, she offloaded it all: the hatred of her father, the hatred of her mother . . .

No. No. *No!* She didn't hate her mother. She had never hated her mother. It was *her father's* fault Mary became an alcoholic, unable to care for her only daughter, riffling through garbage cans, singing loudly at the night, falling down, making her body available to any man who would buy her a drink.

The humiliation. The mocking laughter. The fights Kateri had fought defending her mother's honor, an honor Mary had not cared about . . . the pain, physical and mental. Knowing that her mother didn't love Kateri enough to leave the liquor behind and make a decent life for them both.

There in the deep places of the ocean, Kateri cried salt tears for herself; for her mother; for her father; for the secret, shamed relief she had felt when he came and took her from Mary and into his home, into a place that was clean and normal.

It wasn't her father she hated. Or even her mother.

It was herself for an unwilling betrayal and condemnation of loving, weak-willed Mary.

Fine. Kateri had faced her reflection and seen

the truth. If that was what the frog god wanted, he could have all that.

She was here for a different reason. She was here for Rainbow. Reaching out to the frog god, she silently implored, *Allow me to save Rainbow.*

The large, black, glassy eyes blinked out.

The wave blasted her onto the shore, scraping her cheek on the sand, then pulled away, leaving her gasping and sputtering.

"Hey, lady, didn't anybody ever tell you not to swim alone?" Someone put his hand under her elbow and pulled her to her feet.

She blinked into the face of a teenage boy. He looked both disgusted and concerned. "You okay?"

She stared around the beach.

Early morning sunlight shone on the sand. A few beachcombers strolled down the way, buckets in hand, picking up shells, driftwood, glass floats, anything the waves tossed up. A fire smoldered in a fire pit while all around it, people slept in bags or stood and stretched, or poured water into a pot for coffee. Had they spent the night?

"What day is this?" The empty bottle of port rolled up beside her.

"You must have been on quite a bender. It's Friday." The kid pulled a big strand of deep green, sticky seaweed off Kateri's back and clarified, "Morning."

So she'd spent the night in the depths being sloshed around like laundry in a washer. "Thanks. Now I've got to get going!" She had to see Rainbow while the magic was fresh.

CHAPTER FORTY-THREE

In the still hospital room, Kateri stood over Rainbow and stroked her forehead. Leaning close, she breathed in Rainbow's faint exhalation, then blew her own breath into Rainbow's space. "Rainbow," she whispered. "Listen to me. I went to see the frog god. He made me leave my baggage with him. In exchange for that, my breath is pure. Rainbow, this is your chance to find life again." Again Kateri breathed in Rainbow's breath, then breathed out toward Rainbow's face. "I've been hurt in great ways, and sometimes the pain of recovery is unbearable. But Rainbow, to see the dawn break across the mountains, to smell the pines, to feel alone as if no man has ever stood on this place. I don't know why the frog god cared enough to demand my baggage . . ."

Rainbow's rough, long-unused voice whispered, "Maybe the first time when the frog god consumed you, he didn't like the taste of bitter."

Kateri sighed with relief and at the same time laughed out loud. She said, "Maybe not, Rainbow. Maybe not."

Rainbow opened her eyes and smiled weakly at Kateri. "Your sister was here."

That made Kateri stagger back from the bed. "That bitch! When?"

"I don't know *when*. She asked about the box."

"You could hear her?"

"Heard everything." Rainbow took a long breath. "Couldn't speak. Couldn't move. Wouldn't have told her anyway. But the box . . . is with Margaret."

"Of course!" Kateri felt like slapping her own forehead. Who else would Rainbow trust with the box? Only Margaret Smith, Garik's stepmother and the woman who had run Virtue Falls Resort for more than eighty years.

Rainbow nodded. "You're welcome." She fell asleep with a sigh.

Kateri reached for the call button.

Before she could push it, the door burst open. Peggy hustled in and headed for her patient. She checked the machines, took Rainbow's pulse, lifted her eyelid.

Rainbow opened both eyes. "Do you mind? I'm trying to sleep here."

Peggy burst into tears.

Kateri gave her a hug and a box of tissues and headed toward the Virtue Falls Resort.

Margaret opened her bedroom closet and pointed. "There it is, dear."

Kateri put down her walking stick, reached up to the top shelf and lifted the large, weighty, textured black box.

"You tall girls are so lucky." Margaret had always been a tiny woman, and age had deprived her of inches and agility.

"Thank you for keeping the box." Kateri weighed it in her hand. The raven was heavy. The album was, in her mind, heavier.

"I was glad to do it." Margaret pushed her walker into her sitting room—her suite at the Virtue Falls Resort was both homey and luxurious—and over to her easy chair. She operated the mechanics that lifted the seat, then sank down onto it and lowered it once more. "Rainbow told me you'd come for the box."

"I had to wait until she told me where it was."

Margaret put her palms together. "Her recovery is the miracle I've been praying for."

"Me, too." Although Margaret used a rosary. Kateri went swimming.

"She'll recover completely?"

Kateri searched her mind for the answer. "Yes. She'll be changed, of course. Near death will do that to a person."

"I wouldn't know. I've never been near death." Margaret cackled drily.

A little of the frog god's vision still clung to Kateri, and she used it to examine the tiny, thin woman who unflinchingly stared one hundred years of age in the face. "Margaret, you've got one more grand adventure in you before the end."

Margaret broke into a smile, and her wisp of an

Irish accent strengthened. "Do I? That's a good thing to hear. What are you going to do with the box?"

"I'm torn between giving it to my sister immediately and getting her the hell out of town, or keeping it to frustrate her." Kateri thought of Lilith and having to deal with her constant criticism and said, "I'll give it to her."

"Not without looking to see what is in that box that she so desperately wants?"

"She says it's the raven."

"Is it?" Margaret lifted the receiver on her phone. "Shall I call down for tea, dear?"

"I can't stay." Kateri considered the bright-eyed old woman. "How do you know about my sister?"

"Did you think that the discovery you had a sister wouldn't set the cat among the pigeons? Gossip and speculation, my dear. The lifeblood of any small town. And of course where else could she find a meal even close to the quality she deserves, except at Virtue Falls Resort." Margaret's mouth was puckered.

"Oh, no." That sounded exactly like the kind of compliment Lilith would give. "She's been here."

"Charming woman," Margaret said with patent insincerity. "Tea?"

"I really shouldn't stay. Terrible things are happening."

"Terrible things are always happening. All the

more reason for a fortifying cup of tea." Margaret coaxed, "Cook prepared cream scones today to go with our clotted cream and fresh blueberry preserves."

Kateri was in uniform. She had her cell phone and her radio. Right now, Garik was working with Mike Sun to recover the owner of that fingerprint and her guys were patrolling the roads, making their presence known. "Tea sounds lovely." She placed the box on the floor by the chair opposite Margaret and leaned her staff against it. "But I may have to leave at a moment's notice."

"I remember. When Garik was sheriff, he was always running off to save the world." Margaret called down and ordered. "Don't you have any curiosity? *I'd* love to know what's in that box."

Kateri seated herself. "It's something about my parents, and all my knowledge of them has proved . . . painful."

"Yes, dear, I understand that. But your sister isn't asking merely for the raven. She wants the *box*. There's something of value in the *box*. A truth that's been proven to me time and again over my long years—with the relatives it's a good idea to assume the worst, and if you're wrong . . . well, what a lovely surprise."

Kateri laughed. "I'm glad to hear I'm not the only one with a difficult family."

"There are no functional families," Margaret said firmly.

"My God! Bergen said that exact thing to me not long ago!"

"It's a well-known wisdom."

One of Margaret's room-service servers knocked on the open door.

"Ah! There's our tea," Margaret said. "How are your ribs?"

Surprised, Kateri poked at them with her finger. After being tumbled around in the ocean all night, she would have thought the scab would have broken open. Instead, she had . . . no pain. "They're fine. Apparently the frog god doesn't approve of injuries he didn't inflict. Although actually"—she moved her hips—"everything is feeling better. Perhaps I'll stop carrying my walking stick."

Margaret peered at her. "And perhaps not."

Kateri rubbed the smooth walnut on her staff. "Yes, it does make a handy weapon."

"More important, it makes people underestimate you." Margaret smiled. "As tiny as I am and have always been, I find it's quite the advantage to be underestimated. I imagine in the town's first female sheriff, it's a gift."

CHAPTER FORTY-FOUR

That evening, Merida held her hoodie close around her face, looked up and down the empty street, and watched for movement anywhere—on the lawns, at the windows.

Nothing.

She slipped through the hedge and made her way over the dry, stubbled lawn and up the broken concrete walk to the porch. Every time she came here, the house gave Merida the creeps. But something was wrong and she feared . . .

At times like these, she most missed her voice. If she could, she would stand out here and call his name.

Instead she stepped up to the door and knocked.

No answer.

That meant nothing. He might be out . . .

But why hadn't he called her last night, ordered her to come over? Why wasn't he answering her texts? Since the news about the slashing, her worry had grown.

She gave the door a push and with a rusty creak, it opened.

The foyer was dark, but at the back of the house, she saw a light.

He never would leave a light on, a light that would betray his presence . . . she swallowed hard and tiptoed across the floor, glancing at every shadow, fearing every sound.

The kitchen. The light was in the kitchen. Not much of a light; it was dim and growing dimmer. A flashlight, set on the table at the precise angle to illuminate—Carl Klineman, sprawled on the floor, his arms flung out and his body skewed sideways while pools of dark blood congealed underneath it.

Remember, Helen, you cannot scream.

But she tried.

She clutched her throat and made herself stop straining to produce a sound to express her horror. Even if she could . . . she should not betray her presence by any sound.

Flies buzzed. The body . . . smelled.

She turned to leave, to flee.

But Carl's head was turned toward her, his dark eyes were open and staring, his finger, smeared with blood, had . . . had written something on the floor.

She crept closer. She read what he had written.

Then she heard a noise behind her, whipped around and threw a turning side kick at the man who loomed in the doorway.

The kick never landed.

Benedict Howard blocked her, grabbed her wrist, brought her close and said, "What are you doing here?" He looked beyond her. "And what have you done?"

"Come on." Benedict unlocked the door to the carriage house. "Come in here."

She shook her head. Her face was swollen, her eyes were red and she couldn't breathe from crying so hard. She wiped her nose on the sleeve of her hoodie.

Still she looked gorgeous to him. "You don't want to go in the house, to your rooms. You don't want anyone to see you now."

His porch light illuminated her as she signed, "I can't come in. I need locks on the door. My locks." She looked toward her car. "I should leave, drive away, never come back."

He couldn't let her leave. "Will you be safe if you do that?"

She shook her head. Shook her head again.

"All right. We'll go to your rooms. But there will be people around so don't"—he pulled out his handkerchief and blotted her face—"don't cry. Eyes straight ahead. Walk." Putting his arm around her waist, he walked her through the back door.

In the kitchen, they saw Phoebe.

Benedict said hello.

Phoebe asked what was wrong.

He said Merida had fallen and cut herself.

Phoebe asked if there was anything she could do, asked if they needed a Band-Aid, advised them to go to the hospital and get stitches.

He thanked her. They walked on.

In the entry, they spotted the newlyweds heading up the stairs to their room.

Benedict gave them a hearty, encouraging, go-for-it wave and a smile.

Merida pulled up her hoodie and furtively searched her pocket.

She couldn't have looked more guilty.

Benedict took her key and unlocked the door, then asked, "What's the code?"

She didn't hesitate; she told him and he took that as a sign of trust, the first he'd seen from her. After he had entered the code, she used her thumbprint to get them through the final security device.

He opened the door and held it for her.

She walked in and collapsed on the ottoman in front of the leather easy chair. "I didn't do it," she signed.

"I know." When he had verified the identity of the corpse, everything had changed. They were in trouble.

"I found him . . . dead." Her fingers trembled violently.

"I know," Benedict said again. He locked the door behind them, and not just so she'd feel a sense of security. Finding that body next door had thoroughly spooked him. Add that to the murders around town and the discrepancies in his business accounts, and he suddenly felt as if he were playing the lead in a horror movie. And this room: a long dining table flanked by weapons on the wall, by rows of empty, iron-clad suits of armor . . . at least he hoped they were empty. He didn't believe in coincidences, and he didn't like the number of corpses piling up around them.

"I'm going to check the other rooms." He walked into the next room, up the stairs, through the bedrooms and bathrooms, making sure every lock was secure, noting how she had augmented the safety measures in every room.

True, she was the widow of a wealthy man. But this was excessive, a special paranoia. And he was afraid he knew why.

As he came back into the dining room, he stomped and coughed so she wasn't startled.

He found her with her head in her hands, silently crying, rocking back and forth. "Everything is secure," he told her. Using his cell phone, he made a call to the police. "There's a body in the abandoned house on Mariana Avenue." He hung up, fast, for all the good it would do him.

A light knock on her office door. "Kateri."

Kateri looked up from the paperwork, saw the expression on Bergen's face and said, "You have got to be shitting me. Another one?"

Getting a bottle of water out of the little refrigerator, Benedict sat on the floor in front of Merida and offered it to her. "The police will trace the call, but that's not going to be the first thing on their agenda. At least, I hope not, because this makes me the prime suspect."

She pointed to herself.

"Yes, you, too." He watched her, grim-faced. "That body was Carl Klineman, Nauplius's bodyguard."

She took the bottle of water. She nodded.

"Explain to me what he was doing in Virtue Falls."

Merida was still crying, but she could sign. "He, uh . . . I was running one day and he pulled me through the hedge."

Benedict ran his finger down his own face, indicating he remembered the scratch.

Merida gestured, agitated, trying to convey the words. "Yes. That. He followed me here. He had rented that place."

"Because it was next door to the B and B?"

Merida pressed her finger to her nose. She signed, "He said . . . he said he always wanted to protect me, but my husband . . . Carl said he loved me. He said my husband . . ." Merida tried to open the bottle. Tried again. Couldn't break the seal.

Benedict took it from her, opened the top. "Look. I'm not without sympathy. But damn it, you used me."

Merida started to protest.

He pushed her hands down. "You used me to help keep you safe. Did you think I didn't realize that? Then, although I gave you every opportunity, you never confided in me. You kept vital information from me."

Merida took the bottle and drank.

God, the woman had a way of ignoring what she didn't want to address. She maddened him, and he wouldn't have it. "What did Carl say about your husband?"

She took a last sip of water. "Nauplius was abusive. Jealous. He used to tie my hands so I couldn't speak." Throwing back her head, she laughed without sound. "I'm actually quite good at getting out of any kind of binding." She stopped laughing so suddenly, Benedict chilled at the transformation. With slow, careful gestures, she said, "It's a skill set I wish I'd never had to learn."

He repeated his question. "What did Carl tell you about your husband?"

"Carl said in that last year, he took Nauplius to the doctor for tests, he didn't know for what. But when Nauplius came out, he was mad and he was scared, so Carl poked around in his medical records." Her signing increased in speed.

In the last few days, Benedict had learned a lot. He kept up.

She continued, "Nauplius had received the diagnosis that he was likely to die suddenly, and soon. What scared Carl then was—Nauplius started investigating killers. Carl knew how Nauplius felt about me, that I was his creation."

"How were you his creation? Is the story that you were a beautiful orphaned daughter of missionaries untrue?"

Merida looked at him, head cocked, eyes narrowed.

"I suspected," he said, "when I could find no one who remembered you or your parents in Nepal, or your aunt and uncle in the south."

"You investigated me?"

"I proved who you were not. I never discovered who you were."

She sat back and viewed him as if trying to see the real man.

Uncomfortable; he sometimes thought he didn't know the real man, that he had allowed his aunt and uncle to create him in their images: in reflections of greed, gluttony and self-interest. If that was true . . . she should be afraid.

Merida made some kind of inner decision and sat up straight. She was no longer crying. She signed briskly and matter-of-factly. "I was in an accident. My face was badly damaged. Badly. I was unrecognizable and . . . grotesque. Nauplius arranged for me to . . . look like a normal person again in exchange for my service as his wife."

"Wow." That explained a lot in a horrible way.

"I signed a contract."

"You were an indentured servant."

"Exactly. Drink?" She offered him the bottle.

He took it and drank, appreciating the fact that she shared something lovers shared. Perhaps he was optimistic, but he would read her gesture as belief in him and his good intentions.

She signed, "Carl heard Nauplius say that a wife's life ended with her husband's death. Carl said he believed Nauplius put out a contract on my life, to be executed upon Nauplius's own death."

"That's crazy!"

Merida waved her arm up and down her figure, then around her face, and nodded.

"Yes. If he . . . used your misfortune to create the woman he wanted, then . . . yes, he was crazy." Benedict sorted through his thoughts, put some aside to examine when this crisis had ended. For now, the body next door was what mattered. "Do you believe what Carl Klineman told you? That Nauplius had placed a bounty on your head?"

"For a very long time, I had hoped for the day of Nauplius's death, and prepared. When it came, I left. Vanished. Within twenty-four hours, a woman on Nauplius's legal team was gruesomely murdered. Perhaps that means nothing. But she was beautiful and she was slashed to death." Merida gave an exaggerated shudder. "So yes, I believe Carl."

"Unless he did it."

Merida nodded, up and down, the motion slow and exaggerated. "Carl said he knew a couple of the assassins Nauplius had investigated, but hadn't been able to ascertain who was hired. Carl searched, found me here. He said he came after me to protect me. He said he wasn't the only one who had found me. The contract killer had found me, too."

"That's when the killings started in Virtue Falls. Women. Faces slashed."

Again Merida pressed the tip of her nose. "Carl wanted to take me away, help me vanish permanently. I didn't trust him. How could I? All those years, he did Nauplius's bidding. He watched me, kept me from escaping even for a moment. I couldn't go out to shop, to eat, to work out, without Carl trailing after me."

"Did you never *try* to escape?"

"You knew Nauplius by his reputation. Do you not believe he would somehow have found me and made me suffer? Made me pay for humiliating him in the eyes of the world, the runaway wife who left her aging husband and his fortune behind?"

"It would never have occurred to me that he would *kill* you. Although now . . ." Benedict considered what had happened recently in Virtue Falls. "Yes, Nauplius would have found a way to make you miserable."

"So miserable." She looked down at her hands, then slowly signed, "Also . . . I did sign the contract in good faith. Nauplius did what he'd promised—he rescued me from a life spent looking like a scary Halloween mask. After our marriage, every year, he put money into an account, showed me the proof, advised me on my investments but allowed me to invest as I wished. I believed it was completely likely I would outlive him and be free to live my life. And Nauplius said, with some justification, that Carl kept me safe. I was, after all, the wife of a very wealthy man and kidnappers are notorious for mutilating and killing their victims."

"You believe Carl could have been the killer Nauplius hired—yet every night you sneaked through the hedge to spend time with Carl."

She jerked, flung her chin up, as if Benedict had prodded her with an electrode.

Good. She was shocked. "Yes," he said. "I saw you. Every night since I've arrived, no matter what else you've done—worked, visited with your friend Kateri, gone on a date with me—afterward you pulled on your most casual clothes and your black hoodie and visited Carl Klineman."

"He could have killed me the first time he pulled me through the hedge, couldn't he? But he didn't. So I mostly believed he was sincere. Not enough to go with him, but enough to go to him when he wanted me to . . ." She erased that with a gesture. "He insisted I train in self-defense. He said if I wasn't going to listen to him and leave Virtue Falls, I needed to be prepared to defend myself. Carl had taught me a little when Nauplius was alive. He almost got fired for that; Nauplius didn't approve of a woman who could fight back. But over the last few nights, Carl sharpened my skills. I thought I was safe." She smiled, but it was wobbly and rueful. "Until I threw a side kick at you and you blocked it."

"It was a solid kick. But I'm a third degree black belt. Some nights of working with Carl can't compete." Benedict was factual.

"So I can't compete against a black belt. But Carl Klineman was Nauplius's bodyguard. He was the best. How did someone manage to kill him? Whoever it is—"

"Is scary." She had a point, not one that he liked, and she had admitted something she did not intend. "I said you were using me, and I was right. You believed an assassin was after you and you were using me as a shield."

"I believed Carl about the assassin, and yes, I used you as a shield."

"Why?"

"You know why."

He did. "Because I want you. So you trust me not to kill you."

She scooted forward on the ottoman, signed with her hands between her face and his. "I also trust you to make me forget."

"Forget what?"

"Forget everything but you."

CHAPTER FORTY-FIVE

Merida expected enthusiasm, passion, kissing, sex . . . forgetfulness.

Instead Benedict stood, walked to the window and looked out.

Feeling instantly stupid and rejected, she scrambled to her feet. Maybe, once she'd asked, he was no longer interested. Some men needed the chase. Benedict had not been that way before, but for them, "before" was many years ago.

Maybe, after hearing the sordid details of her marriage to Nauplius Brassard, he wasn't interested. Or maybe he intended to kill her now. She wouldn't have thought so, not without sex, but when it came to Benedict Howard, she had proved herself woefully inadequate in reading his character.

Still. She stood there, feeling awkward, thinking she should call the police herself, knowing she had just discovered a body, one she could not explain and didn't dare try.

Benedict walked to the light switch and flipped it down.

Now, in the distance, Merida heard police sirens.

"The police," Benedict said. "They've come to investigate my call." He turned away from the window and paced toward her across the floor. "And to answer you—yes. I can make you forget."

Oh. First he made sure they would be uninterrupted. *Then* he focused on her.

This kiss was no hands-off seduction. This was body to body, hands, lips, tongues, a blast furnace that incinerated her fears and memories, lifted her to her toes in a futile attempt to get closer to him, to his heat.

The darkness in the room was city dark: night dimly illuminated by the neighbors' porch lights, the sky washed by the distant downtown bars, restaurants and stores. Now red and blue lights flashed through the window and she had the sense that they were hiding, she and Benedict, here in the dining room, reaching for each other in the dark.

He backed her toward the table, lifted her onto the flat surface, onto the ironed linen tablecloth. He stripped off her shoes, her workout pants, her hoodie, T-shirt, bra and panties, and flung them in a wad toward the leather chair. He stepped back and viewed her, perched on the table like a statue of Venus. "My God," he whispered. "My God." As if the sight stung him to action, he disposed of his jeans, underwear and shoes in a hurry and without a bit of grace.

She smiled.

How flattering.

He climbed onto the table.

She scooted back to make room.

He caught her ankle, spread her legs, slid her and the tablecloth beneath her toward him. Leaning over her, he put his mouth to her clit . . . and his heat brought her hips off the table. She writhed, she strained, she came. Violently, explosively . . . silently.

He was not silent. "That's it," he murmured. "That's what I want for you."

Abruptly she was back in the past, years ago, learning to make love, discovering what it was like with a man who reveled in a woman's response, encouraged it, waited for it . . .

She shook her head. *No. Don't remember.*

"Don't shake your head at me," Benedict said. "Don't try to deny me." He got onto his knees, lifted her bottom and pulled her onto him.

She was wet and ready, in a hurry and desperate, but it had been a long time for her and the process was long, slow, frustrating . . . for him.

She came so often she could hardly call it frustrating . . .

When he was finally inside, he began the long, slow strokes that brought them close, broke them apart, brought them close again and earned them intimacy in the most primitive dance of all.

She panted silently, straining toward another climax, a greater climax, one that would sweep her mind free of every terror, every nightmare, every concern.

He moaned, his arms and thighs corded with strain, sweat staining his T-shirt over the breastbone. The wash of red and blue across his face turned him alternately demonic and angelic, and she recognized both in him. He demanded more from her than she could give, and when she gave it, he demanded again. "Come on, darling," he said over and over. "Come again . . . for me. Come again . . . with me."

Finally she did, losing herself completely as one surge of pleasure followed another, faster and faster until he gave a shout that gave voice to pleasure for them both.

Motion slowed. He lowered her hips to the table, sank down on top of her, silent now, his fingers grasping her waist, his gaze fixed on her face as if being inside her wasn't enough. As if he wanted to see inside her.

Merida smiled, then closed her eyes, luxuriating in physical satisfaction, in the heat of his skin against hers, the pump of blood in her veins, the brief moment when she was no longer Merida or Helen or Merry, but simply herself, one woman united with one man in the dance of joy.

Slowly Benedict pushed away, left her body, sat up beside her. The blue and red lights flashed across his body, illuminating all the shadows in brief glorious reveals. His voice seemed deeper, grittier as he asked, "Did I make you forget?"

She nodded, then afraid he hadn't seen, she spelled, "Yes."

"That's good." He lifted one knee, leaned an arm against it. "Because you made me remember."

There was a warning there, a toughness she hadn't heard.

She sat up, shedding satiation and gaining wariness.

Deliberately he turned his head, looked right at her. "Merry. Merry Byrd. Where have you been?"

CHAPTER FORTY-SIX

Merida vaulted off the table, scampered toward her clothes to grab something, anything, put it on, run away.

Because he was going to kill her . . . again.

As she moved, her mind sorted: no T-shirt, she'd be vulnerable if she pulled it over her head; no pants, she'd be vulnerable when she pulled them on; no shoes . . . she snatched up her hoodie, turned and held it in front of her.

Benedict sat on the table in the same position, unmoving, watching.

Of course. Why not? He could outrun her. Because of her paranoia, she had three locks on the door and a chain; they kept her safe, but she couldn't easily get out. And he'd already proven tonight that her puny self-defense moves could not defeat him.

But bless him. He knew exactly what to say to bring years of pent-up fury roaring back. "Merry Byrd, I thought you were dead."

She threw the hoodie aside and advanced on him. If she was going to die, she wouldn't do it cowering behind a feeble piece of clothing. She was going to go down fighting. "You ought to know," she signed. "You killed Merry Byrd."

"No."

"You arranged for that airplane to explode."

"No."

"When I woke in the hospital, I cried for you. You were nowhere."

"When I woke in the hospital, they told me you were dead."

"Who told you I was dead?" *Wait.* "What were you in the hospital for?"

He paused, studied her. "Do you not remember that explosion?"

"Yes!" Except not really. She couldn't remember everything, and she didn't want to. The noise. The fear. The explosion. The heat. *Oh God the heat the pain the death now run now not fast enough.* "I was to solo at last . . . I was doing the preflight check . . ."

He jumped off the table.

She took a compulsive step back.

Now uncaring of the cops, he flipped on a light. He pulled off his T-shirt and turned his back to her.

The skin from his neck to his buttocks was rippled with red scars, testimony to fire and pain.

She shook her head, little disbelieving shakes.

"When you want to talk, you know where to find me." Pulling on his shirt and his pants, he opened the locks and walked out, slamming the door behind him.

The man knew how to make an exit.

Damn him! The coward, leaving her here alone

when she wanted to fight. Picking up one of his shoes, she flung it at the door. She stomped over and fastened the locks. She sure as hell didn't want to think. She had never wanted to think about that day . . .

The police lights flashed against the suits of armor like some freakish, silent music video.

Benedict had recognized her. He had made love to her and somehow, he had known who she was. How was that possible? Because of her body? No, she had been substantially rebuilt on Nauplius's specifications. She had no voice, so it wasn't that. Maybe because . . . because . . . of the way she made love? Because he had never forgotten her?

Merida, don't go there. That way looms heartbreak.

But the fact remained that somehow, he had known her.

Somehow, he had been hurt.

Somehow, she had never known that.

She pulled on her T-shirt and pants, walked to the window and stared out at the street where the police lights flashed. An ambulance was parked at the curb—why? It was far too late for Carl. Men in uniform moved back and forth, and Kateri stood speaking into a radio, her gaze fixed . . . on the B and B.

Merida stepped away from the window.

She had never once opened the mental box

that contained her memories. At first she had been too bound up in the fight for her life. Then Nauplius Brassard had come to her and offered the deal. She could have a life with the kind of face and form that made children cry and grown men turn away. Or she could become his perfect woman and live her life on his terms. He offered a contract.

She had nobly refused. Even then she couldn't speak, but she had written that Benedict Howard would care for her.

Nauplius had laughed.

She had never forgotten that laughter, or the cruel truth he had thrust upon her. Benedict Howard had tried to kill her. If Nauplius hadn't recognized that she was the woman he sought, if he hadn't let the world believe she was dead, Benedict Howard would have already finished the job.

She hadn't believed him.

He showed her the photographs online, of a smiling, debonair Benedict dating a smiling, glamorous model. Current photos! She had checked the dates. She had feverishly sought more pictures, pictures taken while she struggled in the hospital with pain, fever, infection, the loss of her face.

But that didn't mean he had tried to kill her, only that he'd abandoned her in her time of need. Wasn't that bad enough?

Then Benedict's aunt Rose had visited. The fragile old woman confessed her shame for her nephew and his nefarious deeds. At the same time, she had refused to show Merry proof or turn Benedict over to the law. She said she loved him. She said she feared him. She said Merry was safe as long as he believed her dead, and advised her to take Nauplius's bargain. As reparation, she offered to negotiate his contract and get Merry better terms. And she did: because of her, Nauplius paid Merry that annual salary.

The realization that the man she loved had betrayed her broke Merry. The woman she had been—optimistic, cheerful, helpful—disappeared. From that moment, she faced life as it truly was, and she tried never to remember. Not Benedict, not the circumstances of the accident. She had concentrated on the future, and revenge.

But tonight changed everything. Because he had the scars.

How? Why?

Without turning on a light, she climbed the stairs to her bedroom.

None of that helped her know what to do now.

She should shower. She smelled like sex and sweat and him.

She lowered herself onto the bed and shut her eyes . . . and *tried* to remember.

All her life, Merry Byrd had wanted to fly, and for her birthday, Benedict Howard gave her flying lessons. Everything about the experience lifted her heart and each flight was a gift. She embraced the adventure. She loved the freedom of soaring high above the earth. Her instructor, Bob, said he had never seen anyone who was such a natural at the controls. Benedict Howard rode along for every lesson, and every time they landed, he looked at her as if she was the most wonderful woman in the world.

Yes. She was really flying.

At last she was ready for her solo flight.

The message came. Benedict had been detained—business. He couldn't wave to her as she took off, congratulate her when she landed. But he would be thinking of her every moment. She was disappointed. Of course. But he sent flowers, and Merry did as she always did—she took joy in his thoughtfulness.

Bob handed her the list and sent her out to the plane to do the preflight check. He told her he had to speak with his wife— she was ill, in the hospital for tests—but he would join her soon and give the plane the once-over, too, just to be sure. He seemed nervous, but Merida reassured him, told him she was ready to fly on her own and to go to his wife if she needed him.

Merida walked out to the plane sitting on the tarmac. She performed the visual inspection: fuselage, wings, empennage, power plant, the undercarriage. No nicks, dents, loose fasteners. Checked fuel levels, landing gear, wheels, ignition wires, fuel lines . . . Bob kept his plane in prime condition, and she didn't stop until she had given a good mark to everything on the checklist. She was ready to climb into the plane, do the cockpit check, when she heard him call. She turned and waved, so happy to see him . . .

Him. Bob?

No. Not Bob.

Benedict loped toward her, carrying a gift box under his arm, calling, "Merry, wait!" . . .

Merida found herself lying stiff and breathless, straining to remember the following moments.

Nothing. She didn't remember anything until she woke in the hospital, wrapped in bandages and hounded by pain.

The doctors had told her remembering that trauma might be something she could never do.

Once she knew the truth about Benedict, she hadn't wanted to.

But she *didn't* know the truth about Benedict. She only knew what Nauplius and Rose had told her, and what she'd seen online. After living with Nauplius, she now knew how well the wealthy could manipulate their stories.

Maybe after Merry's "death," Benedict hadn't really been out partying.

Merida sat up.

Here in Virtue Falls, he'd had plenty of chances, but he hadn't killed her yet.

So she might as well go ask him what had happened to cause those scars on his back.

CHAPTER FORTY-SEVEN

Benedict stepped out of Merida's room, heard something thump hard against the door's solid wood panels—his shoe, he supposed. He'd made a grand exit, but now he stood in the entry of the Good Knight Manor Bed and Breakfast wearing the bare minimum for decency.

Luckily, the guests were gathered on the front porch, watching the police action. As he started for the kitchen and the back entrance, he caught tidbits of their avid conversations.

"Did you hear what happened next door?"

"Another one?"

"Stabbed?"

"When he got the call, that policeman who hangs around here ran out the door and drove away."

"Sean Weston. He hangs around to visit with that beautiful woman who is mute."

"A man this time. Really? Next door?"

"Is it always like this in this town?"

And finally, in thrilled tones, "Those policemen are coming up the walk. Do you think they'll want to interview us?"

Benedict walked faster.

"Mr. Howard, have you heard the news?" Phoebe came hustling out of the kitchen holding a tray of macaroons and tiny cut-crystal glasses of port. "The police got an anonymous call about a body and—" She stopped. Looked him over from top to toe and tittered. "Oh. My. The police have arrived, but you have *your* alibi. I suppose she has hers, too." She gazed pointedly at Merida's door.

Benedict always took pride in his ability to conceal his emotions.

Perhaps, at least at this time, it was an undeserved pride, for as he walked toward Phoebe, she stopped smiling and moved briskly out of the way.

He walked through the kitchen. Phoebe's handyman sat at the table, hunched over a plate of macaroons, shoving them into his mouth one after another. He was one of those men Benedict automatically despised: sulky, unambitious, blaming his miserable fate on everyone but himself. He looked up at Benedict, scowled and went back to binge-eating.

Benedict walked out the back door and stepped into a different scene, one with law enforcement thick at the curb and in the yard, radios crackling, and the bright glimmer of floodlights through the hedge. He saw Merida's friend Sheriff Kateri Kwinault talking to one of the guests, taking notes. She saw him, too, and waved.

Benedict wondered how long it would take before they traced his call. Wondered, too, how he'd been so lost to all sense that he used his own phone to make that call.

He knew the answer.

Merida made him lose his sense.

Merry. Of all the women he thought she might be, Merry Byrd had never occurred to him. By the time he woke up in the hospital, two weeks after that explosion, she was dead and buried.

They had lied to him.

Apparently, they had lied to her.

The question remained—who exactly were "they"?

A car drove slowly up the drive. The Cipres. They pulled the car in front of him, blocking his path to his cottage.

If he could, he would have walked around them. But he was barefoot. He had to step carefully and even then, gravel bit him on his heel, on the soft flesh by his toes . . . Next time he made a grand exit, he'd grab his shoes.

Dawkins rolled down the window and leaned out into the light of the porch. "Did you hear?" he asked. "Somebody's dead next door. For a town this size, bodies certainly pile up. I told Elsa we should keep going down the coast, but when she met Merida she insisted we stay to help her get her feet under her. And what thanks do we get? She avoids us."

"Yes, dear. I know." Elsa sat in shadow. "You're right. We can move on tomorrow. Mr. Howard,

I've never seen you so informally dressed. Not everyone can get away with it. It takes a man of supreme confidence like you or Dawkins."

"Thank you." The gravel in the driveway dug into the bottoms of Benedict's feet.

"Did you and Merida have a date tonight?"

"No."

"But you've seen her?"

"I believe she is in her rooms."

"Good. With the murders tonight, she shouldn't be out on her own." For the first time, Elsa leaned into the light.

Benedict saw the bruise on her jaw.

Dawkins shot her a glare.

She pulled back into the shadow.

Dawkins drove on.

Key in hand, Benedict limped his way to his cottage, entered and locked the door behind him. Then unlocked it. He'd seen the look on Merida's face; he believed she would be along soon.

He flipped on his computer and while it came up, he made the call to the cruise ship. The connection took a few minutes; he had to explain to the bridge crew member that yes, this was an emergency and he didn't care what time it was there, he had to speak to his aunt and uncle.

While he waited, he brought up his investigation into the business account discrepancies and once again examined the evidence.

The phone rang.

Rose answered. Naturally, she didn't ask if he was ill or had been in an accident or been named in a paternity suit. No, not dear Aunt Rose. In her quavering voice, she said, "Dear! Did you discover what's wrong with our spreadsheets?"

Yes. The businesses are being hacked. He'd known that already, but he'd held off giving them the information until he tracked the perpetrator or at least discovered the reason for it. As of about fifteen minutes ago, he was pretty sure he knew everything there was to know. But he ignored Rose's question, and said, "I'm calling about the past."

"The past." Her voice got sharp and wary. "At this hour?"

"Did you and Albert try to kill Merry Byrd?" To hell with tact; he enjoyed this frontal assault.

"Merry Byrd?" Rose pretended to grope among unsteady memories. "Remind me, who is she again?"

"Have you tried to kill so many people you can't remember who she is? Merry Byrd. The woman I loved."

A silence. He could almost hear Rose sorting through her options. "You know with the death of your parents, we took you in. We cared for you, loved you as if you were our own."

First, she was playing the guilt card. "Thank you, Aunt Rose. That was good of you."

"You don't understand this, because you never

had a child, but when our beloved boy strayed into danger, we always stepped in to rescue you. Remember when you just turned thirteen, got mad at Albert and wanted to run away? You climbed out of your bedroom window and into the old oak, fell and broke your arm. We immediately cut that oak down."

He did remember. That had been a beautiful oak, over one hundred years old, its broad branches gloriously flat, the perfect place for a boy to lounge in the summer. He also remembered coming home from the hospital, bruised and battered, his arm in a cast, and hearing the horror of chain saws dismantling the mighty tree.

His fault. He had known it was his fault. Albert and Rose had made sure of that.

"We did that because we loved you and couldn't bear to see you hurt."

"You did that to punish me for trying to rebel."

"We would hardly be good guardians if we allowed you to roam the streets alone. You would have been hurt!"

Looking back, he thought of other manipulations, punishments, revenges on him for behavior unbecoming to their heir. He hadn't thought of it before, hadn't considered the ramifications on his own character or realized the swift ruthlessness of their reactions. "So you treated Merry Byrd as if she were a rebellion and eliminated her. As if she were the oak tree."

"You were acting out of character, spending time at an orphanage—"

"A day care."

"Coming home with vomit on the shoulder of your best suit. An Armani! You neglected the business. You were losing your edge. We had trained you to know what was important in life—"

"The business."

"And she was subverting your character. After your infatuation faded, you would have returned to normal. Of course we knew that. But we saved you a lot of wasted time and money."

Her gall flabbergasted him. "You murdered her."

"If she didn't die, it wasn't murder," Rose snapped in her take-charge-of-the-boardroom voice.

"Merry would have died if I hadn't been there."

"Exactly." Her voice smoothed again, soothed again. "We made up an excuse to pull you away from the airport. We didn't want you to get hurt. When we heard you were there . . . do you know how much anxiety you caused us when you were unconscious for so long?"

He noted her move from justifying attempted homicide to blaming him for being in the blast zone.

She continued, "The doctors told us you would never recover. They said even if you woke up, you'd have brain damage! Do you think we wanted that?"

"I suppose I should be grateful you didn't press a pillow to my face to save you any trouble."

Her voice sharpened. "Trouble? You were our only chance to pass the business into responsible hands."

She had just skipped over assuring him they would never smother him while he was in a coma to . . . to rationalizing their motives. Their motives for . . . what? More murder?

"Your father was . . . well, you remember him." She huffed in disbelief. "*Irresponsible* was a kind term. But you . . . when you were a boy and visited us, you impressed Albert and me with how clever you were, how quick to learn, how eager to serve. Even at seven you understood what the business meant to the family, and you looked at your father with such wonderment as if you couldn't believe he could throw it all away."

Benedict gripped the phone so hard, his fingertips grew cold. "I loved my father."

"Of course you did, but it all came out for the best."

"*What* came out for the best?"

"All of it. Their deaths, you coming to us, Merry Byrd being hurt and you being hurt, too. Who could have imagined that would happen, or that you would have had such a difficult recovery?"

He breathed carefully, in and out, regulating his intake and his outflow. "It all came out for the best because it gave you time to get her away?"

"Oh, please. As soon as Nauplius Brassard went to her and offered to make her pretty, she leaped at the deal. Look where she is now—a beautiful, wealthy widow! If the two of you had stayed together, she would be nothing but a frumpy do-gooder and you would be frustrated with her lack of foresight."

His door opened.

The beautiful, wealthy widow walked in, and quietly shut and locked the door behind her.

Rose continued harping in his ear. "You'd be always holding some snotty-nosed baby, or opening some women's shelter or giving money to a homeless bum. No, dear, after the air had cleared, your uncle and I were satisfied we had made the right decision in regards to your little infatuation with Merry Byrd."

She had not only admitted to attempted homicide, she justified it, and now she waited for him to agree. What kind of man was he that she thought such a thing? If he hadn't seen Merida Falcon on that transatlantic crossing, recognized her on some primal level, pursued her and recovered the woman he loved . . . would he someday have become the man Albert and Rose wanted him to be? A man like them: merciless, amoral, loving profit above all things?

Merida looked at him, looked hard at him, then went to the electric tea kettle. Still watching him, she filled it with water, plugged it in and turned it on.

"Benedict? Are you there?" Rose asked.

"I'm here." With Merry—but he wouldn't tell Rose that.

"Did you discover what is going on with our business accounts?"

He laughed once, a guard dog's bark of a laugh. "Aunt Rose, I think I did discover what's wrong with our business accounts."

Merida looked surprised, but not alarmed.

With complete assurance, he said, "In fact, I know I did. Let me do more fact-checking and you'll have all the information you need."

"That's good, dear." Rose sounded satisfied, as if she believed she'd talked sense into her nephew. "Now, if you don't mind, I'm old and tired, and Albert and I need our beauty sleep."

"Yes, Aunt Rose. Of course. Sleep now." He hung up, dropped the phone on the floor and sat down in the easy chair next to the bed. His hands dangled between his knees, and he flexed his fingers, trying to get the circulation flowing.

Merry came to him, knelt in front of him exactly as he had knelt in front of her. "What's wrong?"

"Everything . . . has changed. I've been . . . a fool. I didn't recognize you and I didn't realize

. . . all these years I didn't know . . ." He looked down at Merida. "Aunt Rose. She said . . . they tried to kill you. And I think . . . I suspect they killed my parents."

CHAPTER FORTY-EIGHT

Merry made Benedict a cup of herbal tea. She brought it to him, wrapped his hands around it and sat cross-legged on the floor in front of him.

He took one sip and flinched. "What is this?"

"It's chamomile. It's late and you're upset. You can't process caffeine efficiently, not so late at night. Just drink it."

He laughed, stopped, laughed again. "How could I have not recognized you? You're the same as you always were."

"No, I'm not." This scene wasn't how she'd pictured this at all. She had thought she would be a supplicant, asking for the truth. Instead, he looked like ten miles of bad road.

"Organic. Homemade. Herbal. Meditation." He imitated her voice. " 'Everyone can in their own way make a difference.' "

She was embarrassed to look him in the face. "What a *dumbass* I was."

"No. No, you were wonderful." He smiled at her with such charm. "You reminded me that life could be joyous. You taught me I shouldn't give people a handout, but a hand up. You believed in the inherent goodness of mankind."

He had not convinced her. "*Then* someone tried to kill me. As I said, a dumbass."

His smile vanished. "Not someone. My aunt and uncle."

"Why? I didn't do anything to them."

"They had chosen me to inherit the family business and to carry the torch of brutal industrialization and profitable exploitation into the future. You changed me."

"Not for long. Aren't you still their chosen one?" Before he could speak, she said, "I'm sorry. I'm sorry! I appreciate you trying to make me feel better about myself, but your aunt and uncle succeeded. Merry Byrd is dead and she left nothing. Nothing. I should be grateful to them for killing her before she screwed up her life any more. Or yours."

He picked up his phone off the floor and pushed a few buttons. "Video call," he told Merida.

Merida heard a woman's weary voice say, "Hello," and in the background, a chorus of crying children.

He said, "Sounds like we're having an evening there."

"The identical twins are identically teething and everyone wants to cry about it." The voice sounded familiar to Merida.

"Where's your help?" he asked.

"Everyone is here who is scheduled to be here. It's simply one of those nights." The familiar voice called, "Larry, do we have any more *cold* teething rings?"

"I won't keep you long, but I have a friend here who would like to meet you." He turned the phone to face Merida. "Ms. Sandvig, this is Merida. Merida, this is Ms. Sandvig. Ms. Sandvig directs the Baltimore Inner City Day Care and Preschool."

"I know." Merida tried to speak, to express her delight at seeing her old friend once more. When no sound came out—she should be used to that by now!—she gestured, nodded and smiled.

Ms. Sandvig smiled back. "Are you Benedict's new friend? I'm delighted that he found you at last. He was so upset when you disappeared."

Benedict turned the phone toward his face and looked meaningfully at the screen. "Ms. Sandvig. I was hoping you could tell Merida about the work we're doing in Baltimore."

"Oh! Yes, right, Benedict. Merida, I don't know if Benedict has told you anything about our operations, but we provide twenty-four-hour day care for parents in need. Not just women, we help single fathers, too."

"I know." Merida's fingers shook as she spelled. "I used to live in Baltimore."

"Do you know we care for over one hundred children twenty-four/seven? We have our new preschool and after-school programs."

"One hundred?" Merida couldn't believe it. When she had been there, they had never been able to care for more than ten at a time, and turning desperate parents away had been heartbreaking.

"We teach the children so much. When our children go to public school, they perform so much better than their similarly underprivileged counterparts and—"

Benedict turned the phone toward him and made the cut-off gesture.

Ms. Sandvig laughed ruefully. "I'm sorry, Merida, I do tend to get carried away. We can always use help and of course if you can't help in person I promise your donation will be used in ways that will make you proud."

Merida nodded and indicated she would send money.

Ms. Sandvig sobered. "I don't know if you realize how much of our work is possible because of the man sitting next to you. He has given his time and influence in every way, and every penny it took to construct the Merry Byrd Classroom Facility was his and his alone."

Again Benedict made the cut-off gesture.

"All anonymously," Ms. Sandvig said hurriedly.

Merida's lower lip quivered.

Benedict brought the phone back to his face. "Thank you, Ms. Sandvig. I think you convinced her."

"That you're a wonderful man?"

"My secret plan all along." Benedict hung up and said to Merida, "Actually, my secret plan was to convince you that Merry Byrd left a great legacy behind. I would never have helped those people without the lessons Merry Byrd taught me. All these years, I have missed her so much."

"How did you know . . . ?" Such an embarrassing question! But she had to know. "When we had sex, how did you know it was me?"

"All cats are not gray in the dark. All women are not the same while making love. I simply had to forsake the visible and recognize the union of the soul."

She flung herself at him.

He toppled over onto the floor, lost the phone, held her and rubbed her back while she cried. When she'd caught her breath, she signed, "I've been so angry at you. What happened that day? Please tell me what happened."

"You really don't remember?"

She shook her head.

He settled his back against the ottoman and pulled her into his arms as if he needed to have her close. "I wanted to go up with you. It was your solo fight; I wanted to see your face while you were at the controls. I knew you would . . . look like you did when we made love." He smiled at her, smoothed her hair off her forehead. "I got a couple of calls. One from Bob. He told me you *had* to be alone on your solo flight; I couldn't go up with you."

"True," she signed.

"I said I'd come down to see you off. About fifteen minutes later I got another call. Emergency, business, they needed me, they had to have me. I was so used to doing whatever had to be done I sent a message to you and the flowers and headed over to corporate headquarters to put out the fire. About halfway there, I thought— what am I doing? This relationship is first in my life. Not the business." He took a shaky breath. "So I turned and came to the airport. You had just finished the walk-around check and were ready to climb in for the cockpit check when I caught you . . ."

"Benedict! You're here."

He held two gift boxes. "I couldn't miss this."

They smiled into each other's eyes, two fools in love.

"I brought you a present to celebrate your inaugural flight." He offered her the box.

She lifted the lid and looked. Inside were two crumpled pieces of worn leather. She lifted one out; it was an early-twentieth-century flying helmet with flaps that draped over the ears and a strap under the neck.

"The auction house claimed it was

verified to be one of Amelia Earhart's flying helmets." He set down the box, took the leather out of her hands and fitted it over her head. "Merry Byrd, Aunt Amelia would be proud of you."

Joy choked her; she couldn't speak. But she knew a little sign language, so in a precursor of the future, she used her hands to say, "Thank you!"

"You're welcome," he said. Leaning down, he pulled another leather helmet out of the box. "I got one, too. It's not from a famous flyer, but it does have a fleece lining. Apparently it was pretty cold in those old cockpits." He pulled it on and wrapped his arm around her. He pulled her close for a photo, then showed it to her.

She was blushing bright red and irrepressibly beaming. "Get rid of that!" she said. "Geeze, how embarrassing. I look like a kid getting a treat."

"All we need are goggles and a scarf." He opened the other box. "Here they are!"

She laughed at him, at how happy giving her this stuff made him. "Hang on to those. I was heading into the cockpit for the preflight checks."

"I'll wait here."

She climbed into the well-used, much-loved four-passenger Cessna 182 Skyland. The door sealed well, the seat was adjusted correctly. She ducked her head to get into the cockpit, slipped into the pilot's seat, holding her checklist in one hand, and began her preflight cockpit check. The engine fired quickly, the fuel tank was full, the radio cooling fans and instrument gyros sounded normal. She checked the flaps. "That's it." She marveled at how calm she could act when her heart beat so wildly. She climbed down the stairs, removed the wing tie downs and the wheel chocks, and walked to the front of the plane to do the final visual.

He offered her the goggles and the wool scarf.

"Okay." She felt silly, but she donned them. She sniffed. Frowned. She filled her lungs. "Benedict, do you smell that?"

"Yes," he said. "Smells like a fuel leak."

"The engine was fine a minute ago. I checked. I'm going to kill the motor." She climbed back into the plane, turned off the ignition.

Nothing changed. The engine continued to run.

Benedict appeared at the open door, watched her.

She pulled the mixture control all the way to the lean.

The engine ran. The smell got stronger.

Suddenly, decisively, Benedict said, "We need to get out of here."

"But we've got to get the motor to turn off. This is Bob's living. He trusts me to—"

"Smell the gas? Something is very wrong. Merry Byrd, out of the plane. Now!"

She stopped fussing with the gauges, looked at Benedict, looked at the curl of smoke rising from the engine compartment and realized—he was right. Thank God she hadn't released the parking brakes, because the two of them needed to get free of the area.

She jumped onto the tarmac. She sucked in fresh air; the fumes in the cockpit had been thick and getting thicker. Out here, her mind cleared. "Run!"

He grabbed her hand. "Come on!"

He started toward the terminal.

She ran with him, caught up in his alarm, progressing through all the scenarios in her mind. Fuel pump leakage? Wrong fuel? Malfunctioning starter? Damn it, she had checked everything.

He glanced back. "Faster!" He stepped behind her, pushed at her.

She sprinted. Then—

The fireball slammed him into her back, lifted them both off their feet, tossed them through the air. She landed facedown on the asphalt. She felt every tooth and bone break. She felt his dead weight on her back.

Then . . . there was nothing.

"Your aunt and uncle sabotaged the plane?"

"Yes."

"In the hopes of killing me."

"Yes."

"And they got you, too."

"Yes. But as Aunt Rose so blithely announced tonight, it all came out for the best." His voice held a snap, a whiplash of anger that boded ill for Aunt Rose.

"No." Merida wrapped her arms around his neck. "All would have been best if we'd been together."

He rolled her beneath him, kissed her until they had no breath left.

"Come to bed with me," he whispered.

"Of course. I have all the time in the world."

CHAPTER FORTY-NINE

Benedict flipped on the light beside the bed. "The trouble is, we *don't* have all the time in the world. My aunt and uncle know I've found you and their aims haven't changed. They want me to tend the family fortune and they see no reason they should be thwarted."

Merida's afterglow faded all too rapidly. She sighed and signed, "What do *you* want?"

"I want revenge on the people who killed my parents."

She had to be the voice of reason. "You don't know that they did."

"My parents died in a yachting accident, an explosion blamed on a leak in the fuel pump. What do you suppose the report on the airplane explosion said?"

"Fuel pump leak?"

"My aunt and uncle are the kind of people who believe that what worked before will work again. They were almost right."

Merida sat up, sheet to her bosom, and looked down at him sprawled on the pillow. Signing slowly, reluctantly, she said, "I have a confession to make."

"Do you?"

"I believed Nauplius Brassard when he told me you had tried to kill me."

"I know you did."

"Your aunt Rose confirmed Brassard's report."

Benedict got an ugly expression on his face. "Did she?"

She fussed with the ruffles on the pillowcases, gathering her courage, then she signed, "I wanted revenge on you very much. For all the years of my marriage, through all the surgeries and pain of recovery, I made plans. I studied and consulted experts and created a software program that would create a false report of embezzlement in your business and pin the blame on you."

He said nothing. He looked unconcerned. Did he not understand?

She continued, "As soon as Nauplius was dead, I began to implement it."

"I know." Benedict sounded appallingly casual. "Your work is very clever, but Aunt Rose has an eidetic memory for numbers and an obsession with our business accounts. She caught the discrepancies, although none too soon, and set me to investigating them."

Merida hadn't expected to hear that. "Have you . . . been able to do anything about it?"

"I haven't tried."

"Oh." She ruminated on that. "What do you intend to do about it?"

"I suspect if I had access to your computer and your program, I could stop it."

"Yes, you could. Or I could. I don't want you to take the fall for this."

He sat up, turned his back to her and put his feet on the floor. "Or I could divert the evidence of criminal activity to Aunt Rose and Uncle Albert. The people who killed my parents. Who tried to kill the woman I loved, and succeeded in separating us for far too many years."

She looked at the angry scars that rippled down his spine. She thought about what had been done to them—to him—and placed her hand on his back.

He turned around to see her speak.

"I'd like that, too," she signed. "I recognize the tracks of pain when I see them."

"Good. We are in accord about the Howard family business and its fate." He placed his palms flat on the mattress, leaned toward her. "But we have one problem, and it's a big one. As I said, Rose and Albert know I've found you, and to them, you're still a distraction to me, and I'm still their hope for the future. So I suggest they might have hired a second assassin, one unconnected to your dead husband."

Merida laughed. She rolled away from him and laughed. She laughed silently, so amused by his suggestion tears gathered in her eyes and she blotted her cheeks with the sheet.

He watched her, frowning. "You've developed an odd sense of humor, Merida."

"There are two assassins after me? One sent by Nauplius and one sent by your aunt and uncle?" She sobered. "Which one killed Carl Klineman?"

"The one sent by Nauplius," he said promptly. "The thing to remember about Rose and Albert is that they're cheap. They wouldn't pay for an extra killing. They don't like to spend extravagantly for any reason and I can't believe they would do so in their assassinations. Bob, your flight instructor, owned that plane. He serviced it, he loved it, but his wife contracted cancer and he was in dire financial straits."

"You think Bob *fixed* his plane to explode? He was a nice guy!" She saw Benedict's skeptical expression. "I'm not being a fool. I knew him. I met him and his wife. He was normal and nice, and they were in love."

"When Bob's wife died, he committed suicide."

"Oh. Poor guy."

"Yeah, poor guy, he tried to kill you. But you're right—circumstances sometimes drive us all to do things we don't like."

Merida continued, "I wasn't going to accept Nauplius Brassard's marriage proposal. Not even when I thought you had betrayed me. Then the doctors took the bandages off my face and I walked down the corridor." Merida always said things to him she had never told anyone else. Her fantasy about Aunt Amelia Earhart. And now, this. "The other patients flinched and little children cried. I didn't want to be beautiful, but I couldn't face a lifetime of . . . that."

With his fingertip, Benedict stroked the feathers of her falcon tattoo. "I understand. I would have done anything to spare you the pain and the servitude."

"You did do something." She clasped his hand. "The doctors said the only thing that saved my eyes were . . . the goggles. And the leather helmet kept my hair from igniting."

"Aunt Amelia watched over you." He kissed her.

She leaned into him, wrapped her arms around him.

"No." Regretfully, he took her hands away and pressed them to her ribs. "You're in danger. Carl Klineman gave his life to tell us that."

His words sparked a memory, and she sat up very straight. "That's right. You're right. I saw what he did. What he wrote."

"What Carl wrote?"

"On the floor. With his blood. He used his finger dipped in blood. I was trying to read it when you came up behind me. He wrote"—she closed her eyes and tried to visualize it—"WAS ON. Or WES UN. Or . . ." She opened her eyes. "I don't know. I can't remember for sure, and there was so much blood it had blurred the . . . letters." Her memory of the scene would be forever joined with horror and fear, and she rolled back onto the bed to allow her nausea to subside.

Benedict went into the bathroom and came back with a damp washcloth. He put it on her forehead, then wrote down the letters on a note card and studied them. "Was on . . . *something?*" he suggested. "Somebody *was on* something? Or is it a name?"

"I'm not even sure I'm remembering it correctly. One thing's for sure. We can't go back and look."

"God, no. In fact, we need to leave. Now." He picked his clothes up off the floor, flung her clothes at her. "Get up. Get dressed. We need to drop out of sight. Forever."

His urgency sent a jolt of fear through her. "Is that so easy?"

He pulled on his clothes. "You disappeared quite effectively. I discovered you by accident. I suspect the assassins discovered you by watching me. I led them to you. This time we'll go together. It's the only way. We're intelligent. We're tough. We can make our way in the world. Together."

She liked the way he talked. She liked his confidence. She believed him when he said it was the only way. "All right." For the second time that night, she pulled on her workout clothes.

CHAPTER FIFTY

Three A.M. and the cops were gone.

Good Knight Manor Bed and Breakfast was quiet.

Benedict and Merida tiptoed through the kitchen and toward the knight-filled dining room. They went through the ritual of unlocking the door. Benedict walked through Merida's suite and came back to where she stood in the dining room. "All clear. We're alone."

"Thank you." She handed him her computer, showed him the log-in and where she was in her program.

He studied it. He shook his head. "I need my computer. It's got the security setups to get into the business accounts. But if I can view everything together, I can do this. Move the evidence you piled on me to Rose and Albert. The whole business is going to come crashing down around their ears."

"Your reputation will remain unscathed?"

"I think I can salvage it, and with it my part of the fortune." He grinned. "Baltimore Inner City Day Care and Preschool is going to have an impressive nest egg to depend on."

She had to offer him one more chance. "You *could* remain and be Benedict Howard, the mogul who saved the family business."

"Not and be with you. Don't worry so, I know what I'm doing." He frowned. "Come back to my room with me. I'll pick up my computer and work here while you pack."

"You go back, make the changes on the computers, and I'll pack. When I'm ready, I'll call you and if you're done and if *you're* packed, we can leave."

He tried to tell her no.

"It makes sense. We're in a hurry." She felt the pressure building to leave Virtue Falls and their current lives behind.

"We are in a hurry." He pulled her into his arms and looked down into her face. "Lock the doors after me."

She nodded.

"Don't let anyone in."

She nodded.

"Pack light."

She nodded.

"Am I mansplaining?"

She pulled away and signed and smiled. "Yes, but it's very cute."

He kissed her.

But he didn't linger. The night was waning. He had her software to alter, and quickly. They'd made their plans to disappear and they needed to implement them now, before someone suspected or tried to kill Merida, or Benedict or both.

When he left, Merida locked the doors and went

upstairs mentally prioritizing as she climbed.

First from the safe, her technology: the tablet, the computer, cables and gadgets. From her bathroom: toothbrush, birth control, tampons, sunscreen. From her bedroom: running shoes, comfort shoes and her one pair of stilettos.

Benedict liked those stilettos.

In the closet, she grabbed clothes for roughing it, clothes for layering, a dress, simple but easy to dress up or down. She flung it all on her bed, then off the top shelf she retrieved one rolling suitcase light enough for her to carry as needed. She didn't know where they were going. She didn't know how. She wanted to be prepared for everything.

She packed quickly, efficiently, discarding anything that gave her second thoughts. She was tucking her socks into her shoes when—a brief shriek from the attic room above her. A heavy thud on her ceiling.

Merida jumped. She stared up at the quivering antique light fixture.

No other sound . . .

Night pressed in on the windows, making the darkness blacker and deafening. The Cipres roomed up there. What had happened?

Downstairs, she heard someone rap on her door, a quick panicked patter of terror. She ran halfway down the servants' stairs. Ran back and got her phone. Ran all the way down and into the dining room.

The rapping continued, constant, demanding, desperate.

She put her hand against the door. It vibrated continuously, like a trembling hand. She checked the security camera.

Elsa Cipre stood outside, lip split, blood trickling from one corner of her eye. She wore one of her odd black outfits, maybe her version of a nightgown, and glanced around continuously, watching for someone. Watching for . . . him.

Merida had always known there was something wrong with that man. Something suspicious in the way Dawkins watched his wife.

In the way he watched Merida.

She left the chain on, but unlocked and opened the door and peered through the crack.

Elsa whispered, "Please. Let me in. He's going to kill me. This time he's going to kill me."

"Stay here. I'll call for help." She backed away, dialed Benedict. No service. No ring. Damn it, this was no time to have trouble connecting. Dawkins could get here at any moment, and Merida didn't know what she would do. She didn't like Elsa, but that didn't mean she wanted her to die at the hands of Dawkins Cipre. She needed a weapon. A weapon . . .

Suits of armor lined the walls. Each knight held a weapon: battle-ax, spear, flail, sword . . . Sword was best—although it was too heavy for her, it had a point and sharp sides. A lot of ways to hurt someone. Merida tucked the phone under her ear. With both hands, she grasped the sword hilt and pulled.

She heard a click, a rattle and the sound of a chain dropping.

She whirled to face the door.

A blow to the right ear sent her sprawling.

The sword fell back into place. The phone flew out of her hands and tumbled across the floor.

Dawkins Cipre. He'd forced his way in.

Merida tried to get to her knees. She was kicked flat.

A bony body landed on her back. A bony hand gripped her hair and slammed the right side of her head to the floor.

The second impact on top of the already painful lump made Merida's vision go black.

Dawkins twisted first one of Merida's arms and then the other behind her and fastened them together. He said into Merida's ear, "If you had attended my classes, you would have never made such a mistake. I always taught my girls that a chain on the door will only slow a determined intruder, not stop her. Diagonal pliers, my dear. One good strong snip and I was in."

Not Dawkins Cipre's voice.

Elsa Cipre.

Elsa Cipre rolled Merida over.

Elsa Cipre's face swam before Merida's unsteady vision.

Clutching Merida's jaw with her long fingers, Elsa turned Merida's head back and forth. "Tsk. Look what you've done," she said. "Now the side of your face will be swollen, it'll be harder for me to cut the skin around your ear and the results will not be nearly as appealing. If Nauplius Brassard still lived, he would be most unhappy."

CHAPTER FIFTY-ONE

Victim: male, approximately forty, of African descent, no ID, shot and stabbed.

With a sigh, Kateri finished the paperwork for *that* night's murder, then headed in to meet with Bergen, Garik Jacobsen and Mike Sun. The consensus: some of the violence in Virtue Falls was related; some, like tonight, completely puzzling; some gruesome and disturbing; and they all needed a good night's sleep. Mike and Garik headed back to the morgue. Bergen and Kateri played rock/paper/scissors to decide who would stay through the night . . . and as they did, Kateri got a call from the hospital, from Peggy. Rainbow was restless and wanted to see her.

With a good-humored, "Cheater," Bergen shoved her toward the door.

Kateri hitched a ride with Officer Bill Chippen, took a nap on the way, got out and waved her thanks.

The hospital was steeped in that hushed, wee-hours-of-the-morning quiet. On her way to Rainbow's room, Kateri stopped at the nurses' station.

With her normal brisk efficiency, Peggy informed her, "Rainbow is on fluids and doing well. On the other hand, your sister visited, and ever since Rainbow has been agitated and insistent that she see you."

"My sister visited? Again?" Kateri shook her finger at Peggy. "I suspect there's going to be another murder in Virtue Falls, and I suspect I'm going to be the perp."

"Family. Gotta love 'em." A call button went off, and Peggy stood and whisked away.

Kateri entered Rainbow's hospital room to find her friend awake, irritated and in pain. She asked the usual inane question, "How are you feeling?"

Rainbow glared. "Did you get the box from Margaret?"

"I did. I stashed it in the trunk of my car."

"Did you open it?"

"Not yet, but—"

"I don't care why not. Open it. Find out why that aggravating woman wants it so badly."

"Lilith?"

"Your sister. After she visited, I dreamed about her. She was pointing a gun at you, demanding the box. Then I tried to take off my sweater and it choked me and the horse stomped on my foot . . ."

Kateri took Rainbow's hand and petted it. "Have you had your pain medication recently?"

Rainbow looked at the IV going into her arm. "I think about a half hour ago."

"That's good." Kateri settled into the chair beside the bed. "I'll give Lilith the box."

"No! Look inside." Rainbow closed her eyes. "Look . . . inside. Promise."

"I will look inside." Between Margaret and Rainbow, Kateri would never hear the end of it if she didn't.

She felt as if she'd been asleep for five minutes when Moen arrived, grabbed her shoulder and shook her. "Sheriff, come on!" The boy did not know how to keep his voice down.

Kateri lifted her head, blinked hard. "Shh. She's asleep."

"I know, she's in a coma and she's going to die and I'm sorry, but—"

"No. Haven't you heard?" Kateri beamed. "She's asleep. Really asleep. She's going to recover."

"Wow." Moen stared at Rainbow. "She's a tough old broad."

Rainbow's middle finger shot up.

Kateri chuckled.

"What did I say?" Moen asked, honestly bewildered.

"She is neither old nor a broad."

He blushed as only redheaded Moen could blush. "I didn't mean . . . okay. I apologize, Rainbow."

Rainbow gave a little wave.

"Good night, Rainbow. Sleep well, my friend." Kateri herded Moen out the door.

"Sheriff," he said earnestly, "this politically correct stuff is *hard*."

"I know. But cop or not, you're going to have to get it figured out. It's pretty simple. Think before you speak. Always." She followed him toward the exit. "Nothing more was happening when I left City Hall. What happened now?" *Please, God, not another murder.*

"Mike Sun used the . . . the skin from the finger I found to identify the dead maid from the B and B."

"That was good work, Moen."

"Thank you, Sheriff." He held the outer door for her. "I'm still not staying on the force."

"I know, Moen. For the record, I think you're doing the right thing."

"Really?" He stood still in the brightly lit parking lot. "Cool."

Kateri kept walking. "What do we know about the ID?"

He hurried after her. "Garik Jacobsen got the goods on her. I'm supposed to take you to the morgue, because she's not at all who she said she was. She's wanted by Interpol, the FBI, the CIA. A few terror organizations."

Now Kateri stood still. "For what?"

"Her real name is Ashley Kocsis. She's an assassin."

That was the last answer Kateri expected. She hurried after him toward the patrol car. "What is an assassin doing working as a maid at a Virtue Falls B and B?"

"She was sent to assassinate someone." Trust Moen to break the facts down to the basics.

They climbed in.

"Okay. Who?" Kateri answered her own question. "Merida Falcon." She pulled out her phone and dialed.

"No. Benedict Howard." Moen started the engine and took off like a rocket.

She knew he was going to miss driving for her. "I don't think so," she said. "The people who have been attacked have all been female. It's practice. Or maybe someone who really likes killing and hasn't had the opportunity to get to his victim."

Merida didn't answer.

Kateri hung up.

"Benedict Howard is rich," Moen said. "It's always money."

"Not always. Greed. Revenge. Love. Those are the big three. In this case, Merida does have money—she was married to a very wealthy man and her stepchildren hate her." Kateri texted Merida. "So maybe revenge. The question is— who killed the assassin?"

Moen answered almost before she finished asking. "Another assassin. The one who wants to get paid." His pale cheeks got that mottled red coloring that meant he was excited. "Call her."

Kateri hit redial. "She isn't answering."

"*Does* she answer? She can't speak."

"She can sign and she can text. And yes, I already texted her, told her I was afraid for her life and to get back to me right away. She hasn't."

"That's not good."

"No." Kateri's calm façade hid a wealth of anxiety. "What's in the morgue can wait—it's not going anywhere. Head to the B and B."

He handed her the microphone. "Call in the nearest law enforcement unit. They can beat us there."

"No. We've got a paid assassin, one who was good enough to recognize and kill his or her rival. We know he likes to torment his victims, that he's strong, intelligent and meticulous. Like a college professor. We won't want everyone swooping in, sirens blasting, so he gets in a hurry, gets sloppy." Kateri thought hard. "Merida doesn't like Benedict Howard, but he's the kind of man who gets things done. Let me call him . . . not that I have his number, and wealthy men aren't listed in the phone book."

"Phone book? What's a . . . ?"

Sometimes Moen made her feel so old and creaky. "Don't worry about it, kid. I'll call the B and B." She punched in the number and let it ring.

The answering machine picked up and Phoebe's cheerful recorded voice said, *"Thank you for calling the Good Knight Manor Bed and Breakfast . . ."*

"Where's Sean Weston?" Moen asked. "He's got a thing for Merida Falcon. In his free time, he's always hanging around trying to catch a glimpse of her. Maybe he's there now."

"It's really late. You think he's there now?"

"Maybe?" Moen sounded uncertain.

The chill Kateri felt grew stronger. "Maybe he's the killer."

"What makes you say that? He's a great guy!"

"No one thought the assassin was anything but a cleaning woman with four kids and an abusive husband." Kateri pulled out her phone. "Let me call Bergen and Garik, notify them, tell them we've got a situation and we need to go in quietly. They'll know what to do."

As Kateri and Moen drove along, the streetlights gave off an eerie blue illumination that made Kateri wish for a clear night sky and a full moon. But the marine layer, those high clouds off the ocean, had come in and covered the sky, and a few wisps slipped down to coil around the lights like ghosts dancing to unheard music.

Too many ghosts lately. Too many deaths.

Tonight, they needed to save her friend.

Benedict sat down with his laptop and Merida's and, without a twinge of conscience, used Merida's software to move the proof of embezzling from him to Rose and Albert. They would be surprised. But not as surprised as when they discovered his notation beside the unexplained fee they'd paid to a yacht mechanic at the time of his parents' death. He wondered if it would occur to them that murdering his parents was cruel and immoral, or whether they were so lost to decency they'd be bewildered by his defection.

Damn them. They deserved so much worse and yet, for them, nothing could be worse than losing the business. The business was their only love, their only passion, their only need.

Standing, he gathered his computer gear and headed into the bedroom to pack. On the nightstand, he discovered the note card Merida had made depicting Carl Klineman's message.

WAS ON

WES UN

Merida said the letters were blurred and she wasn't sure she correctly remembered them.

WASON

WESUN

WES. The killer was Wesley somebody? Maybe, but that was a big pool to choose from.

WASUN . . .

WA could be Washington. Washington SUN? Was that a newspaper? Was the killer someone tanned?

Benedict snorted and dropped the card. But his brain worried the problem as he packed his clothes. Washington something. WA S UN.

He stood up straight. WSU. Washington State University.

That was where Dawkins Cipre was supposed to teach next year.

Sitting down at the computer, he immediately found Dawkins Cipre, his honors, his teaching credentials. Then he dug deeper.

Dawkins Cipre wasn't on the WSU autumn schedule.

Benedict looked out the window.

Dawkins and Elsa Cipre had the attic room above Merida. One small light shone in the attic. All of Merida's lights were on.

Picking up his phone, he called Merida.

CHAPTER FIFTY-TWO

Elsa stood, dragged one of the heavy dining chairs out and, hooking her arms under Merida's, deadlifted her onto the seat.

Half blind with pain, Merida tried to lunge away.

With her bony fist, Elsa hit her behind the right ear.

Merida retched and blacked out.

She woke seated in the chair with her joined hands behind the chair back.

With calm severity, Elsa said, "I don't like to compromise the finished product, but I will. The important thing is doing the job. And getting paid." She spoke briskly, instructively, like a . . . like a professor.

Merida's vision returned, dissolved in watery agony, returned again. She looked at the door. It was shut and locked.

Elsa saw her. "Have you ever heard the world's shortest ghost story? A man stayed in a bedroom reputed to be haunted and before he slept, he locked all the locks on the door and windows and barricaded himself in. When he was done, he climbed into bed, turned off the light and a cheerful little voice said, 'Now we're locked in safe for the night.' " She laughed merrily. "Just like you and me."

Merida's phone rang.

Elsa located it, lifted her booted heel and stomped as hard as she could.

The glass shattered.

It rang again.

Elsa lifted her heel and stomped, stomped, stomped, each time the force of her blow growing greater. She stomped until the ringing ceased, then stomped again. When she at last stopped, she was breathing heavily. As if her frenzy was Merida's fault, she said, "We don't have an unlimited amount of time. We'll have to get the job done ASAP. *Of course,* I'm prepared and I've practiced, so don't worry. We'll get there!" She removed her ugly, misshapen black cape and spread it on the table, the lining up. She smoothed the material. Scissors, knives, sewing tools, box cutters: their handles stuck out of a myriad of pockets. In that instructional tone, she said, "I found a purse to be an inefficient way to carry the necessities a woman needs. So when I design my clothing, I add a holder for each item. A place for everything and everything in its place. Tonight, of course, I was wearing my cutting cape."

Merida breathed deeply, working through the pain in her head. Okay. She was seated on a heavy wooden chair, her wrists cuffed behind her.

Not for the first time. She'd been held like this

when Nauplius had chosen to exert his power, punish her with the inability to speak with her hands.

Elsa wore black leggings and a black sleeveless racerback tank. Her eccentric clothing had hidden how wiry she was; her thin arms were deeply muscled, her wrists resembled a wrestler's. This woman worked out, ran, lifted weights.

Elsa retrieved a handkerchief and blotted the blood off the corner of her eye. She had that, a split lip and a bruise on her face, but the body bruises Merida had imagined Dawkins Cipre had inflicted didn't exist.

Why not? What was the thump from the attic, the sound of a body falling? What had Elsa done to Dawkins Cipre?

Who was this woman?

With her fingertips Merida explored the fastening that held her hands. Plastic handcuffs with a zip tie. Her left wrist was caught tight enough to cut off her circulation. She'd been unconscious then.

But for her right wrist, she'd been awake, a little, so when Elsa fastened the tie, Merida had stiffened her hand to make it wider, give herself some wiggle room.

Having Nauplius bind Merida with whatever he had at hand—twine, rope, ribbon—had taught her some tricks. Who would have thought she'd be blessing him for that?

Elsa faced her. "Let's see, you must have a million questions. Where shall we start? You may already have guessed Elsa Cipre is my pseudonym, chosen for me by your husband. By the way, he was a charming man, and knew exactly what he wanted. I'm Gloria Meyrick. Have you heard of me?"

Merida shook her head.

"Fame is so fleeting! You already know some of my story. Dawkins was angry with me when he caught me at that absurd woman's quilting group, telling the truth about my background." Elsa plucked a roll of duct tape from one of her cape pockets and tore off a strip. "In fact, I did lead the Home Sciences department at Northeastern Christian University. I *did* demand the best from my students, and I *was* tough on them. Really tough on the ones with potential. Some of the girls complained. One of them, her mother was a lawyer. Her mother took action against me and *that's* when the dean announced Home Sciences was a dated, unnecessary program. He ended my funding." Bringing the tape to Merida, she placed it on Merida's forehead. "Looking back, my mistake wasn't killing the lawyer. It was sewing her mouth shut. That detail gave me away."

Panicked and repulsed, Merida kicked at her with both feet.

Elsa punched her between the eyes.

Merida blacked out again.

She returned to consciousness to find her ankles zip-tied to the chair legs and her forehead taped to the chair back.

"You shouldn't do that, you know." Elsa stood by the table, selecting from among a variety of blades: ceramic paring knife, embroidery scissors, three kinds of rotary cutters . . . "I was in the penitentiary for thirty-one years. No chance of parole. Prison is brutal. One doesn't survive without inspiring fear. When I went in, I already inspired fear. *You* haven't got a chance. That's why, out of all the killers in the world, Nauplius picked me as his first-wave assassin."

She brought over a pair of tiny gold embroidery scissors and held them in front of Merida's eyes. "Aren't these *cute?* They're antiques, the handles are shaped like a crane. They were beyond belief expensive, but Nauplius gave me a spectacular budget to get what I needed to do the job." She clicked the scissors. "They're also the finest embroidery scissors in the world, and don't worry, I have had them sharpened to a fine edge." She tucked them into her cleavage. "I promised Nauplius I would do a good job, and I intend to keep that promise."

Merida pushed her left wrist down as hard as she could, made her right hand as narrow as possible. The plastic edges were sharp; if she was going to free herself in time, she was going to lose skin. A lot of skin.

If she didn't free herself in time, she was going to lose more than skin.

"You're struggling to talk, aren't you? That's so endearing." With a half-smile, Elsa watched her work her hands behind her back. "What I really think I'll like about performing on you isn't only that you can't scream. I rather enjoyed some of that from the other victims, although Dawkins said it got old. But you can't interrupt me! That is delightful."

Merida showed Elsa her teeth.

"Ooh, you're scary." Elsa selected a new blade for her X-Acto knife and locked it firmly in place. "When Nauplius discovered he was doomed to a soon and sudden death, he broke me out of prison, spoke to me about his wishes. He said he had created you, your face was his, and when he died, he would take it back."

Merida worked at moving the handcuffs down and off. She compressed the bones in her right hand, dragging the plastic over her thumb, scraping skin off the knuckle.

"Nauplius was so logical." Elsa sounded admiring. "After I agreed to do as he wished, he gave me a cover story with Dawkins Cipre as my husband—and as my handler."

Blood trickled down Merida's thumb and she shook her hand repeatedly to scatter the evidence. Merida remembered the fit Elsa had thrown about the ringing phone. If she suspected Merida was trying to escape . . . Merida's gaze wandered over the cutting implements. She listened to Elsa's fluting voice, heard the edge of madness that anticipated this job, and looked into Elsa's avid eyes.

Merida shook off the blood again, shook off the pain, and continued to work.

Elsa said, "You escaped us when Nauplius died, and I hated that. I needed to practice. That was the first time I gave Dawkins the slip, when I killed that member of Nauplius's legal team. I *like* to kill lawyers . . . Dawkins caught up with me that time, but then I knew I was smarter than he was. He knew it, too. He was nothing but a historian, an expert in the past. I taught the practical; I knew how to do . . . everything. Cut anything. Soon enough, he was afraid of me. He saw what I was capable of. But he never imagined what I could do to him." Throwing her head back, Elsa laughed, wildly, happily. "He's up there, bleeding to death in slow increments, unable to move, a needle in his brain . . ."

Tears filled Merida's eyes. She shook them away. She was terrified. She was in pain. She was ripping her skin off her hand. Not fast enough, though. She didn't have enough time . . .

Elsa slid the handle of the X-Acto knife into her cleavage, then added the sheathed ceramic paring knife. "Just the two of us . . ." she sang. She caressed the handles of her embroidery scissors, then hooked them onto her shirt.

There! That was it. How perfect. Elsa had placed those blades where Merida could get them. Most were sheathed; obviously Elsa had a care for her own skin. Yet all Merida needed was her hands free. All she needed was . . . she worked feverishly. Sweat gathered at her spine and slid down in cold, agonizing, itchy trails.

Someone knocked at the door.

Merida froze. She looked at the door. Looked at Elsa.

Benedict? Was it Benedict?

Elsa flushed. Her eyes narrowed with irritation. She whispered, "We'll pretend there's no one in here."

The knocking stopped.

Elsa went to the door, pressed her eye to the peephole. "Good. Whoever it was went away."

Benedict. Come back!

Merida jerked, yanked, tore at the cuffs. She *had* to get her hands free.

Returning to the table, Elsa chose one of the rotary cutters. She visually examined Merida's face, then hooked the handles of the diagonal pliers in her cleavage. At last she walked to the chair, where Merida was trapped, handcuffed, bound head, hand and foot. Elsa leaned forward, so close her breath brushed Merida's face. She smelled minty, fresh, not at all like a macabre butcher. She said, "This work takes concentration. Dawkins never appreciated that. He would always pace and urge me to hurry. That's why I tore the first face. Let me assure you, your face will be an elegant work of art." Easing the rotary cutter out of her cleavage, she removed the blade guard and placed it against Merida's temple.

The cool, light touch galvanized Merida. She jerked hard on the nylon handcuff.

Her right hand popped free. Both hands . . . were loose.

Elsa jumped back. "Be careful! Your face is my chef d'oeuvre, my work of art. Do *not* spoil it for me. That would *not* go well for you. I can make you suffer . . . more."

Now. Merida had one chance of success. With her gaze fixed on Elsa's face, she weighed her options. She needed Elsa to lean close again, to concentrate on the task at hand.

Elsa again placed the rotary cutter against her temple. "I always love the first cut," she said. "When it's done well, I mean."

Merida clenched her teeth. That initial incision . . . that's when Elsa's focus would be at its height.

That's when the pain would give Merida the incentive she needed.

Elsa pressed hard.

The blade slid through Merida's skin and onto the bone at her temple.

The pain!

Elsa rolled the rotary blade down toward Merida's ear.

Merida brought her arms around, snatched the diagonal pliers out of Elsa's cleavage. With a violent upward swing, she stabbed them into the soft part under Elsa's chin.

Elsa's mouth opened; blood gushed.

Merida yanked the pliers free.

Elsa fell backward onto the hardwood floor and rolled in agony, shrieking with the volume and the undulation of a fire alarm.

At the door, the handle rattled.

Merida ripped the tape off her forehead; hair came, too, and skin, and that hurt like hell. Leaning over, she used the pliers to clip the zip ties. Standing, she stepped toward the suit of armor.

In the corridor, people shouted.

Swift as a Gila monster, Elsa swiveled and crawled close enough to grab Merida's ankle.

Merida kicked at her.

Elsa slashed her skin with the rotary cutter.

Merida screamed in silent agony, strained and reached. Bolstered by pain-induced adrenaline, she dragged Elsa with her. She grasped the hilt of the long sword, pulled it away from the knight, lifted the heavy blade and swung.

Elsa's severed forearm rested on the rug.

Elsa screamed again and with the other hand

raised her now unsheathed paring knife toward Merida's knee.

With a downward stab, Merida drove the sword through Elsa's back, through her heart and into the floor, pinning her there like exhibit A in the serial killer museum.

The door burst open.

Benedict ran into the room.

Kateri followed on his heels, pistol in hand and pointed at the scene.

Sean Weston in police uniform. Phoebe Glass in her robe. Lilith . . . they all piled into the room. All witnesses to Merida's achievement.

Merida lifted her gaze from the bloody wreckage of her would-be assassin. She wiped at the blood trickling down her face with the back of her equally bloody hand.

Using her tongue and teeth and vocal cords, she slowly and distinctly said, "I saved myself."

CHAPTER FIFTY-THREE

Lacey stood in the door of Kateri's office and barked.

Kateri glanced at the clock, then at the rather surprising report in her hand. "Yes, you're right, it's past time for dinner." Turning off her desk light, she wandered through the patrol room smiling at her guys.

They all smiled back.

Everybody was happy. Everyone felt as if they'd accomplished something great—even though, as Merida Falcon had said, she'd saved herself. But to have the monster off the streets, to know they would see no more mutilated corpses, that was a great thing.

Lacey raced to the outer door and waited.

Kateri opened it and the dog bounded out, license rattling, down the stairs and onto the street.

At the press briefing, even Councilman Venegra had had to offer up a grudging, "Well done." Then he had, of course, asked about John Terrance. But after the gruesomeness of these murders, John Terrance had become a lesser terror and, as Bertha told the entire town, the press and Venegra, she'd put so much buckshot in Terrance, his ass was dragging.

Bertha was now a bona fide Virtue Falls hero.

Truthfully, like Bertha, Kateri hoped John Terrance had died alone in the woods, a pain-filled septic death, one that in some small part made up for the misery he had caused Rainbow. And her.

Kateri and Lacey called on the park across the street—Kateri found herself revisiting the wonderful world of dog poo removal—then Lacey trotted past the Oceanview Café, past the Gem Lounge, headed for home.

Or so Kateri thought. But to her surprise, Lacey missed the turn for their apartment. Kateri called her, but Lacey continued trotting toward the marina, into the cool, softly lit mist that crept off the ocean. The light fog crept over the streets, bringing a magic to the evening. The shops had closed. The restaurants and bars were humming; people greeted her by name, congratulated her on making Virtue Falls safe once more.

Lacey was right. It was a good night for a walk.

As Kateri crossed at the corner of Ocean and Marina, on a quiet stretch of sidewalk, she heard the rolling thump of a suitcase on the sidewalk. No, two suitcases.

Lacey gave a bark and ran toward the sound, disappearing for a long moment.

Kateri heard a murmur of voices, then out of the mist stepped Lacey, proudly leading Merida and Benedict. Merida's hands were bandaged as was the side of her face.

Both pulled a light suitcase and looked dressed for travel.

Interesting.

In her newly found, soft voice, Merida said, "Kateri, I'm so glad Lacey found us. We're off on an adventure, and I wanted to say good-bye." Putting her suitcase onto its four wheels, she stepped forward and hugged Kateri, hugged her hard, looked into her face and hugged her again. "Thank you for all you've done. You've been . . . the truest friend . . ." She choked up, then stepped back and signed, ". . . anyone could ever have."

Kateri recognized the genuine emotion behind the words, and choked up in her turn. "I'm so glad . . . you came to Virtue Falls. I'm glad for whatever help I could render."

"I'm sorry I brought a serial killer with me," Merida said aloud. "I'm sorry I made so much trouble for you."

"I'll acquit you for that. The FBI has been quite forthright about Gloria Meyrick and what a tangled mess that is. Apparently Nauplius Brassard had her removed from prison so neatly that all law enforcement agencies believed she had died. They looked at the killing in Paris and thought it was a copycat murder when in fact, it was Gloria Meyrick herself." Garik had confided that the FBI was scrambling to discover exactly how Nauplius had pulled off the escape and who was buried under Gloria Meyrick's tombstone.

"I've never been so afraid in my life." Merida both spoke and signed, as if she needed to express herself in every way she could.

Benedict twined her hand in his, using special care not to hurt her or disturb the bandages.

Merida leaned her head against his shoulder.

Seeing their affection, Kateri thought of Stag and considered herself the biggest fool in the history of the world.

"Meyrick had a record of escalating violence against her students when they didn't live up to her standards, and when the university cut her Home Sciences program—wow. She stalked and killed everyone she deemed responsible, up to and including the president of the school. It was quite the reign of terror. So, Merry, you won." Deliberately, Kateri used Merida's real name. "You saved yourself and killed the monster."

"She is the bravest, most wonderful woman in the world, but she never has to stand alone again. I've got her back." Benedict smiled into Merida's eyes, and Kateri could not only sense, but also see his steadfast determination to always be with her.

Yep. Kateri was selfish for thinking of herself . . . but she had been so stupid about Stag.

Benedict touched Merida's arm. "Come on, dear, we'd do well to make the tide."

"Headed for the marina, are you?" Kateri fell in right behind him, walking almost on his heels.

Merida followed.

"We are," Benedict said. "I thought after our ordeal, we'll cruise up the coast and into the Salish Sea, visit a few of the San Juan Islands."

Merida's soft voice said, "We've chartered a seaplane for a flight over the area."

Kateri glanced behind.

Merida had that look on her face, the one she had always worn when she talked about flying. "I think if the flight goes well, if I enjoy it as much as I think I will, I might take lessons again, get my pilot's license. That explosion changed so much about my life. I can't allow it to take away my desire to touch the heavens."

Benedict looked back, past Kateri to Merida, and he had a look on his face, too, the kind that said this man adored everything about this woman.

Kateri's heart contracted with both joy for them, and sorrow for her own aloneness. "The islands are lovely this time of year. You'll enjoy it. Hard to trace people out there. Not much for cell service. That reminds me . . . we at the police department have solved one mystery about last night. We traced the call reporting last night's first death to . . . you, Benedict Howard."

He kept going. "Carl Klineman's death, right? Did you discover who killed him?"

Kateri glanced back at Merida and rolled her eyes. Like she hadn't seen Benedict sidestep that accusation. But truth to tell, she didn't much care *who* had called it in. Knowing about that body had saved Virtue Falls law enforcement a shit ton of trouble later. "We traced the bullet to the pistol Ashley Kocsis used in previous killings. However, as to whether or not she killed Carl Klineman or one of the Cipres took the pistol from Kocsis and performed the deed, we don't yet know." Something pinged her consciousness, and she stopped. No jingling license, no tapping toenails on the pavement . . . "Where's Lacey?"

"She went that way." Merida pointed toward the dark van parked at the curb.

"Lacey!" Kateri called. From behind the van, she heard Lacey bark wildly, then growl, deep and angry. Kateri started around the vehicle, hand on her holster.

A man yelped. "Damn you, you little rat!"

A scuffle.

Another yelp.

Deeper growling.

More swearing.

And, muffled by the swirling fog, a gunshot.

Benedict knocked Merida down to the sidewalk and covered her with his body.

Kateri shouted, "Lacey!" and sprinted into the street and around the van, unsnapping her holster and removing her service pistol. She came around in time to see Phoebe's son, Evan Glass, point his pistol at Lacey—who had her teeth sunk into his leg.

"Lacey, go!" Kateri shouted.

Lacey released him and ran under the van.

And the dumbshit shot himself right in the foot. He screamed in pain, dropped the pistol and grabbed for the wound.

Furious and afraid for her dog's life, Kateri kicked her knee against his hip.

Off balance, he fell sideways onto the pavement, rolled and scrambled toward his firearm.

She slammed her knee into his back, smashed him onto the pavement, cuffed him and shouted, "What the hell were you doing?"

"Your dog bit me!"

"You were hiding behind that van with a firearm and you shot . . . at me!" Maybe not, but it would play in court. "At the sheriff!"

"I didn't shoot at *you*. I shot at *her*." He pointed toward Merida.

As Benedict helped Merida to her feet, he said, "I told you my aunt and uncle were too thrifty to pay the price for a good assassin."

"I feel so cheap," Merida signed, and humor leaped from her hands.

Kateri couldn't believe there had been *another* attempt on Merida's life. Really angry now, she improvised. "These good people seem to believe you're an international assassin and worthy of Interpol's attention."

He whined like a mosquito. "No, I'm not! I got this job from my mother. Today! She said I'd be paid for this and I could move on." There was a world of loathing in his tone. "I want to leave, not be here working for *her!*"

Phoebe Glass had a lot to answer for.

Kateri heard sirens; someone nearby had heard the gunshots and called 911. As the first police cruiser pulled up, she called, "Lacey, come on, sweetheart."

Lacey pranced out, proud of her heroics.

Kateri captured her in her arms and hugged her, so happy to hold that warm, wiggling body and know they would be going home together.

She heard the click/roll of two suitcases and looked up in time to see Benedict and Merida vanish into the fog.

She suspected she would never see her friends again.

CHAPTER FIFTY-FOUR

Kateri had promised Rainbow and she had promised Margaret. No more delays. She had to open the damned box.

But for this, she needed to be alone and undistracted. So she took Lacey to Mrs. Golobovitch, who was delighted to dog-sit. Kateri drove her police cruiser to her apartment, parked, tucked the black box under her arm and carried it into the living room. She placed her staff against the wall and the box on the coffee table. Stepping back, she stared at the box, unwilling to again face the contents and knowing they would somehow change her life.

At last she worked up the nerve and lifted the lid.

Edgar Allen Poe's raven looked back, his shiny eyes alive and knowing. Would it tell its secrets?

Nevermore.

Putting the box top aside, she grasped him in both hands, lifted him free, carried him to the bookcase and placed him on the top shelf among her best beloved books. At eighteen inches tall and twenty pounds, the nineteenth-century black cast-iron bird carried the weight of Baltimore literature, art and history on his feathers. More important to Kateri, he exuded the intelligent, devious spirit that Native Americans worshiped. For all that, he deserved a tall perch.

Returning to the couch, she seated herself and pulled the box toward her. She lifted the faded album, wondering how she could be so brave in the face of danger and so terrified by a bunch of old photographs of her father and her mother together. She smoothed the leather cover, picked it up and smelled in the scent of old paper and dust . . . and was transported back to that moment when she had first seen it, first held it, first opened it and thrilled to the contents.

Stupid, stupid child that she had been. She had danced downstairs to her father's study, knocked as she'd been taught, anticipated his summons. She walked sedately across the hardwood floor, over the luxurious Aubusson rug to his desk and waited for him to acknowledge her—which he did after an appropriately lengthy wait.

But this time, she didn't care, because she knew a secret.

His cool, disinterested voice: "Katherine, what do you want?"

She burst out, "I want to say—I found the album and it's . . . . I'm so glad you loved Mama with all your heart."

His already stern face froze into steely lines. "What are you talking about?"

"About this." She pulled the photo out

from behind her back and thrust it toward him.

He took it by the edges, never touching her fingers, and looked at it.

At first, she didn't notice the way his angular face seemed to be carved of harsh stone, unbreathing, unmoving. She was too intent on babbling, "I know that beach where you took those pictures. Did Rainbow take them? She was in some of them, so I thought it had to be her. Uncle Bluster was in one, too. He's dead now, Mama said he drank himself to death, but for a long time, he was like a father to me."

Her real father lifted his heavy-lidded gaze from the photo and stared at her.

Perhaps she shouldn't have said that. To cover up her faux pas, she rattled on. "You were picking up driftwood in one picture, and I recognize that piece. Mama always keeps it in her room on a shelf lined with shells. She said she used to like to collect shells but now she—"

"Where did you find this . . . picture?"

Something was wrong. He wasn't pleased. "I told you. In the album."

"Where is the album?"

"In the attic."

"What were you doing in the attic?"

She swallowed. *Hiding from my sister. Hiding from your wife. Hiding from the servants. Hiding from my loneliness.* She couldn't say any of that. "I don't know."

Her father put the photograph in the right-hand bottom drawer of his desk. "Don't go up there again."

"But—"

"Nothing up there is of any concern to you."

"Pictures of you and my mom!" *You do remember my mother, Mary Kwinault? You loved her once.*

"They are none of your business."

"I want that picture. Give me that picture!" She wanted to lunge at him, hit him, strangle him until he was dead.

At the same time she feared him, feared that icy control, those cold blue eyes, the cruelty that lurked beneath starched white shirts and in ruthless fingers that without remorse could—and did—tear a screaming child out of her mother's arms and carry her away forever.

He picked up his pen. "Is there anything else?"

Kateri choked on bile, on hate, on impotent fury. "You're the most awful father in the whole world. No one loves you. And I hate you!" Whirling, she stomped toward the door. Stomped, when she wanted to run, but she wouldn't allow herself to show fear for that man who hurt her so casually.

His voice stopped her before she stepped over the threshold. "Katherine."

"What!"

He didn't answer.

She faced him. "What?"

"Put on your shoes before you return to my office."

"I'll never come here again." She had never meant anything so much in her life.

"As you wish." He flicked his fingers at her. "Shut the door on your way out."

"My name is Kateri!" She did shut the door, as hard as she could, but the heavy oak and well-oiled hinges did no more than make a muffled thump. She raced to her room before bursting into loud sobs swiftly muffled by her hands, the blankets, the pillows. She fell asleep crying and when she woke up, it was dark and late, she was starving, and she was determined to get up to that attic and take that album. *He* didn't care about it. *She* did. Those were her parents, and that was the only image of her mother Kateri had ever seen with Mary looking radiant and happy.

She slid out of bed and headed up the narrow servants' stairs, two flights toward the wooden attic door. The stairway was cold, airless. She didn't turn on the lights; with no windows she had to grope her way along the bannisters, feel the steps with her bare feet, and all the time, a sense of being stalked grew. She got to the top, slid her hands down the door until she wrapped them around the knob. She turned it slowly, in growing anticipation—but the door wouldn't yield.

It was locked, and remained that way for all the rest of her years trapped in that cold Baltimore mansion.

Rainbow said that in the album Kateri would solve a mystery, and so at last Kateri opened the leather-bound album and leafed through the pages, looking at each photo, seeing her mother young and happy, her father . . . looking happy, too.

Odd. In all the years she had lived with him, he had never been anything but grim and distant with a lurking cruelty that terrified the whole household. While with her mother he seemed almost human. Maybe in his way he had loved her. Maybe.

But what did it matter? He had broken Mary's heart then. Later, when he took Kateri from her, he had broken Mary's spirit. He had been her mother's frog god, shaking the earth and breaking the sea and changing her life from a bright shining eagerness into the long, dim tunnel of hopeless years.

Kateri had forgiven him. The frog god had demanded it. Nevertheless, she was sure he burned in hell.

The album's last pages were blank, black sheets of dull paper filled with nothingness, and Kateri had not yet solved any mysteries.

The very last page wasn't black or dull; it held a sealed tan manila envelope inserted into the binding. Kateri squished it between her fingers. Not much inside. Tearing the envelope, she pulled out—

From the doorway that led into the kitchen, a woman's voice spoke. "You found it."

Kateri came to her feet. She looked up to see Lilith staring at her. Sneering at her.

Kateri looked down at the header and the ornate green border on the mottled security paper.

CERTIFICATE OF MARRIAGE
NEILL PALMER AND MARY KWINAULT

CHAPTER FIFTY-FIVE

"You trashed my house for this?" Kateri held up the paper.

Lilith lunged across the room, reached for the certificate.

Kateri pulled it back, fended her off with a sharp elbow to the rib cage. "My father and mother were *married*? He *married* her? Why?"

Lilith doubled over, gasped. "He said he loved her."

"He said . . . he loved her? My mother? Mary?" The whole world was falling apart around Kateri's ears, all the perspectives were changing. She didn't know how to put the pieces back together.

"He had clearly lost his mind."

Kateri weighed how much force to put into the next blow to Lilith's rib cage. And head, chest, face . . . But she wanted information and she couldn't get it if Lilith was unconscious. "How did you find out?" She lifted the paper. "About this."

"Father *told* me." Lilith straightened up. "He *told* me he married your mother. He *told* me he loved her. I asked where the marriage certificate was, and he said he hid it."

"What did he hope to accomplish by telling you . . . any of that?"

"He was in pain. On medication. He said someone needed to know."

"Deathbed confession? How human of him."

"I suppose." Lilith clearly did not see the humor. "I knew I had to find it before . . . before disaster struck. I sat down and I thought. Thought about his last days and his last words and I knew . . . I knew somehow he'd managed to send it to you."

"Why do you care? Why would anyone care except me? I'm the one who . . . who's suddenly legitimate." Was she? Kateri wasn't sure that a child born of bigamy was legitimate. Hey, maybe Lilith was no longer legitimate.

Kateri grinned.

"*Why do I care?* Your mother . . . and my father. He was a respected man of the community. He didn't love my mother, but at least she had her position as his wife." Lilith glared as if Kateri were guilty of every kind of crime. "And then you. *You!* We found out about you. So unlike him. Such a lack of control on his part. When you came to live with us, I was in high school. Do you know what my friends said? About me having an Indian sister?"

"Native American."

Lilith kept rolling. "Out of control. Savage. Without the slightest smidgeon of civilization or education. I was *humiliated*."

"You're holding a grudge about what happened

in your high school? That was more than twenty years ago!"

Lilith went into her martyr act. "You have no sensitivity to my finer feelings."

"Finer . . . feelings!" Kateri sputtered. "You . . . you locked Merry Byrd and me in the basement and left us to die!"

"Don't exaggerate. It was only a couple of days."

"*You* didn't let us out. We figured out how to get ourselves out." Kateri reined in her temper. "This is squabbling. This is stupid. How did you get in here? Into my house?"

"That's not important."

"I promise it is."

"I may have helped myself to a key while we were at the quilting group." Lilith managed to sound lofty, as if she had managed some noble mission.

Outraged, Kateri shouted, "You *stole* my back door key? Sure. Why not? You trashed my house. You trashed Rainbow's house. You think nothing of breaking and entering. Why would you stop at stealing?" She took a breath, calmed herself and in a reasonable tone asked, "What did you think I was going to do with the marriage certificate?"

Lilith grew deadly calm, looked down, removed a piece of lint from her sleeve.

Illumination struck. Kateri smiled in the

moment of revelation. "You thought I would challenge his will."

"There is money involved," Lilith pointed out.

Kateri felt herself descend to the level of out-of-control savage without the slightest smidgeon of civilization or education. "I don't want his dirty money."

"Of course not," Lilith mocked. "You're too noble for that."

"Let us be clear here. I didn't know there was a marriage, much less a marriage certificate. I didn't know I had the paperwork." Kateri realized she was shouting again. "And even if I had known, I wouldn't have handed it over to you."

"Why not?" Lilith wore that tucked-in lips, snottily superior *I told you so* expression. "If you're not going to challenge the will, why wouldn't you give it to me?"

"Because you never *asked* for it." Kateri found herself flapping the certificate at Lilith. "I knew when you showed up here you were up to something, but you never told me what. Why is everything in your family so shrouded in secrecy? *'Don't look in the attic, Kateri.' 'Don't touch the raven, Kateri.' 'Don't look at the books in the library, Kateri.'* It's like some stupid game you're always playing and *I can't figure out the rules.*"

With that laser focus that marked Lilith's

personality, she asked, "Will you give me the marriage certificate?"

"Why should I?"

Lilith reached into her purse, pulled a pistol, a Glock 43 and pointed it at Kateri. "Because I said so."

Kateri wavered between scornful laughter and sheer terror. This was the woman who had shut two little girls into the cellar and left them to die. At the same time, her hair was perfectly groomed, her makeup was flawless, and she held the pistol limply, negligently, as if the weight hurt her wrist. But . . .

Looking up into those cold blue eyes, Kateri decided that terror was the logical emotion.

What she didn't count on was her own overwhelming wave of fury. "You bitch. If you had ever asked, I would have given you this. I would have thrown it at you to get it out of my house. But oh, no. Like everything else in your family it's all games and guessing and sneaking around and hiding the truth."

"We're *your* family, too."

Kateri gestured widely, ridiculously. "I came into that Baltimore mansion too late to learn all that *crap*."

"You learned more than you think. Do you think you could have succeeded as you have if you had remained here your whole life, dealing with an alcoholic mother, a lackluster education and all the lowered expectations of being raised on a Native American reservation?" Lilith knew exactly how to strike at the truth, at Kateri's pride. "I don't *think* so. I went out to your rez. That place is a cesspool."

The rez was poor, disheartening, but to hear Lilith describe it as a cesspool made Kateri want to slap her—and made her want to cry. "The reservation is the land the government didn't want and used to keep Natives Americans imprisoned. What did you think it would be like?"

"You people should . . . you should do something to improve yourselves."

Kateri noted she was no longer part of Lilith's family, but *you people.* "We are improving. Every day we're improving. Now, we're building a casino." False bravado. She didn't approve of the casino. But if it would improve her people's finances . . .

"That's immoral. Do you know how those casinos operate?"

"I do. After my mother died, I was a dealer. I also know that job kept me alive until I was able to get into the Coast Guard Academy."

"You're lying. You were too young to work in a casino!"

Lilith's ignorant indignation amused Kateri. "There are ways to get a false ID."

"You . . . lied? You falsified legal documents?"

Lilith broke in to houses, stole a key, held a weapon, threatened to kill—and was horrified about a little falsification. "How can *you* enforce the law?"

"I understand the law as it applies to the shady side better than most people." Kateri's gaze flicked to the pistol.

"If you had simply asked Father—"

"For support?" Kateri's resentment rose. "I think not. When I got away from him, I swore I would never accept his help again."

"You did, though. He got you into the Coast Guard Academy."

"He made me eat *dirt* to do it." Kateri had to take deep breaths to continue. "He was an awful man. Why do you defend him?"

"Why do you defend your mother, a hopeless alcoholic and sometime whore?"

Kateri grew cold with rage. This ghastly, manipulative, greedy, shallow bitch dared to malign Mary Kwinault? No. Never. So Kateri said the thing guaranteed to hurt. "At least I know my mother loved me."

Where Kateri's rage was cold, Lilith's flashed like fire. She lunged, slapped Kateri across the cheek.

When she came in for another blow, Kateri caught her arm, twisted it behind her, made her drop the pistol. It landed with a thunk.

Didn't go off . . . yay. Maybe the safety was on.

"Really?" Kateri was furious. "After what you said, you hit me?"

"You deserve it, you filthy . . . you don't even know if you're really part of the family!"

"Did you think your father took me in without checking my DNA? Of course I'm his! Do you think I want to be related to you? To him? God, no!" Kateri flung Lilith's arm away and spun her around.

Lilith had tears in her eyes. From the pain in her arm? Or from Kateri's cruel taunt?

Of course Kateri felt guilt. Damn it. "Look, I'm sorry that I said that about your mother."

"My mother taught me dignity. She taught me to make the most of my assets. She taught me good grooming." From the sweeping, gimlet-eyed glance Lilith shot at her, Kateri knew grooming to be her greatest failure. "From my mother, from our family, you learned to survive in a civilized environment."

"I learned deception. I learned secrecy. I learned that to express my opinions was a sin punishable by loneliness, rejection and heartache."

"You appear to have forgotten it all."

"Virtue Falls is a small, barely civilized corner of the world where some people, at least, allow a woman to speak her mind." Right now, Kateri had never been so grateful to be in Virtue Falls.

"You can have your barely civilized corner of the world. Now give me that certificate!"

"To hell with you, lady!"

Lilith lunged, grabbed the envelope, wrestled with Kateri for control.

Kateri fought back, angry enough to punch Lilith in the face but too aware of Lilith's desperation to do it. Lilith dragged her across the room.

Kateri saw a flash of movement behind Lilith. Someone—a man—stepped through the doorway and slammed his rifle butt into Lilith's head.

Lilith dropped like a rock . . . leaving Kateri facing John Terrance and the rifle that was pointed right at her.

CHAPTER FIFTY-SIX

Time froze. Kateri froze. And what had been terror when she faced Lilith's pistol cooled and hardened to become something more, something stronger. Courage, maybe, in its rawest and most foolish form.

She eased back a step. "John Terrance. I knew you weren't dead."

John Terrance grinned, all triumph and dingy teeth. "You aren't that lucky."

"Obviously not." Her walking stick was leaning against the wall. Her service pistol hung on her belt holster. She didn't dare reach for either one.

He wanted to kill her. He intended to kill her. Options were limited. She needed time. "How did you get in?" she asked.

"Back door was unlocked. Practically an invitation."

Great. Lilith had used her key to get in and like the damned idiot she was, she had failed to lock the door behind her.

Kateri glanced at Lilith's unmoving figure and the giant lump forming on the side of her head. "You hurt my sister, may have killed her."

He poked his mud-splashed boot at Lilith. "Might have. What do you care? I couldn't believe it when I came in the door and you two darlin's were havin' a catfight. Nothing like a couple of women wrestlers to get my juices flowing." He dropped one hand below his belt and cupped his junk. "I always wanted to fuck a sheriff."

"Any sheriff?" Since all the previous Virtue Falls sheriffs had been male.

"I prefer female, but sure. Any sheriff."

Or any knothole in a tree. Maybe being shot by a deer rifle wasn't such a bad fate. She shifted back another step toward her staff. "I *hoped* you had died."

"I'll bet you did." He leaned toward her, skinny, sunburned, his faded blue eyes alight with malice. "I'm all infected on my backside. I can't survive this. I *am* going to die. What do I care what happens next? As long as I get revenge for my boy, for myself."

Crap. This was a suicide mission. He didn't have anything to lose.

"I don't know who killed your boy," she said.

"Bullshit. You ran the ballistics on the bullet."

"The gun's not registered."

"Bullshit. Bullshit!" John Terrance went from coldly pleased to hotly furious in an instant. "You . . . you're lying. You know who killed my boy. *You* killed my boy!"

"I was bleeding on the floor of the Oceanview Café!"

"One of your officers . . ."

"No!" She caught a movement out of the corner of her eye.

Lilith was crawling away.

So she wasn't dead. Thank God. She might be the worst sister in the whole world, but Kateri didn't wish death on her. Kateri moved to the side, away from her walking stick, drawing Terrance's attention from Lilith's slow escape. "The shot that killed your son was from an unregistered handgun."

Lilith scraped the button of her cuff across the linoleum.

John Terrance half-turned. The rifle dipped and wavered.

Kateri said, "But I won't lie to you, Terrance. I don't give a shit who killed your son. As long as he's dead." She screamed a war cry and attacked.

Martial arts favored the underdog. Trouble was, the tsunami and its aftermath had left Kateri with more than her fair share of artificial joints. She didn't jump well, she didn't run swiftly.

John Terrance stood halfway across the room. Before she reached him, the rifle was pointed at her.

She went in low and tackled him around the ribs.

John Terrance staggered.

Over her head, the rifle discharged.

Behind her, she heard wood splinter, glass shatter.

Still hanging onto his waist—he *reeked*—she balled her fist and slammed the junk he had so proudly cupped.

The air whooshed out of him.

She jumped away, stumbled when he grabbed her hair.

He jerked her head back, smashed the rifle holster against her throat.

She gagged, fell to her knees.

"Look up," he said.

When she did, the black eye of his rifle barrel was pointed between her eyes.

"I'm going to enjoy this." His breath, smelling of rot and infection, rolled over her. His eyes, blue and malicious, gleamed with vivid rapture. In slow motion, he wrapped his finger around the trigger. "You're sweating, Sheriff Kwinault."

"You should be sweating, too." Kateri breathed. Just breathed. If she was going to die, she would first put the fear of a god into John Terrance. Today, he would see the frog god. Putting aside her fear, she placed her palms flat on the floor. She looked past the end of the rifle into Terrance's eyes and called on the Lord of the Deep.

Terrance took a step backward. "What's wrong with your face?"

Kateri knew what he saw. The cold green gaze of the frog god looked out of her eyes.

His finger tightened on the trigger.

Kateri prepared to die.

Then . . . salvation! Lilith loomed behind him, raised Edgar Allan Poe's raven over her head and slammed it down on his skull.

Kateri ducked.

His bullet whistled past Kateri's cheek.

Lilith slammed the bird down again.

John Terrance fell to the floor, bleeding and unconscious.

Lilith hit him again. And again. She shouted at him, "You think you can kill her? You piece of crap, not while I'm around. She's a pain in the fanny, but she's *my* stupid, lousy sister." She kicked him in the ribs, lifted the raven again.

Kateri raised her hand. "Wait!"

Lilith paused. Her hair was mussed. She had a livid, growing bruise on her cheekbone. And she was clearly, absolutely outraged. She kicked John Terrance's inert body again. "If anybody's going to kill her, it's me. Goddamn it!"

Kateri staggered to her feet. Her knees were shaking. Her hands were shaking. She laughed too loudly. "You're going to have a black eye!"

Kateri didn't know it was possible, but Lilith got madder.

She turned on Kateri and stalked toward her like a cat stalking an eagle.

Kateri sobered. She caught the raven and pried it out of Lilith's fingers. "You win. I'll give you the marriage certificate."

In a disconcertingly smooth assembly, Lilith pulled herself together. She smoothed her hair. Smiled tightly. "Very sensible of you."

With four words, she made Kateri want to fight her again. Kateri turned away, toward the sprawled, inert body of John Terrance. She needed to restrain him . . . she searched at her belt, but she didn't have cuffs on her.

Honest to God. She didn't have her cuffs with her. She didn't have her pistol on her. She wasn't holding her staff . . . from now on, she'd be armed and ready no matter where she was, even in church, even in her own house, even . . .

Lilith continued, "You will have to come to Baltimore for the reading of the will."

Hostility prickled along Kateri's nerves. She swung back to face her sister. "Why?"

"You're a beneficiary."

Kateri's temper crackled. "I told you. I don't want that man's money."

"Oh, grow up! Your father was rich. It's purely an accident of birth, but you might as well get some benefit out of it!"

Kateri opened her mouth.

Lilith cut her off before she could say the first word. "No! Don't give it to charity!"

Kateri shut her mouth. Was she that transparent

that Lilith knew what she'd intended to say?

"Spend it on yourself. Get some decent clothes. Spiff up your office." Lilith saw Kateri's scorn and went in for the kill. "Buy a house so your darling Lacey will have a fenced backyard."

"Oh." A house. Now that was temptation. Kateri knew just the one. Small, old, but well kept, close to downtown, backyard big enough to plant a few tomatoes and let Lacey run free.

"See?" Lilith was triumphant. "It only took the right incentive to turn you into the same greedy bitch as your sister."

Carefully, Kateri set the raven on the coffee table. She stepped close to Lilith. She pulled her service 9mm semiautomatic.

Lilith's eyes grew wide.

So Lilith was smart enough to be afraid.

Slowly, Kateri released the safety, pointed the firearm over Lilith's shoulder . . .

. . . At the bloodied John Terrance. That murderous bastard sat up and raised his rifle.

Holding center mass, Kateri squeezed the trigger.

The detonation blasted, echoed.

John Terrance's chest exploded. Twice. The force of the bullets threw his arms up, pushed him back against the wall.

Kateri stared, not understanding. Two kill shots? But she'd shot only once.

"Katherine!" Lilith gasped and pointed toward the front door.

Pistol raised, Kateri flung herself around.

Stag Denali stood there, lowering his rifle. "I would have come in sooner, but I hated to interrupt the family reunion."

CHAPTER FIFTY-SEVEN

WELCOME TO VIRTUE FALLS

FOUNDED 1902

YOUR VACATION DESTINATION ON THE
WASHINGTON COAST

HOME OF THE WORLD FAMOUS
VIRTUE FALLS CANYON

POPULATION 2487

The July 4th weekend had begun. The day was warm, the sky was clear and Virtue Falls's sidewalks thronged with happy, sunburned tourists and smug, prosperous locals.

Kateri walked along Main Street, headed downtown toward Town Square Park. She wore a black sheath designer dress topped by a short-sleeved black jacket. Her black flats shouted *expensive*. Her hair had been cut and styled within an inch of its life. She wafted Chanel No. 5 Parfum Grand Extrait in fragrant waves behind her.

Dressed in his signature tailored black jeans and starched white shirt, Stag Denali swung into place beside her. "Been back long?"

"Came here right from SeaTac Airport. Got in town about five minutes ago." And he'd found her right away. That pleased her more than it should.

"I see your sister took you shopping in Baltimore."

"*Dragged* me."

"That afternoon in your house . . . I thought you were going to murder her."

"I wanted to. So badly." Kateri lifted her hand and waved fondly at Moen, who stood across the street, staring at her with his mouth open. "She did save my life, and in retrospect I enjoyed seeing her swing that precious antique raven at Terrance's skull."

Stag grinned. "I wish I'd seen that. Every time you tell the story, I think it's more awesome."

With innate practicality, Kateri added, "Also, I wasn't sure we weren't going to get killed, and I didn't want to go into the afterlife tangled up with her."

"Very sensible. You look good." He leaned close and took a deep breath. "Smell good."

She wanted to begrudge Lilith the effort and embarrassment of shopping, but he was right. She *did* look good. "I clean up well."

"You look better naked."

He was a sweet talker. "You would know."

"Why don't you take your hair down?" He poked at the stiff creation with his index finger. "You resemble your sister when it's fixed like that."

"Don't be mean." Kateri gingerly touched the upsweep fashioned of her own long, dark hair. "It's going to take an hour to pull out the pins and wash out the hair spray."

"So it's a major operation?"

"Painful, too. I'll pull out half my hair with the pins." She'd been gone, but Bergen had kept her up to date with what was happening in town. "I hear that the ballistics on one of the bullets pulled out of John Terrance's chest matched the bullet that killed his son."

"I heard that, too."

She looked him right in the eyes. "You really ought to get that weapon registered."

"Or what?"

"Or I'll have to detain you."

With a touch too much eagerness, he asked, "Will you tie me up?"

She stopped. She glared.

He took her arm and tugged her along the sidewalk. "I already got it registered."

"And already got another one that's not registered."

With a display of false innocence, he widened his eyes. "Hmm?"

He had Thor's looks and Loki's craftiness and if it wasn't for his touching propensity to be in the right place at the right time to save her life, she really would have to bring him in. "Thank you. For killing John Terrance Jr. and making sure John Terrance Sr. bit the dust."

"Does that mean you finally trust me?"

She stopped. She turned and placed her hand on his arm. She looked up into his eyes. "Lilith kept saying I learned things when I lived with my family. Well, I did. One thing. I learned how indifference and exasperation could feel like cruelty, and how the wounds left by cruelty never quite heal. I learned . . . how to be a better person than my father, my stepmother and my stepsister." Hastily she added, "Which isn't saying much, but right now, I'm feeling pleased with myself. And . . . not pleased with myself. Because I learned something else. I learned to be suspicious of everyone."

"Not a bad trait for a cop."

"True. A better trait for a cop is to figure out who the good guys are before the bad guys take me out." She stepped in front of him, stopping him in midstride. "You're one of the good guys. Thank you for backing me up." She took a long breath, bolstered her own courage. "I, uh, I love you."

He laughed at her, and mimicked her. "I, uh, love you, too."

She hadn't expected that. She'd hoped for it, but she hadn't expected it. "Really?"

"Really."

She wanted to kiss him, but other people were on the streets. Little kids. Tourists. Locals. If she did kiss him, she didn't know if she could stop and she didn't think he would, and she *really* didn't think the sheriff of Virtue Falls should be arrested for public lewdness. So she smiled at him, really smiled, and admired the way he smiled back. Her admiration went on for a little too long because someone whistled. She glanced around, and walked on.

Stag caught right up with her. "Did the will get read?"

"Yes."

"How much did your daddy leave you?"

"You wouldn't believe it."

"He stiffed you."

"Left me half a million dollars."

Stag put his hand to his chest and staggered backward. "Good. God. Gertie."

She laughed. "Are those the new swear words for the tough Indian bouncer?"

"I don't swear much. Mostly I beat people up, shoot them and build casinos that will give Native Americans the money to live a better life."

"Fair enough." She loved him. He loved her. He was a good guy, mostly, and she was pretty sure she was leaving a trail of little red and pink cartoon hearts. She should be embarrassed. But she wasn't. She was just happy.

She stopped in front of Mrs. Golobovitch's apartment. "I need to stop and get my dog." She knocked. She heard the barking frenzy that meant Lacey knew who was at the door. Mrs. Golobovitch opened it and Lacey raced out and danced around Kateri's legs. She had ribbons on her ears and a ribbon tied to her collar, and when Kateri sat down on the step and picked up her dog, Lacey smelled clean and felt slightly damp. Kateri held her in her arms . . .

And Lacey sniffed suspiciously. Sniffed her face, her hair, her neck.

Then . . . she turned and looked at Stag for confirmation.

"It's her," he told the dog.

Outraged, Kateri said, "While I was gone, you seduced my dog?"

He flirted with his eyes. "I'm irresistible."

"Every day, Lacey goes with him to work." Mrs. Golobovitch looked pleased to see them together. "But she misses you at night!"

"At night?" Kateri looked sternly at her dog.

Lacey sighed and laid her head on Kateri's shoulder.

"All right then. That's better." Kateri hugged her. "Thank you, Mrs. Golobovitch. I've got a check for you and I brought you a gift from Baltimore."

"I love gifts!" Mrs. Golobovitch exclaimed. "Is it a raven?"

"Uh, no. No more ravens. Edgar Allan Poe's raven went back to Baltimore and with great ceremony was presented to a museum." Kateri put Lacey down and hooked her on the leash. "Mrs. Golobovitch, I'll bring everything by later!"

Stag gave Kateri his hand, pulled her to her feet. They walked on. "What are you going to do with half a million dollars?" he asked. "Buy that house you want?"

She grinned at him. "I already did."

He laughed, picked her up, hugged her. "Good for you!"

Lacey barked and danced.

"Yes, and good for you, too," he said to the dog. He put Kateri back down. "You're going to need a yardman with experience. When I was a kid in Alaska, to make money, I mowed lawns in the summer and strung holiday lights in the winter. I know the trade."

"But I'd be foolish to take the first applicant for the job." Kateri resumed her stroll toward the center of town. Lacey and Stag walked beside her. "How much do you charge?"

"I'll do it for room and board."

"Room and board? For mowing my lawn?" She was enjoying herself far too much. Teasing with Stag, seeing people's reactions to her appearance, knowing that in less than a block she'd be at the city center: Town Square Park, Oceanview Café, City Hall . . . this was Virtue Falls, and here she was at home.

"I'm handy around the house, too." Stag made

his voice low, husky, suggestive. "Good with electrical, fix a leaky faucet, change the light bulbs."

"That's all stuff that has to be done maybe once a year." Kateri's practical streak could not be tamped down by rampant and eternal love. "Can you vacuum? Load a dishwasher? Do the laundry?"

The pause went on long enough that she stopped to look sternly at Stag.

In a normal voice, he admitted, "Yes, I *can* do all that stuff."

"Will you do it without being nagged?"

"Depends on how often you think it needs to be done."

"It needs to be done when it needs to be done." She shook her head and walked on, much to Lacey's approval. "You just failed the roommate application."

He caught up with her. "I've got furniture."

Kateri hesitated.

"Nice furniture." He used that sexy voice again, then added an element of persuasive. "You're going to need it, what with the stuff that got shot up during the final confrontation with John Terrance. Plus I know you're dealing with increased square footage. You'll need a second bed, a better couch, some art for the walls . . ."

"Damn!" She thought furiously. "Okay, we'll split the household chores according to the schedule I devise. You do your laundry, I'll do mine. And you let me drive your car."

Now right in front of the Oceanview Café, he stopped, and in a voice of outrage, he repeated, *"Drive my car."*

She turned and walked backward. "I'm the sheriff. I can handle a car like that."

"Drive my car."

"You can ride with me."

"Drive my car."

"Good. We're agreed." She returned to him, wrapped her hands around his arm and leaned close, going in for a kiss and to hell with public decency.

He stopped her with his hand on her shoulder. He looked into her eyes, and he wasn't smiling. He wasn't teasing. "I only let relatives drive my car."

Lacey sighed a long-suffering sigh and sat down.

"If we were relatives we couldn't do the—wait." Kateri stepped back. "You mean *marriage?*" She should get points for saying it without stammering.

"That's what I mean." He didn't stammer. Not even close. He sounded very sure of himself.

"I never thought that you . . . Believed you would . . ." *Now* she was stammering. "I mean, you're a free spirit."

"I'm a felon. Marrying the sheriff will keep me

on the straight and narrow. Plus I love you and you love me and we make each other happy. Plus your dog loves me. See how easy that is?"

Guy was pretty smart for a bouncer.

Right there in the middle of the sidewalk in front of the Oceanview Café, he got down on one knee. "Kateri Kwinault, will you marry me?"

Faces. In the windows at the café, at the police station across the street. Grins. From everybody on the street, in the park, driving by.

Lacey getting up to stand beside him like his best man. Or best dog. Whatever.

Nothing private about this. But so, so sweet.

Putting her hand on his chest over his heart, Kateri smiled into his serious, handsome, beloved face. "I would be honored."

He took a few moments to let that sink in, then delved into his pocket and came up with a ring box. "I've been carrying this around for a while. I didn't know what you would want, so I got something I thought was pretty." He opened it and showed her.

Crafted of silver, the ring was woven into a mosaic of branches, leaves and flowers.

"Oh." A breathless sigh. She lifted it from its velvet bed. "That's beautiful."

He took it from her and slid it onto her finger.

"It fits and I love it," she said.

He looked relieved. Which was funny, considering that from him, she would have taken a

Band-Aid wrapped around her finger. He kept her hand in his and stood in a nice, long, smooth slow motion.

More pink and red hearts dancing over her head, bobbing and kissing and popping. Could anyone else see them, hear them? She sure hoped not.

He said, "Okay then. What do you want to do to celebrate?"

She gestured at the Oceanview Café. "We're right here. Maybe we could go in for a piece of pie and some coffee?"

"High-roller, huh? You really know how to live it up." He held the door for her.

She walked in.

Stag followed, his hand on the small of her back.

The old farts were griping about politics. Or maybe kids nowadays. Or maybe uppity female sheriffs.

Cornelia sat in her usual chair at her usual table, frowning intently at her computer, oblivious to the conversations around her.

The new waitress, Linda, shouted, "Were you born in a barn? Shut the door."

"Who's that? Who's that?" Deaf old Mrs. Branyon blinked at Kateri, then announced loudly, "My God. That awful Indian sheriff is back. She's in a dress. Did you see she's in a dress? Who does she think she is?"

Like a queen, Rainbow was installed in an easy chair at the end of the counter, graciously accepting flowers and tributes. At the sight of Kateri, her thin, pale face lit up.

Kateri put her hand to her heart. It overflowed with gratitude and love for Virtue Falls and she was sure that, from now on, there would be crimes no more serious than shoplifting, speeding and tourists flashing the locals.

An unsmiling Deputy Bergen stuck his head in the door. "Sheriff, glad you're back. Can you come in to work? Now? We've got an interesting situation on our hands."

Center Point Large Print
600 Brooks Road / PO Box 1
Thorndike, ME 04986-0001 USA

(207) 568-3717

US & Canada:
1 800 929-9108
www.centerpointlargeprint.com

May 20 2019